Kinky Secrets of Alice Trilogy

Copyright © 2014
Cover art copyright © 2014

This book is a work of fiction. Names, characters, places and incidents are either products of the author's imagination or used fictitiously. Any resemblance to actual events, locales, or persons, either living or dead is entirely coincidental. All rights reserved. No part of this publication can be reproduced or transmitted in any form or by any means, electronic or mechanical, without express permission in writing.

Kinky Secrets of Alice Trilogy

Melinda DuChamp

A Fairytale for Adults

Part 1
Kinky Secrets of Alice in Wonderland
7

Part 2
Kinky Secrets of Alice Through the Looking Glass
125

Part 3
Kinky Secrets of Alice at the Hellfire Club
259

Kinky Secrets of Alice in Wonderland

Chapter 1

Down the Rabbit Hole

Alice put the plate back into the picnic basket and then stared at Lewis, who was wiping a bit of lemon meringue from the corner of his mouth with his sleeve. He noticed her staring and grinned. Alice forced a smile back.

She loved Lewis. And although she was only eighteen-years-old Alice believed she would marry him someday. But now that the picnic had ended, she knew what was coming next. And Alice dreaded it.

Lewis moved closer to her, wrapping an arm around her shoulders and snugging her tight. "The pie was lovely, Alice."

"Thank you."

"You're lovely, too."

He moved in to kiss her, which Alice gladly accepted. Lewis was a good kisser, with full lips and a soft, gentle tongue. His hands encircled Alice's waist, easing her back onto the blanket they'd spread over the meadow's grass, and kissed her neck. Alice closed her eyes and wished the moment would last forever.

But it didn't. All too soon, as she'd feared, Lewis was reaching up to unbutton Alice's shirtdress.

She lightly pushed him away. "I'm rather tired, Lewis. Can't we just kiss and cuddle?"

"But I love you, Alice."

"I love you, too. It's just..."

Lewis frowned, then rolled away from her, onto his side. "I know. I'm not any good at sex."

The sad way he said it broke Alice's heart. But, unfortunately, it was true. While Alice enjoyed the intimacy of making love with Lewis, she'd never climaxed with him. She hadn't even come close.

Truth was, Alice hadn't had an orgasm, ever. She didn't know if she even could. It didn't bother her much, except for moments like this when Lewis wanted to fool around. Though she knew Lewis was inexperienced, Alice couldn't help feeling inadequate. As much as he claimed he enjoyed their lovemaking, Alice knew, deep down, he was just as disappointed in it as she was.

Alice reached over, touching his shoulder.

"It's not just you, Lewis. It's me, too. I'm not any good, either."

Lewis twisted his body to face her. "That's why we should practice. To get better. Here, I got you something to help."

He jack-knifed into a sitting position and dug into the picnic basket, pulling out a slender box wrapped in polka-dot paper.

"I was going to save this for your birthday, but I think now is the perfect time."

Lewis handed the package to Alice, who took it cautiously. Normally, she loved receiving presents. But something about Lewis's tone, and the strange shape of the box, made Alice uneasy.

"What is it? A candlestick?"

"Open it and see. It cost almost a hundred dollars."

A hundred dollars was a lot of money. Especially for Lewis, who worked in a shoe store earning slightly over minimum wage. Alice ran her finger along the seam and tore the paper off, revealing a plain white box. And inside that was…

Well, Alice really wasn't sure.

It looked sort of like Lewis's manhood, with a shaft, and a bulbous head. But this was made of white plastic. Near the bottom were two large, rubber ears, sprouting out of the base where hair on a man would be.

"Lewis… is this a…" Alice searched her mind for a word she'd never spoken before. "A *dildo*?"

Lewis beamed. "It's a vibrator, Alice. It's called a rabbit. I found it on Amazon.com. They sell everything, and have the best prices. The buttons on the bottom make it rotate and vibrate, and those ears rub up against you."

Alice immediately dropped the box as if it contained a live snake. "Why would you buy me such a crude thing?"

Lewis's smile faded. "I thought it would help you to, you know…"

Alice immediately felt bad for her knee-jerk reaction. Especially considering how much it cost. She placed a hand on Lewis's cheek. "Oh, Lewis. I don't want plastic and batteries. It's you I want."

"Really?"

Alice nodded.

Lewis moved in to kiss her again, and Alice kissed him back. This time, when he reached to unbutton her dress, she didn't protest.

A moment later, Lewis had his pants around his ankles and he was on top of her.

"You're so hot, Alice."

"Lewis…"

"God, I love your tits," he said, his hand up under her bra.

"Lewis, you know I don't like it when you talk like that."

"Oh… Alice…"

"Why don't we slow down a little? Then maybe I can…"

Too late. Lewis was already finishing up. It hadn't been more than thirty seconds from beginning to end. Which, for Lewis, was a record.

"That was beautiful, Alice. And you're beautiful. I love you so much."

He kissed Alice again, then rolled off of her, onto his back, and tucked himself into his jeans. A moment later he was snoring.

Alice felt like crying. Everything about Lewis was so perfect, except for this. She had barely felt him enter her before he'd finished. Alice buttoned her dress back up, stared at the fluffy, white clouds overhead, and asked them how she could improve their sex life.

The clouds didn't answer. Because clouds don't talk.

Turning away from Lewis, Alice's eyes locked onto the box he'd given her. The rabbit. A terrible gift, one that reminded Alice of her shortcomings.

"Oh, Lewis, what are we going to do?"

Alice wished, more than anything in the world, that she could be a regular, normal girl. She wanted to have those earth-quaking orgasms her friends told her about. She wanted to feel like a real woman, not like a broken doll. Alice truly believed Lewis was the man for her, the one she wanted to live happily ever after with. But she didn't know of any fairytales where Prince Charming couldn't make the princess climax.

"Someday my prince will come," she lamented softly, "too fast."

Then again, maybe it wasn't all the prince's fault.

Alice hesitantly reached for the box, then withdrew her hand before touching it.

What am I afraid of? Alice thought, chiding herself.

She glanced at Lewis again, making sure he was asleep. Alice couldn't imagine how embarrassing it would be if he saw her do what she was thinking about doing. But Lewis was still snoring softly, and if the pattern held, he'd be asleep for at least another hour. So once again, Alice reached for the box. This time she did pick it up, taking a closer look at the rabbit.

If it was designed to look erotic, the designers got it wrong. This toy was decidedly unsexy, and Alice had no desire to get it anywhere near her private parts, let alone put it inside.

She pressed one of the buttons on the base, and almost dropped the rabbit when it began to undulate in her hand. Once the shock wore off, her original assessment remained. This thing looked goofy, not arousing.

Alice pressed another button, and the rabbit's ears began to vibrate.

Hmm. Interesting.

Alice didn't know a lot about her own anatomy. Her mother died when she was young, and her father wasn't very good at answering questions about anything related to the female body. But she knew enough to know the top part of her nether regions was the most sensitive spot, and these ears looked like they would fit perfectly over it.

Alice tested the vibration with her thumb. It was strong. And a dial on the base made it even more intense.

"So," Alice whispered to herself. "Do I wait forever for Lewis to figure out how my body works? Or do I figure it out for myself?"

Alice chewed her lower lip, made her decision, checked to make sure Lewis was sleeping and no one else was around their picnic nook. Then she tentatively lifted the hem of her dress and—

The white rabbit vibrator hopped out of her hands!

Alice sat up, reaching for it, and the rabbit hopped again, off the blanket and onto the grass.

"That... impossible," Alice said.

She rubbed her eyes, convinced this couldn't actually be happening. It had to be a dream, like in some silly Victorian fantasy novel. Getting on all fours, Alice went after the rabbit, reaching out both hands to grab for it, and the vibrator took three big hops and disappeared into the woods.

Alice didn't know how to react. She'd never experienced anything even remotely like this. Though admittedly her experience was limited, Alice didn't believe that sex toys, even the expensive ones, came to life and ran off. But odd as it was, Alice had no choice but to go after it. She would never be able to explain to Lewis how she had lost his gift.

Alice ran into the woods, even though she had forgotten her shoes, and fortunately was just in time to see the toy pop down a large rabbit hole under a hedge.

"Oh dear, oh dear, this is crazy!" Alice dipped down onto her hands and knees and peered into the hole, but she didn't see any sign of the device. It must have hopped further in. There was no helping it, she was going to have to climb in after. Alice started crawling.

The rabbit hole went straight on like a tunnel for some way, and then dipped suddenly down, so suddenly that Alice had not a moment to think about stopping before she found herself falling into a very deep well.

Alice fell and fell for what seemed like an eternity. Down and down and down. The air in the well smelled sweet and exotic, and the longer she plunged, the warmer and more relaxed she felt.

"Surely when I hit the bottom, I will not be so comfortable," she said to herself. "In fact, I'm sure I will be horribly maimed."

But Alice was wrong about that, just as she'd apparently been wrong about sex toys running off, and when she finally reached the bottom, she landed quite gently on a cushion of pink velvet in the middle of a small room.

Her first thought was to find the vibrator, and Alice spotted it even before she'd climbed off the cushion. It hopped past a small table and toward an even smaller door.

Alice scrambled to her feet and dashed after it, but it was through the door and hopping into what appeared to be a beautiful secret garden before Alice was able catch it. She tried to follow, but her shoulders were too wide, and only her head could fit through.

"There must be another way," she exclaimed to herself. Losing Lewis's gift wasn't an option, and she didn't have a hundred dollars to replace it. So she circled the room three times before finally noticing a blue bottle perched on the top of the table.

The blue glass sparkled, the bottle's neck curving alluringly to an ornate cork at the mouth. Alice picked it up, stroking it with her fingers, and saw a label stamped on the cork.

DRINK ME

Anticipation shivered through her. It would be silly of her to bring it to her lips. She didn't even know what liquid was inside. But still... what if she did?

The thought of tasting what the bottle had to offer teased at the back of her mind. Alice pushed it away, but even before she set the vessel back down, the temptation was back. What would it taste like? What would it do? Was it some kind of exotic liqueur? Would it make her tipsy? Downright drunk? Would it shrink her so she could fit through the small door? If so, wouldn't that just be the stupidest thing ever?

Maybe this strange, underground world was messing with her common sense. Or maybe she was just easily manipulated and lacked self-control. Whatever the case, without another thought, Alice opened the cork and took a swallow.

The fluid was thick and silky, and it moved over her tongue and infused her taste buds first with sweetness, then salt, then a flavor she'd never quite tasted before. She took another drink, and another, until the bottle was empty.

Besides the wonderful flavors, nothing happened.
Until...

Alice's body began to grow warm. Not hot or uncomfortable, but languid and relaxed. Her dress felt tight. The heat ran through her bloodstream like warm molasses and collected at a spot between her legs.

A button popped off her dress, the thread simply giving way. Then another followed, until the whole front split open down to her waist. She shifted uncomfortably, her breasts pillowing over the top of her bra, the cups no longer containing her.

Alice ran her hands over her belly, her sides, her back, but it was only her breasts that had grown too large. The rest seemed as normal as ever, except for the heat between her thighs.

She shrugged out of the dress and let it pool on the floor. With the buttons gone, it was nearly worthless, and the bra pinched her painfully as well. Finally, she grew so hot in her nether regions that she slipped off her panties, desperate to keep cool.

"Oh, dear!" she exclaimed. "What do I do now?" But Alice knew there was only one thing to do. She had to wait until the blue liquid's heat wore off and her bosoms shrunk. Then she'd find a way home, whether she caught the rabbit vibrator or not.

Alice paced around the room, wishing for a window she could open to bring in some air, and then she felt it; a delicious, cooling breeze. She followed its source, light and refreshing on her skin, and to her surprise it led her to an open door she'd never noticed before. So cool, so nice, she stepped outside, just for a moment, but before her moment was up, the room had disappeared and she was in a garden much like the park where she and Lewis had their picnic.

Lewis.

She scampered along the edge of the woods, eager to get back to him. She had no idea how she would explain her nudity, nor her burgeoning breasts or her nipples, which were tight and protruding as if she was chilled. But she could wrap their picnic blanket around herself, and cover it all up. And eventually the heat and the throb of pressure building in her secret place would fade and everything would be back to the way it was.

At least she could hope.

But when she reached the spot where they'd enjoyed their lunch, she realized she'd gotten it all wrong. This wasn't the park. She didn't know this place at all. And in the distance she heard the scolding of birds and what might be harsh human voices, and she ducked into the shelter of a trail through the trees before anyone could see she wasn't wearing a stitch of clothes on this bright summer's day.

Chapter 2

Advice from a Caterpillar

Feeling self-conscious and more than a little ashamed, Alice followed the trail into the forest, sticks and pebbles poking her tender, bare feet, twigs from the ominous, overhanging tree canopy pinching at her hair like thin fingers. Soon the sun was just an occasional flicker through the branches, and a cool ground wind blew firmly across Alice's naked body, stiffening her nipples. Quickening her pace, and getting more and more anxious as the woods darkened, Alice glanced down until she could no longer make out the trail. She turned, trying to backtrack, but couldn't find the path she had taken to get there. However, through a break in the tree line, Alice saw the most interesting sight. A field of mushrooms.

But these were unlike any mushrooms she'd ever seen. Dark and enormous, almost up to her shoulders, with thick, fat stems and bulbous heads so big she couldn't wrap her arms around them. The sight of the shrooms both repulsed Alice and drew her toward them, her feet heading into the field on their own volition. Soon she was surrounded by dozens, hundreds, a whole forest of mushrooms, so close together that Alice rubbed against them as she passed. The caps were soft, almost velvety, but firm and unyielding. They reminded Alice of something, but for the life of her, she couldn't remember what.

The potion Alice had swallowed was making her tingle more than ever. Looking around to see if anyone was watching, Alice pressed her palm between her legs, trying to calm the throb. Her hand felt good there, rubbing softly against her as she walked, and Alice thought about her boyfriend, Lewis. Why couldn't he be here right now? More than ever before, she would have liked him inside her. In fact, Alice had never been so eager for it.

She closed her eyes for a moment, imagined Lewis's weight on top of her, kissing her neck softly, his hands cupping her bare breasts, wrapping her legs around him as the tip of his—

"Who are you?"

Surprised, Alice let out a gasp as she opened her eyes and saw a man staring down at her from one of the mushrooms. He straddled it like a biker astride a motorcycle, and indeed he looked the type. Black leather pants. Black boots. A black leather vest over a bare chest. Several days' worth of beard on his face.

His voice was foreign—some sort of European accent—and Alice guessed English wasn't his first language. His arms were muscled, and Alice noticed a tattoo on his shoulder, something that looked like a letter of the alphabet but upon squinting Alice realized was a caterpillar.

"I'm, um, Alice."

The man didn't reply. His dark hair was short, untamed, and he had the deepest green eyes Alice had ever seen. He glared at her like a lion glared at a gazelle. Even more self-conscious about her nudity, Alice lifted her arm across her breasts, tucked her knees together, and bent over to shield herself from his gaze.

"I am Pilar," he said, pronouncing it Pee-larr and rolling the r at the end. Alice figured he might be Portuguese. "Why are you in my mushroom field, Alice?"

"I'm lost," Alice said, close to sobbing. "Will you help me?"

"Stand up straight," Pilar ordered. Though he said it softly, Alice sensed the steel in his voice.

"I'm naked," Alice said, though she realized it was a silly thing to say. He obviously knew that already.

"If you need my help, Alice, we need to trust one another. One way to build trust is for you to do as I say. How do I know you aren't a poacher, in my field to steal my mushrooms?"

"But I'm not," Alice said.

"Then stand up straight so I may see you aren't hiding any poaching equipment."

Fighting embarrassment, Alice forced herself to straighten to her full height. She watched as Pilar swung his leg over the mushroom and dropped to the ground. He walked to her slowly, leisurely, the barest hint of a smile on his lips, and stopped when he was just a few feet in front of her.

"Put your hands at your sides," Pilar said.

"But you can see I'm not holding anything."

"I see nothing of the sort. You could be hiding all kinds of things."

Alice wondered if she should run away. But to where? Back into the dark, scary woods? Into the field of mushrooms that Pilar claimed were his? Though Pilar seemed a bit strange, and rather intense, he hadn't done anything that made Alice believe he would hurt her. Maybe he was telling the truth, and he just wanted to make sure she wasn't a mushroom poacher.

Alice dropped the arm from her breasts, feeling her face flush with shame.

"You are beautiful, Alice," Pilar said.

She blushed even harder. "Thank you."

"Please remove your other hand."

"But I'm surely not hiding anything in *there*," Alice proclaimed.

Pilar stared at her. "As you wish," he said. Then he turned and began to walk away.

"Hey!" she called after him. "Please don't leave me!"

Pilar soon blended into the mushrooms, and Alice realized the fear of being lost and alone was far worse than the embarrassment of a stranger seeing her naked. So she hurried after him, running through the mushroom field, catching up just as he opened the door to a small, wooden shack with mushrooms sprouting on the flat roof.

"Pilar! Please wait!"

He had left the door open, and Alice took that as an invitation and hurried inside the cabin. The interior surprised Alice, because unlike Pilar's rough exterior, this was pleasant, almost cozy. A fire crackled in a cast iron stove, where a pot of tea brewed, filling the air with the scent of peppermint. A large rocking chair, with a red blanket across the back, sat in the corner. Oil lamps on the walls cast a soft, orange glow over everything.

As Alice was looking around, someone stepped from behind the door and grabbed her shoulders, giving her a terrible shock.

"Why are you in my house?" Pilar demanded, his soft voice loud and firm.

"I... uh... you left the door open... and I thought—"

"I did not invite you in my house. You have no right to be here."

"I'm sorry. I'll go."

He leaned in close, his face inches from hers. "Did you steal anything?" he asked, his breath smelling like peppermint tea.

"What? No! Of course not! I just walked in a second ago!"

"I do not trust you, Alice. How can I believe someone I cannot trust?"

"But you must believe me! I'm not hiding anything!"

"I should call the police. They have ways of dealing with liars and thieves."

Alice realized she'd never been this close to a man before, other than Lewis. Pilar was near enough to kiss her. She stared at his mouth, his cruel lips, unable to turn away. The damned throbbing between her legs was becoming unbearable, and without thinking she quickly pressed her mouth to Pilar's, wanting more than anything to feel his tongue in her mouth.

Pilar quickly pulled away. "What are you doing?"

"I... uh..."

"I did not give you permission to kiss me."

"I'm sorry. It's just, I drank this potion earlier, and it is making me crazy."

Pilar raised an eyebrow. "A potion? Was it blue?"

"Yes."

"Did it say DRINK ME on the bottle?"

"Yes. Yes it did."

"And you drank it?"

"Yes."

"What sort of fool would drink a blue potion without knowing what it was?"

Alice didn't know how to respond. She felt like crying.

"This potion, which is making you crazy..." Pilar's voice had lost the rough edge, and now was soft as a summer breeze. "Do you want to stop the crazy feeling?"

"Yes. Can you help me?"

"I can. But you have to trust me. Do you trust me, Alice?"

Pilar released her shoulders. Alice glanced at the door leading back into the mushroom field.

"You can leave if you wish," he said. "The choice is yours."

Looking up into Pilar's deep, green eyes, she said, "Yes. I trust you."

"Come with me."

Taking Alice's hand, he lead her through his cozy cabin to a large, iron door.

"This is my Pink Room of Bunnies," he said.

"How adorable."

"I can get the potion out of you, but to do so, you must be restrained."

"How do you mean?"

"I must tie you up, Alice. That is the only way."

Alice released Pilar's hand, taking a step back. "I don't know. I—"

"Do you know what a safeword is?"

Alice shook her head.

"While you are restrained, if I do anything you don't want, you say the safeword and I stop."

Alice lowered her voice and whispered, "What is the safeword?"

"It can be anything you want."

Alice tried to think, but the throb between her legs was making it hard to concentrate.

"Alice, the blue potion, if you don't get it out of your system, you will go mad. You could even die from it."

"Die?"

Pilar nodded solemnly. "Unless you have release, it could make your loins explode."

"Gosh," Alice said, shuddering in fear. "I don't want that."

"Perhaps you should have considered it before gulping down some strange, foreign liquid. That was pretty damn stupid."

"Do loins explode a lot?"

Pilar looked pained. "All the time."

Alice took another glance at the door, then looked at Pilar's tattoo on his shoulder.

"Caterpillar," she said.

"Yes?"

"Yes what?"

"You called me?"

"I did?"

"That's my name. Pilar is short for Caterpillar."

"Oh. That's an odd name."

"My parents liked insects."

"It's still odd."

"You should meet my sister, Dung Beetle."

Alice made her decision. "I want to use Caterpillar as my safeword."

Pilar's green eyes twinkled. "Excellent. Into the Pink Room of Bunnies, then."

He held open the heavy door and Alice was shocked by what she saw. It was a dungeon.

Shackles and chains hung from the rafters. There was a table with leather straps on it, and a wooden wheel on the wall where a person could be bound and spun around. A steel cage was in the corner, and there was a collection of canes, riding crops, and whips on the wall. Looking at them made Alice feel queer and peculiar.

There were no bunnies at all. And it certainly wasn't pink.

"Caterpillar!" Alice immediately blurted.

"Yes?"

"That's my safeword. I want to quit."

"Why? We haven't even begun."

"You mean to beat me with those whips and rods," Alice said, pointing.

"I hadn't planned on it. Do you want me too?"

"Why on earth would I want you to?"

"Some people enjoy it."

Alice had never heard of such a thing. "You're making that up."

"Not at all. See that strange-looking table there?"

He pointed to something that resembled a small church pew, covered in padded leather. Alice had no idea what it was, but the sight of it made her uneasy.

"What is it?"

"That's a spanking table. One kneels on it and bends over, and the straps hold them in place so they may be thoroughly spanked."

Alice was flabbergasted such a thing existed."Why?"

"Some people are naughty, and need to be disciplined." Pilar stood next to Alice, snaking an arm around her waist, pulling her so close she pressed into him. "Have you ever been naughty, Alice?"

Alice couldn't quite find her voice. Her pelvis was tight against Pilar's, and she could feel his bulge. She tried to squirm away, but he held her fast, and all Alice succeeded in doing was rubbing against it.

"What do you mean?" she whispered.

"Naughty girls should be punished. Tell me you've been naughty, and I'll take you over my knee and slap your bare bottom right now."

Alice stopped trying to pull away. The potion was too powerful, the feeling building within her too good. She rubbed her hard nipples across Pilar's rough leather vest, and tried to grind her hips against him.

"Yes," Pilar said. "You are naughty, aren't you? Perhaps you need a spanking. Something like this."

Pilar brought his hand down on Alice's naked posterior, and the loud slap was almost as startling as the contact. After a brief sting, her bottom began to warm up where he'd smacked it.

Alice squeezed her eyes shut. She'd never felt like this before. This man, this complete stranger, had just struck her. She should go to the authorities, hire a lawyer, file charges. But instead, her whole body began to tingle, and though she hated herself for how she felt, Alice wanted more than anything for him to smack her again.

"I... I am naughty," she managed.

Pilar rubbed the area he'd punished, and then moved his strong, thick fingers lower, between her legs. Alice gasped. No one had ever touched her there before. When she and Lewis made love, he just stuck it in quickly. And Alice had never touched herself. She believed those parts of her were dirty and strange, and treated them as if they belonged to another person.

But Pilar did more than just touch. His index finger lightly stroked her from beneath, first the left side, then the right. She wondered if he had put something on his hand because it was so slick, and then she realized with utter shame it was her own juices.

"Pilar..."

His other hand came down suddenly, smacking her bottom again, and Alice gasped and her eyes and mouth opened wide. The mixed sensations were extraordinary. The tenderness of his fingers, the firm cruelty of his palm, combining together to make her writhe against her own will.

Then Pilar's finger began to slowly enter her.

"I knew you were naughty, Alice."

"Yes," she gasped as he penetrated deeper. "I am naughty."

"Do you want to know what I do to naughty girls?"

"Oh, yes... Caterpillar."

Alice was abruptly released, so fast her legs couldn't support her and she fell onto the floor. She looked up at Pilar, confused and ready to cry.

"What is it? Did I do something?"

"You said the safeword," Pilar said. "So I stopped."

"What? No! I just... it's your name, I was just calling your name."

Pilar's face brightened. "Ah. I understand. So shall I spank you? I can place you in the stocks and whip your butt and thighs with a crop."

Alice couldn't help but stare at the wooden stocks. She instantly imagined herself bent over, her head and hands trapped, Pilar behind her with a leather riding crop, punishing her bare flesh.

An abhorrent, repellant image. So why did it make her quiver so? Why did she want to try it?

"Never mind," Pilar said. "That appears to be too advanced for you. We'll begin with something easier. Stand up."

Alice waited for him to offer his hand, but he simply stood there. She slowly got to her feet.

"Walk over to the wheel."

Alice glanced at the large, wooden wheel, braced against the wall like a giant clock. It frightened her, made her legs weak to the point where she thought she would fall again.

"Walk to it."

Alice did, each step like walking through thick molasses. When Alice reached it, she saw the four thick leather straps on the edges, made to hold a person spread-eagle. In the center was an even thicker belt, meant to cinch around the victim's waist.

Alice trembled, her whole body shaking.

"Lean against the wheel," Pilar ordered.

"I... I don't..."

Suddenly Pilar was behind her, one hand clutching her breasts, the other pressed to her belly.

"This is for your own good, Alice," he said, his fingers descending. "I'm doing it to help you. Do you understand?"

"Uh..."

Once again his finger entered her. But this time he began to move it in and out, like Lewis when they made love. But unlike Lewis, Pilar didn't seem to be in a race to the finish. He moved slowly, luxuriously, until she wanted to beg him to move faster.

"Lean against the wheel."

"Uh... uh..."

"Alice."

"Okay... okay..."

And the next thing Alice knew she was backed up against the terrible wheel and Pilar was strapping her into place. First her waist. Then her hands. Then her left foot. As he knelt down, stretching out her right foot, spreading her legs, Alice tensed up and began to resist. Pilar's head was only inches away from her most private parts, and Alice felt shame like she'd never felt before.

How could she have gotten to this point? A complete stranger, strapping her to a giant wheel? Even more embarrassing, her hips seemed to have developed a mind of their own, and they heaved forward toward Pilar as if trying to touch him.

Then, suddenly, her other ankle was bound, and Alice had never been so exposed in her life.

"Try to get away," Pilar said.

She strained. She pulled. But the wicked straps were tight, and she couldn't close her legs, couldn't get free. Alice was bound there, spread open before a man she barely knew, revealing parts of her even her doctor had never seen. Alice fought tears, a blush creeping up over her whole body, her sore bottom pressed against the rough wood of the wheel. This couldn't possibly get worse.

Then it did. Pilar went to a cabinet and withdrew a length of white rope.

"This is silk bondage rope I received after training with a *nawashi* in Japan. I am going to tie it around your knees and thighs to restrict your pelvic movement and spread you wider."

"Please, don't. I beg of you."

But Pilar didn't listen. He looped the rope around her right knee and up her thigh, then cruelly pulled it back against the wheel and tied it off. Pilar repeated the procedure with the left leg, the rope so tight it forced her pelvis forward. Alice tried to struggle, but it was no use. She had lost all ability to move her lower regions, except for the tiniest of circles.

Pilar was so close she could feel his hot, peppermint breath on her. She chanced a humiliated look down, and could see his lips were almost touching her hair down there.

"This won't do," Pilar said. "I can't see what I'm doing. I must shave you."

"No! Please don't, Pilar. Untie me at once."

But Pilar was back to his cabinet, and when he returned it was with a safety razor, a bowl, and a brush.

He spent a moment twirling the brush in the soap bowl, making a lather. The brush had round, bushy bristles, and when it was sufficiently covered with foam he began to spread it on Alice.

The lather was warm and smelled of sandalwood, and when it touched her she gasped at the sensation. It felt like washing, but not. When she washed herself down there, Alice used a soapy rag and was quick and businesslike. Pilar was gentler, slower. Alice felt as if he was dragging the process out, stroking her left and then right. Up, then down. Sometimes he missed the hair completely, going lower. Alice began to get lost in the rhythm. She closed her eyes, flexing her hips, trying to press into him. But just as she was ready to beg him to put a finger inside her again, Pilar withdrew the brush and began to shave her.

Unlike the gentle rhythm of the brush strokes, the razor was cold, stiff, and unyielding. The pleasant sensations were replaced by panic. What if he cuts me by accident? And even worse, what will I look like when he finishes? A few deft strokes later, and Pilar was done. He brought a pitcher of warm water, pouring it over Alice, washing away the remaining hair and lather, leaving her as naked and vulnerable as the day she was born.

"Would you like to see?" he asked. "I can fetch a mirror."

Part of her did, but she was so mortified at being laid so bare that she couldn't speak. She couldn't understand how Pilar could even stand to look at it. Those parts of her were ugly and dirty. They were used for childbirth and nothing more. Staring at them was abnormal and perverted.

"Beautiful," Pilar whispered.

Alice wasn't sure she heard him right.

"Pink and perfect and beautiful. I know we have just met, but would it be okay if I kissed you there?"

Alice couldn't believe her ears. Why would he possibly want to do something like that?

But her hips began to make a little circle, and Alice couldn't stop the movement.

"One kiss then," Pilar said.

His lips touched hers, and Alice gasped. He was so soft, so tender, and she had an overwhelming urge to press against him. Maybe this is what she'd been missing her whole life. Maybe this was what sex was supposed to be like. She thought of Lewis, her boyfriend, kneeling between her legs, kissing her as Pilar did, and a low moan escaped her throat.

"Thank you," Pilar said, pulling away. "Now it is time to get to work. I'm afraid it is going to take some time, and may be a bit uncomfortable. To fully extract all of the blue potion, I'm going to have to build you up and tease you beyond what you feel you can endure."

"Tease... me?"

"Have you never been teased before, woman?"

"I... I don't know."

Pilar rubbed his beard. "You aren't a virgin."

"No. I have a boyfriend named Lewis."

"Does Lewis satisfy you?"

"He's a very nice man."

"I mean sexually, Alice. Does he satisfy you?"

"I... I love Lewis. Being intimate with him makes me feel close, but... he doesn't really know what he's doing. I'm afraid I don't either..."

Her voice trailed off. Talking about her lovemaking failures was almost as humiliating as being spread open before a stranger.

"To tease is to arouse without release," Pilar said. "Like this."

Immediately, Pilar pressed his face against her. But this time it wasn't a kiss. He began to lick.

Alice began to plead with him to stop, that this was dirty, but it felt like something had ignited inside her loins. Throbbing, but times ten. Pilar licked around her opening, then put his tongue deep inside her, flicking it in and out rapidly. Then he moved up higher, finding a sensitive spot between her lips, and when he touched it the feeling was so intense it almost brought pain. She cried out, and Pilar stayed on that spot; slow, fat, languid strokes until the almost-pain became something else, a warmth that began to spread throughout her whole body.

This was it, Alice thought. This was what she'd heard about. How sex was supposed to be. It felt amazing, and just kept getting better and better. Her hips were bucking now, wanting to capture Pilar's tongue, and he increased his tempo and pressure, pushing his finger up inside her, and the feeling built and built until—

Suddenly Pilar was gone. Alice continued to buck, straining against the ropes and shackles.

"Please! Please don't stop!"

"That," Pilar said, wiping a hand across his glistening chin, "is teasing."

"No!" Alice said. "Please don't stop. It's too cruel to bear."

She almost squealed with delight as Pilar pressed his face to her again. All she needed was a few more seconds, a few more licks, and—

"Do you want me to stop?" Pilar said, pulling away.

"No! God, no!"

Alice was so close. So near experiencing what she longed so much to experience. Her whole life, she'd felt like a broken doll, missing an essential piece. But now she felt like a woman. A full-blooded, sexy woman. Alice wanted sex. She wanted it so bad she almost felt like crying.

"Do you want me to lick you again?" Pilar asked.

"Yes!"

"Or would you prefer I mount you?"

The thought made Alice shudder.

"Oh, mount me," Alice said, close to tears. She'd never used such a vulgar command before. "Please mount me!"

Pilar stood up. Alice eyed the bulge in his leather pants. It seemed monstrous.

"Do it," she begged. She felt like her lower regions were on fire.

"Would you like it if I spanked you now?" Pilar asked. "What if I took the riding crop and tapped you where I just shaved? Would you like that?"

The very idea was abominable, but Alice was so excited that if anything touched her there, even something as terrible as a riding crop, it would send her right over the edge.

"I... I would like that."

"Beg me to spank you."

"Please... Pilar. Please spank me."

"Beg me to lick you again."

"Please. Lick me, Pilar."

"Do you want me inside you?"

"Yes! Oh, yes!"

"No," Pilar said.

Alice cried out in frustration. She tugged against her bounds, thrusting her hips into empty air without relief.

Pilar reached out, gave her cheek a tender caress, and then moved his hands to her breasts. His rough fingers found her nipples and began to tug.

Alice's breath caught in her throat. Somehow all of the burning in her loins had suddenly transferred to her breasts.

"Harder," she said.

Pilar gave each a small pinch, and Alice grunted in appreciation.

"I'll be right back," he said, releasing her.

No! No, no, no!

Alice squirmed and strained and begged for him not to leave. She felt completely out of control, more frustrated than she'd ever been in her life. This teasing was intolerable, and she thought about using the safeword just so that wicked Pilar would untie her so she could touch herself.

However, she didn't say the safeword. Because deep down, Alice realized she liked being teased.

It made no sense. It was like being hungry, and not being able to eat an apple only a few inches away. Or being terribly hot and thirsty and denying yourself a cool glass of lemonade. Or having an irresistible itch on your arm and being unable to scratch it.

But it was more than that. Alice yearned to know what other ways Pilar could torment her. She wanted to see how much teasing she could take before she burst. The throb had become a steady thrum of pleasure. Pilar's tongue on her most intimate parts had awoken some primitive beast in her.

A beast that demanded to be fed.

"Let him try to tease me beyond endurance," Alice said to herself, stiffening her upper lip. "I can handle anything he does. Even the riding crop. This can't possibly get any more intense."

Pilar came back from the cabinet with a leather bag. "Did you say something, dear Alice?"

"I said you can tease me however long you like. I can take it."

"Is that so?"

"Indeed."

Pilar reached his hand between her bare legs, rubbing her wetness, beginning the slow and steady rhythm again. Alice wanted to buck against him, to beg him to go faster, but she set her jaw and refused to give him the satisfaction of even a moan. But when Pilar took his hand away, Alice once again had to fight to not cry.

"Poor little Alice. How she suffers so."

Pilar reached into his bag and took out a small, golden chain. On each end was a wooden, spring-action clothespin.

"These hurt somewhat going on," he said. "But the real sensation begins when they are pulled off. The feeling is tripled."

Pilar pinched some skin of her inner thigh, and clamped the clothespin down. It brought a brief pinch of hurt, but then only pressure. Alice thought, wickedly, how it would feel clamped down elsewhere on her body.

"See?" Pilar said. "Not bad at all. But when I remove it."

He pulled off the clothespin, and the pinched bit of skin seemed to burn like she'd been struck with a wooden cane.

"Oh!" Alice cried out. It hurt, but as with the spanking, the sensation melded with the feeling in her shaven area, heightening the intensity of her longing.

"I shall clamp these onto your nipples," Pilar said.

"No, you can't!" Alice said.

"I can. And I will."

Then his hand was between her legs again, rubbing and teasing. Alice clenched her jaw, watching as he brought up the clothespin, pinching the end so it opened like a tiny bird's beak. He touched her nipple with it as she watched, helpless. Then he clamped it upon her.

Alice screamed. Not from pain. As before, somehow the heat between her thighs connected with the sensation in her breast, and a wave of pleasure hit her like a slap.

Panting now, her breath in short gasps, Alice watched as Pilar opened up the clothespin's partner, circling it lazily around her areola as the fingers of his other hand thrust inside her with increasing speed.

"Do you want me to clamp this on your nipple?" he asked.

Alice couldn't answer.

Pilar slowly began to withdraw his finger, until it barely touched her entrance.

"Yes!" Alice blurted out.

"Beg me."

"Please, Pilar!"

The clothespin bit into her nipple just as he roughly entered her again, two fingers this time, going in and out with increasing speed. The pinch in her breast grew to encompass Alice's whole body, and her eyes squeezed shut as a wave built inside her unlike anything she'd felt previously, and then—

"Not yet," Pilar said, withdrawing his hand. "You aren't ready."

"I'm…" Alice gasped, "I'm ready."

"I think not."

"I really think I am."

Pilar shook his head.

Alice wanted to scream. To cry. She was torn between wanting to strangle him, and begging him to touch her again.

"How about," Alice said while panting, "we trade?"

Pilar narrowed his eyes. "Trade what?"

"Keep touching me, and I'll…"

"You'll…?"

Alice blurted out the most daring thing she could think of. "I'll kiss you… on your private."

Pilar laughed.

"What's so funny?" Alice asked, the blush rising again, her hips yearning to brush against him.

"Dear Alice, when I'm done with you, you'll be begging to deep throat my cock and swallow every last drop of my essence."

Alice had never heard such vulgarity directed at her. As aroused as she was, the very idea was ludicrous. Just saying she would kiss him there was as outrageous as she could possibly get. There was nothing he could do to her to make her do *that*.

Pilar seemed to drink in the expression of disgust on her face, and reached into his bag again and held up a…

"What is that?" Alice asked.

It was shaped like Lewis's manhood, but made of black plastic and quite a bit larger. There were also tiny bumps across the surface.

"This is one of my smaller models," Pilar said.

"You call that small?"

"It's about the same size as I am. I don't have the bumps though. Open your mouth."

Alice shook her head. "No. Absolutely not. I don't care if you keep me here and tease me for eternity." And secretly, part of her hoped he would. But Alice wanted no part of putting that plastic monstrosity in her mouth.

Pilar took something else out of the bag with his other hand. It was bigger, but not shaped like a body part. She recognized it from the store Sharper Image when she visited the mall. It was a back massager. An eighteen inch handle, with a soft rubber ball on the end that vibrated.

A back massage? Now? It didn't make sense, although Alice was rather tense in the shoulder.

Without saying a word, Pilar switched on the massager—

—and pressed it between her legs.

Alice gasped. The feeling was so intense, so acute, it made everything that happened previously that day seem trivial.

"This is a Hitachi Wand," Pilar said. "The most powerful massager in the world. Right now, you're experiencing the low speed. This is the high speed."

He pressed the switch.

The sensations doubled.

Alice feared she would pass out. The pleasure began to multiply exponentially, until her whole body was reduced to pure sensation. Alice couldn't think, couldn't talk. She became a complete prisoner of her own greedy desires. Just a few more seconds and she would—

Pilar took the wand away.

Alice screamed with a frustration so great she had no doubt they could hear it all the way back home.

"Open your mouth," Pilar said.

Alice couldn't take it anymore. This had to end. "Caterpillar," she said.

"Yes? That's me."

"Release me."

"Is that what you want?"

"I can't take this anymore. I—"

And then the massager was against her again. When Alice cried out, Pilar slipped the black plastic member in her mouth.

Alice gagged, trying to spit it out, to repeat the safeword. But then she lost her mind again to the vibrations.

Pilar continued to tease her. He would rub it up and down her legs, missing the most sensitive spots on purpose, driving her mad. When he did place it against her, he shut off the power. Even so, just rubbing against it was heavenly, but each time Alice got close to reaching her peak, Pilar would pull away.

Alice had no idea how long it went on. Minutes? Hours? But at some point, she resisted trying to spit out the thing in her mouth, and had begun to suck on it. Suck hard. She wanted that black thing deep in her throat, far as it could go. Alice imagined it was Lewis. Then she imagined it was Pilar. Before she knew it, Alice was concentrating so hard on the dildo she didn't even notice Pilar was no longer teasing her. With no stimulation at all, the feeling in Alice began to build again. Her breath came faster, and as she sucked, her womanhood seemed to ignite. She was getting just as much pleasure and arousal from sucking a piece of plastic as she'd been when Pilar was touching her.

Then the terrible man began to tease her with that as well. Pulling the plastic out of her lips. Touching it to her chin and cheek. Making her strain and beg to have it in her mouth again.

"What do you want, dear Alice?" Pilar asked.

"Let me suck it, Pilar. Please."

"It?" he asked, rubbing it against her cheek. "Or would you prefer me?"

Alice shuddered. What had seemed so abhorrent before was now all she wanted in the world.

"You. Please, Pilar. Let me take you in my mouth."

"I think you are ready."

Suddenly the wheel spun, and Alice was hanging upside down. Her face was inches away from Pilar's pelvis. She whimpered as he unbuttoned his leather pants, and when he released himself he was fully erect. So big. So stiff. Alice opened her mouth, wide as she could, moaning for it. Pilar brushed the tip against her lips—its velvet softness reminded her of the mushrooms—and then eased it inside her cheeks.

At the same time, Alice felt her shaven parts suddenly filled with something long and hard. It made her scream around Pilar's manhood, and some overloaded part of her brain recognized it as the dildo she's just had in her mouth. Pilar worked it in and out of her, picking up speed, and she tried to match that speed with her own efforts.

Then, abruptly, he pulled out of her mouth.

"NO!" Alice screamed. Now she did begin to cry, her whole body shaking at the cruelty of it.

But the toy inside her began to move faster and harder, and then suddenly the back massager was pressed against her as well, right on her most sensitive spot. The sensation was so strong Alice screamed again, and then Pilar rammed himself back into her mouth, and the pleasure overtook her, finally pushing Alice over the edge. All the build-up, all the teasing, crescendoed in a mind-blowing, frenzied climax that went on and on and on, and just as it began to die down and Alice thought there was nothing left in her, Pilar took the Hitachi up to the higher speed, reached down, and pulled the gold chain, yanking the clothespins off her nipples.

Alice felt as if she left her body. As if she no longer existed, except as pure sensation. The orgasm locked every one of her muscles, and she cried out around Pilar's manhood and shook and trembled and rode wave after wave until she was ragged and sweaty and completely spent.

Pilar pulled out and turned the wheel so she was once again upright.

"Pilar…" she said, out of breath, flushed, feeling more like a woman than she ever had before. "Thank you for—"

And then he was inside her, filling her, thrusting slowly. Unlike Lewis, who always seemed to be anxious to finish, Pilar took his time. Alice didn't think she had anything left, nothing more to give. But the feeling was impossible to resist. She sighed. She shuddered. Soon she was matching his thrusts, and the wave was building again inside her. Pilar moved his hands up her body, to her breasts, her nipples, which were wonderfully sore as he rolled them between his fingers. And then he was cupping her face, his thumb at the corner of her mouth, and she began to suck it, which turned her on even more.

"I'm coming," Pilar said, and incredibly, Alice was once again as well. His thrusts became faster and faster and then his whole body seized and he held her tight and Alice screamed until he finally put a hand over her lips and politely asked her to shut up.

Alice was exhausted. But she felt she needed to thank him for what he'd done. Maybe she could clean his house, or help harvest some mushrooms or whatever the heck he did with them.

"You've been very kind to me," Alice said. "Is there anything I can do to repay you?"

Pilar laughed. "You already did, dear Alice. I enjoyed it as much as you."

"That hardly seems possible," Alice said, blushing.

"How many times?"

"Excuse me?"

"How many times did you come, Alice? We need to make sure we got all the potion out."

"I... well... I guess I'm not sure. I mean, there was at least two, but it may have been more than two. It was all so intense I don't know if it was a bunch close together, or one really long one that wouldn't end. I don't have any experience in this area."

"You mean you've never come before?"

Alice shook her head.

"Well then, we're going to have to take some drastic measures to be sure you no longer have any of the potion in you. Apologies, dear Alice."

"Apologies? Heavens, what for?"

Pilar produced another length of rope from his bag. He began to wind it around the Hitachi wand.

"Pilar, what are you doing?"

Without answering, he tied the vibrator to Alice's waist, so it hung between her legs, the soft ball pressing her swollen lips.

"We won't bother with the teasing this time. I have some chores to do around the house. Yell for me when you get to—I don't know—fifteen. That should be enough."

He switched on the vibrator, instantly making Alice cry out. She squirmed and struggled against it, but there was no way to escape the sensations.

"Pilar, please... I'll go mad."

"You'll do fine, Alice dear."

Alice thrashed. "It's too intense!"

He put the black dildo back into her mouth, and then found another, even larger, dildo in his bag. It had a thick, elastic strap on the end of it. He forced it up into Alice, filling her completely, and fastened the strap around her thigh so it stayed in place. Already the pleasure began to overpower Alice, the orgasm building rapidly.

"I'll check on you in half an hour," Pilar said.

A half hour? That was torture! Her eyes implored him not to go, but at the same time Alice didn't want to spit out the dildo. The sensations were overpowering.

"Let me tell you how beautiful you look, suffering like this. I should call in the townspeople, sell tickets for them to watch."

Alice shook her head, mentally begging him not to do that. She would never be able to handle such humiliation.

Pilar chuckled to himself, walking away as the orgasm swallowed her.

Chapter 3

Pig and Pepper

The half hour went by quickly, and yet lasted longer than a lifetime. When Pilar returned and untied her, Alice's legs felt like rubber, and she could barely walk. She wanted nothing more than to curl up near the fire in his cozy cabin, sip peppermint tea, and then sleep the afternoon away.

"Goodbye now," he said, throwing open the door.

Alice pouted. "Can't I stay?"

"No."

"But I want to stay. Here. With you." She'd only just met the man, yet he'd given her everything she'd longed for, everything and much she hadn't even known existed. "Please?"

"Don't be silly, Alice. You have things to do, and so do I. Now, go."

Alice didn't have things to do, at least not in this strange place, but the way he'd said it, so forceful and sure, she didn't want to contradict. And she did want to go home. Very, very badly.

"Might I at least have something to wear?" she asked.

"Nonsense. A woman as beautiful as you, it would be a tragedy to cover you up. But the woods out there can be rough on bare skin. Just a moment."

Alice waited, and thirty seconds later, Pilar appeared again, holding a cardboard box.

"You look to be a size seven," he said.

A seven would be a bit tight on her, especially since her breasts still felt a bit swollen, but Alice would be thankful for any dress he gave her.

But when Pilar opened the box, it didn't contain a dress. Or a skirt. Or pants.

It was a pair of black leather boots, with pointed heels and silver buckles at the thighs.

"Here you are," he beamed.

Alice had never worn any such footwear. They looked to be made for strippers. Or prostitutes. But the trail was indeed rough on her bare feet, so she sat in the doorway and with great effort tugged them on.

"Magnificent," Pilar said. "They make your legs and bottom look incredible."

"Thank you. I—"

But he had already slammed the door.

So Alice forced her incredible-looking (but still rubbery) legs to carry her through the mushroom field, and peered up to see the sun glistening on their dew-kissed caps. She'd been in Pilar's cottage for what seemed like an eternity, and although her balance was wobbly and the spot between her thighs deliciously sore, she didn't feel the least bit tired.

She felt brilliant.

Alice walked in the direction Pilar had pointed, and soon she cleared the forest of mushrooms and came upon a ranch-style house with pink shutters. For a minute she stood looking at the house, wondering if whoever lived there could direct her to the path home, when suddenly a man wearing a police uniform with big lettering on his shirt stepped out of the forest and walked to the front stoop. There he set down the boom box he was carrying and simply stood, staring at the door.

"Aren't you going to knock?" Alice said. She wasn't sure what had made her feel so bold. Normally she wouldn't talk to

43

a strange man like this, even a police officer, and it wasn't until he turned and looked at her that she remembered that except for the boots, she was still completely nude.

Alice drew one arm across her breasts, and covered the shaved spot with her hand.

He would probably give her a ticket.

Instead he looked at her, staring with an intensity that made Alice want to shrink away. It wasn't a mean or hateful stare, or a crazy one.

No, this stare was... *hungry.*

"My, aren't you a pretty thing," he said, the tip of his tongue poking out his mouth and running across his perfect white teeth. "What is your name?"

"I'm Alice."

"I'm Dick. Are you here for the party, Alice?" Dick's eyes seemed to devour her.

"What party?"

"This is Wonderland. There's always a party. The Queen is playing croquet, but that's invitation only. The Hatter and the Hare are doing their tea thing, as usual. And I am here for the Duchess."

"What kind of party is the Duchess having?" Dick's stare was making Alice feel weird, and she wished desperately for something to cover herself up.

"This is a rainbow party."

Alice frowned. "I don't know what a rainbow party is."

"It is a lot of fun. Do you like having fun, Alice?"

"Yes. But I really do need to get back home."

"Well, I do hope you'll stay. You've got the prettiest lips. And your legs and bottom look fabulous in those boots."

"Thank you," Alice said, blushing.

"But your tits..."

Alice began to slouch, the blush getting worse.

"They are magnificent. I would love to have mammary intercourse with you."

"I don't know what that is, either."

"Perhaps, if you join us in the party, I can show you."

He chuckled a little and smiled. It was a handsome smile, and Alice felt the throb between her legs return. She couldn't help but wonder if Pilar's treatment hadn't done the trick, if she still had a bit of the potion still in her. Why else would she be so wanton?

"So why don't you knock on the door?" she asked, covering up again.

"Because it is open already." Dick turned the knob and they went inside.

The door led right into a large kitchen, which was full of smoke from one end to the other. Someone Alice assumed was the Duchess sat on a three-legged stool in the middle. A beautiful, buxom woman, she wore a dress with a plunging neckline, and every time she moved, she flashed a glimpse of nipple. Behind her, a large cauldron simmered on the fire, appearing to be full of soup. The rest of the kitchen was dark, cloaked in shadows, and in the corner, Alice saw something that looked like a white snake poking through the darkness.

As she stared, she realized there was a man standing behind the snake. The man had a round face with an enormous smile that seemed to cover half of it. He held a tablet computer in one hand, its screen glowing, and he grasped the snake in the other. Only the snake wasn't a snake at all.

"Please would you tell me," said Alice, a little timidly, for she was not quite sure whether it was good manners for her to speak first, "why that man is tugging on his privates?"

"His name is Cheshire," said the Duchess. "And he likes to look at naked breasts, that's why." And as if to demonstrate, she twisted in her chair and her dress fell open to expose a huge bosom.

"Thank you, Duchess!" Cheshire called, his hand a blur.

The Duchess smiled, then she took a deep breath and bellowed, "Pig!"

At first Alice thought the woman was yelling at her, or at Cheshire, and then she realized she was looking at the policeman. Flustered at how rude the Duchess was and feeling uncomfortable about how fast the man in the corner was now tugging, Alice backed away and let Dick step past her. He hit a button on his boom box, and music started playing. Before Alice knew what was going on, the cop began gyrating to the beat and taking off his uniform.

The cheap shirt and plastic badge went first, revealing sculpted muscle. With one move, his pants were off as well, leaving him in the smallest pair of underwear Alice had ever seen.

"Are you a stripper?" Alice asked.

"Didn't the shirt give it away?" Dick said.

Alice glanced at the shirt and noticed, for the first time, it had printing on it that read STRIPPER in large letters.

"My badge says, *You have the right to remain naked.*"

"I'm sorry, I didn't know."

"Duchess calls me *pig* because that is crude slang for police officers, which is how I dress as part of my act."

"Doesn't that offend you?"

"No. It turns me on. Aren't you turned on by crude and vulgar words?"

"Well, I... I don't know."

"When I said your tits were magnificent, did that arouse you?"

Alice didn't know how to answer. She was embarrassed by the question, and uncomfortable being gawked at by the man in the corner, pleasuring himself. "I... I..."

"You seem flustered."

"I *am* flustered," Alice said.

"Don't you like strippers?"

Dick pressed his muscular body against Alice, bumping into her heaving breasts, his bulge brushing the tip of her femininity.

Alice kept staring, and she felt shame in doing so, even though she couldn't turn away. Even worse, she wanted to put her hands on Dick's chest, to run them over his six-pack abs, and most of all, take off his underwear and see what that bulge looked like underneath.

Terrible, obscene, shameless thoughts that made Alice's mouth go dry.

"I need to go," she said.

"Please stay," Dick said. "I strip for the Duchess, and she gives me a rainbow. It would be wonderful if you helped her."

Alice watched the clutch of his buttocks as he danced and the bounce of the package in front, not knowing what to do. She should leave, right away, but whenever she tried to get around Dick, he stepped in front of her, gyrating and grinding. Every time he bumped her, it caused another tingle in Alice, and she was becoming increasingly, uncomfortably aroused.

"Come here, naked girl." The Duchess said in a sharp tone. "I'll show you what a rainbow party is."

Alice did as she was told, grateful to get away from the stripper.

"Isn't he delicious?" the Duchess asked. "Look at the size of his bulge."

Dick's bulge was, indeed, formidable. The Duchess motioned him to come closer. When he did, she pulled the scrap of fabric down until Dick sprang free. He wasn't quite as long as Pilar, but almost as thick as Alice's wrist, and as she looked at him, his manhood flexed upward, as if reaching for her.

"Mmm," The Duchess said. "Isn't he just lovely?"

Alice had forgotten how to talk.

"Let's make a beautiful rainbow, shall we Alice?" The Duchess reached into her clutch, pulling out a handful of small cylinders. She spread them onto the floor, chose one, and pulled off the cap and twisted, revealing a length of deep, red lipstick. Puckering up, the Duchess gave her lips a thick coat, then beckoned Dick closer.

Grabbing him roughly, the Duchess opened her mouth and slid his member deep into her cheeks. Dick stopped dancing, and instead stood incredibly still, a deep moan emanating from his chest. Her lips stretched wide to accommodate him, and the Duchess slowly, incredibly, was able to take all of him in, right down to the root.

"Thank you, Duchess," Dick said. Alice tore her eyes away from the spectacle and looked at Dick's face. His eyes were closed, his mouth open, and he panted in obvious ecstasy.

Slowly, the Duchess pulled her head away. When he popped free, there was a red lipstick ring encircling his member near the base.

"Your turn," the Duchess said. "Pick a color."

Alice was astonished. As arousing as it was to see Dick react to the Duchess's actions, Alice had never done anything like that before. She'd taken Pilar in her mouth, true. But she'd been half-insane with lust at the time, unable to control herself. And even then, Alice hadn't known what she was doing. Pilar seemed to enjoy it, but Alice's technique was amateurish. The Duchess knew exactly what she was doing. She seemed to be in complete control.

"But... I don't know how," Alice protested.

"Nonsense. You just put on lipstick and take him in your mouth."

"I don't know what I'm doing."

"I'm sure Dick won't mind if you practice on him. Dick?"

"I wouldn't mind at all, Alice," Dick said. "Practice all you like."

The Duchess picked up a tube of lipstick, extending it. The color was deep blue. She cupped Alice's chin in one hand and smeared a thick coat across her lips.

"There. Now make the second band of color in the rainbow."

Dick was right in front of her face, bobbing there, still glistening from the Duchess's attention.

"I can't," Alice said, leaning away.

"See how much he wants you?" the Duchess said.

"Please, Alice," Dick said. "Please take me in your luscious mouth."

Alice thought about getting up, running for the door. But that damnable throbbing in her nether regions had gotten worse, and Dick looked so earnest and needy. Maybe she could try it, just once.

She parted her lips, slightly, and moved them to the tip of Dick's extension. As on Pilar, the head was soft but firm, and as Alice wrapped her lips around it, Dick cried out.

She immediately jerked her head away in alarm. "I'm so sorry! What did I do wrong?"

The Duchess laughed. "Nothing, dear. The poor boy was simply overwhelmed with pleasure."

"But all I did was put it in my mouth."

"Trust me, Alice. There is no man in the world who wouldn't want a woman to take him in her mouth. It is the ultimate in control. They'll do anything for it. Watch." She turned to the stripper. "Dick, get down on your knees and put your head under my dress and I'll put you in my mouth again."

Dick immediately obeyed. Alice watched, fascinated, as the Duchess began to ride Dick's mouth like it was a carousel horse. She was rough, smearing her juices all over poor Dick's face, and it took less than a minute for her to shudder and cry out in release. Then she told Dick to stand, and took Dick's full length into her throat in a sudden, violent movement.

Dick cried out, "Thank you, Duchess!"

The Duchess bobbed her head twice, and then withdrew.

"Now put your mouth around him and see how far you can take him in, Alice."

Watching the scene had made Alice's throbbing become oh so terribly worse. She wished she had the courage to order Dick to lick her, as he had the Duchess, but that was far too embarrassing to even think about. But she did manage to open her mouth, wider this time, and slowly suck Dick in between her cheeks.

"Yes," Dick said. "Oh, yes. That's so good."

"Now bob your head, Alice," the Duchess said, entangling her fingers in Alice's hair and guiding her back and forth.

Alice began to get the hang of it, but went in too deep and began to gag. She spat Dick out.

"I'm so sorry, Dick."

But Dick's eyes had rolled up into his head, and his hips were bucking uncontrollably. He didn't seem to mind at all that she'd gagged.

"New color," the Duchess said. "How about a pretty orange?"

She did up her lips and swallowed Dick, also using her hand to stroke the base of his shaft. After a few pumps, it was Alice's turn again. Alice selected a bright pink shade of lipstick, even though pink technically wasn't a color in a rainbow. She imitated the Duchess's actions, using her hand as well, and Dick began to whimper and shake.

"What a lovely rainbow," the Duchess said, admiring the multicolored smears of lipstick on his manhood. "Don't you think so, Dick?"

"Uhng... ungh... ungh..." Dick said.

"They're so stupid and pliable when you get them to this state," the Duchess said to Alice. "Right now, if you asked him to, he'd lick your boots."

"But why?"

"Because men are pigs," the Duchess said. Then she stood up. "This has been lovely, but I must attend the Queen's croquet game. She sent an invitation to me, and she gets cross when guests are late. Please finish off Dick for me, Alice."

"Excuse me?"

"Make him climax. He's been a dear boy, and deserves his reward. "

"But, I don't know how."

"It's easy, really. Just remember the song." The Duchess started singing along with the music.

I speak severely to my boy,
I beat him when he sneezes;
For he can thoroughly enjoy
The pepper when he pleases!

"That doesn't make any sense," Alice said, wrinkling her brow.

"And why should it?" the Duchess said. "It was written a hundred-and-fifty years ago. But I will say the soup has a lot of pepper in it, and next to the soup is an ice bin. I know that Dick enjoys both. Use your imagination, Alice. You have the power here. Look how badly he wants you. He'll do anything you ask if you give him the attention he desires. Now I must be off."

And with that, the Duchess left.

Alice swallowed, her throat gone dry. She thought of Pilar, of all he'd shown her. But as much as she'd already learned about herself, he'd been in control. Alice hadn't had to do things on her own. And like she had told the Duchess, she didn't know how.

"Don't be afraid. You're doing an excellent job."

Alice turned in the direction of the voice, met Cheshire's grinning face, and all she could think about was running out of this strange house and getting back to safe, sweet Lewis, who never put her on the spot, never leered, never tried anything new, and never asked anything of her beyond laying on her back and opening her thighs.

"I like to watch," said Cheshire, stroking furiously. "I watch movies. Live shows. Some people around Wonderland let me peep in windows. And let me tell you something, Alice. You are *very* sexy to watch."

Alice wasn't sure if it was proper to thank a man who was staring at her, wanking, so instead she just politely curtsied.

"Dick likes the soup," Cheshire said. "The peppers in it are most titillating. Isn't that right, Dick?"

"Uhng," Dick said. The poor man didn't appear to know where he was.

Alice couldn't leave him in such a terrible state, so she decided to at least try. She lifted the spoon from the cup, and fingers trembling, she brought it to her lips. It smelled heavenly, like roasted chicken and potatoes, like sweet curry and succulent vegetables too varied to name. She took a sip.

Heat spread through her body, like a spicy wildfire. She let the spoon drop into the cup, then the cup crashed to the floor.

"It's so hot." Peppers overwhelmed her senses and made her body feel as if it was burning.

Dick locked eyes with her, his pleading for release.

"Come to me," she said.

He instantly responded, standing directly in front of her. She looked down at his member, hard and strong and ready. Alice shouldn't want this. Pilar was one thing. He'd overwhelmed her. No one could blame her for that. But here she could do whatever she wanted. Walk out the door and find the white rabbit vibrator. See if it could show her the way home.

Only...

Only...

Only she wanted to know what he'd taste like when he climaxed. She wanted to feel him against her tongue.

Alice lowered herself to her knees.

"Okay... I guess you can put it against my lips," she told him.

Her mouth still burned with pepper. When he brushed against her, Alice wrapped her lips around him and slid him over her tongue until he was halfway down her throat.

With a grunt, he surged deeper in her mouth, and she could imagine the sting of the pepper in her mouth on his tender skin. She pulled back slowly, as the Duchess had done, and as she reached the tip, she teased him with her tongue.

He grunted again.

Like a pig.

Figuring that was a good thing, Alice took hold of him at his root with one hand and flicked and circled and licked. Each stroke of her tongue brought a grunt and a flex, as if he was her puppet she could make perform to her whim.

"You have magnificent tits."

She'd almost forgotten that Chester (or whatever his name was) was there. And for a second, the flush of embarrassment washed over her again, but then Dick gave a mighty grunt and a little whimper, and she brought her focus back to him.

"More soup," Dick begged. "Please."

Alice had heard Lewis beg her before, but not like this. Dick's pleas aroused Alice, almost to the point where she was ready to climax herself. Unlike Lewis, whom she pleased out of love and obligation, Alice wanted to please Dick because…

Because…

Well, because it was *fun*.

Mammary intercourse, wasn't that what he'd mentioned? Maybe she could do that. It wasn't hard to figure out. But first…

Alice lifted a full cup of soup, and added a cube of ice from the bucket so it wasn't so hot. Then she splashed it onto her chest, the liquid dribbling down between her breasts.

She poured a little more of the soup on her body. It coated her skin, stung her nipples, making them tingle and burn. Alice cupped her hands on either side of her mounds, pushing them together, her nipples jutting, then she slid his manhood in between.

He grunted again, this time sounding like it came from the bottom of his being.

Alice moved up his shaft, the tip of him vanishing into her cleavage. Then she glided down, watching him grow, push forward, his head purple, burning, wanting. And when he had fully emerged, she licked him.

He cried out, and she could feel his thighs tremble.

Like she had trembled at Pilar's hand.

Tease him, that was what Pilar had taught her.

Alice circled Dick, taking her time, flicking and tormenting with her tongue, then plunging him back down between her breasts.

Between her tits. Alice embraced the vulgar word, owning it, letting it empower her.

In fact, Alice had never felt so empowered. Perhaps there was something to this.

She moved one way, she could make Dick grunt. She flicked with her tongue, light like a butterfly landing, and she could bring on a whimper. She brought him deep down into her throat, and he cried out.

The feeling was amazing.

Every few minutes, and the grinning man in the shadows would make similar, approving sounds. Where his watching had once creeped her out, Alice now found it strangely compelling, and she thought that must make her extra naughty. She imagined what he saw. Her licking and fondling and rubbing her body over Dick, but also, when she lifted from her boots to run her body up the stripper's length, Cheshire would moan, and on some level, she realized he must be looking at her, at her bottom, between her legs, at her shaved area. And instead of moving so he couldn't see, or running away, which is what she probably should have done if she'd been a good girl, she spread her thighs to give him a better view.

It was delightfully wicked.

She brought Dick into her mouth again, deep this time, until she could feel hair tickle her nose.

"Please grab them," he said, his voice hoarse. "Please grab my balls."

He started rocking against her, thrusting his length into her mouth, and they began to swing like pendulums.

She brought her hand up under him, cradling them, feeling their weight. She rolled them lightly between her fingers, seeing how it made him quiver. Dick moved faster, harder, grunting and groaning. Alice thought of Pilar, of the pleasure of being teased, of the luscious pain.

She pulled away, letting him slide from her lips.

"Oh, please don't stop. I beg you."

Alice smiled. "So beg."

His eyes widened, and she could imagine that was just how she had looked. "Please take me in your mouth again. You are so hot. I'm so turned on right now."

"How do I make you feel?" Alice asked.

"So good. I'm so close. Please, please let me come."

"I'm hot," Alice said.

His gaze skimmed down her naked body, glistening with soup. "Yes, you are so very hot."

"Yes, you are," echoed the grinning man.

"I meant, my mouth and skin are hot from the pepper."

Alice reached for the ice bucket and took several pieces into her mouth. Then she took Dick's shaft as well.

The ice was delicious and cold and wet. She cupped a chip in her tongue, then ran her tongue up the underside of his manhood.

He groaned. He grunted. He cried out.

She brought her mouth lower, under his stiff length. Cupping and licking with iced tongue, she made him whimper and beg, his hips thrusting as if he no longer had control, as if he was all hers.

So this is what Pilar meant, she thought. *This is why he enjoyed himself as much as I.*

"Please," begged Dick.

Alice smiled up at him, then stepped away. She remembered what the Duchess said.

It was ridiculous and wrong and she shouldn't do it. "Lick my boots," Alice told him anyway.

He immediately dropped to his knees and began lapping at the black leather like it was the most delectable thing he'd ever tasted. She took more soup, poured it down her belly, letting its greasy warmth tickle between her thighs.

"Now you taste the soup."

He grunted, then ran his tongue over her boot tops, up to the hinge of her thighs.

"Can I put my tongue inside you?" Dick asked. "Please?"

His pleading was sweet, his begging irresistible. And it *did* sound like a keen idea.

"What do you think, Cheshire?"

"Wait just a moment. I'm out of tissue." There were sounds of frantic movement from the shadows, and then the tear of a box being ripped open. "Okay, go ahead."

"Sit," she ordered Dick.

Dick sat.

"Lie down on your back," she said, and to her delight (and still a bit of surprise) he did.

She walked slowly around him, letting the heels of her boots click on the stone floor. A flush of heat stole over her skin, a little embarrassment at the two sets of eyes on her, yet not only that.

Strength.

Power.

Alice had something they wanted, and she could give it if she pleased.

She placed a boot on either side of Dick's head, leaving him to stare up at her most private spot, the spot that was now bare to the world.

She focused on him, on his *cock*, letting that word roll over her mind, tasting it with her thoughts, just as she'd tasted him.

Then she squatted over his face. "Lick me."

The first lick of his peppered tongue made heat wash through her, stinging, searing. She'd thought Pilar had been enough for her, forever, that she wouldn't want—couldn't want—anything more.

She was wrong. "Keep going."

He did. With pepper and with ice, he moved his tongue over her, slowly like Pilar, then fast and frantic, like Lewis, only this lasted much longer.

The pressure built in her, as before. More and more. Faster and faster. She thrust herself against his mouth, her breasts bouncing, and all the while she could see the glazed look on the smiling man's face, watching her, wanting her.

Dick uttered, "Please," through the vee of her thighs, the word sending pleasure and pain and need crashing through her.

Leaving her legs straddling him, she moved down his body, flicked and teased with her tongue, and then took his entire length deep into her throat, just as the Duchess had when she branded him with the bright red lipstick.

"Oh, Alice, you are the best!"

"Seconded!" Cheshire yelled, grunting along with them.

Then Alice climaxed as Dick flexed and moaned and another taste filled her mouth, salt joining the pepper.

Alice managed to swallow all of it, more out of courtesy than anything else, and realized she didn't mind at all. In fact, it was something she'd be happy to try again.

The experience seemed to completely exhaust Dick, who dropped to his knees with a dazed expression on his face. He managed to sort-of look at Alice, though his ability to focus seemed compromised.

"Best. Ever," he said.

Alice wanted to tell him how sweet that was to say, and how good it had been for her as well, but Dick was already curling up on the floor with his eyes closed.

What was it with men and wanting to sleep afterward? Alice felt energized. Alive, vibrant, ready to take on the whole world.

"Agreed," said Cheshire from the shadows. "That was tremendous, Alice. Thank you for a wonderful show."

Alice peered into the dark corner. "I don't understand, sir. You were touching yourself."

"Yes," Cheshire said. "That's what I do."

"So how could any one time be better than any other time if it is always you doing the touching?"

Cheshire chuckled. "I never thought of it that way. Consider this, dear Alice. Sex is only partly about friction and bodily fluids. The majority of it takes place in the mind. The body responds to what the mind desires. When we see something arousing, or read something arousing, our bodies respond because we can imagine ourselves in that situation. Watching you turned me on, because I saw what you did to Dick, and wanted to be him. I fantasized it was me, and my climax was very nice as a result."

"Wouldn't it be better to experience the real thing?" Alice asked.

"Fantasy is real, Alice. The outcome would be the same whether it was by my own hand, or your lovely mouth. Or any of your other lovely parts."

Alice touched one of those parts, which moments ago had been pressed against Dick's face. While that had been delightful, Alice wouldn't have minded if Dick had entered her as well. Alice was satisfied, but had discovered her body's capacity to accept more pleasure than she'd ever thought possible.

"So, Cheshire," Alice said delicately, "if I were to come over to you, perhaps we could—"

"A lovely offer, Alice. But I'm no longer a young man, and my refractory period is perhaps longer than you would feel obliged to wait. However, if you do come here, I would be pleased to bestow a gift upon you."

Alice brightened. A gift may not be as nice as being vigorously penetrated, but it was a good consolation prize.

"I do hope it is some clothing," Alice said. "I so need something more to wear than these boots."

"Indeed it is, Alice. Though I must say, those boots make your legs and bottom look extraordinary."

Alice hurriedly walked over to the corner of the room, her heels clicking rhythmically.

"Mind your step," Cheshire warned. "I have been here a while, and the floor is slippery."

She traversed a minefield of spent tissues and slick stains, and then reached Cheshire, who was naked, flaccid, and standing next to the largest bottle of hand cream Alice had ever seen. It had to contain several liters.

Cheshire caught her staring and said, "I buy in bulk. When one masturbates as much as I, chaffing can become life-threatening."

"I'm sorry."

"Sorry? No need. See?"

Cheshire offered his hand. Alice took it lightly.

"My!" she exclaimed. "You have the softest hands I've ever known!"

"And look at my grip," Cheshire said. He dug his hand into a nearby box of walnuts and cracked them using only his fingers. "Care for one?"

Alice was actually a bit hungry, so she picked out the nut meat from the shells and ate them.

They tasted like hand cream.

"Anyway, here is the gift I promised you," Cheshire said, holding up what appeared to be a black pair of panties.

"Underwear!" Alice squealed, snatching the gift. But when she examined them more closely, they were unlike any underwear she had ever seen.

"It's a garter belt," Cheshire said.

"What is it for?"

"For holding up stockings, of course. They are terribly sexy, and a personal favorite of mine."

"But I'm not wearing any stockings," Alice said.

"I just gave you a garter belt, and now you demand stockings from me as well?"

Alice shook her head, flustered. "No, I—"

"Kidding," Cheshire said, grinning his wide grin. "I also have some of those for you." He squatted down next to Alice's boots. "May I?"

Alice nodded, figuring it was impolite to say no, and Cheshire removed her left boot. He then took her foot in his hands, kissed it, and for some reason, sniffed it deeply.

"Have you ever had your toes licked?"

"No! Why would anyone want to do that?"

"Certainly you would never form an opinion about something without trying it first?"

Alice thought it over. "I suppose I wouldn't." At least, not anymore.

"You should consider it at some point. You have lovely feet."

Cheshire reached behind him and produced a black stocking. He helped Alice into it, and then its twin, and showed her how to hold them up with the clips on the garter belt.

"These are very odd stockings," Alice said. "They aren't warm at all."

"Fishnet stockings aren't meant to be warm. Fishnet stockings are meant to make the wearer feel sexy, and to arouse all that see her."

Alice remained dubious. She put her boots back on and studied the look, unsure if she liked it or not.

Cheshire apparently did. He was reaching for the hand cream pump and tugging on himself again, his eyes glued to Alice's legs.

Alice thought it rude for him to waste his arousal on himself, when she was feeling so empty and in need of being filled. But he had just given her a present, so she didn't say anything.

"Well, thank you, Cheshire."

Cheshire nodded, his hand tugging himself even faster. It made Alice feel very self-conscious, and the shame of being watched was returning. He seemed to be a nice enough fellow, but being on display like this was off-putting.

"I, um, have a question, Cheshire. I really do want to get back home, but I don't know how."

"Why? Aren't you enjoying Wonderland?"

"I am, yes, but..."

"Have you tried clicking your ruby slippers together three times?"

"What?"

"Sorry, wrong book. Would you mind bending over for me?"

Alice hunched down. "I'm not really comfortable with that."

"You were earlier. You were putting on quite a show."

"Well, I don't know what came over me. Normally I'm quite shy and reserved. This is really the first time I've ever been naked in front of anybody."

"Not even in front of your boyfriend?"

Alice frowned. "I never have time to get naked in front of him. He's... quick."

"Sounds like a turtle I know."

"A quick turtle? That's ridiculous."

"Would you squeeze your nipples for me while slowly rolling your tongue across your lips?"

The question made Alice *very* embarrassed. She slouched even further, putting a hand over her breasts.

"Try the Hatter and the Hare," Cheshire said. "They might be able to help you get home."

"Where might I find them?"

"Take the trail in the woods. But both are quite mad."

"Who are they mad at?"

"Mad as in crazy, Alice. Wonderland is filled with crazies and cuckoos and nutjobs. It is quite your good fortune to run into someone as sane and lucid as I am. Now, before you go, could you bend over for me and spread your cheeks apart while singing the theme from *Happy Days?*"

Alice nodded a hasty goodbye, then hurried to the front door and left the Duchess's cabin, fleeing back into the woods, embarrassed and inappropriately aroused and hoping this Hatter and Hare could help her leave this strange, uncomfortable place.

Chapter 4

A Mad Tea-Party

Alice followed the path to its end, coming to what seemed to be someone's front yard. The strangest table Alice had ever seen was set out under a tree in front of a house. It was only the size of a leather loveseat, and one end crested then plunged down into a valley, like a rollercoaster, before rising again to a smaller peak. Three men were gathered tightly on one end, a nice-looking one wearing a top hat and suit, a rather bleary chap who slumped between them, fast asleep, and a third wearing a bunny costume. The two sat on either side of the sleeping man and used his back as a cushion, resting their elbows on him, talking over his head.

Embarrassed that she was totally naked but for her boots, garter belt, and stockings, Alice ducked behind a nearby bush.

"What are you doing?" the man with the bunny costume asked.

"I'm naked."

"Are you? That must be why I can see your bush."

Alice frowned at the greenery. "This isn't my bush."

"Then why are you in it?"

She wasn't sure if he was complaining about her trespassing or was worried about the bush, but he didn't seem to understand her point. "I'm naked, and I don't wish to be seen. So I'm hiding in this bush."

"I don't believe that you're naked. Let us see for ourselves."

Now this really didn't make sense to Alice, but very little did in this strange place. And since she left the Duchess's house, the hollow ache in her most private place had grown worse, demanding to be filled. So despite knowing it was naughty to do so, she stepped out from behind the bush, covering her vulnerable parts as best she could.

The two men who were awake stared, but it was the bunny who again spoke. "You're not naked. You're wearing boots."

"Boots aren't clothes."

"Maybe not," continued the bunny man, "but they make your legs and bottom look divine."

Alice stood there for a long while, and no one said a word. Aware of the afternoon sun glowing on the white curve of her breasts, and her nipples tightening to hard nubs under their gazes, she grew more and more uncomfortable. "May I sit?"

"There's no room," said the handsome man in the hat.

The statement was ridiculous, and it occurred to her he must have said it just to give her a hard time. But when she looked into his face, he had a kind and interested expression, and she recognized the gleam she had seen in Pilar's eyes, in Dick's eyes, and in Cheshire's.

He looked as if he wanted to touch her. To kiss her. To do dreadful and delicious things.

Maybe they all were mad, as Cheshire had suggested. Maybe she was mad, too. Her deepest place felt terribly vacant, and she was even starting not to mind these men looking at her nakedness… at least a little.

"Are you sure there's no room? Not even if I sit very close?"

"How close?" the Hatter asked.

She slipped her bottom onto the ground beside the strange table.

"I'm sorry, that's not close enough. I'm afraid you will have to leave."

To Alice's surprise, she didn't want to leave. "But I can't sit any closer at this odd table."

"You think our table is odd?" said the bunny man.

"I don't mean to offend you, but most tables are flat, so the cups and saucers don't slide off."

"Are they?"

"Yes."

"Well, this isn't most tables." The man in the hat gave a harrumph. "It's a sex chair. But that doesn't change the fact that if you want to stay, you must sit closer."

Alice didn't believe there was any such thing as a sex chair, but she thought it might be rude to say so.

"Are you going to sit closer?" The Hatter asked, and he and the rabbit man stared at her, and there wasn't a bit of rudeness in their eyes. In fact they even smiled. "Please?"

And at that, Alice felt *she* would be the rude one if she didn't at least make an effort. So, with a feeling of supreme naughtiness trilling up her spine, she plopped one hip on the edge of the leather top of the curvy, slopey-slanty sex chair table, her nipples jutting only inches from their faces.

The men stared and time ticked by. Alice thought they might have fallen into some kind of trance.

"Are you okay?" she finally asked.

"We're giddy," said the Hare.

"Why wouldn't we be?" echoed the Hatter. "A naked stranger is sitting at our table."

"I wish all of our tea parties were this good," the Hare said.

"Well, shouldn't we do something?" Alice asked. "Other than just sit here?"

"What do you suggest?" the Hatter asked. His eyes glinted with wicked possibilities.

Alice wanted to say something exciting. Something outrageous. But, once again, her embarrassment got in the way.

"May I have some tea?" she eventually asked.

"Tea?" The Hatter frowned, as if he'd never heard the word before.

"Yes, tea. Isn't this a tea party?"

"No, we're not really interested in politics."

"I mean the kind of party where you serve tea. The beverage," Alice clarified. "Or is this a costume party?"

"Why would you say that?" asked the man in the rabbit suit.

"Because you're dressed as a bunny."

"I'm the March Hare," he said.

"And I'm the Hatter," said the other, facts she'd already surmised based on what Cheshire had told her. "And this," he pointed to the sleeping man, "is Dorien. Dorien Maus."

The man gave a snore, as if in hello.

"Dor Maus for short," the Hatter said. "Even though the work we're parodying is in the public domain, it should be noted that parody is protected under the First Amendment as part of free speech, just in case."

Cheshire has said they were mad, and he was spot-on.

"My name is Alice." She looked at the March Hare. "And I'd like to know why you're wearing a costume."

"Because I'm a hare, Alice," he said to her breasts.

"But you're not. You're a man. You're just dressed as a hare."

The Hare stuck out his chest and proudly began to recite:

> *The rabbit has a charming face,*
> *Its private life is a disgrace.*
> *I really dare not name to you*
> *The awful things that rabbits do.*

"You people are batty," Alice said, meaning it.

"Not batty," said the Hare. "I'm *harey*. Or, more technically, *furry*."

"People who dress up as animals are called *furries*," the Hatter whispered to her. "They believe they are the costumes they wear. It's an odd kink, that's true, but judging others is quiet dull and repressive."

"I don't mean to be dull, or to repress anyone, but he surely is a man," Alice insisted. "Those rabbit ears are attached with a headband."

"I am a rabbit," the Hare said, "who also happens to wear a rabbit costume."

"No you're not."

"Can you prove I'm a man?" the Hare asked.

"Yes, I can, if you'll take off your costume."

So he took off the lower part of his costume, revealing he was naked underneath. Naked, and very aroused. Not quite as big as Pilar, but the Hare's manhood curved upward in a way that Alice found quite erotic.

"Do you wish to touch it?" the Hare asked.

Alice did, but again shyness prevented her reply.

"I would so like it if you did," the Hare said. "And stroking a rabbit's foot is lucky."

"But that's not a foot!" Alice insisted.

"True, I'm only seven inches," said the Hare. "But doesn't it have a nice, upward arc to it?"

Alice agreed. "Yes, it does."

"So touch it."

"Well, I don't want to be rude." Alice reached out and ran a finger up the underside of the arch. "See?" she said, feeling him twitch under her fingertips. "You are a man."

"No," said the Hare, "I'm a well-endowed rabbit. The Hatter is a man." And he pointed to the Hatter who had peeled off his pants and shirt and was wearing a different hat, a rakish fedora this time.

But Alice didn't care about his hat. She was focused on the hair that sprinkled his chest and trailed in a line as if pointing down to the thick staff jutting between muscular thighs. Something quivered deep within her.

The Hatter smiled. With one swoop of a powerful arm, he cleared the few cups that had managed not to already have slid off the odd table and pushed the sleeping Dor Maus onto the ground as well.

"Now lean forward, put your hands on the table, and spread your legs wide," he said.

Alice wasn't sure how to respond to that. She knew boldness was within her, as Pilar, the Duchess, and Dick had coaxed her into try things she otherwise never would have. But Alice still lacked the confidence needed to be so daring.

"I... I can't. I wish I were a little bolder."

"What for?" the Hatter asked. "Being a small rock wouldn't be much fun."

"Unless you were a rock star, perhaps," added the Hare.

"What? Oh. Not boulder with a *u*. Bolder, as in without fear."

"We knew that," the Hatter said. "We were making a stupid pun."

"Which we must apologize for," said the Hare. "They weren't funny when that hack Carroll did it back in 1865, and they certainly have no place in an ebook of mommy porn."

"What are you both talking about?" Alice asked.

"*Mommy porn* is a crude label applied to erotica read by discerning, intelligent women who seek something more adventurous in their reading choices," the Hare said.

"What?" Alice said.

"Perhaps you should Google the word *metafiction*," the Hare suggested.

"What does any of this have to do with wanting to be bold?" Alice demanded, thoroughly confused.

"We all feel fear, Alice," the Hatter told her, resting a kind hand on her shoulder. "Being bold is a chance to show that you control your fear, and won't let your fear control you."

"So lean forward and spread your legs wide," said the Hare.

Alice bit her lower lip, her heart beating twice as fast as normal. She knew they were right. Both about the stupid puns, and the fear. So, summoning up some reserve of courage Alice didn't know she had, she decided to comply.

Standing at the lower end of the curvy contraption, she leaned forward on her hands, her bottom tilted in the air, her breasts slung forward, nipples nearly brushing the leather cover.

"So, what next?" Alice asked.

"Now we play a game," the Hatter said.

"What are the rules?" she asked, since everyone knew all games had rules.

"There's only one rule," said the Hatter. "To enjoy yourself. Because after all, that's what games are about."

"So why do I have to stand in this position?" Alice didn't want to be disagreeable, but if they wanted to play the type of game Alice thought they did, there were other, more conventional positions to do it in.

The Hatter winked and stroked himself. "You'll see. And it will be fun."

He lay down on the chair with his face beneath her mounds, his legs on either side, and his thick shank thrust straight up to the sky, purple and corded with veins and hair curling around its base. "Do you like to have fun, Alice?" he asked.

And Alice thought about Pilar and how full she'd been when he shoved himself inside her, and how empty and hollow her special place had felt when she'd left the Duchess's rainbow party.

"Yes, I like to have fun," said Alice, and a shiver of anticipation prickled her skin.

The Hatter smiled up at her, her nipples directly under his mouth.

"Your tits truly are magnificent, Alice," he said and teased the tight, throbbing nubbins with his tongue, then sucked and nibbled until she thought she might scream from the building sensations.

"Do you like this game, Alice?" asked the Hare.

"I do so far," she said with a puff of breath.

"Good. Then it's my turn."

The Hare circled behind her bottom and peered between her legs. For a moment she thought he would lick her. She wanted him to lick her. But he didn't. He merely stared.

"Your womanhood truly is beautiful, Alice."

Warmth flushed through her, and she felt utterly exposed. "But I don't even have any hair down there."

"You will in a moment," the March Hare said. Then he stepped behind, grabbed her hips, positioned himself at her opening, and thrust his curved shaft deep inside.

Her body clutched around him. She lurched forward and just then, the Hatter sucked her right nipple hard into this mouth, and she cried out.

Alice's muscles contracted and spasmed, like they were being pulled by rubber bands, and she thought her legs would collapse like a telescope. But the Hare circled his arm beneath her belly and cradled her to him, all the time driving into her and making her clench deep down with unspeakable pleasure.

She could feel something more, a force swinging and slapping against the sensitive bump between her legs, and realized it was the rest of the Hare's man parts—his *balls*, as Dick had called them—and the rhythmic *slap, slap, slap* sent another spasm arching through her.

This was, indeed, a better position, and a better game, than she ever could have imagined.

"I have another game to play, Alice," said the Hatter, the low timbre of his voice vibrating between her breasts. He scooted his body further beneath her until she could feel the stubble on his chin prickle against her most tender place and he started licking in time with the March Hare's thrusts. The Hatter's thick, purple staff, like one of Pilar's mushrooms, rested against her nose. On its tip, a tiny drop of moisture glistened like dew.

"Would you like permission to take my cock in your mouth?" the Hatter asked.

Alice blushed at his use of the word. But she managed to say, "Yes."

"Yes, what?"

Alice was finding it difficult to concentrate, between the nipple licking and the Hare pumping into her from behind.

"Yes, I'd like permission…"

"To?"

"To take your…"

"My what?"

Alice stared down at it, so big and inviting. The word was so naughty, so vulgar, but she wanted it badly.

"I'd like permission to take your… your… *cock* in my mouth."

"Permission granted."

Sighing with relief, Alice placed a hand around the thick base and licked it up with the tip of her tongue.

The Hatter tasted different from the stripper, different from Pilar. Salty, yes, but with a certain sweet note that made her want to lap at him endlessly. It never occurred to her that men would taste different. Before she came here, she hadn't wanted to taste them at all.

But now?

Now she'd probably wonder what every single man she saw walking down the street tasted like—not that she'd try to find out, of course not, girls like her didn't do such things—but thinking about what Lewis might taste like turned her on even more.

She cupped her lips around the Hatter's thickness and slid down to his root. She could feel a groan work through his body from his loins through his belly, into his chest, and finally tickling her as he slathered her breasts with lips and tongue.

And from behind, the Hare kept going and going and going, as if his batteries would never wear out.

Alice felt the climax growing inside her, building like a tidal wave, and then, quite amazingly, the pleasure tripled when something touched her most sensitive spot. With the Hatter still in her mouth, she looked down between her legs and saw he had reached up his hands into her cleft, flicking her grateful clitoris as the Hare continued to plunge in and out.

The sensations overpowered poor Alice, and she began to scream around the Hatter's manhood. It went on and on and on until she simply couldn't stand up anymore, and she fell down onto her knees with both men slipping out of her simultaneously.

"Are you okay, Alice?" the Hare said, his face awash with concern.

"I'm... fabulous," she said, smiling wide.

"Then let's try a new game," said the Hatter, and he spun around on the sex chair and leaned against the steeper rise. "Sit on my lap, Alice."

The Hare helped Alice to her feet, and she stared down at the Hatter's member, which thrust up from his lap and seemed to be growing thicker and longer by the second. "Where would I put my bottom? There seems to be no room."

The Hatter winked. "Have you ever wondered what it feels like to be so totally full that you thought you might burst?"

"You mean like when I go out to dinner and eat too much when I should have taken the leftovers to go?"

"No, that's not exactly what I mean."

"Then what do you mean?" She couldn't look away from his long rod, it was if she had fallen into a trance herself.

"I mean what if you sat in my lap? And I filled up your bottom?"

He couldn't mean what he was saying. "Filled it up with what?"

"With my cock." And to illustrate, he took hold of it and began to stroke.

Next to her, the March Hare did the same with his charming curved shaft.

And as much as she liked these two men, and as much fun as she was having with their game, and as much as she wanted to be bold, Alice gave her head a shake. "I think that would hurt."

"Have we hurt you so far?" asked the March Hare.

"No, but I think the Hatter will be too big."

"How about me?" The March Hare angled his hips to thrust his length in the air.

Alice shook her head. "No, I'm afraid that even though it's curved in that charming way, yours is too big, too."

The Hatter climbed off the sofa or table or sex chair or whatever it was and nudged the sleeping Dor Maus with his toe. "Wake up, Maus, and take off your clothes."

And as absurd as the order was, the man woke and disrobed as if it was the most natural thing in the world, then he stared at her bare breasts and glistening nipples with wide and hungry eyes.

And even though she'd just had the Hare inside her and the Hatter deep in her mouth, Alice still felt ashamed she was naked in front of this new man.

"How about him?" The Hatter reached down and tugged at the man's privates. "Is he a more comfortable size?"

And Alice examined Maus. Five inches if he was lucky, the man's member was chiseled like a sculpture, and was possibly the most attractive one she'd yet seen. And before Alice quite knew what she was doing, she nodded, and Maus was taking the Hatter's place on the sex chair and pulling something that glistened on his perfectly formed part.

"Sit on his lap, Alice," the Hatter crooned.

"Sit on his...?"

"Yes."

"With his...?"

"Yes."

"In my...?"

"Yes."

"But, isn't it..." Alice blushed something terrible and whispered, "dirty?"

"Dirty?" Maus bristled. "I just took a shower this morning."

"I meant, my..."

"Your bottom?" the Hatter asked.

"Yes." Alice hung her head in shame.

"Well," the Hatter said. "Only one way to find out."

Suddenly he, the Hare, and Maus were on their knees behind Alice, as the Hatter, now wearing a light band on his head like a medical doctor, spread her cheeks apart.

"My!" Alice yelped.

"Looks very clean to me," the Hatter said.

And then Alice felt something warm and wet where she'd never felt anything warm and wet before. She almost fell over again.

"Tastes fine, too," the Hare said.

"You're going to have your body your whole life, Alice," the Hatter said. "There are no parts you should be ashamed of. And certainly no parts that are dirty." He smiled and gave her a devilish wink. "Unless, of course, you *like it dirty*."

Alice wasn't sure what to say, what to. No one had ever licked her there before. And no one ever wanted to put anything in there, either.

But Alice thought about all the other new things she'd tried that day, things she never could have imagined, and she'd liked them all. And although she knew she probably shouldn't, that no decent girl did things like this, Alice decided to take a chance and be bold.

"Okay," she said. And a millisecond after the words left her lips, Maus was back on the sex chair and the Hatter and the Hare had whisked Alice off of her feet and begun to lower her, legs parted, onto him.

Alice could feel his tip probe at her bottom, and she started to have second thoughts. "I can't—"

"Just relax and let me glide inside," said Maus, his voice gentle and soothing as a gentle rain. "I'm using a lubricated prophylactic. If this hurts too much, let me know, and I'll stop."

"How shall I let you know?" Alice asked.

"A phone call?" the Hatter suggested.

"Semaphore?" added the Hare.

"Do you have semaphore flags, Alice?" asked Maus.

"I meant," Alice said, "if I'm screaming, you might well think I'm enjoying myself and won't stop. Can we use a safeword?"

"Very well, a safeword," said the Hatter. "And our safeword today is *cock*."

Alice flushed at the thought of saying that word. "That's so vulgar."

"But sometimes vulgar is exciting, isn't it?"

Alice didn't reply, but she hoped she wouldn't have to use the safeword. This game was embarrassing enough.

"Now relax and I'll enter you very slowly," said Dor (she figured she should call him by his first name, since he was about to enter her bottom), and he slid between her cheeks.

Alice relaxed, and little by little, he inched inside. And she could feel herself stretching, but there was no pain, at least none but the pleasant kind. She was worried he'd be revolted, but the sounds he made were of the happy variety, sighing and moaning.

Then Dor started moving, slowly, tenderly, and she stared up at the tree bows overhead and lay on her back on top of him, and actually had to admit this strange fullness felt deliciously good.

The Hatter slung a leg over the chair as if he was climbing aboard a motorcycle, and on his head now was indeed, the type of leather cap Alice had seen bikers wear. And he snuggled up against her and his huge shaft pushed into her other opening.

If Alice had thought she felt full before, she was mistaken. For a second, she thought it was too much, that she couldn't take it. The Hatter was so big, and Dor already occupied her bottom. But then the Hatter eased deeper and deeper and her juices flowed and her body relaxed and then the two of them started rocking in time, Dor behind and the Hatter in front.

"Oh," Alice said. "Oh, my."

She could feel both men inside her, as if they shared the same space. Her whole lower area was glowing with sensations, and the sensations were building upon each other, getting more intense with every stroke.

"This..." Alice said. "This is..."

"It's what?" the Hare asked.

"*Oh my.*"

Then the Hatter reached up, his fingers finding her nipples, and Alice let out a sharp cry that scared all of the jays off the dead birch tree in the yard.

"How about me?" said the Hare. "Is there a game I can play?"

Alice nodded, reaching for him, her hands shaking.

"What are the rules?"

Alice was unable to articulate anything. She was too lost in pleasure. She looked at the Hatter, thrusting into her, and pleaded for him to help. He brought his fingers against her right above where he'd entered and he played and stroked until she screamed out again, scaring a family of squirrels out of their nest, where they dropped to the ground and bounced like furry brown balls.

When she'd recovered enough to think, Alice peered up at the Hare. With her bottom claimed by Dor, and her womanhood overflowing with the Hatter, there was obviously only one game left to play. She opened her mouth wide, trying to get him to understand.

"You want to play dentist?" the Hare said. "I'm to examine your teeth?"

The rhythm continued. Back and forth and back and forth until Alice felt she was going to lose her mind.

"My... my... my rules," Alice said, struggling mightily to get the words out. "You have to... put it... in my mouth."

"*It*?" he said.

"Your..."

"My?"

The Hatter did something with his fingers again, and Alice screamed so loud the dog ran and hid under the porch.

"Your... man part."

"Which part?" He frowned, still not following.

"Your..." she ogled his sweet, curved shaft, hoping he'd follow her meaning.

"I don't understand," he said.

The Hatter's thrust and Dor's parry grew faster, and Alice could feel another orgasm roaring up fast as a freight train.

"Your cock! Your cock!" she cried.

And the other two stopped.

"Please, keep going," Alice begged frantically, bucking against them and sending her breasts bouncing.

"That was the safeword," said the Hatter.

Of course it was, and she'd forgotten. But she didn't want to be safe now. She wanted to be totally filled by all three men. She wanted them to send her over the edge and then go over along with her. "I'm... I'm being bold and changing the rules," she gasped. "Can I do that?"

"You can do anything you want," said the Hatter. "All you have to do is figure out what it is."

Alice didn't have to think about that, not right now, which was probably good, because she was beyond thinking. "I want three cocks inside me right now."

"But wait," said the Hare.

Alice stared at him. "*Wait?*"

"What's a tea party without tea bagging?"

She was almost frantic, wanting him in her, needing him. "Why are you talking about tea bags? I want your cock in my mouth."

"I'll show you." He took hold of his manhood and lifted it, then he straddled her hear and lowered his other parts—his balls—down to her lips.

Immediately understanding his odd request, Alice opened her mouth and took them inside. And although she still didn't see what this had to do with making tea, she sucked and she rolled until he tensed up with a groan. Then he plunged his cock between her lips as the other two rocked her, and an orgasm crashed through Alice so fierce she was sure she'd become as mad as they were. It was followed by another, and another.

"I'm coming," cried Dor.

"Almost there," moaned the Hatter.

Alice sucked the Hare harder, hoping to make him climax at the same time. And then Dor cried out, his hips spasming, and the Hatter bellowed deep, pressing his cheek into Alice's chest and holding her tight as he shuddered, and the Hare's hot essence shot into her mouth and dribbled down her chin, and Alice literally exploded with pleasure.

Okay... Alice didn't really *literally* explode. But it was pretty damn epic.

Their energies spent, the Hatter helped her up off the sex chair.

"I have to buy one of those," Alice said, blowing out a huge breath and eyeing the chair.

"Amazon.com," said the Hare. "They sell everything, and have the best prices."

Dor began to snore.

"Does he always sleep so much?" Alice asked. She felt lovely and content and a little sore, and just about ready to curl up and go to sleep right beside him.

"He can't sleep for long. He's invited to play croquet with the Queen."

"Were you two invited?" Alice asked, looking from the Hatter to the Hare.

"Of course we were," said the Hare. "Weren't you?"

"She must be," said the Hatter. "Why wouldn't a beautiful and sexy woman like Alice not get an invitation?"

And although Alice was embarrassed, she had to shake her head. "I have no invitation."

The Hatter frowned. "Are you sure? Maybe you should look inside you."

Alice frowned. "What do you mean? Search my soul and see if I deserve to go?"

"No," the Hatter said, pointing to her nether-regions. "I mean *inside* you."

Alice stared down between her hairless legs. "There's a croquet invitation in *there*?"

"Check and see."

Alice reached a hand down there, then hesitated. She *never* touched that part of her. And had certainly never reached inside. Squeezing her eyes shut, hating every moment, the put a single finger in and moved it around.

"There's nothing," she lamented.

"Go deeper."

Alice did.

"Deeper."

"There's nothing," she yelled, pulling out her hand in anger and humiliation.

"Of course there is nothing," the Hatter said. "Who ever heard of such a ridiculous thing?"

"So why did you make me do it?" Alice demanded.

"Because it was really hot," he answered.

The Hare nodded in agreement.

The Duchess was right. Men were pigs.

"Well, I have to get dressed," the Hatter said. "I can't play croquet like this. It would cause a scandal."

The Hare nodded. "And sunburn."

And as they dressed, the Hatter in his suit and the Hare in his costume, Alice again felt self-conscious about her nudity. "What about me? I have no clothes."

"You have boots," the Hatter said, studying her, and if she wasn't mistaken, his manhood started to grow again. "And they make your legs and bottom look stupendous."

"I have something for you to wear," said the March Hare. And he reached into the discarded furry pants of his costume and pulled out a leather bra. "Put this on."

Grateful to finally have something that covered her breasts, Alice slipped the bra on. But though the leather contraption fit her perfectly, it was like no bra she'd ever worn before. Made of leather straps and silver buckles, the apparatus surrounded each of her breasts, hefting them high. But it left most of her fleshy mounds totally bare, her nipples protruding luridly in front of her.

"I can't wear this," she said.

The Hare made a face. "Of course you can. Look in the mirror. You're wearing it right now.

"But it doesn't even cover my nipples."

"Your nipples are delicious, Alice," said the Hatter. "Why ever would you cover them? They should be seen and tasted and suckled by the world. But…"

"But what?"

"You're right. The look isn't quite complete." And so he took off his leather motorcycle cap and plopped it on her head. "There, that's perfect. We'll see you there. Just walk through that hedge."

"Don't be late," added the Hare, and the two of them walked away to the house and left her.

Alice looked down at sleeping Dorian Maus, then shrugged. It had been the loveliest tea party she'd ever attended, but now that it was over, what was there to do but continue on her way?

Chapter 5

The Queen's Croquet-Ground

Alice wasn't sure what croquet was, because she lived in modern day America and not nineteenth century England. She had never seen croquet on YouTube (though one of her favorites was that adorable little baby panda sneezing), and the sad fact is that most teenagers are, by their nature, rather dense, and Alice was no exception. She thought it may have something to do with knitting, recalling that she once received a terrible birthday gift from one of her elderly aunts, who had croqueted a sweater.

But she had never met a queen before (other than a rather flamboyant boy in her science class who painted his nails pink and called everyone *girlfriend*) so Alice was both excited by the prospect and a little nervous. If anyone knew how Alice could get back home, it was probably a queen.

She walked through the hedge, as instructed, and it lead to a clearing with a green, lush, carefully maintained lawn hemmed in by bushes trimmed in the shape of playing cards. Her spiky heels dug into the sod, making walking awkward, but anyone watching would have agreed that her legs and bottom looked awesome. However, no one was watching, which suited Alice fine. Even though she'd been naked for what felt like forever, she still hadn't gotten used to it, and every time she met someone new it was embarrassment and humiliation all over again. Alice once heard it said that more people were afraid of speaking in public than dying. She understood completely. But there was one thing worse than public speaking; public speaking while all of your private parts were showing.

Sounds of conversation and laughter broke through the bushes, and Alice followed them until she reached a crowd of people. Considering all the weirdoes she'd recently met, these people were dressed more or less normally. Alice had heard it called business casual. No ties or suits, but the men wore pleated pants and long sleeved shirts, and the women wore fashionable skirts and tops. It made the ridiculous outfit Alice was wearing even more outrageous.

She hobbled up to the group, which seemed to be circled around four people hitting colored balls across the lawn with large, wooden mallets.

So that's croquet, Alice thought. *How ridiculous. Haven't these people heard of PlayStation?*

Three of the players were men, but one was a woman. She was tall, in a red dress that clung to her every curve, and she wore red boots that had heels just like Alice's. Her hair was deep red, pulled back in a severe bun, and her bright red lips formed a heart when she pouted, which at the moment she was doing. Alice immediately knew this must be the queen. The woman radiated power, and authority in a way Alice had never known, and everyone buzzed and flocked around her as if she was the center of the universe, some people looking timid and frightened, some looking infatuated.

Also, she wore a gold crown, which kind of made it obvious.

"Has anyone seen where my red ball went?" the Queen demanded, hands on her hips.

There was shrugging from the three men she played with, and intense murmurs from the crowd of a dozen.

"If that ball isn't found immediately," the Queen said, "you shall all be publicly paddled!"

Alice couldn't think of anything worse than that, and apparently everyone agreed, because the next few seconds were a frenzy of frantic searching, everyone climbing all over one another to find the Queen's ball. Alice was pushed, bumped, and shoved, and she wound up flung into a hedge and on all fours. And there, under the hedge, was the red croquet ball.

Alice snatched it and stood, holding it triumphantly over her head.

"I found it! I found it, Your Majesty!"

All at once the crowd went silent and still. They parted, forming a circle around Alice and staring intently as the Queen approached. Alice inwardly shrank, placing an arm across her bare nipples, lowering the hand with the ball to shield her naked loins. A blush crept up her cheeks, getting worse as the crowd began to whisper and point at her.

"And who are you?" the Queen said, her voice loud and mean.

"I'm Alice. I found your ball."

Alice held it out, meekly. The Queen slapped it away, and it went rolling under another hedge.

"You shall not speak unless spoken to," the Queen said.

"But you just spoke to me."

"Silence!" the Queen ordered, pointing a finger at Alice's face. The Queen's nails were glossy and red. "This croquet party is private and can only be attended if you have an invitation. Do you have an invitation, Alice?"

Alice wasn't sure whether or not to answer. She didn't like being yelled at. It added to the humiliation of being naked in public. She wished, more than anything, to just disappear.

"You refuse to answer?" the Queen asked. "So be it. Guards! Off with her clothes!"

One of the men in the Queen's croquet game, a man in khakis and a polo shirt, approached Alice and grabbed her arm. "My Queen," he said, "she doesn't seem to be wearing much in the way of clothes."

"Is that so?" the Queen asked.

"Just a hat, boots, a garter belt, stockings, and a demi bra, Your Majesty."

"So it seems. Tell me, why are you dressed that way, slut?!"

Alice was shocked by the vulgarity. "I'm not a slut!"

"You are certainly dressed like one," the Queen said.

"But these are the only clothes I have!"

"The only clothes you have? If those are your only clothes, then you must be a slut!"

"But I'm not!"

"Seize the slut!"

The next thing Alice knew, guards were holding both of her arms, stretching her out so she could no longer cover her body. The Queen approached, then spent a moment looking Alice up and down. Her gaze felt like a laser, burning Alice's skin wherever it focused.

"Everyone, look at Alice's bare breasts," the Queen said.

The crowd came in for a closer look. Alice struggled, but was held firm, exposed to all.

The Queen reached out, pinching both nipples. "See how her nipples are erect?" the Queen said. "Who but a slut would have erect nipples at a croquet game?"

More murmurs, many people agreeing. "Yes, she does." "Those nipples are certainly hard." "Only sluts get horny playing croquet."

"But you just pinched them!" Alice said.

"And look at these boots!" the Queen said. "Thigh-high leather with spiked heels! Who but a slut would wear spike heeled boots to a croquet game?"

Again the crowd mumbled in agreement.

"But you're wearing spike heeled boots!" Alice cried.

"Mine are red," said the Queen.

"What is the difference?" Alice said.

"More proof!" triumphed the Queen. "Who but an oversexed slut couldn't tell the difference between black and red?"

"I swear, I'm not a slut!" Alice declared.

"Oh, really?" the Queen asked, smiling. She glanced down, below Alice's belly. "You have no hair down there. Who else but a slut shaves off all of her hair?"

"That wasn't me!"

"Of course it is you. I'm looking right at it."

The Queen ran her hand down Alice's belly, between her legs.

"So smooth," the Queen said, gently working a finger inside of Alice.

Alice's lower lip quivered. "Please don't."

But the Queen didn't stop. And even after all of the days' erotic encounters, Alice felt herself responding.

"Everyone!" the Queen said, "look how wet this little slut is."

The crowd got even closer. Alice wanted to die. Her face burned bright red, her ears felt aflame, but the Queen's fingers were expert in how they coaxed pleasure out of her. Her Majesty seemed to know exactly where to stroke, and how long and hard. Alice was helpless to control her body, which began to gyrate to match the Queen's fondling.

"Feel her nipples," the Queen ordered the crowd. "See how hard they are."

A procession line formed, one stranger after another lining up to tweak and stroke Alice's tortured breasts.

"And how wet this slut is!" the Queen declared. "Touch her and see!"

The guards lifted her up, spreading her legs apart. Alice watched, horrified, as hand after hand began to caress her most sensitive parts. Some began to take pictures. Some tasted her with their tongues. Men and women. It was the most embarrassing, humiliating moment in Alice's whole life, but no matter how hard she tried, she couldn't stop her hips from moving.

"Such a greedy little slut."

"She's so wet."

"Look how badly she wants it."

"Feel how tight she is."

"Shaved and spread open for all to see."

"She should be ashamed."

"Do you hear how she moans when I touch her like this."

As the never-ending line continued, Alice felt herself getting closer and closer to the point of release. She tried to stop it. Nothing in the world could be worse than having an orgasm while all of these people watched. But even though she shut her eyes and tried to think other thoughts, Alice's body kept responding to the groping, the teasing, the licking. And though she didn't want to admit it, the comments and the eyes on her were making it more intense. Somehow embarrassment magnified the pleasure, making it impossible for Alice to calm herself down. It was unbearable, and Alice knew if she did come, it would destroy her.

Then someone began to kiss her mouth. Someone with soft, full lips and a clever tongue. Alice opened her eyes and saw it was the Queen.

"There is nothing wrong with being a slut," the Queen said, smiling. "But you should own it. Let it empower you. Sexuality should be enjoyed, not repressed. And no good can come from pretending you're something that you're not."

"But I swear, Your Majesty!" Alice said, her voice getting higher and louder because she was so close to the edge. Someone worked fingers inside her while another licked her most sensitive spot, right where her lips met. Both nipples had wet, hungry mouths on them, kissing and nibbling. There was even a finger in her bottom or maybe it was something more, she couldn't quite tell. The sensations, coupled with the taunts and stares and pictures being snapped, were overwhelming Alice until she was afraid she'd start screaming and never stop.

"You really believe you aren't a slut?" the Queen asked.

"Yes!"

"Everybody halt!" the Queen ordered.

At once, the crowd stopped their groping of Alice, immediately backing away. The guards released her. Alice's whole body quivered, and she was panting like she'd just run a mile. But even though she'd been very close to climaxing, Alice was grateful to be left alone. She knelt on the lawn, covering up her breasts, trying to stop shaking.

"For lying about being a slut," the Queen declared, "Alice is sentenced to a public paddling!"

Alice's relief turned to raw terror. "What? No! Please, no!"

Instantly, Alice was grabbed and dragged across the croquet ground and taken to a large open area where a strange sort of table awaited. Alice recognized it from Pilar's Pink Room of Bunnies. The sight of it caused Alice's throat to seize with fear.

A spanking table.

The table was made of wood, the top and the kneeling rest covered in padded, black leather. Alice was forced to her knees and bent over, her wrists fastened to the table's legs with leather cuffs. Her legs were also spread and cuffed to the terrible device, and Alice felt both afraid and demeaned, especially as the onlookers began to *ooh* and *aah* at her. A moment later the Queen appeared before her.

She was holding a wooden paddle, similar to the kind used to play ping pong. It was heavily varnished, making it shine in the afternoon sun.

"So, slut, how many times shall I paddle your bare bottom?"

Alice couldn't take her eyes of the paddle. To be spanked with that... in front of all these people... it was too much.

"Well?" the Queen demanded. "How many times?"

"None! Have mercy, Your Majesty!"

"Perhaps I shall. But you must show your queen obedience, Alice. Can you do that?"

"Yes." Alice was so frightened her whole body shook.

"Tell me how many times I should paddle you. If the number is too tiny, I shall multiply it by ten."

Alice had no idea how to answer. She hadn't been spanked since she was a child, and the experience terrified her. What did the Queen think was too tiny a number? Five? Ten?

"Twenty," Alice said.

"Twenty," the Queen cooed, rubbing her hand across Alice's back. She cupped one of her buttocks and held the paddle up to Alice's lips.

"Kiss the paddle, Alice."

Alice couldn't imagine anything more outrageous. Kissing the very implement that was about to cause her pain was intolerable. But then the Queen was flicking her fingers across Alice's most sensitive parts, coaxing a moan from her, and Alice pursed her lips and kissed the wretched paddle.

"Now lick it, Alice."

"Please, don't make me."

"Lick it and make me believe you like it, or your ordeal will get worse."

Alice didn't believe her ordeal could get any worse, but the Queen was using a flicking motion with her thumb, a movement so intense it felt like Pilar's back massager. No longer trying to resist, Alice gave the paddle a long, slow, sexy lick, as she felt dozens of eyes burning into her. If that wasn't bad enough, the action made Alice somehow lose control of her hips, and they began to buck involuntarily, pressing up against the Queen's hand.

Alice was so embarrassed she wanted to die.

"Look! The slut licks the paddle!" the Queen declared.

The crowd gasped.

"And look how she moves her hips!"

More gasps, and some camera flashes. This was intolerable. Alice's whole body burned with a blush, but she still couldn't stop wiggling her bottom.

"Alice, I have sentenced you to be paddled for being a slut. The number you have chosen is twenty. Is that your final number?"

Alice wasn't sure how to answer. The Queen's fingers were making it impossible to think. Was this a chance to save herself from the number being multiplied by ten?

"Forty!" Alice squealed, praying it was high enough.

Another gasp from the onlookers.

"You heard her! Alice begs to be paddled more times!" the Queen said. "Who else but a slut would do that?"

And then the Queen's lovely fingers were withdrawn, and she walked behind Alice, continuing to pat and caress her buttocks, which the spanking table position high in the air for all to gape at. Then the Queen began to recite a poem, which made perfect sense given the situation.

> *Twinkle twinkle little slut,*
> *Now we'll spank you on your butt,*
> *Everyone will stand and watch,*
> *As you bare your hairless crotch.*

"What is with you people and your stupid rhymes?" Alice asked.

The Queen raise the paddle high, and Alice was infused with the same kind of adrenaline-fueled fear as when she was at the doctor's and about to be given a shot.

"Wait!" Alice pleaded. "Shouldn't I have a safeword?"

The Queen paused. "A safeword?"

Alice nodded frantically. "If things become too painful, I say the safeword and you stop."

"But my dear, a paddling is *supposed* to be painful."

"Please, Your Majesty! You must allow me a safeword. I beg you."

The Queen's brows furrowed, and she said, "Fine. Your safeword is *more*."

"Thank you, Your—"

A loud *crack!* thundered across the croquet area as the paddle landed on Alice's left buttock, cutting off her next word.

Surprisingly, it didn't hurt much. Pilar's spanking had carried more weight and force. But the surprise and suddenness of the blow made Alice cry out.

The second and third strikes came quickly, and now a definite heat had settled into her bottom. Strangely, it matched the heat between her legs, and by the fourth smack Alice realized with great astonishment that she wasn't minding it too much.

With five and six, the stinging began, but Alice was able to bear it.

At seven smacks on her left buttock, Alice really began to feel it. The Queen wasn't hitting her any harder than before, but each seemed to build upon the last. Though she wasn't able to tune out the gawking crowd around her, Alice had begun focusing on the lick of the paddle, the sensations it produced. She found herself anticipating the next blow, almost willing it to come.

But the Queen didn't swing. Instead, her hand moved between Alice's legs and began to stroke rapidly. Alice cried out, the pleasure from the caress and the sting from the paddle blending together until they seemed to be one and the same.

"Tell the crowd, Alice," the Queen purred. "Are you a dirty little slut?"

Alice shook her head. She could never say those words. They were too embarrassing, too vulgar. She would have been humiliated to say them to Lewis, whom she planned to marry some day. But to this group of strangers? Naked and bent over a spanking table? No way could she debase herself like that.

"Very well," the Queen said, and then began a flurry of paddle strokes, so fast they sounded like applause. Alice's legs were tense, her muscles locked, and she set her jaw and tried to brace herself against the onslaught, but it came so fast that all she could do was cry out. Right when Alice was certain she couldn't bear another blow, the Queen switched buttocks, focusing on the right one and giving the burning left one a rest.

But all too soon, her right rump began to heat up and sting something mighty. Alice struggled against her bonds, trying to pull away from the paddle, but there was no escape.

"More!" Alice yelled, reaching the peak of her endurance. "I beg you!"

The Queen stopped, and Alice let out a long sigh of relief. The sigh became a moan as the Queen roughly jammed two fingers inside her, working them in and out.

"The slut begs for more," the Queen said, "even though she has completed her sentence!"

"No!" Alice cried. "Please don't."

"How many more would you like, slut?"

"No more, Your Majesty! Please! I beg you!"

"A thousand? I can form the crowd in a line, give them each a chance to paddle your splendid bottom."

"No! Don't! I... I..." Alice squeezed her eyes shut. "Five more!"

"The slut wants *five* more!" the Queen shouted.

The audience cheered.

"Count them, Alice. If you lose count, we shall start over."

Again the paddle struck Alice's tormented bottom, lighting it up as if she'd sat upon a stove.

"One," she said, fighting tears.

"Louder."

"One!"

The Queen returned her two fingers to Alice's honey hole, thrusting once and making Alice gasp. Then the fingers were removed and the paddle came down again.

"Two!" Alice yelled.

The Queen's fingers again entered Alice, this time pumping in and out twice. Then the paddle once more.

"Three!"

Three lovely strokes, and once again Alice's bottom began to buck. When the paddle hit the fourth time, Alice moaned, and she couldn't tell if it was from pain or pleasure.

"Four!"

The Queen's delicious fingers penetrated Alice four times, using a downward angle that hit a spot Alice had never felt before. A spot inside her, just behind the clitoris, that was so sensitive it felt as if it was her clitoris being stroked. Through all of her adventures that day, no man had managed to hit that spot.

"That is your G-spot," the Queen said, wiggling her fingers.

Alice screamed. She was very close to coming.

"No one knows how to please a woman like another woman," the Queen said. "I know your body better than you do."

Then the fingers were withdrawn and the paddle came down for the fifth time, and again Alice screamed, her bottom ablaze, her womanhood dripping wet, waiting desperately for the Queen's fingers to return.

But they didn't.

"Look how she wiggles and writhes!" said someone in the crowd.

"Such a little slut!"

"She loves the paddle!"

"Look how wet she is!"

"She's about to come!"

Alice *was* about to come. She needed to, so badly. The taunts only made her desire worse.

"The sentence is complete!" the Queen roared. "Release the prisoner!"

The guards quickly unstrapped Alice's wrists and ankles, and all Alice could think was, *No! Please don't stop now! I want more!*

Alice fell to her knees, desperately wanting to beg for it, but her shame overwhelmed her need.

"Look at you," the Queen said. "Trembling and on the verge of a glorious orgasm. Now do you admit you are a slut?"

A hush fell over the crowd. Alice glanced at them, saw their judging stares, and her face turned bright red and she was forced to look away, toward the spanking table.

If I tell the Queen no, will she spank me again? Alice thought.

"No," she said, trying to look defiant. "You must spank me again, Your Majesty."

The Queen smiled. "No, Alice. That does not seem a fit punishment for you. If you won't admit what a dirty little slut you are, I have a different sentence for you."

Alice's mind reeled. At this point, anything the Queen did to her would be glorious.

"Tie me up and tease me?" Alice asked, shuddering at the memory.

"No."

"Force me to suck a man's member?" Alice's loins tingled at the thought. "As he licks me?"

"No."

"Force all the men here to make love to me?" Alice asked. The very idea was almost enough to cause her to swoon.

"No, Alice. Because you fail to embrace your inner slut, you are hereby sentenced to…"

Alice held her breath.

"Public masturbation!"

The crowd applauded.

Alice cringed. This was dreadful. Simply dreadful. Alice had never masturbated before. And to do this in front of a crowd of people… there was no way.

"I can't," Alice said.

"You can. And you will. Stand up!"

Alice stood on shaky legs. She was still wildly turned on, but an orgasm was the furthest thing from her mind. She couldn't do something so personal, so private, in public. Especially since she didn't know how.

"Please, Your Majesty," Alice whispered. "Anything but this."

"Face the crowd," the Queen ordered.

Alice did, but her head hung in shame.

"Look at them, Alice. As you touch yourself, I want you to look at each man and woman in turn. If you break eye contact at all, I shall extend the sentence."

Alice's lower lip trembled, and she looked up and stared at a tall man with a mustache.

"Put your finger in your mouth and suck it, Alice," The Queen said.

Alice forced her index finger between her lips. She was so mortified her knees knocked together.

"Get it nice and wet, Alice."

Doing this, while the man stared, felt dirtier than anything Alice had done all day. She wanted to close her eyes, pretend she was somewhere else, but the Queen's threat loomed large in her mind.

"Pinch your nipples with your other hand," the Queen ordered.

Alice continued to suck her finger, and with her free hand lightly tugged at her left breast.

"Harder, Alice. Stroke them and tweak them, one after the other."

Alice did, a tiny shock of pleasure rippling down to her loins.

"Look at everyone in the crowd, not just one person. And moan while you play with your breasts."

Alice looked at a woman next, someone older with short, blond hair. She moaned as the Queen told her, feeling like a bad actress reading for a part.

"Now tease yourself with your wet finger. Circle it around your clitoris, but don't touch it."

Alice trailed her hand down her breastbone, leaving a trail of saliva. She touched her pubic bone, just above her clitoris, and began to draw a circle around it.

"Slower," the Queen said. "And don't stop tugging those nipples."

Alice slowed down, moving her eyes to the next person. A man. A very attractive man, with a broad chest and strong arms.

"Moan. And gyrate your hips."

Alice let out a louder moan, and began to move against her wet finger. Having this cute guy watch her was the height of embarrassment, but at the same time Alice was having a hard time circling her clitoris without touching it.

"Now move your hand from your nipple and slide a finger inside yourself."

Alice couldn't do this looking at the handsome guy, so she turned her attention to the next person in the crowd and saw it was the Duchess. Like Alice, the Duchess was also touching herself, one hand fondling a generous breast, the other up under her skirt.

"Flick your clitoris like I did to you," the Queen said.

Alice did, and this time her moan was sudden and very real.

"Move your other finger in an out."

Alice obeyed, surprised at how intense the feeling was. She tore her eyes away from the Duchess and looked at the next man in the crowd. It was Cheshire, who, as could be expected, had whipped it out and was tugging mightily on the tip. Rather than be shocked this time, Alice felt some inner need to excite him. She began to move her hips faster, and her moaning became rhythmic, animal grunting.

"Now tell the crowd what a dirty little slut you are."

"I'm..."

"Say it."

Alice glanced at the next person, Pilar, who was giving her a happy thumbs up. She worked herself harder, the orgasm which had eluded her minutes ago now building up again.

"I'm... a..."

She looked at the next person and realized it was the Hatter, only this time he was wearing a fireman's helmet and bunker pants, his hairy chest bare. He gave her a sly smile, then winked.

"A dirty little slut, Alice," the Queen said. "Tell everyone."

"I'm... a... oh... oh..."

The March Hare stood next to Hatter. He was wearing the top of his bunny costume, but not his bottoms. And speaking of bottoms, Maus was behind the Hare, and he seemed to be entering him the same way he'd entered Alice earlier. Alice had never seen two men doing such a thing before, and for some reason it made her even wetter.

"She gives amazing oral love!" a male voice yelled. Alice sought it out, and saw Dick, waving at her from the crowd. "You are so beautiful, Alice!"

Alice's hands worked faster, knowing just which spots to touch. She flicked her index finger. She found her G-spot. The wave inside her was coming up fast, so fast, and in just a few more seconds she was going to—

"Halt!" the Queen ordered. A moment later she was on Alice, grasping her wrists.

Alice cried out, her hips still bucking, desperate to be touched again.

"You may not come until you admit what you are."

"Please, Your Majesty."

"Say it!"

Alice was sooooo close. She again stared at the crowd, many of whom were now masturbating. Alice tried to pull away from the Queen, but her grip was too strong. Then she tried to press against her, desperate for release.

"SAY IT!"

"I'M A DIRTY LITTLE SLUT!" Alice bellowed. And upon saying the words, something within her snapped, and she began to orgasm without any stimulation at all. It doubled her over, making her whole body shake, and the Queen put her hand between Alice's legs and Alice began to scream without any control at all, "I'M A SLUT! I'M A SLUT!" over and over until the pleasure became so unbearable she collapsed onto the lawn, the whole world spinning, her juices squirting out of her and drenching the Queen's hand.

For a moment, it seemed as if time stopped. No one moved. No one spoke.

Then, incredibly, the entire crowd broke out in thunderous applause.

And Alice, for the very first time ever, wasn't embarrassed anymore. In fact, she felt glorious.

"Take a bow," the Queen said. "You were splendid."

Alice bowed, and suddenly she was surrounded by people, patting her on the back and congratulating her.

"Good work," Dor Maus said.

"I knew you had it in you," Dick agreed.

"Look how far you've come," said Pilar. "I'm so proud of you."

The compliments seemed to go on and on, until the Queen yelled, "Enough! Back to croquet!"

A moment later, the crowd had abandoned Alice, leaving her behind as the game continued. Alice didn't know what to do next. Follow them? Search elsewhere for home? Certainly home had to be somewhere.

"That was a terrific performance, Alice," Cheshire said. He was clutching his cell phone. "I recorded the whole thing. I think I'm going to wank to it right now."

"I saw the Hatter and the Hare," said Alice.

"And Dor Maus, too. I know." Cheshire pointed to his phone. "I got it all here. Was hiding in the bushes."

"They couldn't help me."

"It looked like they helped you plenty," Cheshire said, waggling his eyebrows.

"They couldn't help me get home!" Alice said.

"You still want to go home? Don't you like it here?"

"I do. But I have responsibilities. A job. A boyfriend."

"The quick one? Why would you want to go back to him?"

"Because I love him," Alice said.

"I see. Well, I suppose you could ask Mock Turtle. He's self-important, and far too eager, but he might set you on the right path."

"Where do I find him?"

"Just click your heels together three—"

"You already used that joke," Alice said, sighing dramatically.

"Oh. Truthfully, I don't know where that bore is. But the Duchess does." Cheshire pointed to the Duchess, who was walking away with the crowd.

"Thank you, Cheshire."

"You're welcome. Would you mind if I took just a few seconds of video of you bending over?"

Alice was about to refuse, but then she thought, *why not?* She bent over for Cheshire, wiggling her bottom, not embarrassed in the least bit. She even spread her cheeks and sang what she knew of the theme to *Happy Days*.

Cheshire immediately dropped his cell phone and began to abuse himself with reckless abandon. Part of Alice feared he'd actually tug it completely off. But rather than worry about that, she nodded a quick goodbye and went to the Duchess, who was waiting for her turn at play, twirling a croquet mallet in her hands.

"Duchess, do you know where the Mock Turtle is?" Alice asked.

"Hello, Alice. Splendid show you put on. I'm having another lipstick party tomorrow, if you'd like to attend."

"Thank you for the invitation, but I do need to see Mock Turtle. I was told he might help me return home."

"A possibility. But he might not assist you. I'm afraid he only cares about himself."

"Please," Alice said. "I've been here a long time. I'm sure my boyfriend is getting concerned."

"Very well. Follow me."

Alice followed.

Chapter 6

The Mock Turtle's Story

"So what exactly is a Mock Turtle?" Alice asked the Duchess as they strolled through the woods. "Is it another dreadful pun?"

"Not that I'm aware of."

"Is he going to recite silly, pointless poetry to me?"

"Probably."

"Is there any way to skip it?"

"On an ereader? It isn't easy. See the clearing in the trees there? It leads to a beach. That's where Mock Turtle lives. Good luck to you, Alice."

The Duchess gave her a warm hug, and then left. Alice continued on through the clearing and saw a man standing next to a large body of water. At first glance, she thought it was Lewis. He had the same build, same features. But the face was different. Where Lewis had a sweet smile and beautiful eyes, Mock Turtle looked as if he'd just sniffed something unpleasant. From forty feet away, Alice could see his scowl. It was so disconcerting that she considered turning around and going back.

"Who goes there?" he yelled, spotting her.

Alice almost ran. But she didn't. The old, frightened, unsure Alice would have. But she was the new bold, fearless Alice, who got what she wanted.

"I'm Alice. Are you Mock Turtle?"

"Who wants to know?"

Another lunatic. "Me," she said, rolling her eyes. "Alice."

"Approach so I may look at you."

Alice tromped across the beach, her sharp heels sinking into the stand, but she managed to reach the man without falling over.

"Those boots are hardly proper attire for the beach," he said. "But they make your bottom and legs looked superb."

"Are you Mock Turtle?"

"I am."

"But you aren't a turtle. You aren't even a furry."

"A what?"

"You aren't wearing a turtle outfit."

"What about my mock turtleneck sweater?" he asked.

"You aren't wearing one."

"But I have one, at my house. It's blue."

Alice folded her arms, becoming annoyed. "You're called Mock Turtle because you sometimes wear a blue, mock turtleneck sweater?"

"No. Mock Turtle is my pen name. I'm a writer."

Alice softened a bit. "Really? I love to read."

"I'm a poet," Mock Turtle said proudly.

"Oh." Alice made a face. She should have known. "Poetry sucks."

"Don't disparage poetry. I shall make up a poem on the spot, about you, if you allow it."

"How about I pay you twenty dollars not to?"

But it was too late. Mock Turtle began to recite.

Little Alice,
Stole a chalice,

Why'd she do it?
She won't talice.

"Get it?" he asked. "Won't *talice*? *Tell-us*?"

"It's dreadful," Alice said.

"Oh, I have worse than that," said the Mock Turtle, and proceeded to prove it:

There was a girl named Susie,
Who drowned in a Jacuzzi,
She boiled like a potato,
And really tasted greato.

"If I had a gun, I'd eat it," Alice said. "But I'd shoot you first."

"Last one," said Mock Turtle.

"Promise?"

"I promise."

"Can I get that in writing?"

Mock Turtle launched into it:

When I need reference media,
I go to Wikipedia,
A dictionary is too slow,
And Wiki is much speedia.

"Ugh," Alice said. "I think I actually threw up in my mouth a little."

"A poet's job is to provoke emotion," Mock Turtle said proudly.

"You actually make money writing things like that?"

"Not yet. So far the snobbish literary journals have refused to publish any of my work. Do you know why?"

"They have standards?"

"Envy!" Mock Turtle declared. "They can't stand that I have this talent, flowing through my veins, like some poet with poetry talent in his blood."

Wow, this guy was clueless.

"I know a man named Nolan, who had a spastic colon—"

"You promised no more!" Alice said, shoving Mock Turtle to shut him up. "I need to get home, and I was told that you could help me."

"Help you get home?"

"That's what I just said."

Mock Turtle tapped a finger against his chin. "Well, I could help you, Alice. But I'd want something in return."

Alice narrowed her eyes. "Is it to recite another poem? Because I'll turn around right now."

"No. But you are quite beautiful, and I also couldn't help but notice, quite naked. If you allowed me to make love to you, I could show you how to get home."

Alice didn't find Mock Turtle attractive, he was much too sour, but she was a pro at pity sex, and if she had to appease him to get back home, it didn't seem like such a bad proposition. Besides, he might actually surprise her and be amazing at making love, like the many people she'd encountered that day.

"Fine," Alice said. "Where would you like to—"

In a flash, Mock Turtle's pants were around his ankles, and he was franticly rubbing up against her, trying to kiss her neck.

"Uh! Uh! Uh!" he groaned.

"Hey!" Alice said. This scenario was disappointingly familiar. "Slow down and we can—"

But it was too late. Mock Turtle had spurted all over her thigh, without having even entered her.

"That was the most unsatisfying experience I've ever had," Alice chided him. "And that's saying something."

"Sorry," he said, sheepishly looking at the ground. "It's just that you're so beautiful, and—"

"SEIZE HIM!"

Alice spun around and saw the Queen tromping down the beach toward them, surrounded by several guards. They immediately rushed at Mock Turtle, grabbing his arms.

"Your Majesty, what are you doing here?" Alice asked.

"The Duchess told me where you'd gone. This man has a seedy reputation, and as I'd suspected, my instincts proved correct."

"What did I do?" Mock Turtle cried.

"Nothing!" the Queen retorted. "That's the problem! Mock Turtle, I hereby accuse you of being a greedy, selfish lover, who cares not for his partner's needs. If convicted of these charges, the penalty is…"

"Spanking?" Alice asked. She wouldn't mind seeing the annoying little poet spanked.

"No," the Queen declared. "Death!"

"Death?" Mock Turtle, true to his name, turned green.

"Death?" Alice repeated. "You certainly take your orgasms seriously here in Wonderland."

"Yes, we do."

"But he's just a pathetic, selfish lout who doesn't know any better," Alice said. "Surely death is too strict a punishment."

"The trial shall begin immediately," said the Queen. "Off with his clothes."

The guards stripped Mock Turtle of his wardrobe, ripping it so severely Alice couldn't salvage any of it to wear herself. Though, quite honestly, she was beginning to really enjoy parading around naked.

"Alice, I subpoena you as the star witness." The Queen pointed at her. "This man's life hangs on your testimony."

"Be merciful!" Mock Turtle begged.

Alice looked from the Queen, to Mock Turtle, and back again, wondering what she was going to do.

"To the courthouse!" the Queen commanded.

Not seeing any other choice, Alice followed the procession. This was going to be interesting.

Chapter 7

Who Stole the Tart?

The trial took place in a courtroom which was like no courtroom Alice had ever seen. In fact, it looked like a New Orleans bordello, or at least what Alice imagined a New Orleans bordello would look like, as she'd never been in one. Draperies of red velvet covered windows and walls, held back with ornate chains of gold. Plush carpet stretched wall-to-wall. Members of the jury lounged on opulent chaise lounges and wavy sex chairs and contraptions involving wooden crosses and leather swings and hanging chains. It wasn't the least bit official-looking.

But Alice didn't mind.

Her three tea partiers were there on the chairs, acting as the jury, Alice supposed. And they seemed to be the only three members. The Hatter wore a cowboy hat this time and nothing else but a pair of western chaps that framed his burgeoning manhood. The Hare donned his usual bunny suit, though still only the top half. And Maus wore the most beautiful ring around his beautiful masculinity and nothing else.

The Duchess was there, and Pilar too, standing next to Mock Turtle. But before Alice could truly get her bearings, a curtain parted and Dick strode in and stopped front and center.

"Hear ye, hear ye, court is now in session," Dick said. Although he was wearing a police hat and a belt with a nightstick hanging from it, he wasn't wearing anything else, and he was very aroused. Apparently people enjoyed court more in Wonderland than they did back home. "The honorable Queen presiding. All rise."

The Queen made the obligatory grand entrance, splendidly wrapped in a thin layer of what looked like red rubber, or latex. It was skin tight, shiny, and there were holes for her nipples and her feminine parts. She wasn't completely shaved like Alice, but her nether hair had been artfully shaped into a heart. Alice also noticed a glint of silver, and she realized with a pleasurable shock that the Queen had earrings *down there*. Each of her lips was adorned with a silver ring, as was her clitoris. Alice could barely imagine what it felt like to have a ring in that most sensitive spot and how it would feel if stroked. Or licked. Or during penetration. Would a man's soft thrusting tug against it with each stroke? When he entered her completely, would he press against the ring?

The Queen had similar, larger rings in her nipples, and they were connected with a length of chain. Seeing Her Majesty's secret jewelry made Alice feel funny, and she had to press her hand to her loins to calm the sudden throb.

"I said, *all rise*," Dick announced, scowling at Mock Turtle.

Turtle was completely naked, his ankles and wrists in cuffs. "But I *am* standing," he whimpered.

The Queen rolled her eyes. "Alice? Can you make the defendant rise?"

"How so?" Alice didn't understand.

The Queen pointed at Turtle's manhood, which hung limp and flaccid.

"Ah," Alice said. She approached Turtle, and reached down to stroke him. Almost immediately, he sprang to full attention and began to moan and buck.

"Bailiff!" the Queen thundered. "Secure the defendant!"

The Queen quickly pulled a red ribbon from her hair and passed it to Dick, who stormed between Alice and Turtle and quickly tied it in a large bow around the base of Turtle's member.

"Make sure it is tight," the Queen said. "I won't have him leaking all over my courtroom."

"It is tight, Your Honor."

"Alice! Take Turtle in your mouth and make sure he cannot climax."

Alice obediently dropped to her knees. She eyed Turtle's protrusion dubiously. Though she'd never seen Lewis's this closely, or for this long, it seemed awfully similar to her boyfriend's. Not entirely trusting the bow, Alice slowly brought Turtle to her lips and sucked hard, cupping his balls in her hand and gently tugging them, expecting the hot spurt any second.

Turtle moaned and shook and thrashed his head back and forth in apparent ecstasy.

But he didn't come.

"The defendant is secure," Dick said.

"Alice, you may release him. But first, give his nipples a twist."

Alice wasn't sure why the Queen wanted her to do that, but with Turtle still between her lips, she raised her hands and tweaked his nipples. His whole body seemed to tremble, and he cried out as if lovesick.

This was easily the most fun trial Alice had ever been to.

She released him and took her place on a chair next to the Queen's bench. The court reporter, Cheshire, sat nearby, with one of those tiny typewriters on the desktop in front of him. His hands weren't poised on the keys, however, but busy in his lap.

"Very good," said the Queen. "Now the prosecution can begin. Your opening statement?"

"Yes, your honor." The Duchess stepped forward. A leather corset wrapped her waist, from the bottom of her naked breasts to the garters framing her woman's mound. Stockings like Alice's covered her legs and on her feet were a pair of leopard high heels. "Mock turtle is charged with being a greedy, selfish lover, who cares not for his partner's needs."

"Call your first witness," the Queen said to the Duchess.

"I call Alice."

Alice walked to where Dick was standing.

"I need to swear you in," said Dick. "Put your hand on my cock, please."

This seemed strange to Alice, but since everything was strange in Wonderland, she was getting used to going with the flow. She placed her palm on Dick's protruding member.

His eyes rolled back a little in his head, and his hips began to thrust, rubbing his velvet head against her hand.

After a dozen strokes, Alice spoke up. "What about the swearing?"

Dick blinked. "I would never swear at you, Alice. You're so beautiful and sweet."

"I didn't mean the cursing kind of swearing."

"Okay. Now could you wrap your fingers around me a bit tighter? Maybe lick your hand first and get it nice and wet?"

Now Alice was confused. "But you're the bailiff. Don't you have to make me promise to tell the truth?"

"Oh, of course. But I would never swear you in on my cock. I use a bible for that."

Alice thought that maybe she should feel put out, but she liked the feel of Dick's cock, so she gave him a few more strokes before insisting he pull out a bible and properly swear her in. And through all of this, the queen and the lawyers and the jury and especially the court reporter watched. Although as far as Alice knew, Cheshire didn't record a single word, since every time she looked his way, he was diligently abusing himself.

"Sit in the witness chair," the Queen ordered and pointed to a black leather swing that hung from the ceiling on four chains.

But when Alice approached the contraption, she had no idea how to get on it. "I'm sorry, Your Majesty—"

"Your Honor," corrected the Queen.

"Your Honor," said Alice. "But I'm afraid I don't understand how this works."

"You've never been in a sex swing before?"

"No."

"Baillif! Assist Alice!"

With a boost from Dick that somehow involved him touching her bottom, fondling both breasts, and administering a tender pinch to her feminine lips, Alice found herself suspended in midair. The swath of black leather supported her back and butt, and her feet were in stirrups. The only way to sit comfortably was for Alice to bend her knees and spread her legs wide, for the whole courtroom to see. Alice immediately understood why this was called a sex swing. Any man—or woman—had full access to all of Alice's private parts, and she could be easily moved, turned, and manipulated as if she weighed nothing at all.

It turned her on something fierce.

"What do you have to say, Alice?" asked the Duchess.

There was only one thing that popped into her mind. "Those stockings and heels make your bottom and legs look spectacular."

Alice glanced around the room, and everyone from the Queen to Pilar to the jury nodded in agreement.

"Why, thank you, dear," said the Duchess. "I appreciate the compliment. But I'm sorry, I now have to ask you some tough questions."

Alice braced herself as much as she could in a swing.

"You were at the beach with Mock Turtle, and he made love to you. Is that correct?"

The Duchess wasn't kidding. That *was* a tough question. And Alice wasn't sure how to answer. "Well... he..."

"Did he make love to you or not?"

"Well, he sort of tried... I guess."

"I need a more specific answer."

Mock Turtle gave her a pleading look. The experience with him had been outrageously unsatisfying, but Alice didn't want the poor man to be sentenced to death for it.

"The witness will answer the question," ordered the Queen.

"I'm sorry, but that's the only answer I can give."

"Then let me be more specific," said the Duchess. "May I approach the witness?"

"By all means," said the Queen.

The Duchess looked sympathetic. "Now some of these questions might be tough, Alice, but just do your best to answer. Okay?"

Alice nodded, not sure what would come next.

"When Mock Turtle made love to you, at any time, did he lick your pussy?"

Alice shuddered at the vulgar word. "Um, no."

"No, *what*?"

"He didn't, um, do any licking," she said.

"He didn't lick *what*?" repeated the Duchess.

Now Alice had been in Wonderland long enough to know that the Duchess wanted her to say that word. But even though Alice formed her lips and moved her tongue to pronounce it, she couldn't get any sound to emerge.

"May I assist the witness, your honor?" The Duchess asked the Queen.

"Please do," said the Queen, fondling her gavel.

Alice was hoping the Duchess would assist by saying the word for her, but instead she brought her face between Alice's thighs.

"Did he do this to your pussy?" And she darted her tongue between Alice's sensitive nether lips and swirled around Alice's nub in the most electrifying way. It was almost too intense. But the swing prevented Alice from closing her legs, even as the Duchess continued to torment her in short, piercing stabs.

"Oh... oh... unh..."

"Is that a yes or a no?" the Queen asked.

"No," Alice managed after the Duchess pulled away. "He certainly didn't do that."

"How about this?" The Duchess dipped back into Alice's special entrance and ground her mouth against Alice, devouring the whole of her with slow, fat licks of her tongue. She went up, and down, as if Alice was a wall she was painting, and when Alice tried to buck to make her speed up, the Duchess slowed even more.

Alice couldn't think, let alone answer. She thrust her hips against the Duchess's mouth, and the word she was trying to say came out as an unintelligible gasp.

"Answer the question," the Queen ordered.

"He... he... he didn't... do... that."

"How about this?" And the Duchess rose up between Alice's legs, then claimed Alice's nipples in her mouth, one at a time, kissing, licking, sucking, then slowly moved up to Alice's lips, where she kissed her and plunged her tongue deep.

The kiss sent heat spiraling through Alice, and she could taste her own juices on the Duchess's tongue, and for some reason that thrilled her even more. The Duchess's nipples brushed her own, and Alice raised up her hips and the friction of the Duchess's fishnet stockings sent her over the edge, making her climax quite audibly.

When Alice finally stopped screaming, the Duchess turned to the Queen. "She's taking an awfully long time to answer simple yes and no questions, Your Honor. May I treat the witness as hostile?"

The Queen's heart-shaped lips curved in a heart-shaped smile. "Please, do."

"Dick?" said the Duchess, extending her hand.

With a dazed look on his face, Dick handed her his baton. And Alice couldn't help noticing the device looked an awful lot like Pilar's dildo. It even had the little bumps and ridges on it.

And that was exactly how the Duchess used it, starting by teasing Alice's nipples, and then slowly bringing it down between her open legs. The Duchess rubbed it across Alice, over and over, until it was slick with wetness.

"Did Mock Turtle do this to you?" She penetrated Alice, filling her.

Alice groaned, her eyes closing in rapture.

"What was that?" the Queen asked. "Read that back to me."

Cheshire imitated Alice's gasp without missing a stroke.

The Queen frowned. "Is that a yes or a no?"

"Noooo," croaked Alice, barely able to breathe.

"Did he try this?" Pumping it in and out, slowly and deliciously, The Duchess coated the stick with Alice's juices as Alice tried in vain to stop her hips from bucking.

"Oh... oh... oh... oh... no..."

"How about this?"

And with the baton still deeply inside Alice, The Duchess gave the swing a spin. Alice began to twirl while impaled upon the stick, screaming all the while. The feeling was so amazing, so intense, that coupled with the dizziness of the rotation, Alice came very close to blacking out. When the swing finally came to a stop, Alice saw that the Hatter and the Hare, the Maus and Cheshire, Pilar and the Queen and Dick were all stroking themselves and staring at her. And all Alice could think of was how good she felt and how much she wanted it to go on forever.

Then the Duchess pulled the baton out of Alice, and Alice almost cried. "Please... don't stop..."

"I'm finished with this witness," said the Duchess, and she walked briskly to the back of the room.

The Queen turned to Pilar. "Your witness, Mr. Caterpillar."

"My witness?" Pilar stood and smiled. "I'll take her back to my Pink Room of Bunnies and pry the truth out of her. I don't care how long it takes. Hours. Days. I'll make her come so many times she'll beg for me to stop. But I won't stop. Not until I break her."

"Oh, please do," Alice said, whimpering.

"I'm afraid you can't," answered the Queen. "This story is already longer than the original it is parodying, and you need to get on with it. What say you?"

"I say, put Mock Turtle in the pillory and flog him for his heinous crimes."

"You're his defense attorney," the Queen reminded Pilar. "How do you defend your client?"

Pilar glanced at the Mock Turtle, naked and pouting, his tortured member twitching with no immediate hope of release. "Oh, there's no defense for not seeing to your partner's needs."

"Can I get a new lawyer?" Mock Turtle asked.

"Bailiff! Gag the defendant!"

Dick swaggered over to Turtle, and forced a red rubber ball into his mouth. It had a leather strap attached to it, and Dick wound that around Turtle's head and buckled it in place. Almost immediately, a line of drool fell from Turtle's chin.

Alice had never seen such a terrible device. It made Turtle look so pathetic. So helpless.

It was such a turn on, Alice dropped her hand to her womanhood and began to rub.

"Can I be gagged too?" she asked.

"Perhaps later," promised the Queen. "Call your next witness, Duchess."

"I think it's time to put Mock Turtle on the stand."

The Queen shook her head. "You can't call the defendant as a witness. Only the defense attorney can do that."

"Then that's what I'll do," said Pilar.

And Dick didn't ask Mock Turtle to place his hand on his cock, but he swore him in anyway. Turtle mumbled his response around the gag.

"Can you read that back?" the Queen asked.

"Mmphhh-mmmbbaa," repeated Cheshire.

"Your witness," said the Queen to Pilar. "Ask your questions."

"Oh, he doesn't have to answer to me," said Pilar.

"Prosecution?"

The Duchess shook her head, now busy using the baton on herself. "He doesn't have to answer to me, either."

The Queen focused on Alice. "They're right, you know. There's only one person he must answer to, and that's you."

"But I don't—"

"Then I will sentence him immediately, and judging from the evidence I've seen, the sentence is death."

"But isn't that for the jury to decide?"

The Queen peered at the jury box. Hatter was busy riding Hare, and Hare had his mouth full of Maus.

"The jury seems preoccupied," the Queen said. "Mock Turtle, for the crime of ignoring your partner's needs, I sentence you to—"

"Wait!" Alice shouted. She couldn't let Mock Turtle die, not when she might be able to save him. She didn't have a clue how she would do that, but if there was anything Alice had learned in her time in Wonderland, it was that being timid never got her anywhere. It was time to be bold. "I have some questions for Mock Turtle, and before he is sentenced, he needs to answer to me."

"Very well, Alice. Ask away." And Alice thought she could detect a note of pride in the Queen's voice.

Alice tried to remember all the courtroom shows she'd seen on TV, but she doubted much of what she'd seen would apply here. Best as she could recall, Matlock didn't have a sex swing. And on *Law and Order*, the judge never wore latex. Alice hadn't seen *Boston Legal*, but she'd heard good things.

Alice looked around the room, hoping for a bout of inspiration, and she noticed an odd chair with a tall back, short legs, and a round seat with a hole in the center. It almost looked like a toilet, but there didn't appear to be any plumbing, and it had another odd hole in the front at the base, and leather straps on the sides with buckles on them.

The ideas popping into Alice's mind were embarrassing, or at least they should have been. But instead of embarrassment, Alice felt a renewed tingle between her legs.

"What kind of chair is that?" she asked.

"It's called a queening chair," answered the Queen.

"Why is it called a queening chair?" Alice figured if anyone would know such things, it would be the Queen herself.

"Because it will make you feel like a queen," came the answer. "The accused lies on his back, beneath the chair, with his head and hands secured in place. The seat has a hole in it, directly above the prone man's face. When a woman sits upon it, the man has complete access to her. She could sit comfortably there for hours."

Alice swallowed the large lump in her throat, and waited until the shiver had passed. "If it would please the court, I would like the defendant to be locked into place under the chair."

The Queen smiled. "Oh, it would please the court, all right. Very much."

Dick escorted Mock Turtle to the chair and directed him to lie on his back, his face staring up through the space where the chair's seat should be. His ball gag was removed, and his neck locked in place. His wrists were cuffed on either side of the chair.

"You'll require this," the Queen said to Alice, handing her a stiff, black riding crop with a fat swatch of leather on the end. "If he doesn't follow your orders, give him a little swat."

Alice approached the queening chair, her legs shaking. She stared down at Turtle, his poor ribboned member stiff and turning an angry purple color, his eyes pleading up at her through the oval hole in the chair's seat.

"I'm sorry," he told Alice. "Forgive me."

And she almost did, right there, and was just turning to ask the Queen for mercy when Turtle continued with, "I've even written a poem to express my remorse."

The frown creased Alice's face immediately, and before he could begin to recite she moved to the chair and settled her bottom. It was a curious sensation, because the opening in the seat relaxed Alice's pelvic muscles, so everything down there hung low, like a ripe fruit ready to fall from the vine. Alice could feel Mock Turtle's hot breath directly upon her. She stared down, seeing his chin between her legs, and adjusted her position—

Right onto his mouth.

Alice wanted to rub herself all over him, grind upon him, force him to deliver the pleasure he'd denied her earlier with his selfishness and his haste. But she controlled herself.

Control, Alice thought. *Is that what this has been about all along? Controlling our own lives, and the pleasure we both give and receive.*

"Lick me," she ordered Mock Turtle.

He began in such earnestness it was as if he'd been waiting his whole life for someone to give him that command. His movements were so frantic, Alice felt as if he had two tongues. First he began beneath her, toward her bottom, and then penetrated her stiffly, making Alice clench the queening chair's arms and dig in her nails. Turtle's tongue drew upward, but to the side, missing her most sensitive spot. Then to the left, slow and soft. Then the right again, stopping to once again pierce her opening.

"Higher!" Alice yelled. And she used the riding crop to give him a flick on his stiff manhood.

He yelped, and then began to lap at her most sensitive spot, using his mouth and lips and taking her into his mouth and sucking gently.

"Order him to clean you all over," the Queen said.

"Lower," Alice said, once again using the crop, this time on his inner thigh.

Alice moved forward in the chair, capturing his flicking tongue with her backside, as Hare had done at the tea party. But rather than just one lick, Turtle seemed intent to devour Alice. If she'd ever thought that part of her was dirty, it wasn't after Mock Turtle finished his warm, wet assault.

She smacked him again with the riding crop, not because he was doing anything wrong, but because Alice simply liked doing it. Once again she changed positions, giving him full access to her clitoris, ordering him to suck her as he had before.

And then Alice felt the wave begin to crest in her again, and she pressed herself down onto Turtle's willing mouth, eyeing his stiff member, wanting it to fill the ache inside.

"You may get off the queening chair and use him as you wish," the Queen said, reading her mind.

Alice stood up, immediately dropping to her knees, and spreading herself wide, she slid down Mock Turtle's stiff manhood. She cried out, and the jury and the rest of the courtroom began to applaud. It was then that Alice not only forgave Mock Turtle, but also forgave Lewis for his inexperience and naivete.

"I have reached a verdict," the Queen declared. "Mock Turtle, you have been sentenced to..."

The entire court held its collective breath.

"To be trained by Alice!" the Queen ordered. "You shall remain her sex slave until you learn how to satisfy her completely. Case dismissed!

Alice smiled happily at the Queen's verdict as she furiously rode the Mock Turtle's member, with its ribbon tied around the base so he would stay stiff as long as she desired. He moaned in appreciation.

"Thank you for saving my life, Alice," he said between grunts. "All I needed was someone to teach me what to do."

And when she looked down at his face through the hole in the queening chair, he was no longer Mock Turtle.

He was her boyfriend, Lewis.

Chapter 8

Alice's Evidence

Alice opened her eyes, the white rabbit vibrator bringing her close to yet another glorious orgasm.

She'd lost count of how many she'd had, how many fantasies she'd dreamed up, but after endless, constant ecstasy for over an hour, Alice wanted more.

She wanted the real thing.

Turning on the picnic blanket, she stared at Lewis, still snoring, completely oblivious to the bliss she'd been experiencing, the change she'd gone through.

"Wake up," Alice said, giving him a shake on the shoulder.

Lewis's eyelids fluttered open. "Oh, hey, Alice. Sorry, I must have dozed off." His gaze dropped, focusing on the white rabbit still buzzing and undulating inside her. "Hey! You're using it. That's great, I—"

Alice switched off the rabbit and tossed it aside, no longer needing it.

"Take. Off. Your. Pants," Alice ordered. "Now."

Lewis didn't waste any time, and in a flash his pants were off and he was reaching for her.

"No," she said, pushing him back. "You aren't allowed to touch me unless I give you permission."

"I don't understand."

"Think of it as a game," Alice said. "If I do anything that makes you uncomfortable, or that you don't like, you can say a safeword and I'll stop. Your safeword is…" Alice searched the fantasies she'd been so recently occupied with, and came upon the perfect one. "Wonderland."

"Wonderland," he repeated. "Got it. So what are you going to—"

Alice silenced him with a kiss, her tongue penetrating his mouth as her hand sought his manhood, stroking and pulling on it until it was quite still. She'd never touched Lewis there before, and was delighted to discover how long and thick he was, with the same delightful curve as the March Hare in her fantasies. Lewis moaned, immediately beginning to buck his hips.

"Hold still, she demanded.

Incredibly, Lewis listened. Alice reached up, pulling the blue ribbon out of her hair, and then deftly tying it around the base of Lewis's member.

"What are you doing, Alice?"

She hesitated only the slightest of moments, then said with authority, "Your cock belongs to me. You shall only come when I allow it. First, you shall satisfy my needs."

Lewis's eyes became wide as the plates on which they'd eaten their picnic lunch. Alice placed her hands on her boyfriend's shoulders, then swung a leg over, straddling him.

"Reach up and play with my tits."

Lewis did so eagerly. He squeezed her breasts, then his fingers found her nipples, rubbing and pulling and causing delightful sensations up and down Alice's spine. She moaned, rubbing herself on Lewis's chest, electric ripples of pleasure making her tremble. Then she moved higher on him, her knees on either side of his ears, until he stared directly up into her.

"You are going to lick my *pussy*, Lewis," Alice said, and the vulgarity of the word was so exciting she was already on the verge of orgasm.

"Yes," Lewis said, his tongue stretching out and reaching for her.

Alice had never noticed before, but Lewis had the longest tongue she'd ever seen. She lowered herself onto it, slowly, pausing when only the very tip touched her, waiting there as he traced the outline of her feminine parts, over and over. She pressed closer, and Lewis entered her with his glorious tongue, moving it in and out until Alice had no choice but to cry out. She wanted nothing more than to squat fully down, as on the queening stool in her fantasies, but instead she pulled back again, teasing both Lewis and herself, drawing it out and heightening her anticipation and pleasure.

Alice did this several times, until she felt ready to burst, and then she grabbed Lewis by his hair and ground his mouth into her, smearing her juices all over his face as he worked his magical tongue. The feeling was so overwhelming that Alice's whole body spasmed uncontrollably, and her climax was so loud she scared a group of jays out of a nearby tree.

She considered going for seconds, pressing against him greedily, wishing she were completely bare down there and deciding Lewis would shave her when they got home. Then Alice slid down his body, his manhood bumping her between the legs as she slid over it, then standing straight at attention as she wrapped her hand around the base.

She licked Lewis, up and down his length as if enjoying a popsicle on a hot summer day. Lewis began to buck and moan, and she ordered him to stay still.

"I can't," he groaned. "It's too intense."

"Then use the safeword," she said, teasing him by running her tongue under his purple head.

Lewis shook his other head, his hands clutching the picnic blanket.

Alice took Lewis in her mouth, slowly, inch by delicious inch, and the very idea of what she was doing, coupled with Lewis's trembling, was such a turn on she was on the verge of another orgasm. Alice began to suck him, bobbing her head up and down, stroking his shaft with increasing speed as Lewis began to cry out, begging for the ribbon to be untied.

"Not yet," Alice said, pulling off of his manhood and then moving up his body again. She knelt on either side of his waist, lowering herself to him, once again stopping to tease herself. Alice clutched Lewis, hard, and then rubbed him all over her womanhood, using him as she'd used the rabbit vibrator, brushing his velvet head against her lips, her clitoris, then placing just the first inch inside her and moving in small circles.

"Please!" Lewis begging. "I can't take much more!"

"You'll take whatever I dish out," Alice said. "You are my slave, Lewis. My sex toy. I can do with you as I wish. Say it."

"I'm… I'm your slave."

His words were just as intense as his tongue upon her.

"Louder!"

"I'm your slave, Alice! I'm your sex toy!"

Alice dropped suddenly, impaling herself upon Lewis, the sudden fullness taking her breath away.

"My tits," she managed to gasp.

Lewis obediently reached for them, working her nipples as she rode his length, faster and faster, until she couldn't prevent the climax from overtaking her. Seeking the ribbon, she released the bow knot from Lewis's manhood and ordered him, "Come! Come for me!"

He did. So did she.

And for the very first time—for real and not as a vibrator-fueled fantasy—Alice felt like a complete woman.

She collapsed into Lewis's arms, happy, exhausted, and completely satisfied. For the moment, at least.

"Wow," Lewis said. "That was amazing. I didn't know it could be like that. You're… you're incredible, Alice."

She snuggled against him. "You did pretty well yourself."

"I did?"

"Well, you'll need a bit more training. But I think you're going to work out just fine."

His eyes got wide. "You mean, it could always be just like this?"

"No."

Lewis's happy expression faded, and he looked like his puppy had just died. "No?"

"Not just like this. I have a lot of other things for us to try," Alice said.

"Really?" he asked, perking up again.

Alice thought about the many things she'd done in her fantasies. All the scenarios. All the toys. All the role-playing she and Lewis could do together.

"I have a great many ideas, in fact, and I think they will keep us busy for a long, long time."

Lewis reached out and embraced her. "I love you, Alice. I love you so much. When can we start?"

Alice smiled wickedly, placing her hand on Lewis's head, pushing him down to her nether regions.

"There's no time like the present," she said, wrapping him with her thighs.

Part 2

Kinky Secrets of Alice Through the Looking Glass

Chapter 1

Looking Glass House

One thing was certain, the *white* kitten had had nothing to do with it—it was the black kitten's fault entirely. For Snowball had been having her face washed by the old cat for the last quarter of an hour (and bearing it pretty well, considering), so she *couldn't* have had any hand in the mischief.

Alice held up the sexy halter dress she'd been planning to wear to her first real college fraternity party and studied the large, ugly snag right at boob level. "You had to play with this, didn't you?" she scolded Creampie, the black kitten.

The kitten rolled around on her futon, as if he couldn't care less, while the mother cat, Alice's dear Felcher, finished with the white kitten's bath.

Alice threw the ruined dress onto the floor and eyed her naked body in the full length mirror. She'd heard horror stories about the freshman fifteen—those extra pounds co-eds famously put on in their first year at college from too much fast food and beer—and she was adamant about not letting that happen to her. But lately, she couldn't seem to prevent stuffing her face with chocolate, causing most of her sexiest clothes to no longer fit, and that was all Lewis's fault.

She still couldn't believe what she'd seen that morning after Lewis had stayed over. Alice had walked in the bathroom and—oh my dear—he'd been standing in front of the mirror wearing her frilliest, laciest, pinkest panties and stroking his stiff manhood through the silk.

"Lewis! You're gay?" had been the only words that she'd been able to push through her lips.

Of course, he'd denied it, claiming he just found wearing pretty, girly things to be a turn-on. But she hadn't believed it for a moment. Lewis—her Lewis—was obviously not interested in women other than their underwear, and so she'd broken up with him on the spot.

Now weeks later, Alice was horny as she could possibly be, and her dear little mischievous kitten had ruined her chance to go to her first frat party and find some sexual release. There was even a good chance that Lewis would be there, and she could never have him see her looking fat in clothes that didn't fit, whether he was gay or not.

And all this because of a kitten.

Alice took a deep breath and decided not to think about the cats anymore, because that would be frightfully boring to read about. But sex, on the other hand, was always fun, so with this in mind, dear reader, she peered into her underwear drawer, and rather than selecting a bra and panties, she dug out a long cylindrical device from underneath the underthings.

The white rabbit.

Alice ran a finger from the base of the device, over the two ear-like stimulators, and up to the firm yet flexible tip. She'd once been told that sex is only partly about friction and bodily fluids. The majority of it takes place in the mind. If she had nothing decent to wear to the party, so be it. She would find her release right here.

Alice returned to the mirror and stared at her nakedness. Her breasts were full and high, being that she was only eighteen, and her nipples had already hardened into nubs, tingly with anticipation. She switched on the rabbit vibrator and began to circle each breast, the spiral growing tighter and tighter until the delicious pulsations caused her nipples to grow so erect and rigid, they cast shadows on the floor.

What would the frat boys think if she showed up at their party with breasts bared and nipples protruding as if begging to be sucked and teased?

What would Lewis think if she let the whole party of men fondle her?

The prospect of all that male attention focused on her made a delicious throb start between her legs.

Alice moved the head of the rabbit down, over her belly, tickling and teasing.

Lewis had shaved her secret garden, and even though she hadn't had sex since the breakup, Alice had kept it smooth, though she wasn't certain why. Now she sat on the edge of the futon and opened her thighs wide in front of the mirror.

Even though Lewis had seen her special place down there many times, Alice had never really had the occasion to look. Not completely. Not altogether. But now seeing herself spread open, she was somewhat fascinated with her delicate, pink folds, the shape of her clitoris, the deep mystery of her most private place.

What if she went to the party bare from the waist down? Or best yet, totally naked? Would the frat boys touch her and lick her? Would they all take off their own clothes, their masculinity hard and straining to plunge inside her?

A tremor built inside her loins. A hunger. A need.

Alice toyed with her opening, moving the vibrator around and around, but never really touching the place she wanted to touch most. Her nether lips glistened, her juices flowing in abundance, and when she finally nudged the rabbit between her folds, her need was so immediate she made a keening noise deep in the back of her throat. It filled her so completely, so utterly, and she felt the rotating beads undulate and brush against her G-spot with each gyration. Alice watched, shuddering, as she stretched open to accommodate the rabbit's full length, imagining it wasn't a sex toy, but instead a lover ravenous to satisfy her.

"Oh, yes," she said to her fantasy man. "Yes. Harder."

One stroke, then another, and Alice's legs were already trembling.

"Do it harder. Just like that."

Alice met her own thrusts, finding the rhythm she liked. She wanted so badly for this to be real, and not plastic and batteries. To be giving a man as much pleasure as she was receiving.

Then her hips started bucking, and she slid off the bed.

"Oh, heavens!" Alice exclaimed. Embarrassed, she glanced around, even though she knew no one but the kitties were watching.

Hmm. She eyed herself in the mirror, sitting on the floor, legs splayed and rabbit still buried inside. A dirty, wicked thought entered Alice's head: What would it be like if someone really was watching her? Watching everything she was doing to herself?

Alice withdrew the device and climbed to her feet, the idea spinning through her mind and causing the excitement already thrumming within her to ripple over her skin. "If someone was watching me through the mirror, what would he like to see?" she asked no one in particular. "Would he like to see me do this?"

Alice leaned forward, letting her breasts sway in front of her, nipples lurid and inviting. She spread her legs wide and slipped the vibrator into her slick slot, angling from behind.

"Oh, yes. If someone was watching me through the looking glass, he would like this," Alice said, even though she really couldn't know. But Alice knew that she liked it, and when in the act of pleasuring oneself, that was the only thing that mattered.

"Would you like to see me come?" she asked the mirror.

She flipped the switch and the rabbit sprang to life (not literally, although that was not out of Alice's realm of imagination). The hum electrified her, and for a few minutes, it was all she could do to keep her balance. But as she recovered, she began to move the device, pulling it out to her outer lips, then sinking it deep into her pleasure cave.

Out. In. Out. In.

Every time she went deep, the rabbit's "ears" touched her most sensitive place, and every time they touched, she let out a little yip. The pressure built within her, bringing her close to what she wanted, close to the edge. Her hips started to thrust. Her breasts started to buck and swing. They swung faster and faster—

—and she spilled forward and fell through the looking glass.

Though she hardly knew how she had gotten there, Alice landed on her hands and knees on the cushy throw rug in the mirror image of her room.

"Oh my, that was athletic," said a male voice.

"Quite so," said another. "And she's such a hottie."

"My word, is that kind of position even allowed?" queried a woman.

"I'm sure it isn't. I'll consult my book," said another woman in an authoritative voice that sounded as if she was scolding while looking down her nose.

Alice shook her head, trying to clear it, then she sat on her bare bottom and turned to face the voices. She was unsure of where she was, or how she'd gotten there, or who they were, but the thought that they'd been watching gave Alice a terrible thrill. The rabbit had somehow slipped out of her, leaving Alice throbbing with unresolved need.

But with all of these people in the room, Alice secretly hoped she wouldn't need the rabbit anymore.

Two men sat at a small table in front of the mirror, staring at her, one wearing a red bathrobe and one dressed in white.

Both were handsome and older, maybe even as ancient as their (gasp) *forties or fifties*, and both wore crowns on their slightly salt-and-pepper heads. A woman stood near them dressed in a white lace bra, garter belt, stockings and heels, her knees apart and her private place open for all to see. She wore a silver tiara atop her platinum blond updo, and on the table in front of them, a chess board was spread, the pieces poised mid-game.

Alice blinked her eyes, but when she opened them, the three were still there. "Are you—"

"Two kings and a queen? Why yes, we are, dear," the woman finished for her.

Alice should have felt embarrassed, as any girl lying naked on the floor in front of strange royalty might. But her first thought beyond how in the world she'd fallen through the mirror, was how rare it was these days to see people playing that particular game.

"Are you playing chess?" she asked.

The kings glanced down at the chess board in front of them with confused expressions on their faces. "Of course not," said the White King. "A chess game wouldn't be all that interesting for a twenty-first century audience to read about. We were watching you masturbate through the mirror."

The Red King nodded. "I loved when you bent forward at the waist and your tits bucked with each stroke." He brushed aside his robe to reveal his erect manhood folded in one fist.

Even the White Queen nodded. "Yes dear, your tits are quite magnificent. Such perky nipples."

Alice rubbed her eyes. Surely she must be dreaming. She couldn't have fallen through a mirror; that wasn't even believable in fairytales. But when she opened her eyes once again, the kings and queen were still there, only the Red Queen had joined them. And dressed in red leather pants and matching bustier, she was frowning something awful.

"The position you used was not approved," she said.

Alice had no earthly idea what the queen was talking about. "The position—"

"You were leaning forward, showing off those jutting nipples and lush breasts of yours and plunging the vibrator in and out, in and out, in and out from behind. I'm afraid I can allow neither the leaning forward position nor the fantasy of men ogling your bare breasts through the looking glass."

Alice glanced at the kings, who now both had spread open their robes and were holding their stiff shafts in hand, ogling her bare breasts.

"But that wasn't a fantasy," Alice explained. "The two kings really were watching me through the looking glass. They are watching me now."

"We all are, dear," said the White Queen, and she slid a hand between her legs and began to stroke the glistening wetness there.

The Red Queen shook her head severely. "I'm sorry. This won't do. Only the ruling queen can decide which fantasies and positions are allowed on this side of the looking glass, and you're not a queen at all."

Alice scrambled to her feet, feeling very embarrassed, not from the nudity and the staring and the masturbation, but from the realization that she'd offended a royal; quite a horrific prospect indeed.

"I must apologize, Your Highness," she said as she curtsied. "I didn't mean to offend. Truly. I'm not familiar with the rules."

The Red Queen's frown faltered, then slid from her lips, replaced by a satisfied bow of a smile.

"Very well, then. I like a young woman who knows her place. I shall teach you the rules right now."

She picked a thick, leather bound volume from a bookshelf, carried it to the table, and plopped it open, scattering chess pieces far and wide.

"Now here," said the Red Queen, extending a long finger tipped with a ruby red nail, "are the acceptable positions."

Alice and the two kings and White Queen gathered around her and peered down at the book.

"But your majesty," Alice said. "There's only one position here. The woman is lying down and the man is on top of her."

"The missionary position," said the Red King, nodding his head sadly.

Alice had heard of that name for it, and the position reminded her of the way she and Lewis used to make love before she'd learned many sexy lessons in Wonderland (now available exclusively for Kindle).

"Is that the only position acceptable?" Alice asked.

"There are others. Just look for yourself."

Alice did, slowly turning the pages of the book. On each page, the couple was in the same exact position, the woman on the bottom and the man on the top. Only in one picture, the woman was raising one arm. In another, she was raising two arms. In a third, the man and woman were both raising an arm and holding hands. The fourth depicted the woman and man each raising an opposite arm. In the fifth, the woman was raising an arm and smiling.

"But except for a bunch of silly arm raising, they are doing exactly the same thing."

"No," the Queen scolded. "There is a different name for each position. That means each position is different. See? This is *Missionary Holding One Hand*. And this one is *Missionary Kissing on the Cheek*. And this one here is *Missionary While Watching Lifetime For Women*."

Alice had to admit she thought the Red Queen was loopy, not that Alice would ever dream of saying that aloud. A queen is a queen, and since Alice wasn't a queen, she couldn't possibly disagree with authority.

"What about different positions?" Alice asked. "Such as the woman on top?"

The Red Queen frowned. "Forbidden."

Alice looked at the other three royals, and noticed neither king was paying attention. Instead, they were staring intently at her nudity and stroking themselves. The White Queen wasn't looking at the book either, instead winking at the White King every so often, pinching her nipples through the white lace bra, and smiling as if she had a glorious secret.

The Red Queen cleared her throat, bringing Alice's attention back to her. "Forbidden positions have also been catalogued in this book, but it is forbidden to look at them."

"Well, shouldn't we be able to look at them so we can be sure we don't do any of them?" Alice asked.

"The little tart has a point," said the White King.

The Red Queen sighed dramatically. "Very well," she said, flipping open the book. "This travesty here is called the *Open Fire Hydrant*."

It was, indeed, and appropriate name for it.

"And this is, *Camel In Repose*."

"I can sort of see the repose action," Alice said, squinting, "but I don't understand the camel reference."

"It refers to the hump, dear," said the White Queen. "There is also a two humped camel variation."

"Also forbidden," the Red Queen snapped. "And look at this nasty one; *The Leaky Faucet*. Just look at that mess they're making."

"Delightful," the Red King said, though he said it in a very sad way.

The Red Queen seemed not to hear her husband. "Check out this abomination, *The Spinning Noodle*. I don't see how that is even possible unless both partners are double jointed."

Alice wasn't sure it was possible either, but the explicit pictures were making her ache with desire. She wondered if it would be rude if she were to touch herself.

"Show her *Reverse Layup with Happy Ending*," suggested the Red King.

"How about *ER Visit*?" suggested the White. "That one is quite a challenge."

"We should stop this," said the Red Queen, her face getting brighter than her outfit. "I have not approved those positions. And fantasizing about them is off limits, too."

"Even fantasy is forbidden?" Alice asked. The Red Queen had mentioned that before, but Alice still found the idea shocking.

"I have forbidden everything I am uncomfortable with or don't understand," said the Red Queen. "Tolerance is a slippery slope to debauchery. Why, we wouldn't want people strutting about, making love in any perverted way they please, would we?" she asked the other royals.

They grumbled a non-coherent reply.

"Am I allowed to touch myself?" Alice asked, her fingers eagerly anticipating the answer.

"Yes, of course you are," the Red Queen said. "But only in bed at night, with all the lights out, and not for more than eight seconds."

"Eight seconds?" Alice said. "But, that's not long enough!"

"That's all I need," said the Red King, even though he was touching himself right that moment and had been doing so for far longer than eight seconds.

Alice was just about to point that out, when the White Queen gasped.

"Oh, my!" she said, walking to the window and peering outside. "Whatever shall we do?"

The Red Queen's attention snapped around. "What's wrong?" she demanded.

"I think there's a problem in the courtyard, Red Queen. I believe they are all too bored to continue making love."

"Take care of it."

"As you wish," said the White Queen and peeled off her bra, unleashing a very attractive pair of breasts with long, erect nipples.

"Not that way," said the Red Queen. "You are far too much of a slut, White Queen. If it were up to you, all manner of fantasies and positions would be allowed, and then where would we be?"

"Having fun?" muttered the Red King.

"Tolerant of others?" whispered the White King.

"Harrumph!" sputtered the Red Queen. "We need order in Looking Glass Land. Only with order can we have conformity, and conformity, as we all know, is the only path to happiness. I'll have to take care of things myself."

And so she stormed out of the room, leaving Alice and the others with the book.

The White Queen sidled up to Alice, her breasts still bare, one nipple brushing lightly against Alice's. "While she's gone, let us look at more of the fun positions."

She stared flipping through the book, while the kings ogled and stroked.

"What's that position called?" Alice asked, pointing.

"*Agonizing Cramps.*"

"And that one with the one man and two young women?"

"*Impending Divorce.*"

"What are those three people doing?"

"*Knot of Rectums.*"

"And that single man, in the corner?"

"*Frightened Virgin.*"

"What's that one called, where she has her legs up over his shoulders and her arms behind her in a twist?"

"*Quadriplegia.*"

"How about this one, where he puts it in her bottom while hitting her in the back with a rotten fish and calling her vulgar names in French?"

"*Joyful Sunset.*"

"And that woman on her knees, surrounded by eight men touching themselves?"

"*Emergency Trip To The Hairdresser.*"

"How about that man who has two other men in his hands?"

"*Carpal Tunnel.*"

"That woman over there, eating pie?"

"That's an ad for Weight Watchers, dear."

"Oh. How about those five old men, with all the girls climbing on them?"

"*Aerosmith.*"

"There certainly are a lot of banned positions," Alice said. "How about this girl held upside down on the table, all greased up with lard?"

"*Impending Lawsuit.*"

"The man who has the rope around his neck while he's touching himself?"

"*Cautionary Tale.* It's also known as *Dead on Arrival* and *Twitter Meme.*"

"How about that woman with her whole fist in her mouth?"

"I have no idea," said the White Queen. She turned to the White King. "Do you know the name of this position?"

"Can't say I do, but her boyfriend is one lucky bastard."

The White Queen turned to a new picture, a position like Alice had never imagined in her wildest dreams.

"I can't believe THAT!" said Alice.

"Can't you?" the White Queen said in a pitying tone. "Try again: draw a long breath, and shut your eyes."

Alice laughed. "There's no use trying," she said: "one *can't* make love in such an impossible position."

"I daresay you haven't had much practice," said the White Queen. "When I was your age, I always did that for half-an-hour a day. Why, sometimes I tried as many as six impossible sex positions before breakfast."

Alice studied the photo again. She'd have to think about that, and even as she did, standing there with the kings and queen, she could feel the ache between her legs grow stronger.

"If I were you, dear, I'd get out of here while she's gone."

Alice snapped out of her reverie. "Gone? Who?"

"The Red Queen," said the Red King.

The White Queen nodded. "We're having a swinging party, and you don't want to be part."

"A swinging party?" Alice said. She glanced around the room but saw no swings. Perhaps they were in the garden. "I love parties."

"Not this one, you won't," said the White King with a sigh.

"Why not? Are the swings outside?"

"There are no swings, dear, although sex swings are delightful fun."

"Yes, they are," said the Red King with a sigh.

"How do you have a swinging party with no swings?"

"A swinging party, my dear, is a party where couples gather and have sex with other couples."

Well Alice wasn't a couple, not since she broke up with Lewis, but the idea of the swinging party sounded naughtily enchanting. "And I can't join, because I'm not part of a couple?"

"Oh, you can join," said the Red King.

"We'd love to have you join," said the White King.

"It would be wonderful to have you, my dear," said the White Queen. "Attractive and charming women such as yourself are welcome at virtually any swinger's party. You don't need to be part of a couple."

"I find the three of you to be attractive and charming, too. So why shouldn't I love *this* swinger's party?"

"Because my dear, at a swinger's party on this side of the looking glass, we must all follow the Red Queen's rules."

Alice pictured that for a moment. Missionary position. No fantasies allowed. "Oh, I see. But can't we change the rules?"

The White Queen slowly shook her head. "I'm afraid the ruling queen gets to set the rules for fantasy and sex on this side of the looking glass."

"Funny," mused Alice. "On my side of the looking glass, fundamentalist religion does that. Although most people only pretend to be pious, so enforcing their rules is not all that successful most of the time."

"I say we all try to jump through the looking glass!" said the White King, throwing a fist in the air.

"I say we get in a quickie before the Red Queen gets back," said the Red King, rubbing his stiff member against Alice's thigh and cupping one of her breasts and one of the White Queen's in each hand.

"What do you think we should do, Alice?" asked the White Queen.

"Well," Alice said, wrinkling her brow. "I don't rightly know. Should I even have a say?"

"Everyone should have a say," said the White King.

"But you are all royalty. I'm just plain, regular Alice."

"There's only one answer to this problem," the White Queen said.

All three turned to look at her; Alice and the two kings.

"Alice has to become a queen."

If there was something she could say that would have shocked Alice more, Alice didn't know what it was. "A queen? Me?"

"Certainly!" said the White Queen. "You'd make a fabulous queen."

"Yes, you would," said the White King, lowering his head to suckle Alice's nipple.

"Yes, you would," said the Red King, now behind her and probing between her legs with his rigid manhood.

"Yes, you would," said the White Queen, dropping down to her knees and preparing to lick between Alice's thighs. "You just need to have an open mind."

"That's all I need to become a queen?"

The White Queen toyed with Alice, using the tip of her tongue. "That's all you need."

"I daresay, you have the rest of the requirements already," said the Red King, rubbing his hardness over her bottom and between her legs as if coating himself with her nectar.

A thrill swept over Alice, the physical pleasure of three people making love to her, and the delight of imagining that she was a queen.

She would have a crown, of course, or maybe a tiara of diamonds. And she would wear beautiful dresses and attend parties and everyone in her kingdom would adore her.

"Please, can you take it in your hand?" the White King asked, stroking her fingers with his stiff rod.

Alice was very anxious to be of use, so she gripped his member in her palm and started working up and down over his rigid length, soft skin and prominent ridge.

"Oh, yes."

She felt a pressure behind at her opening, and tilted her bottom upward in response.

The Red King's fat member slid into the hungry wetness of her enchanted tunnel. He gripped her hips and delved deep, just like she'd done with the rabbit, just like she'd imagined a man doing when she was watching herself in the mirror.

The White King took one of her nipples between his teeth, giving her a gentle nibble. He cupped both breasts in his hands, massaging and kneading and making Alice feel wonderfully thrilling sensations while he pumped his shank into her tight fist.

"Your tits are so hot, Alice," he said. "I want to spill my essence all over your nipples."

Alice had never heard of such a thing, but it sounded interesting all the same. Perhaps it was something reserved for royalty; something she could try once she'd opened her mind enough to become a royal herself. Maybe some of those pretty, queenly dresses she'd wear would be designed to leave her breasts bare, for just such an occasion.

"The rest of you is hot too, Alice," muttered the White Queen between licks, and her enthusiasm rippled through Alice in trembling waves.

"I'll say!" The Red King bellowed, taking another deep plunge. "Alice has the hottest box in Looking Glass Land!"

Alice wasn't sure if it was polite to say thank you to such compliments or not. But truly, the more the kings and queen licked her and teased her and explored her and thrust into her, the hotter she felt, and the more queenly.

The White King had just started making loud grunting sounds and the Red King had just settled into a driving rhythm and the White Queen had just slathered Alice's sex trigger with a good, fat lick of ecstasy when a voice cut the room.

"This is NOT an approved position!"

The White Queen fell back on her haunches. The Red King pulled out of Alice's special place. The White King reluctantly gave her nipples one last tweak, and then they left Alice to face the Red Queen's wrath.

"Leave this party at once!" she shouted.

Alice cowered away. "I'm so ever sorry, Your Highness."

"Don't *sorry* me. I was going to invite you to our very proper party, only to discover that you—with those perky nipples and shaved special place—are a troublemaker. To the courtyard with you! There you will learn the simple joys of *Missionary While Cross Stitching* and *Missionary With Eyes Closed Hoping It Ends Soon*."

"But the mirror is my only way back home," Alice said, backing up. Although if she was honest, she didn't want to go home, not just that minute. She wanted The Red King to be thrusting inside her, and the White Queen to be licking her, and the White King to anoint her nipples with his essence. But of course, she couldn't say any of that to the Red Queen.

"To the courtyard, or I will have you arrested and taken to the HDO!"

The two kings and the White Queen gasped in unison.

Alice didn't like the sound of that, whatever it was. So naked and aroused and totally unsatisfied, she dashed from the room.

Chapter 2

The Garden of Live Flowers

Alice raced through the house, not wanting to be arrested. Not that she was all that excited about going to the courtyard where only the missionary position was allowed, but Alice feared what would happen if she disobeyed the fearsome Red Queen, whom Alice feared quite fearily. Fear fear fear!

So for the courtyard she ran, seeing the patio door in the distance, and tripping over a book that had been placed conveniently in the middle of the floor for the purposes of this plot. Rubbing a stubbed toe, Alice picked up the doorstopper of a tome, cursing that the royals in this house still hadn't adopted ebooks, which wouldn't have stubbed her toe nearly as bad, or even at all. On the cover of the book was a strange word in a language Alice didn't know.

YKCOCREBBAJ

She puzzled over this until she realized, "Duh! It's a looking glass book! If I hold it up to a mirror, I can read it the right way!"

But Alice didn't even attempt it, because upon opening the book she saw lines of prose that looks suspiciously like quatrains and stanzas, which meant it was a book of poetry.

Alice despised poetry. She found it to be the most self-indulgent, most useless, most boring type of art. She'd rather watch a meth-addled performance artist scream incoherently about Martians while throwing rotten eggs at the audience than read poetry. Especially old poetry, and the copyright on this book said 1871. That sealed the deal that she would never, never, never, no way, no how, read this poetry book, because everyone knows nothing worthwhile was written before 1970, which was when Judy Blume released *Are You There God? It's Me, Margaret.* Everything prior to that was boring and stuffy and full of itself.

"I'm not going to read this," Alice said. "Never, never, never, no way, no how."

Then she opened it up and held it up to a mirror and began to read. After all, how was Alice supposed to open her mind, as the White Queen said, when she refused to even open a book?

JABBERCOCKY

'Twas horcky in the HDO,
Beased so long they mersycried,
Empty was the bordello,
Tolerance had up and died.

Beware the Jabbercock, my girl!
The pole that jabs the secret patch!
Torment shall make her toesies curl,
She was so shunned, they bandersnatch.

A soul condemned to face the beast,
By missionench, so crimson mean,
But pleasure fiftyfold increased,
Made her then the Golden Queen.

The Jabbercock shall masturbate,
Poor Golden Queen with fiendish chode,
But she shall rise and liberate,
And jabbing pole shall overload!

*One, two! One, two! And through and through
Until the machilit the smoke,
The souls condemned, they came and flew,
While Golden Queen BJ'ed her bloke.*

*Freedom rang in Kingdom high!
Snowballing and hot bukkake!
Gokkun, felching, and creampie!
Queen shall wed the panty jockey!*

*'Twas horcky in the HDO,
Beased so long they mersycried,
Empty was the bordello,
Tolerance had up and died.*

"Well," Alice said. "That was awful."

She tossed the book aside. Not only did it make zero sense, with all of its made-up words, but there was a smarminess to it that reminded Alice of grammar school, being condescended to by an underpaid teacher's aide who would have rather been travelling through Europe than dealing with children.

"Knight!" The Red Queen screamed from the other room.

Alice didn't wait to hear the rest but ran out the patio door and onto a stone courtyard littered with small beds. On each of the beds, reclined a naked woman, and on top of each naked woman was a timidly thrusting man.

Alice even recognized some of the positions from the Red Queen's book. One couple doing missionary was doing it with their faces together: *Missionary Touching Foreheads*. The next were holding hands: *Missionary With Hands Held*. Another watched a TV show about a woman dying of cancer who was being stalked by her boyfriend after her daughter who needed a kidney transplant was kidnapped: *Missionary While Watching Lifetime For Women*.

Alice stood and stared at the copulations for a few minutes, unsure what to do. It was a titillating scene, to be sure, and Alice felt like she should be aroused by it. After the Red King's quick exit from her love cave, The White King's final tweak of her nipples, and the White Queen's forced abandonment of Alice's pleasure folds, Alice was feeling rather lustful. Maybe as long as she watched the missionary position with its endless variety of arm raising and other nonsense, it would be within the rules for her to touch herself.

She tried cupping her breasts in her hands and teasing her nipples. She tried spreading her legs and massaging her most sensitive spot. She tried walking closer to the couples. She tried standing on one foot. She even tried out some arm raising of her own. But nothing seemed to work. Watching these obviously bored couples going through the motions without even making a peep was depressing, not arousing. Alice wished she had her rabbit vibrator, but that damn thing seemed to disappear on a regular basis.

"Psst!" someone said from beyond a hedge. "The garden is more beautiful from up here on the hill."

Alice turned in that direction, but she couldn't see anyone.

"Psst!" Came the voice again. "If you don't get out of there quickly, you'll be planted in one of those beds for sure."

"Who said that?" Alice asked. "The tree?"

"Trees don't talk, dumb ass. Hurry up!"

Alice took one last glance at the fornicating people, none of whom was looking to be having an enjoyable time at all, and then she scampered through a gap in the hedge and down a twisty-turny path until a green lawn opened in front of her. Lounging on the lawn were three nude women, one with dark skin, orange hair and tiger stripes tattooed all over her body, reaching down to the sculpted hair around her special place; one with pale pink hair, voluptuous curves and glittering rings piercing lush rosy nipples; and one with her brunette hair tied in pigtails and her shockingly fair body looking fresh as dew in the morning.

Alice glanced around, but there were no beds here, no missionary position, not even any men.

"What is this place?" she asked the women.

"We're the wild flowers."

Now this made no sense to Alice. "I'm afraid I don't understand. Although the three of you are beautiful, you're not flowers. Not literally."

"Sure we are," said the orange one with tiger stripes. "I'm Lily."

"And I'm Rose," said the pink woman with the lavish breasts.

The last, who looked delicate and sweet and the same precise age as Alice (because, of course, the youngest she could possibly be in this book is eighteen), giggled. "I'm Daisy," she said with a southern twang.

"I'm Alice. So you are flowers because you have flower names."

"Now you're just stating the obvious," said Lily.

Alice frowned. She hated being scolded, even by exotic-looking naked women. But scolding, as much as Alice detested it, always made her want to try harder. So try harder, she did. "And you're wild, because you have colored hair and tattoos?"

"I don't have colored hair or tattoos," said Daisy.

"Then why are you wild flowers?"

"We're the ones lucky enough to escape the beds," said Lily with a naughty wink.

"Oh, I get it. Flower beds."

"Yes," said Rose, "Violet, Dahlia, Iris, Pansy, and Marigold are all stuck in the beds, following the Red Queen's rules."

"So you don't follow the rules?" asked Alice, a wicked thrill making her nipples tighten.

"Of course not," said Lily, who seemed to be the leader. "We're wild, after all."

Alice already liked this place much better than the courtyard of beds. "So you can do anything in any position and follow your sexual fantasies?"

"We certainly can," said Rose, and as if to prove it, she began to play with her abundant breasts, pulling and twisting the sparkly rings until her nipples jutted out from her pillowy areolas, more erect than any nipples Alice had ever seen, even the White Queen's.

Now Alice had always found women's curves to be beautiful—they were the subjects of paintings and sculpture, after all. But never in a million years did she dream she would find another woman's breasts this arousing. The sheer lavishness of Rose's made her want to touch them, to suckle them, to caress them with her own.

And it wasn't just Rose's, she realized. Lily's breasts were much smaller, but perfectly rounded and firm. Her nipples were tight as well, jutting hard like bullets, dark against Lily's rich, chocolate skin.

And then there was Daisy, hers white and pure, her areolas pink and delicate, nipples perky.

And as Alice drank in the variety of mammary beauty, she found herself fondling her own. Her mounds were larger than Daisy's or Lily's, yet half the size of Rose's plush curves. But they had a firmness that felt good in her palms, and she'd liked the weight of them bouncing when the Red King had thrust into her. Alice's nipples tingled, and she played with them while recalling the lovemaking. The yearning within her reached a fever pitch.

"You like looking at tits, Alice?"

Alice flushed a little. "I suppose I was staring. I apologize."

"No need," said Rose. She rose to her feet and stepped close to Alice. "But there are some things more fun than staring. Like touching. Would you like to massage mine, Alice?"

Alice looked at those sumptuous breasts, the soft, puffy, cloud-like areolas and prominent nipples just inches from her own. Rose was wearing some sort of lotion that glistened like vegetable oil, and Alice couldn't help wondering if Rose's breasts would feel slippery if Alice stuck out her chest, leaned forward and pressed hers to them.

Sweat bloomed on Alice's skin, and wet heat pooled between her thighs. She pulled her gaze away, not sure where to look.

Lily and Daisy stood and stepped close to her, as well. Now wherever Alice directed her eyes, there were soft mounds to touch and erect nipples begging to be licked and sucked and…

"Um… Are there any men around?"

Lily smiled slyly. "Have you ever rubbed your tits against another woman's nipples, Alice?"

Alice's throat felt dry, and to her horror, her nipples tingled, hard and erect at the thought.

"Um… I like it when men suck my nipples. Especially when another man is thrusting into me from behind."

Rose arched her back and brushed her prominent nipples against Alice's as the White Queen had done earlier. Only the White Queen had not been wearing jewelry, and the addition of the silver rings embedded with diamonds made a shiver ripple over Alice's whole body and zing straight to the core of her femininity.

"You liked that, didn't you, Alice?" asked Rose and rubbed against Alice again, and her skin was indeed slippery.

An involuntary moan issued from Alice's lips. She had to get ahold of herself. "I like it when men…"

"You sure talk about men-folk a lot," said Daisy, as she dipped her delicate fingers into the V between Alice's thighs, making her gasp. "And yet, you are mighty wet. Mighty wet."

"Do our tits turn you on, Alice?" Lily took Alice's hand and cupped it over a tattooed breast. Her nipple poked between Alice's fingers.

Alice rolled it with her fingertips despite herself. "I'm… I'm not gay."

"Well, bless your heart. You don't have to be gay, Alice." Daisy slid her finger against one side of Alice's clitoris, then the other, sending powerful tremors through Alice's body.

"She's right, you know, Alice." Lily slid a hand under Alice's bottom and skated a finger inside her pleasure tunnel. "You just have to enjoy yourself."

"Are you enjoying yourself, Alice dear?" asked Rose, pressing her bodacious breasts firmly against Alice's and gliding her nipples up and down.

Alice was confused… and incredibly turned on… which confused her even more. "But if I enjoy myself, doesn't that mean I'm gay?"

"Well, I'm gay," said Daisy.

"And I'm gay," said Rose. "Is there a problem with that?"

"No," Alice said, and for the first time, she really thought about that question and what she was feeling, and realized that *was* really how she felt.

Could it be that she had accused Lewis of being gay when really it was her who was a lesbian all along? "I guess I have to be gay then," she concluded aloud.

"You don't have to be anything," said Lily. "We are what we are. There shouldn't be a *have to*."

"But I'm having sex with three women," said Alice. "So I must be a lesbian, right?"

"I'm not a lesbian," said Lily. "I enjoy both men and women. If anything, I'm more partial to a good, stiff cock. But I'd say I'm pansexual."

"What do you mean? You're turned on by pots and pans?"

Lily laughed. "I'm attracted to all people, regardless of gender. I just like sex. Giving and receiving pleasure. Perhaps you're like that as well."

Now Alice was really sweating and throbbing and tingling. She was also still confused. "So I can like both playing with your nipples and having sex with a man?"

"You can like anything you want, Alice. Just as you should be tolerant of what others like."

And Alice couldn't argue with that, but truth be told, she couldn't argue with anything right then, with Rose's nipples stroking hers, Daisy toying with her sensitive nubbin, and Lily plunging two fingers into her special place. Alice was unable to focus on anything but how good she felt.

Except, maybe, that she wanted to make the others feel good, too.

She ran her hand down Lily's belly and over the pubic hair sculpted with tiger stripes.

"Now you're getting the idea," cooed Lily and spread her legs.

Lily was as wet as Alice, and as Alice slid her fingers over her stiff clitoris and dipped into her garden of delight, she felt a thrill that she must have excited these three as much as they'd excited her.

Next she lowered her mouth to one of Rose's generous nipples and ran her tongue over the stiff peak.

"Oh, honey," Rose said on a breath.

Alice suckled and licked and massaged the full mounds.

Daisy dropped to her knees and began to lick Alice in the precious spot where Daisy's fingers first had fondled. And between Rose in her mouth, her fingers inside Lily, and Daisy lapping at her center of desire, Alice's legs started to shake. "Oh my," she exclaimed around Rosie's big breast. "I think I might fall."

And all four began to giggle and laugh.

"Have you ever tasted a woman, Alice?" Daisy drawled, smiling up at her, lips and chin glistening with Alice's juices.

"No," Alice answered politely. Just a short time ago, she would have been flabbergasted at the idea, but now it was sounding like something she'd like to try. "May I?"

And Daisy reclined in the grass and spread her pale legs wide to the bright afternoon sun. She was shaved smooth, just like Alice, and in her center emanated the most delightful golden gleam.

"She's right, you know, Alice." Lily slid a hand under Alice's bottom and skated a finger inside her pleasure tunnel. "You just have to enjoy yourself."

"Are you enjoying yourself, Alice dear?" asked Rose, pressing her bodacious breasts firmly against Alice's and gliding her nipples up and down.

Alice was confused… and incredibly turned on… which confused her even more. "But if I enjoy myself, doesn't that mean I'm gay?"

"Well, I'm gay," said Daisy.

"And I'm gay," said Rose. "Is there a problem with that?"

"No," Alice said, and for the first time, she really thought about that question and what she was feeling, and realized that *was* really how she felt.

Could it be that she had accused Lewis of being gay when really it was her who was a lesbian all along? "I guess I have to be gay then," she concluded aloud.

"You don't have to be anything," said Lily. "We are what we are. There shouldn't be a *have to*."

"But I'm having sex with three women," said Alice. "So I must be a lesbian, right?"

"I'm not a lesbian," said Lily. "I enjoy both men and women. If anything, I'm more partial to a good, stiff cock. But I'd say I'm pansexual."

"What do you mean? You're turned on by pots and pans?"

Lily laughed. "I'm attracted to all people, regardless of gender. I just like sex. Giving and receiving pleasure. Perhaps you're like that as well."

Now Alice was really sweating and throbbing and tingling. She was also still confused. "So I can like both playing with your nipples and having sex with a man?"

"You can like anything you want, Alice. Just as you should be tolerant of what others like."

And Alice couldn't argue with that, but truth be told, she couldn't argue with anything right then, with Rose's nipples stroking hers, Daisy toying with her sensitive nubbin, and Lily plunging two fingers into her special place. Alice was unable to focus on anything but how good she felt.

Except, maybe, that she wanted to make the others feel good, too.

She ran her hand down Lily's belly and over the pubic hair sculpted with tiger stripes.

"Now you're getting the idea," cooed Lily and spread her legs.

Lily was as wet as Alice, and as Alice slid her fingers over her stiff clitoris and dipped into her garden of delight, she felt a thrill that she must have excited these three as much as they'd excited her.

Next she lowered her mouth to one of Rose's generous nipples and ran her tongue over the stiff peak.

"Oh, honey," Rose said on a breath.

Alice suckled and licked and massaged the full mounds.

Daisy dropped to her knees and began to lick Alice in the precious spot where Daisy's fingers first had fondled. And between Rose in her mouth, her fingers inside Lily, and Daisy lapping at her center of desire, Alice's legs started to shake. "Oh my," she exclaimed around Rosie's big breast. "I think I might fall."

And all four began to giggle and laugh.

"Have you ever tasted a woman, Alice?" Daisy drawled, smiling up at her, lips and chin glistening with Alice's juices.

"No," Alice answered politely. Just a short time ago, she would have been flabbergasted at the idea, but now it was sounding like something she'd like to try. "May I?"

And Daisy reclined in the grass and spread her pale legs wide to the bright afternoon sun. She was shaved smooth, just like Alice, and in her center emanated the most delightful golden gleam.

"What is that?" Alice asked.

Lily laughed. "Why don't you kneel down and find out?"

So Alice did, and she discovered Daisy's womanhood was pierced like Rose's nipples, but the jewelry adorning Daisy was as golden as the center of a… well, a daisy.

"Daisy has a piercing. It makes the clitoris more sensitive," Rose explained. "The same as the jewelry in my nipples."

"Taste her," Lily urged.

So Alice lowered her head to Daisy and ran a fat lick over the petal of soft skin. Daisy moaned, her hips shuddering.

Did I do that? Alice thought. She licked again, and Daisy cried out, even louder.

"Do it gently at first," Lily told her. "Then harder as she gets closer to coming."

"How will I know?" Alice asked.

Lily smiled. "Oh, you'll know. Also, lift that luscious little bottom in the air. I have something for you."

Alice did as instructed. She tongued Daisy softly, making her mewl like her kitten, Creampie, did when she was hungry. Daisy's nectar turned on Alice something fierce, and she was surprised how much she liked the taste. So wet and hot, with a tiny bit of tang. Alice licked her up and down, and then side to side, and then made little circles around the gold ring.

Rose lay down next to them, bringing her hands first to Daisy's breasts, then to Alice's, rubbing and tugging and pinching.

Daisy clutched Alice's head, her hips bucking. "Oh yes," she moaned. "Yesssssss."

"Do it harder!" Lily said. "And stick your butt out!"

Alice began to tongue Daisy with more pressure, using her chin and lips as well. She worked the clit ring, tugging it this way and that, sucking it into her mouth over and over as fast as she could.

"Give it to her!" Alice heard someone yell. It was a man, his voice coming from the garden. She stopped just long

153

enough to look up on the ridge, and saw several of the couples had stopped their missionary sex and had gotten out of bed to stare at Alice and the wildflowers. The men were tugging on their members mercilessly, and the women were fingering themselves, their eyes wet with lust.

Then Alice screamed, for a man had penetrated her from behind just as Rose pinched Alice's nipples. It was stiff and thick and filled her up so completely and wonderfully. She turned to thank the man for doing her such a nice favor, and saw it wasn't a man at all. Lily was behind Alice, wearing a pair of black leather underwear that had a rubber dildo in the front.

"Strap-on," Lily said, pounding into Alice. She brought her fingers to Alice's clit, matching the stroke of her hips. "Finish off Daisy."

Alice buried her face in Daisy, wanting to devour her, each stroke of her tongue matching the thrust of Lily's hips. Daisy began to scream, and Lily had been right—Alice *knew* she was coming. She pushed two fingers inside Daisy's slot, jamming them in and out as she continued to lick, feeling her own wave cresting as Lily pounded into her.

"OH MY GOD!" cried Daisy, grabbing Alice's hair, pressing up into her as spasms shook her whole body. And then Alice was screaming as well, deep in her throat as Rose pulled her nipples and the crowd above cheered and applauded.

"Change positions!" Lily yelled.

While still in the throes of orgasm, Alice was pulled off of Daisy and flipped onto her shoulders, her hips held up in the air as Lily continued her thrusting. Alice watched Lily's breasts bounce with each plunge, then stared, wide eyed, her mouth open in ecstasy, at the ridge where the people watched. Two men continued to furiously pull on their long shafts, their hands blurry, but several couples had returned to their beds, or the hedges, or the grass, making love in different positions with vigor and throaty lust, even as their eyes continued to devour Alice and the flowers on the hill.

Then Alice's view of her audience was blocked as Rose lowered herself onto Alice's mouth. Alice immediately began to lick her and nibble on her, putting her hands on Rose's hips to pull her closer. Rose was extremely wet, and tasted sweeter than Daisy, coating Alice's face as she ground against her.

Somehow, Alice's hips stayed elevated, Lily continuing to drive into her, and then another feeling joined it.

A tongue. A glorious, ravenous tongue.

As Lily made love to Alice with the strap-on, Daisy had moved her face to where they were joined, and Lily gave her enough space to lap at Alice's clitoris while she was being thrust into.

Rose reached down, seeking Alice's tender nipples, riding Alice's tongue with a frenzy. She began to groan, and then her thighs locked around Alice's neck and for a moment Alice thought she might smother, and somehow that made what Lily and Daisy were doing even more exciting, and Alice climaxed a second time, screaming into Rose.

Then Daisy abruptly pulled back. "The Queen, she's coming! I can hear her footsteps!"

And all three women moved away from Alice, leaving her squirming and confused on the grass. When she was able to get her bearings, Alice saw the Queen was staring down at them. Only she wasn't wearing red leather. Instead she sported a white garter belt, stockings and shoes, her breasts and special place still bare for the world to see. And in her hand, she held a bundle tied with a bow.

The White Queen.

Alice blew out a breath of relief, and then began to tremble uncontrollably.

"I see you've opened your mind a bit, Alice," said the White Queen, smiling at Alice and the other three naked women in turn. "That's a good start. You're on your way to becoming a queen."

Alice could feel the three wild flowers staring at her. She managed to sit up, with help from Rose and Daisy.

It was Lily who spoke first. "You're going to become a queen?"

Alice blew out a big breath. "I'm... um... trying my best to open my mind so I can."

Then the three wildflowers, and the Queen as well, jumped up and down with an oddly out of place cheer that would have been more at home in a sex movie aimed at teenaged boys than an erotic fairy tale like this. And when the White Queen's breasts had stopped bouncing, she handed Alice the package she carried.

"A gift for you."

"Thank you." Alice unwrapped the package, hoping it was a pair of thigh high boots to make her legs and bottom look marvelous. Instead, it was clothing.

"Thank you," Alice said.

Alice wasn't sure what kind of clothing, exactly, but Lily, Rose, and Daisy were already dressing her.

"There," Lily said. "All done."

Alice looked at her new outfit. The white blouse and short, plaid skirt made her feel as if she'd just stepped out of an adult Japanese anime, only her hair wasn't blue. Her pumps were, though, and they almost glowed next to her crisp white ankle socks.

Well, at least the outfit covered most of her bare bottom, and except for being very thin fabric, the blouse covered her nipples. That was better than she'd done in Wonderland.

"Now you'd better go," said the White Queen. "The Red Queen is bound to come out any minute to check what positions are being used, and I'd like to slip in a little fun before she does, if you know what I mean." And with a wink, the White Queen walked back down the path and disappeared behind the hedge.

Alice glanced this way and that, unsure what to do next. "So which way does one go to open her mind?" she asked the three.

"You should go into the Sunny Bunny Fun Field of Happiness. I bet you could open your mind there." Rose answered.

"Where is that?"

Lily extended one arm in a point. "Through the hedge, there's a path. Go to a fork, and make sure you go left, not right."

"What's right?"

"Dreadful Famine Disease Povertyland." Daisy supplied.

"That does sound dreadful," Alice said.

Daisy shrugged. "Everyone has their kinks."

"Goodbye, Alice," Lily said. "It's been a lot of fun."

The women all shared a warm hug, and then Alice was once again on her way.

Chapter 3

Looking Glass Insects

Feeling tingly all over, Alice walked through a grassy field so green it looked artificially dyed. The ground seemed to suck onto the heels of her blue pumps with every step, and her tight outfit, though flattering, wasn't very warm. The gentle breeze kicked up under her plaid skirt and tickled Alice between her legs. She shivered, feeling her nipples harden under her white blouse, and she looked down and saw their stark outline through the thin fabric.

"It was kind of the Queen to give me these clothes, but they are rather revealing," Alice thought.

Unsure of where to go, Alice walked up a gentle slope and peered down into a valley filled with bright daisies, lush apple trees, and brightly colored birds singing playfully. She felt as if she'd stepped into a Disney cartoon.

"I half-expect the animals to start talking," she said to a fat bumble bee as it buzzed past her nose.

"Fuck off," said the bee.

Alice pouted at the insult. "Why, I never!"

"That's not what I've heard, you little slut," the bee said.

Alice thought about swatting the unpleasant insect, but realized it might sting her. Or worse, call her more names. So instead she continued to walk into the valley of the Sunny Bunny Fun Field of Happiness, and eventually came upon a rugged-looking man sitting under a tree. He wore peasant's clothing: a tan shirt, open at the chest, which appeared to be made of some rough material like burlap, and brown pants with a hole in the right knee, their cuffs tucking into black boots. Though the clothes appeared rough hewn, they were very clean, and the man looked comfortable in them. He had shoulder length black hair, in need of a comb, and a face in need of a shave. He was playing with a Rubik's Cube, and had managed to complete both the red and the green sides.

"Hello," Alice said.

The man glanced up at her, but rather than make eye-contact, he seemed to be focusing up her skirt.

"That's rather rude," she said, placing a hand between her legs to hide from his stare.

"What is?" he asked.

"Staring at my private parts."

"If you didn't want me to stare, why didn't you put on panties?"

Alice frowned. "I don't have any."

"That proves you want people to stare. You don't even have any panties to put on. How about you stand over me right now, let me have a nice, long look?"

Alice felt herself blush at the suggestion, and a wicked part of her almost wanted to do it. But she didn't even know who this man was.

"You're thinking about it, aren't you?" he asked.

Alice chewed her lower lip.

"You have nothing to be ashamed of, you know. Your womanhood is quite beautiful."

Alice felt the aforementioned womanhood grow warmer. "Really?"

"Like a big, pink flower."

"A flower?" Alice said, and she giggled thinking about Lily, Rose, and Daisy. She supposed the description made some sense, although before now, she never would have described it that way.

"Yes. I bet it smells nice, too. I think it would look perfect on a book cover."

"Well, thank you, I suppose. But I doubt that will ever happen."

"You never know," the man said, offering his hand. "I'm Gnat."

"Nat?"

"No. Gnat. With a silent G. Short for Gnathan. And you are?"

Alice took his hand, "I'm Alice."

Gnat's hands were rough with calluses but pleasantly warm.

"What brings you to the Sunny Bunny Fun Field of Happiness, Alice?"

"I'm looking for…" Alice chose her words carefully. "An open mind."

"I could help with that," Gnat said, lips turning up into a bright smile.

"Really?"

"Really. And it will give me a break from this." He held up the Rubik's Cube. "This puzzle is like a penis, you know."

"How so?"

"The more you play with it, the harder it gets."

Alice giggled. "Well, Gnat, I think I'd enjoy that."

"The puzzle? Or my offer to open your mind?"

"Your offer, Nat."

"Gnat. The G is silent."

"Gnat," Alice said.

"Well, then, lie down next to me and we'll begin."

Gnat released her hand and patted the ground, inviting Alice to have a seat. She did, and the grass was soft and cool under her bare bottom. Her imagination ran amok with the possibilities of what Gnat might do.

"What next?" Alice asked, tilting up her chin and expecting to be kissed.

Instead of kissing her, Gnat reached into a leather satchel and removed a coiled up length of clothesline.

"I'm going to tie you up. Have you been bound before, Alice?"

Alice nodded, her nether parts becoming tingly at the memory.

"Some people like to be bound and then spanked, or caned."

"Mmm-hmm," Alice said, not admitting she'd tried that herself with a certain degree of enjoyment.

"But I'm not really into that. I'm into something else."

"What?" she asked, genuinely curious.

"I'll show you." Gnat held out the rope. "May I?"

Alice nodded. Gnat didn't undress her. Or kiss her. Or even talk. He laid her gently down on her back, and then began winding the rope around her body in an intricate design. Gnat was so focused on this, that Alice felt more like she was posing for a portrait than engaging in some kind of sexual activity. Just as her interest was beginning to wane, Gnat bent her legs and fastened her ankles to her thighs, exposing her delicate parts. Gnat then tied her thighs so they were wide open.

"Okay," Gnat said. "Try to get away."

Alice had been in bondage before, but never this elaborate or constricting. She had very little freedom of movement. Her arms, hands, shoulders, waist, and legs were all so thoroughly wrapped up she practically felt swaddled.

"I can't," Alice said, straining to wiggle. "I can't move at all."

Gnat smiled, then bent down and gave her the sweetest, most tender kiss on the lips. Alice sighed, giving in to it, his soft tongue making her whole body seem to melt.

"It is so exciting to see you like this," he said. "You're so beautiful."

"Beautiful?" Alice was dubious. "I must look like a fly in a spiderweb."

"Your helplessness is beautiful," Gnat said. "For example, what if I were to do this?"

Gnat trailed his hand downward, touching her lightly between the legs. He drew a slow outline around her femininity with a single finger. After a complete circle, Gnat pressed lightly on Alice with his full palm and twisted it lightly, causing a most pleasant sensation.

"Oh, my," Alice said.

"See what I mean? I can touch you like this, and you can't do a thing to stop me."

The last thing Alice was considering was trying to stop him, but since her position was compromised she knew it was important to establish the rules of this game.

"Shouldn't I have a safeword?" she asked.

"I'm not going to hurt you, Alice. I promise."

"But what if I want you to let me go?"

"Is that what you want?" Gnat asked. His palm moved up, and his fingers slipped between her folds, entering her.

Alice answered with a gasp. She was beginning to understand what a turn-on being helpless was. Instead of resisting, Alice raised her hips so he could penetrate her deeper and reach her G-spot.

Surprisingly, Gnat withdrew his hand completely, and instead began lightly rubbing the inside of her thigh, nowhere near her sensitive parts.

"Please," Alice whispered. "Touch me."

Gnat brought his hand back, and began stroking her lightly. His touch was so delicate that it almost felt like a tongue. Alice moved her hips as best she could, however the ropes didn't allow for much leeway. But even though he was taking his time, Gnat knew exactly what he was doing. He began stroking her outer lips, then the more sensitive inner ones, making his finger slick with her juices. Then he slowly circled inward until he hit her most sensitive spot. Gnat took it in his fingers and wiggled his hand, sending a shock of pleasure through Alice just as intense as her vibrator. She cried out, the pleasure cresting as he eased two fingers inside of her and began to work them in and out.

"You're so sexy, Alice. So beautiful and sexy."

Alice began to pant. Her hips had taken on a mind of their own, thrusting at Gnat's fingers as if trying to capture them.

"Do you like this, Alice?"

"Yes," she said, closing her eyes and concentrating on the building pleasure.

"How about this?"

He put a third finger inside her, while his other hand continued to tug on her clitoris, and Alice felt the orgasm coming up so fast that she began to cry out—

Then Gnat withdrew his hands completely, leaving her bucking and humping the empty air.

"Please!" Alice pleaded. "I'm so close!"

But Gnat's hands had moved up to her breasts. He pinched and pulled at her hard nipples through the thin material of her blouse. While that felt wonderful, he was neglecting the part that would take her over the edge, and she tried to thrust her hips at Gnat, desperate to touch any part of him at all.

"Do you like me playing with your nipples?" he asked, rolling them around in his fingers. "They seem especially sensitive."

"They are," Alice said, unable to swallow.

"When I touch them, does it make the heat between your legs worse?"

She bit her lower lip. "Yes."

"Would you like me to stroke both at the same time?"

"Oh, yes."

Gnat continued to rub her nipple, and then once again put his hand on Alice's womanhood. But his touch was too soft. Too slow. Alice wanted it faster. Harder. And whenever she tried to press against him, he withdrew.

"This..." she said, quickly becoming out of breath, "this is cruel."

"Oh, but Alice. We've only just begun to play. Are you close to coming?"

Just saying the word *coming* almost made Alice come, but once again Gnat had stopped all stimulation, leaving her frustrated.

"Are you close, Alice?"

"I am so close. Please, Gnat."

He slipped a finger inside her again, moving it in a beckoning motion, making her breath catch. Alice could feel the orgasm coming, but right before her body clenched, Gnat withdrew.

"No!" she said, her eyes welling with tears. "Please oh please, Gnat. Your teasing is more than I can handle."

"This is called orgasm denial," Gnat said, lightly brushing a tear off her cheek. "I keep you at the edge of orgasm, but you can't come until I allow it."

"For how long?" she squeaked, her voice hoarse with desperation.

"For as long as it pleases me."

Alice was so hot down there. She wanted to be taken, not teased, but had no idea how to convince Gnat to satisfy her needs.

"Don't you want to make love to me?" Alice asked.

"Indeed. And I will."

"Now. I want it now. Please."

"Not yet, Alice. You aren't ready."

"But I am ready!" Alice pleaded. The very thought of him entering her made Alice ache in a way she'd never ached before.

"The longer you sustain a state of high arousal," Gnat said, "the greater it will be when you do come."

"Aren't you aroused?" Alice asked, desperate to somehow convince Gnat to enter her.

"Very."

Alice wiggled in frustration. "But I'm bound. I can't touch you, or give you any pleasure."

"I'm getting pleasure from teasing you, Alice."

He roughly entered her with two fingers, making Alice scream in a combination of shock and joy. Gnat began to move them in and out, faster and faster, until Alice was about to be overtaken by a gigantic—

"No!" she cried when he removed his fingers again. "Please! I beg you!"

"Begging is a turn on," Gnat said.

Alice tried to undulate closer, to get Gnat to touch her again. If only she could rub up against his knee. Or his wrist. She only needed a little bit more…

"I'll give you anything," Alice begged.

"It will all be worth it. Trust me. I've been to the HDO."

Gnat traced his finger around her nipples, flicking them through the blouse, making Alice wish he'd taken off her clothes.

"What are you talking about?" she asked, squirming uncomfortably. "What is the HDO?"

"When people offend the Red Queen, they are taken to the Hall of Denied Orgasms. It is run by a close friend of mine, the Knight. His job is to pleasure the men and women who are held captive there, taking them to the brink of orgasm without letting them come. He can do this for hours. Or, if the offense is severe enough, for days."

"It sounds dreadful," Alice said, clenching her teeth as Gnat squeezed a nipple. She wondered if she hadn't taken the wrong fork in the road, and was actually in Dreadful Famine Disease Povertyland. Being helplessly teased for hours, or days, without orgasm was more than Alice could bear to think about, especially when she was so close to coming right then.

"It isn't dreadful, Alice. It's beautiful. All of those writhing, begging people, so desperate to be allowed release. Instead, they are brought to the brink, over and over, using all manner of dastardly technology."

Gnat moved his hand between Alice's legs again, and was stroking her so lightly she knew she'd go insane.

"Technology?" she grunted.

"Sex machines, Alice. Intricately designed to stimulate for extended periods of time."

Alice began to weep. "How can you get turned on, being so cruel?"

Gnat appeared thoughtful. "Everyone gets turned on by different things, I suppose. For example, Alice, some women get aroused by giving oral sex. Does that excite you?" Gnat moved his face next to hers, his breath hot on her ear. "Taking a man in your mouth?"

Alice blushed, and thinking about it made her loins burn. "Oh... actually... yes."

Again he moved his hands away, now drumming his fingers on her bound inner thigh.

"But why, Alice? What do you get out of that experience?"

Alice was finding it hard to speak. She was too focused on Gnat's hands.

"Pay attention, Alice. Why do you like giving men head?" He took his hands away, and stared down at her with his arms folded over his chest.

"Oh, please, Gnat..."

"Answer the question."

What was the question? Something about why she liked to take men in her mouth?

"I'm... not sure, really," Alice said. "I like hearing the sounds the man makes. I like him wanting me badly."

"You like being in control of his pleasure."

"Yes."

"That arouses you?"

Alice nodded.

"And women?"

"Women?" echoed Alice.

"I was buzzing around the garden earlier and saw you with those flowers. Did you like to lick them for the same reason? Did you enjoy the way they responded? The way you controlled their pleasure?"

Alice thought about the response she'd gotten from Daisy and Rose. "Yes... I did."

"And it arouses me to do things to you while you're tied up and helpless. Things like... this."

Gnat lowered his head between her legs, his unshaven cheeks pressing against her bare, quivering flesh. She felt his mouth press against her folds, his tongue slipping inside, and the pleasure was as strong as an electric shock.

"Oh, yes, Gnat. Yes..."

But Gnat didn't lick. Didn't stroke. Didn't move. Alice tried to push against him, but his hand gripped her tied thighs too tightly, preventing any movement on her part.

"Please, Gnat. Oh, please."

He stayed still.

"Gnat!"

Not the slightest movement. Just heat and pressure, so terrible Alice felt ready to burst.

"Lick me!" Alice shook her head back and forth. "Gnat! Lick me!"

He didn't.

Alice didn't know what to do. There was a man's mouth between her legs, pressing against her, and rather than being in ecstasy Alice felt like pulling her hair out in frustration.

But maybe she didn't need more than just him being there.

Even though Gnat wasn't actively trying to pleasure Alice, the feeling grew in her anyway. The weight of his lips, his tongue. The very thought of him down there. Knowing she was bound and helpless, at his complete mercy. Remembering the things he'd already done to her, and would continue to do.

Yes, Alice didn't need more than just a simple touch. She could make herself come. All she needed was a few more seconds and—

Gnat pulled away again.

Alice spent a very unladylike few seconds calling him every dirty name she could think of. As she did, she watched Gnat slowly unbuckle his belt. His pants fell free around his ankles, and he sported a lovely, throbbing erection. A glistening pearl of dew leaked from the tip, and Gnat rubbed it with his thumb, lubricating his soft, velvety head. Then he grasped himself firmly at the base.

"Would you like to put this in your mouth, Alice?"

The very suggestion made Alice's whole body clench and thrum.

"Please," she said. "Oh please."

Gnat lowered himself to his knees, his manhood bobbing before Alice's face. She stretched her head toward him, mouth open, trying to capture it. Gnat rubbed the head over her lips, the outside of her cheeks, and then pulled away.

He's going to tease me like this as well? Alice thought. *This man is dreadful!*

But tease he did. Gnat would put just the tip into her mouth, just enough for her to get the tiniest taste, then quickly withdraw. He did this again, and again, and made it even more unbearable by talking to her.

"Do you want it?"

"Yes."

"Beg me for it."

"Please, Gnat. Oh please."

He placed it on the tips of her lips, making Alice stretch out her tongue.

"Do you want me to touch you?"

"Yes."

"You've made me so hard, Alice. Perhaps I should mount you right now."

"Yes!"

"Or maybe I'll let you suck me. You seem so eager to."

"Yes! Please!"

Gnat, however, did not accede to her wishes. He never allowed Alice to take him fully into her mouth, to suck on him as she so desperately desired. He just continued to tease her until the longing became so unbearable, Alice was positive that if she could lick him for just a few seconds she herself would come, even without any stimulation at all. She had never been this turned-on before. It was maddening.

Then, as if her prayers were answered, Gnat crawled down between her legs, his manhood poised above her garden of delights.

"Oh, Gnat..."

But he didn't enter her. Instead, holding his erection like a paintbrush, he drew little circles around Alice's lips with his head, barely putting it inside before withdrawing.

Alice's fists clenched. She set her jaw. She thrashed her head back and forth. It was all too much.

Still, Alice was determined to get her way, and if she concentrated, Alice knew Gnat's teasing would be enough to make her explode. Alice squeezed her eyes shut, grinding her teeth, concentrating on the sensations. She only needed a few more seconds to reach her peak, just one more stroke, one more rub—

And then Gnat was standing up, stroking himself vigorously.

"No!" Alice cried out, her whole body shaking.

"It must be so uncomfortable, being so close to coming," Gnat said. "And look how I can pleasure myself. Why, I may come on your breasts and just leave you like this."

Alice wanted to scream at the injustice of it. Yet the thought of Gnat spurting his essence all over her nipples added to Alice's furious arousal.

"What can I do?" Alice said. "Please! Tell me!"

"You are already doing it," Gnat said, his hand a blur. "You see how excited I am. All because of you, Alice. Wouldn't it be fun to do this to me? To bind me up and make me plead for release?"

Alice nodded, but she didn't want to think about that now. Right then, all she cared about was blessed release.

"Look how wet you are," Gnat said. He knelt down and Alice screamed when he touched her between her legs. "Have you ever been this wet?"

"No," Alice panted. "Never."

"So warm and wet. Do you like what I'm doing to you?"

"No! It's torture!"

Gnat frowned, withdrawing his hand.

"No! I mean, don't stop! Please, Gnat!"

"So you want me to keep teasing you?"

Alice didn't know how to answer. But when Gnat's fingers grazed her again, she gasped, "Yes!"

"You've been so kind to me, I'm going to let you come."

"Oh, yes!"

"Just another half an hour of teasing."

"NO! PLEASE!"

But Gnat was merciless. He would stroke her, then stop. Lick her, then stop. Once he even entered Alice, so quickly that her brain barely had time to register the pleasure before he was gone again.

It was such beautiful agony. Such delicious torture.

Alice came close to orgasm, too many times to count, but Gnat knew her body amazingly well, and would always pull away before she could reach her peak.

By the time thirty minutes had passed, Alice no longer existed. Every bit of her personality was gone. Every memory, every thought, had been wiped away. Gnat had reduced her to nothing but instinct. A helpless, clawing, mewling animal, existing only to pursue pleasure. He got her to the point where a single stroke of his finger across her mouth was enough to make her come. Where a soft breath on her thigh was enough. Where the mere words, "Would you like me to rub your clitoris?" were just as arousing as being vigorously tongued.

Alice's clothes were drenched in sweat. The ropes that bound her were wet. She could no longer form a thought, or a sentence.

"So beautiful," he said, running his hand through Alice's damp hair. "You've suffered enough. I'll make you come, now."

Alice could scarcely believe it, and then Gnat was driving his manhood into her, impaling her, filling her. He wasn't going to pull away this time. He was thrusting hard, gripping Alice's hips, plunging into her with the speed and power she'd been yearning for since he'd tied her up. It was so needed, Alice could scarcely believe it, and the surprise was every bit as powerful as the soul-freeing relief.

Alice screamed with pleasure as her mind, and her body, snapped like dry kindling.

It started with a spasm, as all her orgasms did, muscles clenching down deep, so strong it overtook every cell in her body.

But it didn't stop there. It kept going, kept deepening, widening, until all she could feel was scorching heat, all she could see was white light, and all she could think…

Well, she couldn't think at all.

It was like an explosion, only slowed down, where each burst of fire built and billowed and crescendoed just as another was building behind it. Again and again and again, and Alice had no control over her body or the lewd words coming out of her mouth. She was a prisoner to her own unending ecstasy. Gnat kept pounding into her and each thrust added to the all-consuming inferno where every second she'd been teased was rewarded with a life-shattering jolt of pleasure, which seemed to go on and on.

"I'm coming!" Gnat said, and those words sent Alice up yet another precipice, and she joined him as he cried out, his spasms joining hers until Alice could no longer tell when he ended and she began.

Eventually, his movements ceased, and Alice felt like she was a tire with all the air let out. A very happy tire.

When Gnat finally pulled out of her, he planted a sweet kiss on her forehead and said, "So, did that open your mind at all?"

Alice didn't answer. She felt drugged. Out of sorts. Wonderful, and satisfied, but as if she'd suddenly awoken from deep sleep.

"Alice? Are you okay?"

She peered up at Gnat, having to concentrate for him to come into focus. "Oh, my, yes."

"Would you like me to tease you for another three hours?"

Gnat began to move his hand between her open legs.

"NO! I mean, that's kind of you to offer, but I believe I'm losing circulation in my fingers."

Alice knew that was from her clenching her fists so tightly, not the ropes, but she couldn't bear being teased again. Especially for that long.

"Fair enough." Gnat pulled one strand of rope, and Alice's legs were instantly freed. It was nothing short of magical. "So what was your impression of orgasm denial?" he asked, rubbing her wrists and getting the circulation flowing.

She blew out a long breath, both happy to be untied, and a little saddened as well.

"The build-up was dreadful. But the pay-off was spectacular."

"If you come by here again, I can teach you how to do the same to me, if you'd like."

Alice decided she would like that, and thanked him for the offer.

"So where are you off to, now?"

Alice tried to stand, but her legs wouldn't support her. Gnat had to help Alice to her feet and keep an arm around her waist.

"Well, you could go through the orchard and meet with Tweedle Dee and Tweedle Dum. If you want to open your mind, I'm sure they could help you with that."

"They aren't into orgasm denial, are they? I don't believe I could handle that again so soon."

"No. They are into something else entirely."

"What exactly?"

"You'll see," Gnat said, smiling. "Just follow the sun through the orchard, and look for the sign on the tree."

"Thank you, Gnat."

"Thank you, Alice. Are you sure you don't want to play for a bit longer?"

Alice touched herself, and while she did want to go again, she didn't want to be tormented for hours first.

"Perhaps some other time, Gnat. But I do appreciate you opening my mind."

"It was my pleasure, Alice."

"Mine, too. See you, Gnat."

Alice gave Gnat a kiss on the cheek, then began to follow the sun through the orchard, onto her next adventure.

Chapter 4

Tweedle Dee and Tweedle Dum

When Alice reached the end of the orchard, she found several signs nailed to the last tree. The first was marked TWEEDLE DEE IS SEXY. Beneath that was TWEEDLE DUM IS 2X SEXY. Under that was TWEEDLE DEE IS 4X SEXY. This went on for eight more signs, getting up to TWEEDLE DEE IS 2,000,000X SEXY and by then there was no tree left.

Alice found a path behind the tree, which she followed until she reached another tree, which was also covered with signs that went up to TWEEDLE DUM IS 999,999,999,999,999,999X SEXY. Beneath that was another sign that read YOU'RE BOTH SEXY! LEAVE ME ALONE! It was signed THE TREE.

Alice found the whole thing very queer. A few steps later, she came upon two short, rotund, decidedly unsexy gentlemen whom she also found very queer, as evidenced by them kissing one another.

"No, my dear, you are sexier," said one between smooches.

"You are too kind," replied his partner. "But indeed you are much sexier."

Each was no taller than her shoulder, and they had largish heads and protruding bellies and could have been twins except one of them had an erect member that curved upward, whilst the other's curved in a decidedly downward fashion.

"Excuse me," Alice said, "But are you Tweedle Dee and Tweedle Dum?"

"It depends," said the one with the upturning member. "Whom do you think is sexier?"

Alice didn't want to be cruel, as she didn't find either of them sexy in the least, but she went with the safe bet. "I find both of you equally sexy."

"Preposterous," said one.

"Unheard of," said the other.

"Inconceivable."

"Ridiculous."

"Outrageous."

"Unbelievable."

"Gelastic."

"Gelastic?" Alice asked. "I've never heard of such a word. What does it mean?"

"It means preposterous," said one.

"Unheard of," said the other.

"Inconceivable."

"Ridiculous."

"Outrageous."

"Unbelievable."

"Please stop," said Alice, who had an urge to slap them both in their gelastic heads. "I'm seeking to open my mind, and I was told to look for Tweedle Dum and Tweedle Dee."

"I am Tweedle Dum," said the downturned member Tweedle, "and my much sexier partner is Tweedle Dee."

"Not true," said Tweedle Dee.

"But you are Tweedle Dee," insisted Tweedle Dum.

"Indeed I am. But I am not the sexier partner. That indeed is you."

They once again began to kiss, whilst engaging in something that Alice could only describe as penis fencing.

"Are you brothers?" Alice asked.

"Of course not," they answered simultaneously.

"My brother's name is Irving," said Tweedle Dee. "He lives in Dubuque, Iowa with his wife and kids and works at a meat processing plant."

"I am an only child," said Tweedle Dum. "Besides, Amazon.com doesn't allow incest erotica."

"But you look so much alike," Alice said, growing more annoyed.

"Plastic surgery," beamed Tweedle Dee. "I have had over a dozen procedures to look more like sexy Tweedle Dum."

Tweedle Dum nodded and smiled. "And I have had more than a dozen procedures to look like sexy Tweedle Dee."

"But you are the sexier one."

"No, you are."

"No, you are."

"No, you are."

"No, you are."

"No, you are."

"No, you are."

"No, you are."

"Will both of you sexy bitches shut up for a moment!" Alice said. She wondered if Gnat had simply been teasing her in a different way by sending her here. These two men were opening Alice's mind to the possible delights of homicide, not sex.

"What is your name, young lady?" one of them asked. Alice had forgotten which was which.

"I'm Alice."

"Well, Alice, tell us again what you seek."

"An open mind," Alice said. She almost added, "and no more talk of which of you ugly little farts is sexier, or I'll scream." But she didn't add that, because it was mean.

"Well, Alice. The best way to open your mind is with an excruciatingly long poem."

"Oh, please don't."

"You don't like poetry?"

"I really despise it. Can't you teach me open-mindedness with a hard spanking? Or through some sort of sexual escapade? Really, I'd even prefer being tied up and teased for hours than listening to—"

"A poem it is!" said the other one. "I shall now recite the very, very, very long poem, THE WALRUS AND THE CARPENTER. It is the longest poem I know."

Alice cringed, looking for a path to escape, but a Tweedle grabbed each of her hands, then held hands themselves, and they all began to swing in a circle as the terrible poem was recited.

> *The financier D. Walrus*
> *Always paid his debts in checks*
> *But when he paid the Carpenter*
> *It was with anal sex.*
>
> *"The time has come," D. Walrus said,*
> *"To give you what you're due,*
> *I'll mount you like a priceless stamp,*
> *For I'm in love with you."*
>
> *"Outrageous!" cried the Carpenter*
> *"You're like some raging bull!*
> *I cannot work for orgasms!*
> *Or when my bum is full!"*
>
> *As Walrus thrust, he pictured, thus:*
> *The sweet, white cliffs of Dover,*
> *Plus it was hard to hear his friend*
> *Whilst he was bent over.*
>
> *"What was that?" Walrus inquired,*
> *"Did you say something, dear?*
> *It's mighty hard to hear you*
> *As I'm thrusting up your rear."*

"I wish to be paid differently!"
The bowed carpenter pleaded.
"Preferably in a way
Rear entry isn't needed!"

Walrus grabbed his tender hips
And his thrusts picked up speed,
"But surely, my dear carpenter
It's precisely what you need!"

"I've watched you build my kitchen
And I really have to say
Any man with such good taste,
Must certainly be gay."

"That might be true," came the reply,
"But you, sir, take advantage.
Plus your manhood is so large,
That I can barely manage!"

D. Walrus knew just what to do,
And growling like a hound,
He used his hand to give his friend
A welcome reach-around.

The Carpenter cried out with joy,
His hips began to spasm
And he joined D. Walrus
In a mutual orgasm.

D. Walrus gave him a wet kiss
They shared a tender hug,
Neither of them showed concern
For the stains on the rug.

"So... shall I go and cash a check?"
D. Walrus asked his friend.

"I just made a big deposit..."
"Yes, you did! In my rear end!"

The Carpenter then laughed aloud,
"It's been a long, long while,
Since a benefactor paid me
With bareback doggy style."

"But I still need cash," he stated,
Because sex won't buy me bread,"
So cheap D. Walrus countered with:
"What if I give you head?"

The Carpenter considered it,
And then gave his consent,
A blowjob seemed more urgent
Than promptly paying rent.

D. Walrus dropped down to his knees,
And slurp-slurped up his dingus,
Which he was much better at
Than awkward cunnilingus.

"Oh my! Oh my! Oh me, oh my!"
The Carpenter extolled,
Then he filled Walrus's mouth,
With his hot and salty load.

From that day on, they were a pair,
And both their lives were great,
They wed in San Francisco,
Fuck Proposition Eight!

"What is Proposition Eight?" Alice asked. She was surprised the poem wasn't as bad as she'd feared, and even more surprised because she felt she'd learned something.

"It was a Constitutional Amendment passed in California to ban same-sex marriages," Tweedle Dum said solemnly.

"Why, that's abhorrent!" Alice proclaimed. "People should be able to marry whomever they want to!"

"We agree," said Tweedle Dee. "But this country is still firmly stuck in Puritan times when it comes to sex. Did you find the Walrus and Carpenter poem offensive?"

"No. I thought it was lovely. Though the meter was off a few times."

"It's a hastily written parody," said Tweedle Dum. "No one is trying to win a Pulitzer here."

"There's no danger of that happening," said Alice. "But I do have to ask you something. It's about my boyfriend, Lewis. I dumped him because I caught him wearing my underwear."

Tweedle Dee gasped and fainted, falling into Tweedle Dum's arms. Then Tweedle Dum stood him back up, and he gasped and fainted, falling into Tweedle Dee's arms. They repeated this an irritating number of times until Alice wanted to club them both to death.

"Enough!" she finally demanded.

"You hate us, because we're gay!" Tweedle Dum decried.

"No, I hate you because you're annoying little bastards. How about trying to teach me about tolerance instead of playing around?"

"Dear Alice," said Tweedle Dee, his face a picture of serenity. "Human sexuality is a strange and beautiful thing. No one knows where we get our preferences. Could be our genes. Could be early life experiences. Could be from viewing too much Internet porn. Sexuality, no matter what type, is completely natural as long as there is mutual consent. But when we start condemning others for their choices? That's evil."

Tweedle Dum pointed a finger in Alice's face. "It is none of your business where I stick my dingus, unless I'm trying to stick it in you." He sidled up to her, slipping a hand around Alice's waist. "Is that something you'd like?"

"I... I... I don't know," Alice stammered. "What about diseases?"

"We're both regularly tested. Plus we use condoms."

(Of course, in Alice's fantasies, no one actually used condoms, but in real life, she recognized the need for them and was very responsible.)

"I... I thought you were gay," she said.

Tweedle Dee shrugged. "We swing both ways."

"But, aren't you married?" she asked, looking at their ring fingers and seeing gold bands.

"We just told you we swing."

Oh yes, Alice had learned about swinging from the kings and queens. "Do you only use the missionary positions?"

"Were you sent by the Red Queen? Are you here to spy on us?"

Both the Tweedles' members shriveled and shrank right before Alice's eyes, like helium balloons on a cold day.

"Heavens, no! The Red Queen banished me to the courtyard."

"But you're not in the courtyard now," Tweedle Dum said.

"I escaped with The White Queen's help. I'm trying to expand my mind so I can become a queen myself."

"When you're a queen, will you regulate fantasies and sex acts?"

"Heavens to Betsy! No, of course not!"

"You're not judgmental about the sexuality of others?"

"A thousand times no! Why would you even think something like that? I am very open-minded and tolerant."

But either Tweedle Dum or Tweedle Dee didn't believe her, or the specter of the Red Queen's rules had frightened them deeply, because both of their members hung flaccid and sad beneath their bellies.

Then Tweedle Dee (or perhaps it was Tweedle Dum) said something that made Alice feel even worse. "You do realize that the only people who declare they are open-minded so adamantly are those with closed minds, right Alice?"

Alice didn't know how to answer that, so she looked down at her pumps and tried not to cry.

"I'm so sorry," she said. "I don't want to be closed-minded. And I feel terrible that I've ruined your charmingly curved erections." She sniffled. "Is there any way I can help you get them back?"

Tweedle Dee looked at Tweedle Dum, and Tweedle Dum looked at Tweedle Dee.

"We have an idea," they said in unison.

Alice brightened. "You want me to suck one of your stiff quarter rolls while the other one slides into my slot of riches from behind?"

"No," said Tweedle Dee. "I'm afraid that won't cut it."

Disappointed, Alice pondered for a moment. "I know! You want to stick one of your love rockets into my bottom while the other one plunders my secret garden with his shaft of pleasure?"

"No," said Tweedle Dum. "I'm afraid that isn't good enough either."

"And also," said Tweedle Dee, "Your euphemisms are annoying. Why must you purposely be annoying, Alice?"

Now Alice was getting frustrated. Again she found herself wanting to kill the odd little Tweedles, but due to the lingering heat of Gnat's teasing and her own lascivious suggestions about what she could do with their charmingly curved members, she didn't want to bludgeon the strange little men any longer. Now she wanted to hump them to death.

Alice unbuttoned her thin white blouse and cupped her breasts together, nipples jutting excitedly at the duo. "How about mammary intercourse?"

"Don't be silly," the Tweedles said.

Alice stood there, feeling like an idiot, holding her bare breasts in her palms. "What then?"

"Stand there, just like that," said Tweedle Dee.

"Just like that, except spread your legs apart," said Tweedle Dum. "And lift your skirt."

Alice did as they asked, tucking the front hem of her skirt into the waistband to reveal the shaved area between her legs. She still felt a little silly, but that was overridden by the anticipation of what they might do, now that her breasts were bare and her thighs were open.

"Now what?"

"Watch." And with that, Tweedle Dee took ahold of Tweedle Dum and Tweedle Dum took ahold of Tweedle Dee, and with two strokes of each other's lengths, both the curve up and the curve down were stiff as could be.

"Are you ready now?" asked Alice, and she spread her legs farther apart, the cool air caressing the (very!) wet heat between.

"Keep watching," said Tweedle Dum, and he fell to his knees and took his partner's shaft deep into his mouth.

Tweedle Dee moaned, and his eyes turned back a little in his head.

Alice pinched her nipples, rolling the sensitive nubs between her fingers as she watched the show, wondering when they'd get to her.

Dum cupped Tweedle Dee while he sucked and licked and did all manner of appealing things with his (very!) talented tongue. And as he bobbed and weaved, putting his energy into the task, his own member bobbed and weaved and swayed heavy between his legs, and Alice found herself wanting desperately to take him into her hands.

"Don't," said Dee, as if reading her thoughts. "We're not at all ready for you yet."

So she stood there while they traded places, Tweedle Dee doing the sucking and flicking and bobbing and weaving, his curved upward tool stiff and glistening and hanging temptingly like delicious fruit waiting to be eaten.

And Alice slipped one hand from her breast and glided her fingers into the wetness between her open thighs.

Now the two returned to penis fencing, rubbing one hard length against the other. And as Alice caressed herself in small circles and played with one soft mound of breast, she could feel building that sense of pressure and heat and emptiness. And she was looking at two things that would be perfect to fill it.

"May I please?"

"Please?" said Tweedle Dee.

"Please, please, please?" begged Alice.

"Please, please, please?" echoed Tweedle Dum.

Alice had no idea what else to say. In all honesty, she'd never had to try too hard to get men interested in making love to her. Never had to try at all, really. Not on either side of the looking glass. And now she was standing in front of these two erect and ready shafts with her nipples protruding and her special place dripping with want, and these two men she'd hadn't even found attractive refused to let her touch them.

And yet, she wanted nothing more. Somehow, while watching their coupling, these unappealing little men had become very appealing indeed.

This land through the looking glass really was a backward kind of place!

She cleared her throat. "May I please put your long, hard cocks in my mouth and lick them with my tongue?"

The Tweedles stared at one another and then looked back to her. "Certainly! Why didn't you ask that in the first place?"

And although Alice definitely should have felt put out and frustrated and longing to kill them both over that last remark, instead she got down on her knees in the green, green grass and began to lick the two crossed shafts as they rubbed against one other.

She ran her tongue over Tweedle Dee's ridge and underneath to his swinging sack. Then she worked her way back to the place where they crossed and lavished her attention on

Tweedle Dum. Pretty soon she couldn't tell Dum from Dee or Dee from Dum, it just seemed like one big pleasure pretzel that existed simply for her pleasurable pleasure.

Each man grasped a breast and played with her pulsing nipples. Tweedle Dee would moan, then Dum would moan. Tweedle Dum would groan and then Dee would groan. With each flick of Alice's tongue, the men would respond. Each lick of their balls, they'd bellow like elk.

Finally Tweedle Dum caressed her hair, causing her to look up at him. "Let's try this," he said, and he poked the tip of his shaft between her lips.

She took the down curve in her mouth, sliding all the way to Dum's root. And while she sucked and played with her tongue, the up curve's head rested against her cheek, as if waiting in turn. After several strokes, she moved to the other, working back and forth between the two. Then she took them both, their heads rubbing one another inside her mouth, their tastes mixing and mingling into an intoxicating cocktail.

Sweat slicked her skin and her breasts bounced and swayed and her nipples brushed against the men's legs. If her mammaries could talk, they would have asked to get in on the fun, but since that was ridiculous, even on this side of the looking glass, Alice had to see to their satisfaction herself.

She took one man's shaft between her mounds, licking as his head surfaced, then plunging him down to be encased in her flesh. The other moved around behind her, and she could feel her short skirt lifting, cool air quivering over her wetness, and an upward curve probed her slick opening.

Alice spread her thighs wide and reclaimed the down curve with her mouth, and Tweedle Dee sank into her, filling her just as she'd imagined while using her rabbit in front of the mirror.

"Oh, that feels so good," she said, then sucked Dum hard.

Tweedle Dee gripped her hips and started pumping, his balls slapping her sensitive nub with each plunge.

"Now this is fun!" Dee called. "Are you having fun, Alice?"

"Mmmph," came her best reply.

"Yes, this is fun," said Dum from above her. "Are you enjoying yourself, Alice?"

"Mmmph," she answered again.

But if they could understand her words, they would have heard her say, "Oh my heavens, yes!" Because with a cock in her mouth and a cock in her slot, Alice was having a WONDERFUL time. And all of her reservations about them being gay or being round and unattractive or being annoying as all hell seemed petty and silly and nothing but a distant memory.

When Tweedle Dee got tired, he sat down on the grass. Alice climbed upon his lap, and sank onto his stiff upturned pole. Then Tweedle Dum stood over Dee, his manhood thrusting into her mouth.

"Oh, what a view," rhapsodized Dee. "Dum looks so sexy thrusting into your sweet mouth. I can see his balls swing against your chin. Don't you think that's a lovely view, Alice?"

"Mmmph."

Tweedle Dum stared down at Dee. "Oh, what a view," he said, "I can see Dee driving up into you and making your tits buck like you're in a rodeo. Don't you think that's a lovely view, Alice?"

Alice pulled her head back and glanced up at Tweedle Dum. "Look, you want me to talk, or suck?"

"I'd vote for the sucking," helpful Tweedle Dee offered.

"Agreed," said Tweedle Dum. "Please get back to it, Alice."

"Gladly."

Alice took him as deep into her mouth as she could, all the way to where her tonsils would have been if they hadn't been removed when she was seven. Soon she found the perfect rhythm, sucking on Dum while bouncing on Dee, her breasts jostling freely and the pressure building inside her like a boiler about to explode.

And so she did, the feeling growing and growing until she couldn't ram down on Dee fast enough or suck Dum hard enough. And she shattered and screamed out, and wave after wave of orgasmic contractions hit her.

When the waves of ecstasy ebbed, she grabbed ahold of Tweedle Dum's love handles and sagged against his legs.

"You're not tired, are you, Alice?" he asked.

"You're not tired, are you, Alice?" echoed Dee.

And together they said, "Because we have a lot more fun in store for you."

So although Alice was tired, she couldn't deny they were still hard. Really hard. And if she'd learned anything in her time beyond the looking glass, it was that she had to do her best to pleasure others if they took the time to pleasure her.

"Bring it on, boys," she said with a smile.

And they did.

They tried all manner of combinations, those three in the field that day. Dum on Alice and Dee on Dum. Dum on Dee with Alice underneath. Alice sucking Dum and Dee sucking Alice.

And the best part? Alice was pretty sure none of it was approved by the Red Queen.

Finally Alice lay back in the grass almost too tired to move, and Dee and Dum were on either side of her, kneeling on the grass, their members still hard as could be and stretching full length over her when Dee announced, "I'm ready to come."

"I'm ready to come, too," agreed Dum. "And I have a grand idea. We just need you to do something for us, Alice."

Alice propped herself up on her elbows and eyed their everlasting erections. She'd lost count of her orgasms, but these two odd little men had given her so many that she felt limp as a dish rag. Still, she wanted this to be just as fabulous for them as it had been for her, even if she wasn't sure how she'd find the strength to see them through.

"What would you like me to do?"

"Just take off your blouse and lie back in the grass, Alice dear," said Dee.

That sounded like a grand idea, and Alice shrugged the open blouse off her arms and relaxed in the grass. "Now what?"

"Now raise your skirt to your waist and spread your thighs wide," said Dum.

Alice did as he asked.

Dee looked down at her exposed center and nodded approvingly, his upturned shaft following the bob of his head. "Now pull your arms tight to your sides and fluff up your tits."

"Fluff them up?" Alice repeated. "How do I fluff them up?"

"Kind of squeeze them together a little with your arms."

"Yeah," added Dum taking hold of Dee's hard member and stroking. "Make your nipples point right up at us."

"Yeah, like they're begging," Dee said, grabbing ahold of Dum.

Alice did as she was asked, her arms acting a bit like a pushup bra. Her mounds surged together, looking and feeling more voluptuous than she ever remembered. Her nipples were incredibly hard, but Dee and Dum pinched and teased them anyway, until they strained upward, as if (indeed!) begging to touch the men's vigorous poles.

"Now bring both hands between your legs and touch yourself," said Dee. "Make yourself come."

Alice hadn't been sure she could make herself come again, as tired as she was, but all this tit fluffing and nipple begging was making her feel hot and wet all over again. She slid her fingers on either side of her clit, then dipped two fingers into her special place, clit, special place, clit, special place, imagining it was both the Tweedles penetrating her at once.

Above her, the Tweedles pumped one another with their hands. Faster and faster their fists flew, one curving up and one curving down, until one and then the other began to thrust with his hips and moan.

And then Alice started moaning too, the quiver between her legs escalating as she watched the curved shafts and tight balls bob above her. And a wave of ecstasy crashed over her, seizing her muscles, and shuddering and quaking, and she didn't stop but pushed for another.

And then the Tweedles cried out, one after the other, and their essence streamed from their stiff rods and kissed her breasts, warm and glossy and smooth. And then they were rubbing their hardness over her, cock against nipple, slick skin against slick skin.

And another wave crested and crashed, and Alice added her cries to the mix.

And when they were done, Alice knew without a doubt what her nipples had been begging for, because it was exactly what they got.

"Well, thank you for a wonderful time, you sexy gentlemen," she said, still out of breath.

Tweedle Dee and Tweedle Dum each wiped off a breast, taking great care to flick and pinch and toy with her nipples while they were doing it. "You have lovely feminine parts, Alice," said Dee.

"Thank you," said Alice.

"Yes," said Dum. "All your parts are quite lovely."

Alice sat up, but the two kept wiping, their members thick and ready once again, only this time Dee's was turned down and Dum's was facing up.

Curious.

"Have you ever thought of showing off your lovely parts with a bit of sparkly jewelry?" Dee asked.

"Oh my, yes. That would be divine," concurred Dum.

Alice remembered Rose's sparkly nipple rings and the beautiful golden gleam brightening Daisy's clit.

"It would be beautiful, that is for certain, but I'm not sure I'm daring enough to try something like that."

Dee smiled. "You should at least talk to the White Queen, see what she says."

"The White Queen?"

"She's a queen. The one who wears white," Dum explained.

"I know who she is. I've met her before. But she doesn't wear any jewelry, if you don't count the tiara on her head."

The two looked at each other. "She doesn't wear much of anything at all."

"That's true," agreed Alice, thinking of the White Queen's bare breasts and special place. "Although it seems that on this side of the looking glass, very few people wear much at all. But what I don't understand is why I should talk to her about jewelry."

"Well, that's simple enough," said Tweedle Dee. "She does piercings at her store. Ye Olde Sex Shoppe."

"Where is that, exactly?" Alice asked, becoming curiouser and curiouser.

Tweedle Dum pointed with his member, now very much as stiff as before. "You just follow the path through the trees."

"There sure are lots of paths through the trees around here," Alice mused.

But neither Tweedle Dee nor Tweedle Dum was listening; they were too busy kissing and stroking each other again.

Alice had to wonder if they ever had a problem with chafing. But she didn't ask, because a discussion about it wouldn't be very sexy, and quite possibly rude.

Besides, much as she'd enjoyed the three way, she really hated talking to the annoying little bastards.

"Thank you so much," she called. "I believe I'll pay her a visit."

"Mmmph!" they both said, their mouths full of each other.

Alice set off on her way.

Chapter 5

Wool and Water

Alice followed the left fork in the path, and for once it was a nice, paved path with no sticks to trip over or tree branches to snag her hair or dirt that her heels sunk into. When Alice reached the end of it she found a sign nailed to a tree that read WRONG PATH, GO BACK. Alice wasn't sure how the sign knew where she was going, but there wasn't anything beyond the tree but a patch of stinging nettles, and since Alice had an aversion to stinging of any sort, she walked back to the fork and took the right path, which was filled with sticks to trip over and branches snagging her hair and dirt that tugged at her high heels. And stinging nettles.

When she finally reached Ye Olde Sex Shoppe, Alice was in a grumpy mood. Her mood went from grumpy to venomous when she saw a sign on the front door that read CLOSED FOR UNBIRTHDAY PARTY.

Alice didn't know what an unbirthday was, but guessed it was something stupid and annoying. For all the good sex she'd had in Looking Glass Land, it certainly had its fair share of stupid and annoying people and customs. Alice frowned, her brow furrowing, as she wondered where to go next, when the door suddenly swung open and the White Queen appeared. Breasts and special place still bare for all to see, she wore a white garter belt and fishnets, and a white boa. The feather kind, not the kind that eats small children.

"Alice! How are you, dear? Did you come for my unbirthday party?"

"I'm afraid I don't even know what an unbirthday is," Alice said.

"No worry," said the Queen. "As it is both stupid and annoying. But I did get some wool and water for unbirthday gifts, thereby explaining this chapter's odd title. So why are you here?"

"Actually, I was sent here by Tweedle Dee and Tweedle Dum—"

"Excellent lovers, but also stupid and annoying."

Alice agreed on both counts, but didn't want to appear rude. "They mentioned you do piercings."

The Queen smiled wide. "I do. In fact, when I opened my shop, I was going to call it *Houses of the Holey* and put a big lead zeppelin in the storefront."

"I don't get it," Alice said.

"It was the seventies. I did a lot of drugs. I also have a Ficus I named Robert."

"Excuse me?"

"Robert Plant."

"Isn't he that singer in the Rolling Stones?"

"You're making me feel old. Come in."

The Queen held open the door, and Alice walked inside. She'd never been in a sex shop before, and for some reason expected it to be dimly lit and dirty. Instead, the lighting was bright and uniform, with stock neatly arranged on racks. It could have been a local convenience store, but rather than snacks and sundries, the wares on these shelves were decidedly more... *personal*.

Alice stared at a display of movies, their covers depicting every type of coupling imaginable, and some that were almost beyond imagination.

"Organized according to kink," the White Queen said. "Orgies, three ways, gang-bangs, all the group stuff, is in this section. Next to it is oral, which is always popular. Then gay, both women on women and men on men. Anal is next to that."

"Apparently a lot of people like anal," Alice said, noticing the section was larger than any of the others."

"People often like to watch the stuff they can't get at home."

Alice picked up a film called *Butt Plug Babes 37*. "They make dildos for your butt?" she asked, looking at two naked women on the cover who appeared to be enjoying the activity.

"Of course. But they're shaped differently, so they don't fall out. Sort of like an American football, with a base on the end so it doesn't get lost. I think I've got the brand used in that video, if you'd like to see it."

Curiosity overcame Alice, and she nodded. The White Queen lead her past an aisle displaying various cuffs, restraints, hoods, whips, paddles, and chains, and to a whole wall of butt plugs. She selected a pink one, and held it out for Alice. It was roughly the size and shape of a lemon, with a flat base on one end.

"That's gigantic," Alice said.

"There are smaller models, for beginners. The anus is simply packed with sensitive nerve endings. Have you ever done any butt play?"

Alice blushed. "Nothing quite so large."

"You think this is large? We have a lot bigger. In dildos as well. Take a look at this one."

The White Queen walked an aisle over, and picked up a box that held a dildo thicker than Alice's arm.

"That's not a sex toy," Alice said. "That's a murder weapon."

"You'd be surprised how wide you can stretch when properly aroused."

Alice had been properly aroused countless times, but she didn't think she'd ever be aroused enough to accommodate that abomination.

"So you want a piercing?" the White Queen asked. "Where were you considering it?"

"Um... well... the usual places, I suppose."

"And those are?"

Alice fidgeted. Surely the White Queen knew. Why embarrass her by making her say it?

"Alice, if you're too embarrassed to say it, you probably shouldn't get it done."

Oh. That's why.

"Well, my nipples," Alice said softly. "And my... clitoris."

"Nipples! Excellent! A piercing will dramatically increase sensation. But clitoris? That's so rare I've never actually done one. Very risky. Very precise. And that's one part of the female anatomy that you don't want to hurt or damage."

Alice frowned. "But, in the garden, I saw Daisy."

The White Queen nodded. "Ah, yes. That's not a clit piercing. I do not recommend piercing the clitoris. Daisy has what is known as a *clitoral hood piercing*. She had a vertical bar inserted in the thin skin that covers her clit. It is the easiest, and quickest healing, of any genital piercing." The White Queen leaned in closer like a conspirator sharing a valuable secret. "And the sensations are out of this world."

"Really?" Alice asked. "I don't mean to be rude, but how can you know for sure, if you don't have one?"

"I have a clitoral hood piercing, a triangle piercing, a labia piercing, and a fourchette. But when my husband and I visit the Red Queen, I remove my jewelry, because she forbids it."

"She's not a very nice person," Alice said.

"No. She's a boring bitch."

"I thought you needed an open mind to become a queen," Alice said.

"That's one way. The other way is to do what she did."

"What's that?"

The White Queen lowered her voice. "Defeat the Jabbercocky."

"I've heard of that, in a confusing poem. I—"

"Please," the White Queen said, holding up her palm. Her eyes brimmed with tears. "I don't want to discuss the Jabbercocky, Alice. I had a terrible experience in the HDO, and don't wish to recall it."

"I'm sorry," Alice said. She was bursting with questions, but the White Queen seemed ready to sob.

"It truly is a terrible place. I hope you are never sent there." Then she brightened. "Now let's get you up in the chair and poke some holes in you."

Alice had never liked needles, and while she'd felt rather confident on the walk over—wrong path and stinging nettles notwithstanding—the thought of having needles stuck into her most sensitive parts was quickly becoming a badder and badder idea. But rather than object, she obediently followed the White Queen past racks of lubricants, adult magazines, and love dolls ranging from cheap inflatable bachelor party gifts to full-sized models that looked more real than many of the people Alice went to college with. The piercing room was through a doorway draped with hanging beads, and there was a comfortable-looking leather recliner in the corner, next to a hanging print of a Georgia O'Keefe painting of a flower that looked more like something else. Upon closer inspection, Alice noticed someone had altered it; the pistil in the overtly feminine flower had a silver bar pierced through the tip.

"Sit sit sit," the White Queen said. "We'll start with your breasts, I think."

Alice sat, legs stiff in front of her, every muscle tense. She didn't want to get jabbed, especially in such sensitive areas. "I think I'm changing my mind."

"Are you sure? I certainly wouldn't do anything without your consent, but I really do think you'll enjoy the jewelry. Everyone does."

Her mind racing for an excuse, Alice suddenly remembered that she couldn't possibly get a piercing. "I… I don't have any money," she said, for the first time in her life relieved to be broke.

"Nonsense," the Queen said. "There is no money in Looking Glass Land. We use the barter system here."

"But I have nothing to barter with," Alice said, close to whining.

"Of course you do, my lovely little dear. Haigha! Hatta!"

Alice thought the Queen had begun speaking gibberish, but a moment later two men popped into the room. The first was wearing flared jodhpurs and tall black boots and a tweed jacket over his hairy chest. A beret perched on his head and he held a megaphone in one hand and a riding crop in the other.

His companion carried a large camera, and although he wore sunglasses, the rest of his body was bare. His erection curved up toward the ceiling, more charming and generous than Tweedle Dee's… er, Dum's… er, whatever.

Of course, Alice recognized them from her journey to Wonderland.

"Hatter!" she exclaimed, grinning. "March Hare!"

"No, it is Hatta and Haigha. We went to Boston recently and forgot how to use the letter R," said Hatter… no, *Hatta*. And it couldn't have been true, because he pronounced *recently* and *forgot* correctly.

"Hare, um, I mean *Haigha*, what happened to your lovely rabbit suit?"

"Cleaners," he said. "It gets awfully soiled with bodily secretions, as you can imagine."

"He's a regular walking hot zone," said Hatta. "When the Lysol stops working, steam cleaning is required."

"Where is your friend, Maus?" Alice asked.

Hatta shrugged. "Sleeping, as usual."

"Can you gentlemen begin a two camera set up?" the Queen asked.

Hatta and Haigha nodded, going into a closet and dragging out various pieces of equipment. As they set up three point lighting around Alice, she asked, "What's happening?"

"We're going to make a movie," Haigha said.

"*Alice's Sexual Piercing Adventure*," Hatta said. "We're pornographers now."

"You see, Alice," said the Queen, "we shall make a movie of this event. That is what you offer in barter. I'll do the piercings, and you sign the model release."

Haigha thrust a piece of paper and a pencil at her.

"I'm not sure I want to be in a movie," Alice said. "Especially one that will involve me crying."

"There will be no crying, Alice." The Queen's eyes twinkled. "Trust me."

"But…" Alice's voice trailed off.

"You're afraid," the Queen said.

Alice nodded, ashamed.

"Everyone who sits in that chair is afraid, Alice. Bravery doesn't mean you have no fear. Bravery is simply getting control over your fear. Do you want me to help you be brave?"

"I don't see how you can," Alice said.

"I'll be right back."

The Queen left and Alice read over the release and signed it. Then she fidgeted, becoming more and more nervous as Hatta and Haigha set up lights and loaded their cameras.

"Have you made many movies?" Alice asked, more out of nervousness than genuine curiosity.

"But of course," said Hatta. "Did you see *Fluffy Mr. BunnyToes Goes Balls Deep in Ass*?"

"I also acted in that one," Haigha said proudly.

"You were Fluffy Mr. BunnyToes?" Alice asked.

"No," said Haigha, "I was Ass."

"That role had such depth," said Hatta.

"I'm afraid I missed it," Alice said.

"We also did an all male vampire movie," Hatta said. "*Jackula*."

"Jackula?" Alice said.

"It's not blood he sucks," said Haigha. "Hatta starred in that one. Remember your final scene?"

"It was certainly a mouthful."

"How about *The Jubjub Bird's Golden Shower Extravaganza*?" said Haigha. "Did you see that one?"

"I don't know what a Jubjub bird is," Alice said. "Or a golden shower."

"It's just as well," said Hatta. "They are both rather messy."

"How about *Dear Grandma Muffleton's All Stud Gang Bang*?" asked Haigha.

"She's eighty-five years old, and takes on an entire high school varsity football team," said Hatta. "And she got halfway through junior varsity before breaking a hip. What a talent."

"I found her charming," said Haigha. "We dated for a while afterward, but she eventually said I was too old for her."

"A shame," said Hatta. "I miss how her pelvis creaked when she made love. It was like sexy time with a bag of crisps."

"Hatta does enjoy his snacks," observed the White Queen, returning with an armful of colorful boxes and packages. She set them on the table next to Alice's chair.

"What are those?" Alice asked.

"As you know," the White Queen said, "the female orgasm is a marvel of human physiology. Pain tolerance goes up 100% while a woman is climaxing."

Alice eyed the boxes, saw they contained various items from the shelves.

"So we're going to use some toys," the Queen continued, "and pierce you when you're coming. You won't feel any pain. Can you disrobe, please?"

"I really won't feel a thing?" Alice asked.

"Oh, you'll feel quite a bit," said the Queen. "But it won't be pain."

Alice slowly removed her blouse and skirt, immediately aware that the cameras were capturing her nudity.

"I missed seeing you naked, Alice," said the Hatta scanning her body through his lens.

"Uh, thank you." She lowered herself into the chair.

"I also missed feeling you naked, Alice," said the Haigha, taking his curved manhood in his free hand as he angled for a shot of her breasts.

"Ah, thank you, Haigha."

Alice had to admit, she liked having Hatta and Haigha, and the Queen, staring at her body, and the cameras only added to her arousal. Imagining men and women she didn't know staring at her nakedness was naughtily titillating.

Then the Queen unwrapped the first package.

Alice stared. "What in the world is that contraption?"

The Queen smiled. "This is a Sqweel."

It looked like a large pizza cutter, without the long handle. Or a particularly large snail that had a wheel for a body. The outer shell part covered half the wheel, with buttons on it that could be pressed while being held. The wheel itself was covered with tiny, pink plastic paddles that looked like—

"Are those tiny tongues?" Alice asked.

"Indeed. The Sqweel is meant to stimulate oral sex."

The Queen put in some batteries and pressed a button. The center wheel with the tongues began to spin around rapidly, until they were a blur.

"You want me to put that between my legs?" Alice asked, growing a little worried.

"Hold out your hand."

Alice did, and the Queen squirted a dollop of strawberry scented water-based lubricant onto her palm. Then the Queen used the Sqweel to lap up the lube. Incredibly, it did feel as if Alice's hand was being rapidly licked by little tongues. It was undeniably erotic and a shiver worked over her bare skin and tightened her nipples.

"Magnificent," said Haigha, focusing his camera on her face and breasts.

"Spread your legs, Alice," the Queen said.

Alice did, cool air caressing her wetness.

"So sexy," Hatta said, dropping to a knee to get a better angle between her open thighs.

Alice had never been filmed before, especially without clothes. She wasn't sure what to do. "Should I look at Hatta's long lens, zooming in on my feminine parts, or should I watch the Queen move the Sqweel up to my nether region?"

"Whatever you do, it will be hot," said Haigha. "Just show us how good it feels."

Then the Queen's Sqweel was touching her, and Alice said, "Oh my."

"It isn't as hard or intense as a vibrator," the Queen said. "But once you warm up to it, the sensations are quite marvelous."

The tongues zoomed right in on her clitoris as if they were hungry for it, and Alice warmed up to the device quickly. It didn't feel like many little tongues licking her, but more like one endlessly long tongue, stroking upward with gentle, almost delicate motions that went on and on and on. Then the sensation changed entirely, making Alice clench her fists; the Queen had turned the Sqweel upside down.

"Well," Alice said, her breath beginning to quicken. "That is quite... that's... well."

"Lick your lips, Alice. Don't be shy about it."

Alice did, and it felt delightfully wicked.

"Pinch your nipples."

Alice pinched, surprised by how stiff they already were. "Moan a little."

She moaned. But everything was feeling so good, Alice couldn't tell if her moan was for the camera, or entirely natural.

"Good. Very sexy. Now thrust your hips."

Alice did, and soon her hips were moving on their own accord. She continued to pinch and moan, and now Hatta's pants were off and he was stroking himself with his non-camera hand.

"Take the Sqweel," the Queen said. "Use it as you see fit."

Alice hesitated. "I've… I've never really used toys with another woman before."

"Never had vibrator parties with your girlfriends, where you practiced French kissing and deep throating cucumbers?"

Alice shook her head.

"You missed out," the Queen said. "But we're catching up now. This switch controls the speed. Just move it in whatever direction you fancy."

Alice took the Sqweel and followed the Queen's instructions. She tried sideways. She tried sideways in the opposite direction. She varied the pressure. She switched it to its top speed, and felt the familiar pressure building in her loins. Requiring no further direction, she gyrated and panted and cooed and pinched her nipples harder than she ever had before.

"Amazing," Haigha said. "You are so sexy when you're aroused, Alice."

"Imagine all the men who will be watching this," Hatta added. "They'll all be stroking themselves, wishing they could be licking you in place of the Sqweel."

Yes, she could feel their eyes. She could feel their tongues.

How many people will watch this movie and get off? Alice thought. She moved the Sqweel as Hatta zoomed in close enough to lick her himself.

"Arch your back, Alice. Stick out those incredible breasts."

"You're so beautiful. Come for the camera, Alice."

Haigha got so close to Alice that his lens was almost touching her cheek. Alice tried to imagine what she looked like, to picture who would be watching this movie later, and that added to her mounting pleasure. Then the Queen was at Alice's breasts, and Alice panicked for a moment, thinking it was the needle.

But it wasn't. The Queen held two small, purple objects.

"Nipple clamps," she said. "The weights have vibrators in them."

First the Queen attached one to the right nipple, then to the left. The pressure was just on the cusp of being painful, but instead it made her very aware of her nipples, and even more aware of the camera. Then the Queen squeezed the clamps and the vibrators roared to life, sending an electric burst of stimulation coursing through Alice's body.

"Oh my. Oh my, oh my, OH!"

Sqweel lapping between her legs, nipples buzzing, Hatta and Haigha caressing her body with their cameras like voyeuristic lovers, Alice could no longer hold it in.

The orgasm crashed through Alice before she was prepared for it, her lower body lifting up off the chair, her hips bucking against the Sqweel and its relentless, delicious tongue-lashing. A moment later, Alice was penetrated by something long and thick, and it pumped in and out of her with the Queen holding its base. Alice rode out the orgasm, then reluctantly pulled away the Sqweel to see what was being done to her.

The Queen was plunging a flesh-colored dildo into her, over and over, and it felt very good indeed. But Alice was confused, because it seemed to be attached to something that looked like a large ray gun.

"It's a Drilldo," the Queen said. "Watch."

The Queen held the device inside Alice, and then there was a loud *WHIR* followed by them most curious sensation.

The dildo was spinning!

Indeed, the Drilldo was a common dildo attached by some means to a cordless drill. It rotated within her, like Alice was being drilled, but with a much more nerve-tingling result. If Alice had thought her orgasm was peaking, the Drilldo had other ideas. Starting slow, no more than a full turn per second, Alice felt the dildo's fat head churn against her G-spot, teasing it over and over. It was unlike anything she had ever experienced, and though her juices were flowing aplenty, the Queen had apparently slicked it down with more lube because the action was delightfully smooth.

Then it began to pick up speed.

Alice reached her hands out, fingers spread, her eyelids fluttering. She had always wondered what it would feel like to spin upon a man's stiff member, and the sensation didn't disappoint. Just as she began to hit another crescendo, her nub began to buzz once again. But this was more intense than a vibration.

"An Eroscillator," the Queen said over the noise. She was holding something that looked like a gold electric toothbrush against Alice's clit. "The tip oscillates 3600 times a second. How does it feel?"

Alice answered with an "Uhh." She noticed Hatta between her legs, working the Drilldo, to which he'd attached his camera. What a curious angle; one Alice wished to view.

As if reading Alice's mind, the widescreen TV on the opposite wall turned on, with a live feed of the proceedings. Half the screen was Haigha, panning between Alice's vibrating nipples and her ecstatic expressions, the other half was a super-close view of Alice's special place, the Drilldo and Eroscillator doing their work.

This was a much bigger turn-on than the looking glass in her apartment, and Alice's squeals reverberated back at her in stereo sound.

"Come again Alice," said Haigha, his camera in her face. And another image crossed the screen; his lovely erection, right next to her breasts, twitching and jerking and begging to be touched. She reached for it, grabbing his glans, and the feeling of his stiffness in her hand overloaded her senses.

Between the whirling Drilldo and the intense Eroscillator and the vibrating nipple clamps and the images on the TV and Hatta between her legs with a camera and Haigha's hard curve in her hand, Alice lost complete control. She screamed. She shook. She thrashed. Her body had become a slave to orgasm, and Alice felt as if she were melting and floating at the same time.

When the White Queen removed the nipple clamps and replaced them with surgical clamps from her nearby autoclave, Alice watched with curious detachment. The first needle pierced her right nipple with a little more than a sting, and not an unpleasant one at that. When the second needle entered her, Alice cried out again, not in pain, but in pleasure, and she watched a close up on the TV as the Queen inserted a gold ring.

The Eroscillator was removed, but the Drilldo was still doing its thing, and Alice pulled Haigha closer, aching to have him in her mouth. Her tongue shot out, licking a drop of moisture leaking from his tip, and from the corner of her eye she saw the Queen's gloved hands holding a cotton swab between her legs, easing it between the top of her clit and the thin skin that covered it.

"Perfect," the Queen said. "You're a perfect candidate. "

"I'll say," said Hatta.

"Just a quick sting, dear."

Alice watched, transfixed, as the Drilldo churned inside her and the White Queen used a sealed needle to put a tiny, golden barbell through her clitoral hood. There was only the quickest of pinches, and then the Drilldo was out and all three spectators were standing away from Alice, gazing at her admiringly and touching themselves vigorously.

"My, that was erotic," said Hatta.

"I'd film you anytime," said Haigha.

"You did a great job, my dear," said the White Queen.

"That was it?" Alice said, still panting. "It doesn't hurt at all."

The Queen nodded. "Normally, a hood piercing takes about a week to heal, and a nipple piercing about two months. But in Looking Glass Land, all healing is instantaneous."

"That's amazing," Alice said.

"We also have the best bouillabaisse here," said Hatta, smiling. "That might not be as dramatic as instant healing, but try to find a bowl worth eating anywhere outside of Marseilles."

"Also," said Haigha, "In Looking Glass Land, *Seinfeld* was never cancelled. Season twenty-three was hilarious. Kramer becomes President."

"That Kramer," Hatta said, slapping his thigh.

Alice swung her feet over the side of the chair, lightheaded and still tingling all over.

"I must say, that was much better than I'd anticipated." She stared down, looking at the lovely rings in her breasts.

"Give them a pull," the White Queen said, proudly.

Alice gave each a tentative tug, and it felt like a lover nibbling on them, multiplied threefold.

"Goodness," she said. "That is a lovely sensation."

"Now stand up and take a few steps."

Alice did, and the bar in her hood rubbed gently against her clitoris, making her shiver.

"Why, I can't wear this!" Alice protested. "I'll never be able to get anything done! How am I supposed to live my day-to-day life if I have an orgasm ever few steps I take?"

"I'd call that living very well," said Hatta.

"It would sure make jogging more fun," said Haigha.

"I'd like to film Alice jogging," said Hatta. "Naked."

"Alice naked?" asked Haigha.

"Both of us naked," said Hatta. "You, too."

"That would be hot," agreed Haigha.

The White Queen patted Alice's shoulder. "You're still aroused, dear. When that wears off, you won't even feel the piercings, unless they are directly stimulated."

"Oh." So she could have the sensation just when she wanted? This was getting better and better. "How did the movie turn out?" Alice asked.

"Spectacular," said Hatta.

"Arousing," said Haigha.

"Beautiful," said Hatta.

"Exciting," said Haigha.

"It will make you a superstar, Alice. You are easily the sexiest woman who has ever starred in an adult film."

Beaming with pride, Alice dressed quickly, and as her arousal level dipped, so did the stimulation her piercings provided.

"I can't thank all of you enough," Alice said.

"Why not?" asked Hatta. "Have you run out of thank yous?"

Back to the nonsense, Alice thought. She so preferred the constant climaxes to the silly wordplay.

"Where are you off to next, Alice?" the Queen asked.

"Well, I'm still trying to open my mind," Alice said. "Where do you recommend I go?"

"This is Looking Glass Land, Alice. Just follow a path through the woods. It will take you somewhere interesting."

"Just avoid the ones that dead end at stinging nettles," said Hatta.

"But how do I know which ones dead end at stinging nettles?"

"I just told you. Those are the ones that have stinging nettles at the dead end."

Alice kept her tongue firmly in cheek, bid goodbye to the trio, and went off in search of more mind-opening experiences.

Chapter 6

Humpty Dumpty

Still buzzing from the experience at the toy shop (and feeling her new piercings rub against her most sensitive parts with each step), Alice followed yet another path through a clearing and came to thirty yards of board fence, nine feet high, that a boy named Tom Sawyer was whitewashing—

Wait... oops. Wrong nineteenth century classic.

Still buzzing from the experience at the toy shop, Alice followed yet another path through a clearing and came to a high wall, which Humpty Dumpty sat upon.

Alice knew it was Humpty Dumpty because she was familiar with the nursery rhyme, and because this man was egg-shaped and perched precariously on a wall, but most of all because he waved at Alice and said, "Yo, baby. I'm Humpty Dumpty."

As Alice approached, she noticed something odd. Well, odder than an egg man from a nursery rhyme sitting on a wall. This particular egg man, although sporting a light beard and a deep, baritone voice, was wearing women's undergarments. Chiefly a bra, panties, and nylon stockings, which made his stubby legs look like sausages ready to burst from their casings.

"Why, you're dressed like a woman!" Alice declared.

"So are you."

"But I *am* a woman. My name is Alice. You're a man."

"What gave it away?" Humpty Dumpty asked. "Was it my masculine bulge, threatening to burst through this Frederick's of Hollywood g-string?"

"It *is* rather obvious."

"Don't you think I'm sexy?" he asked, gyrating suggestively and pursing his lips which, shockingly, were painted bright red.

Alice couldn't imagine anything less sexy, but she'd already been down that road with the Tweedles and had learned her lesson, so she changed the subject.

"Aren't you worried you'll fall from there?" Alice asked.

"Why?"

"Because of the poem, of course." Much as she loathed poetry, Alice began to recite. "Humpty Dumpty sat on a wall, Humpty Dumpty had a big fall—"

"No, you're getting it wrong. It's Humpty Dumpty sat on a wall, Humpty Dumpty had a big *ball*. Which I do. Two of them in fact. My testicles are bigger than peaches. I'm sure you can see them from there."

Alice could. And they were, indeed, bigger than peaches.

"They're also full of peach juice," Humpty Dumpty said, his voice tinged with pride.

"They aren't."

"They are. If you'd like, you can have a sip from my straw." Humpty grabbed himself through the panties.

Alice was confused. Not about the peach juice—she knew that was nonsense. But that this man in ladies' underwear was apparently coming on to her. "You want me to... to put your member in my mouth?"

"I can think of worse ways to spend the next thirty seconds."

"Do you," Alice searched her mind to remember the term, "*swing* both ways?"

"Naw. I mean, I have no problem with those who do, but I'm strictly a ladies' man myself."

Alice was perplexed.

"You look perplexed," Humpty said.

"You're wearing feminine underthings," Alice stated. "Aren't you gay?"

"Don't you know the rest of the rhyme?" Humpty cleared his throat, spat, then began to recite:

Humpty Dumpty sat on a wall,
Humpty Dumpty had a big ball,
All the King's wenches and all the King's chicks,
Lent him their panties and then sucked his dick.

"If you like women," Alice said, "why do you dress like one?"

Humpty shrugged. "It gets me off."

"Why?"

"Can't really explain why. Are you gonna come up here and start sucking, or what?"

"But it doesn't make any sense."

Humpty laughed. "If you really expect human sexuality to make sense, you're more naive than you look, Alice."

Alice didn't like being called naive. In fact, she was working hard to be more knowledgeable.

"So you're a," Alice searched for the term. "Transsexual?"

"No. I'm a man trapped inside the body of a man. Got a buddy named Earl, she's a transsexual. Sweetest broad you'd ever meet. And plus size, like me. She just let me borrow this gorgeous Christian Dior pencil skirt, and I'm thinking about moving away and not leaving a forwarding address so I don't have to give it back. I wish I had his taste. And his hips."

Alice still didn't understand. "Do you have both male and female private parts?"

"No. Just male. And they aren't very private. I can whip them out and show you, if you want."

How rude. He really was a bad egg. And Alice was still confused.

"You seem still confused," Humpty said.

"I am." Alice pouted. "My boyfriend—*ex*-boyfriend—I caught him in the bathroom, wearing my panties."

"What color were they?"

"Pink."

Humpty laughed, and rubbed his bulge. "Pink is my favorite, next to black and red and yellow and green and blue. Did they have frilly lace on the top?"

"A bit."

"They sound lovely. Your ex-boyfriend has good taste."

"I... I thought he was gay."

"Could be. Or he could just be a cross-dresser."

Alice had heard the word before, but didn't know quite what it meant. "A what?"

"A transvestite. A heterosexual man who likes to wear women's clothing. It's a fetish. Deriving sexual excitement from an object. In this case, female clothing."

"Men who aren't gay do that?"

"Climb up on this wall, baby, and I'll show you how hetero I am."

Alice noted that the lump in Humpty's panties had gotten larger as he stroked himself.

"I'm afraid I still don't understand," Alice said.

"When you put on a nice dress, and high heels, and make-up, and jewelry, does it make you feel sexy?"

"Yes," Alice said.

"Me too."

"And you aren't gay at all?"

"No. But I'm willing to pretend I'm gay if you come up here and give me a hummer. In fact, I'll pretend to be whatever you want. An alien. A dinosaur. Red Foxx. A Denver omelet. You name it."

Alice buried her face in her hands. She was beside herself with guilt. All this time, she'd been sure her boyfriend Lewis was gay. But he'd been telling the truth when he said he loved her and found her attractive. He just liked wearing her clothing.

"Oh dear," Alice said, ready to cry. "I made a huge mistake."

Humpty patted the wall. "Poor thing. Come up here, girl. You can tell me all about it while you're blowing me."

The tears came. "Can't you see I'm upset?"

"You know what can stop those tears? Giving me vigorous head."

"Can you please stop thinking about oral sex for just five minutes?"

Humpty laughed. "Ha! Show me a man who can do that!"

Alice really began to cry now. "Lewis loved me. I thought we'd be married some day. But I dumped him for no reason."

"Wow. You're such a bitch."

Alice fell to her knees, her whole body racked with sobs. She had ruined Lewis's life, and hers, all because she'd let her biases and prejudices override her feelings and common sense.

"Why don't you just apologize and win him back?" Humpty asked.

Alice sniffled, staring up at him. "Could I really do that?"

"Why not? Don't you have an open mind now?"

"I think so."

"You'd better. Or else I'm going to write KEEP AN OPEN MIND on a club and beat you over the head with it, like we've been doing to the readers."

"I've got to go back home and talk to Lewis," Alice said. "Which way do I go?"

"Where is home?"

"On the other side of the looking glass."

"I don't have the slightest idea what that means. But you could follow this path to Lion and Unicorn Park. There's an orgy going on there right now. Lots of people. Maybe one of them will be able to help you. But be careful."

Alice wiped away a tear and smiled shyly. "I think I'll be okay. I've been to an orgy or two."

"It's not that. I heard the Red Queen is planning to raid the park. You don't want to be arrested and have to face the Jabbercocky."

The word rang a bell, and Alice recalled that horrible poem she'd read earlier and the word being repeated by the White Queen.

"What's a Jabbercocky?" she asked.

"It's a sex machine, in the Hall of Denied Orgasms. Meant to cause unbearable arousal in women."

Alice frowned. "The White Queen didn't want to talk about it. She said the Red Queen beat the Jabbercocky, and that is why she's allowed to rule Looking Glass Land."

Humpty spat. "The Red Queen. She's an unfeeling bitch. Do you know how she beat the Jabbercock? She fell asleep. Can you imagine? I weep for her poor husband."

Alice thought about the Red King and how eager he was, and how hard, and how long. "But the Red Queen and the Red King have swinging parties with other couples. He seems to have a lot of sex."

"Yes, on this side of the looking glass, everybody has sex with everybody. But the Red Queen believes all sex should be boring, and she'll only allow the Red King to come during boring sex. Even the Jabbercock couldn't turn on the Red Queen."

"I read a poem about it. In a book."

"Turning on the Red Queen?"

Alice sighed and rolled her eyes. "No. The Jabbercocky."

"Did you like it?"

"No. I thought the author was full of himself."

Humpty laughed, then began to recite:

Carroll's lyrical endeavor,
Thinking made-up words were clever,
Read a hundred-plus years later,
Only prompts my inner hater.

"You can say that again," Alice said. "But please don't. I hate poetry. Though I do wonder what that Jabbercock poem meant."

"You want I should explicate it for you?" Humpty asked. "Could have some relevance."

Alice sighed. "I suppose. Will it take long? I do have an orgy to get to." And she had to admit, that even after the very many lovely experiences she'd had today, the thought of an orgy made her start to tingle all over again.

"I'll make it quick. Which, incidentally, is the line I use picking up women. Let's go through it, stanza by stanza."

Alice winced, but nodded. Humpty began.

'Twas horcky in the HDO,
Beased so long they mersycried,
Empty was the bordello,
Tolerance hsad up and died.

"Horcky means horny and unlucky," Humpty said. "Beased is bound and teased. Mersycried is those who cry for mercy. A bordello is—"

"I know what a bordello is," Alice said.

"Slut," Humpty said, then continued.

Beware the Jabbercock, my girl!
The pole that jabs the secret patch!
Torment shall make her toesies curl,
She was so shunned, they bandersnatch.

"So far, the poem is about being taken to the Hall of Denied Orgasms and being mercilessly teased by the Jappercocky," Humpty explained.

"What's a bandersnatch?"

"A woman was shunned and exiled from the kingdom. Get it?"

"No."

"They banned her snatch."

Bandersnatch. Alice rolled her eyes. The only thing worse than poetry was poetry with bad puns.

"Shall I continue?" Humpty asked.

"I really wish you wouldn't, but I guess you should."

Humpty cleared his throat, spat, and went on.

A soul condemned to face the beast,
By missionench, so crimson mean,
But pleasure fiftyfold increased,
Made her then the Golden Queen.

"A missionench is a wench who only allows the missionary position," Humpty said.

Alice nodded. "Crimson mean. That's the Red Queen?"

"That's her."

"So who is the Golden Queen?"

Humpty rolled his eyes. "I have no idea, blondie. I wonder who it could be? Insert sarcastic emoticon here."

"Excuse me?"

"I'll continue."

The Jabbercock shall masturbate,
Poor Golden Queen with fiendish chode,
But she shall rise and liberate,
And jabbing pole shall overload!

"So the Golden Queen takes on the Jabbercocky," Alice said. "What's a chode?"

"It's a penis that is wider in girth than it is long."

Alice laughed. "You're kidding! Such a thing doesn't exist."

Humpty pulled down his panties, exposing a very short, but extremely thick member. It looked like the top of a fire hydrant. It was even bright red like one.

"Oh, wait," Humpty said. "That's my toy fire hydrant. Hold on."

He tossed that aside, exposing a very short, but extremely thick member. It looked like a penis, only shorter and wider.

"And you wanted me to put that in my mouth?" Alice said, shocked. "I don't know if I could even fit my lips around it."

"But think of the fun you'd have trying."

Alice did think about it, and her thoughts made her aware of her piercings. She shifted uncomfortably from one leg to another, but that only made the feeling worse.

One, two! One, two! And through and through
Until the machilit the smoke,
The souls condemned, they came and flew,
While Golden Queen BJ'ed her bloke.

"So she beats the Jabbercock," Alice said. "I'm guessing machilit is a portmanteau of machine and lit. Maybe it lights on fire and starts to smoke?"

"Good guess. And then she gave her boyfriend a blowjob. Want to practice on me?"

Humpty grabbed himself, and he was so thick his fingers couldn't fit around it.

"Maybe later," Alice said. "Finish the poem, if you please."

Freedom rang in Kingdom high!
Snowballing and hot bukkake!
Gokkun, felching, and creampie!
Queen shall wed the panty jockey!

"So everyone went free, and debauchery returned to the kingdom." Humpty said. "Are you familiar with all of those words?"

"I'm not sure."

"Snowballing is passing a man's essence from mouth to mouth by kissing. Creampie is when a man's essence leaks out of a body part. Felching is sucking a man's essence out of the body orifice where it was deposited."

"But I named my cats Snowball, Felcher, and Creampie!" Alice said, shocked by the definitions.

"Slut," Humpty admonished. "And, of course, bukkake and gokkun are Japanese terms."

"What do those mean?"

"Do I look like Google?" Humpty asked, tugging on his chode.

"No, but—watch out!"

While pleasuring himself, Humpty had lost balance, and he plummeted off the wall and fell right at Alice's feet.

"Oh, my!" Alice knelt beside him. "Are you okay?"

"I'm fine," he said, sitting up.

"You are?"

"Of course I am. It was just a small fall. What, did you expect me to break into a million pieces?"

"Well, I—"

"I'm a man, not a 95% chemical compound of calcium carbonate crystals stabilized by a protein matrix."

"Huh?"

"I'm not an egg. I just have a gland problem, exacerbated by an eating disorder."

"But, the Humpty Dumpty poem…"

"Does the poem ever say that I'm an egg?"

Alice ran through it in her head. "No, I guess not."

"Do eggs get hard-ons?" he said, gripping himself.

"Not that I've heard of."

"Then drop it with the egg nonsense. Now help me up, and I'll accompany you to the orgy at Lion and Unicorn Park. I was planning on warning them about the raid anyway."

Alice helped Humpty up, and in doing so got a closer look at his member. It couldn't have been more than four inches long, but it was indeed equally as wide.

"Impressive, ain't it?" Humpty said, shaking his hips.

"Yes," she said, shyly.

"You're thinking about what it would feel like inside you."

Alice blushed, but nodded.

"The raid isn't scheduled for another hour, so we got some time. Go ahead and use me."

Alice considered it. The idea was kind of crazy, Humpty Dumpty wasn't appealing at all, but she really *did* want to know what that fat monster felt like, and it had been more than 2500 words since the last sex scene.

"Okay," Alice said. "But go slow and easy."

"Low and sleazy, that's me. Now lemme see those titties."

Alice paused a moment, then shrugged and pulled her blouse up over her head without even unbuttoning it, her breasts bobbing free. Humpty grabbed them in his fat fingers, rubbing his thumbs over her nipples until they stood at attention, the golden rings swinging proudly.

"You're very beautiful, Alice."

Alice didn't return the compliment, because Humpty looked a lot like a fat, pink toad, if fat pink toads dressed in women's underwear. But he was doing a pretty good job with her nipples. And his prick was magnificent.

She reached down and couldn't even fit her hand completely around it. The head was oval and—go figure—egg-shaped. Alice tugged on the foreskin, surprised by how hard Humpty was.

"How do you find pants to fit?" she asked, genuinely interested.

"I only wear panties, remember? Can you help me with my bra?"

Alice felt for him, for often she had a hard time with the clasp as well. "I know a trick. Pull it around backwards, so you can undo it in front."

He followed instructions, and easily unhooked the undergarment, letting it drop to the ground. Then he kicked off his very large strappy sandals—honestly they had to be a size 15 triple wide, and he was Alice's height exactly. And although his face wasn't anything to look at either, his eyes were bright and twinkled with mischief, which Alice found quite erotic.

He skimmed one of his hands down her belly and entered her with a finger, making Alice squeak with surprise. His finger was larger than some men she'd known before Lewis, not that she'd known many, of course.

"You're so wet," he cooed. "That's hot."

Humpty moved his finger in and out so rapidly, it made Alice's knees weak. Seeming to sense this, Humpty grabbed her bottom with his other hand, both holding her up and pressing her closer to his clever jabbing. Alice stood there, pinned by his enormous hands, as he worked her slot with more speed than she'd ever known.

"Oh my oh my oh my OH MY!" Alice cried out, squirming against him, her new piercing intensifying the wonderful sensation.

"Do you like this?" Humpty asked, breathing hot on her neck.

"Ugn... ugn... yes..."

"I can go slower, if you want."

Cupping her butt cheek firmly, he slowly withdrew his chubby finger, wiggling it as he did. Then he teased her lips and ran his moist fingertip along her most sensitive part, making Alice's whole body clench. She squeezed her eyes shut, concentrating on the sensations. Ever so slowly, Humpty inserted the finger again, all the way to the last knuckle, moving it back and forth like a scolding parent. Alice ground her hips into his hands, grunting, then crying out when Humpty's thumb stroked her clitoris, tingling her barbell.

Alice began to come, and as she did Humpty used his other hand—the one squeezing her rear—to insert a finger into her other opening. It was only the tip, but it stretched Alice wide and made everything happening in front even more intense. Alice clutched his shoulders, digging her nails in, and screamed as she climaxed, shuddering and clenching as Humpty worked his fingers back and forth, back and forth, using her body as his own personal Chinese finger cuffs while she rode the wave.

When Alice's senses returned, she opened her eyes and stared at Humpty, who was grinning with apparent satisfaction.

"Want to see if you can get your mouth around it?" Humpty asked, the corners of his eyes crinkling.

Alice swallowed, and nodded, because right now she wanted that more than almost anything.

Humpty released her and Alice sank to her knees, staring into the eye of his monster. With one hand she weighed his gigantic balls, which were not only big as peaches, but heavy as the fruit, too. Alice's other hand grasped him at the root, pulling back his skin. She gave the head a slow, tentative lick, and seriously doubted she could fit something that wide into her mouth, let alone anywhere else in her body.

"Oh, yeah," Humpty said. "Get it nice and slick."

Alice continued to lick, alternating with full-lipped kisses. She sucked on the side as if giving a hickey, and Humpty moaned. Then, sticking out her tongue so it covered her lower teeth, Alice opened her mouth as wide as she could, and tried to force the massive head into her mouth.

It went in, just barely, and filled Alice so that her cheeks bulged out. She began to move her head back and forth, but couldn't do any real sucking because it was simply too big. From the sounds Humpty made, he seemed to be enjoying it. But in truth, Alice wasn't. Her jaw was stretched too far, and the whole process was uncomfortable. She kept going, however, partly because of the wonderful orgasm Humpty had just given her, and partly because she hoped he would climax, because Alice didn't think she'd be able to fit this massive member in her secret garden.

Humpty seemed to sense her discomfort, and he pulled free and then caressed her sore cheeks.

"Congrats," he said. "Not many women can do that. You have a big mouth."

"Thanks, I guess."

"Want to try sex?"

Alice chewed her lower lip. "I don't know. I'm not sure I can handle you."

"Won't know until you try," Humpty said, winking. Then he was lying on his back, hands clasped behind his head, fat toes wiggling.

Alice's early comparison to a fire hydrant was appropriate. She stared at his manhood in awe, sure there was no way she could ride something that wide.

"I thought your tits were beautiful before. You should see them from underneath." He said the words softly, reverently, and yet Alice felt them in her core. "Play with your nipples a little, will you?"

Alice did, and her nipples tingled and peeked in front of Humpty's appreciative eyes.

"I wish I could film a porno of you right now. Every guy on earth couldn't help stroking his pole to the sight of those luscious tits."

The appreciation in Humpty's voice made her wish Hatta and Haigha were here right now recording her newest adventure. Humpty's comments and the enthralled look on his face were making her feel like gold.

Hot gold.

"Do you like hearing me talk dirty, Alice?"

"What do you mean?"

"Do you like me saying crude and naughty words? Like when I talk about your tits?"

Alice thought she probably shouldn't, but she had to admit she kind of did. "It's exciting. A little forbidden, I guess."

"How about pussy? Would you think it was hot if I said that word?"

She felt a little thrill down below. "Yes, I guess it would be hot."

"Okay, let's try this: Will you show me your pussy, Alice? Will you stand over me and give me a peek?"

Alice *knew* she shouldn't do that. But again, it was exciting. Thrilling, even. So she stood over Humpty, a leg on either side of his head, her thighs spread wide.

He reached for his member and started fondling. "You are so sexy, Alice. So wet. Do you like me staring at your spread pussy?"

She swallowed into a dry throat. "Yes, I do."

"Can you touch yourself while I watch?"

She did, and sensation zinged along every nerve.

"How wet are you, Alice?" Humpty asked.

"Wet."

"Really wet? Check and see."

She slid her fingers over herself, then deep inside, feeling the orgasm building again. "Yes."

"Dripping? Because I think I can see you dripping for me, Alice."

"Yes, I'm dripping."

"For me? Staring up here at your pussy and your jutting nipples? Are you dripping for me, Alice?"

He was crude and rude and her legs felt weak. "Yes, for you."

"For which part of me, Alice?"

"For you, Humpty."

"For which part? Say it, Alice. And say it dirty."

"I don't know if I can."

"I think you can, Alice. I think an amazing, sexy woman like you can do anything. Now what are you dripping for, Alice?"

"For your huge cock, Humpty. I'm dripping for your cock."

"My huge cock wants to be inside you, Alice. Inside your dripping wet garden. The beautiful garden I'm staring at right now. Do you want that, Alice?"

"Yes, Humpty."

"Do you want it bad?"

She did. She was so wet. She was so ready. "I want it bad, Humpty."

"Then lower your smoking hot self over me, Alice. Let me fill you. Let me impale you."

Alice moved lower, positioning herself over his manhood, and began to slowly drop down. When the tip bumped against her, Alice's first reaction was to do as Humpty suggested and impale herself upon it. But she feared if she went too quickly, she'd split in half. So instead, she rubbed herself over him, her opening and her clit, moving, moistening, teasing herself into a frenzy.

She really was dripping for him, and it didn't take long to coat him with her juices. Then she moved her opening just above the soft apex of his glans, and gently eased onto his fat, rigid head, and then all the way in, to the hilt.

Her body filled. Her skin stretched. The rim of her opening felt hot, almost burning.

"You feel so good, Alice. I knew you would feel this good."

She gasped in a sharp breath, then another.

"I love how your breasts bounce when you do that. Do it again, Alice." And his fat fingers found her nipples, teasing and flicking.

And Alice found herself moving, slowly, carefully, but moving all the same. He was so big, her muscles could do nothing but clench, and as her body gripped him, and she slowly thrust herself on him, in and out, in and out, the heat kindled into fire and the fire started to consume her.

She'd had a lot of orgasms that day. So many, she'd totally lost count. But between the thrusting and the stretching and the gripping and the friction, Alice totally lost control.

Her screams echoed over all the paths through all the trees in Looking Glass Land, and she suspected that the spasm of her muscles and the fire in her loins would never stop. Then finally Humpty gave out a shout of his own and his hips bucked several times.

"Damn," he said. "That was epic."

Alice felt him grow soft inside her, and with some effort she slid free.

"Oh my heavens, Humpty. That was something else."

"Wasn't it, though?" Said Humpty, and then the most peculiar thing happened.

Humpty hugged her.

And it wasn't a lecherous hug, and it wasn't crude or dirty or mean. It was sweet and warm and made Alice feel nice inside.

"Now let's go to the orgy and get us some tail!" he said, and they didn't bother dressing (except for Alice slipping on her blue pumps) but simply hurried through yet another path in the woods, this one warm and humid like a warm and humid tunnel or cave or something totally unerotic like that.

Chapter 7

The Lion and the Unicorn

After all the sex she'd had in the past eighty-odd pages, Alice was feeling quite sated, and the closer she and Humpty came to Lion and Unicorn Park, and the more annoying sticks and mud and nettles they had to wade through, the less Alice felt she needed more sex.

"So tell me something, Humpty."

"Something, Alice."

"No, I mean answer a question."

"Okay then. My answer is yes."

"I haven't asked the question yet."

"Maybe not, but that's my standard response to any question directed to me from a hot woman. Especially one who is completely naked, such as yourself."

Alice supposed that was fair, having read a bit on the subject of testosterone and the male sex drive, so instead of commenting, she just went ahead and asked her question. "Do I have to have sex with everyone I meet in Looking Glass Land?"

"Are you talking about everyone *you* meet? Or everyone *your genitals* meet? Because by then, Alice, you're already having sex."

Alice shook her head. She'd come to like Humpty, but she realized that like Tweedle Dee and Tweedle Dum, she liked sex with him much better than conversation. But since he was walking with her now, and she wanted to know the answer to her question before she arrived at the orgy, she decided not to get too annoyed. "Do I have to have sex with everyone I see, whether I want to or not?"

"Didn't you want to have sex with me, Alice?" The poor egg-shaped man looked a bit bereft.

Alice had to be honest, because honesty is a heroic trait and she is the heroine of this story. "Not at first, no. But then you kind of grew on me."

"I grew really hard and thick, and you wanted to try out the chode."

She glanced down at his outrageously wide member, which was back to being rigid and bouncing with each of his fat-legged strides. "Actually, yes."

"Did it stretch your mind, Alice?"

"I think so, yes." Truth be told, it had also stretched other parts, parts that were still a bit sore. "But if I don't want to have sex with someone in this place, can I decide not to? Because it seems that I'm humping everyone in sight."

"Only you can answer that, Alice."

Alice thought about that for a few steps. "I don't seem to be very discerning."

"Maybe you're just becoming more open-minded." Humpty shrugged. "Just because you fantasize about something Alice, doesn't mean you necessarily have to do it in real life."

"In real life, I haven't slept with anyone since I broke up with Lewis." And right then, she felt like she wanted to cry again for what she had done to him. "And I most want to be with him."

Humpty looked bored. "That's nice."

"But on this side of the looking glass, I seem to be having sex at the drop of a hat with everyone I see."

"That's because this is a sexual fantasy, Alice."

"What?"

"A fantasy. Think about it, Alice. Why would you fantasize about someone you *didn't* want to have sex with? I mean those individuals wouldn't even *be* in your fantasy in the first place. That would just be a waste of time. And pages."

Alice supposed that made a lot of sense, and as she continued down the path with Humpty, she could feel her piercing rub between her legs and the hot sun and cool breeze caress the rings in her bare nipples, and by the time they arrived at Lion and Unicorn Park, Alice was hoping to meet some new people, because she felt quite wet and ready to have sex with them, both immediately and vigorously. That, after all, was the point of fantasy.

The first people they encountered when they entered the park were the wildflowers, Lily, Rose and Daisy, along with several women Alice had yet to meet. They were in a circle, alternating being on their knees and on their backs, so the flower behind could lap at the nectar in front.

"Hello, Alice," said Daisy. "How do you like this position? I just made it up."

"It's very nice, Daisy." And Alice meant it. Watching each of the women lick the other, their faces glistening and breasts heaving with desire, was making her want to touch herself again. "What is it called?"

"Why a Daisy chain, of course," she answered. "Would you like to join us?"

Alice might consider it, if not for having developed a special aversion to groan-worthy puns. But she didn't have much of a chance, because Humpty was already jumping in, pushing his large-eggy body between Lily and a woman with long, pendulous breasts that Alice swore she'd seen within the pages of an old National Geographic in her grade school's musty library (and found quite exciting when she was young). Humpty directed the woman to sit on his face, and Lily opened her mouth wide (very!) and managed to fit Humpty inside.

Alice watched for a while, but then continued on her way. Now that she understood she didn't have to feel guilty for having sex with everyone she bumped into in Looking Glass Land, she was eager to meet some new faces… and, um, other body parts.

The next frolickers she encountered was a group of men milling around on the grass. Alice looked at each in turn, she realized she had seen every single one of them before. Not in Looking Glass Land, but in Alice's day-to-day life.

The first was a handsome black man she recognized immediately as her professor for Math 101. He was so handsome and creative and nice, that all the girls seemed to have a crush on him, and although Alice had only been to a few classes thus far, she was no exception.

Next to him stood a Samoan wrestler Alice remembered seeing in a match on TV. He had tattoos on his beefy body, but the most striking were circling his face.

There were other men, too. A cute actor from a romantic comedy Alice had Netflixed three times. A pro football player she thought was hot. A biker wearing leather and chains who she'd once spotted walking into a bar. Her favorite member of a boy band, back when she was a screaming preteen. The cop who'd given her a speeding ticket last week. A Latino heartthrob she'd swooned over on *Dancing with the Stars.*

Some of them wore leather, their bodies crisscrossed with straps and studs. Some of them had jewelry decorating their members, their sacks, their faces and nipples and tongues. Some were clean cut, but carrying a gleam in their eyes that was shocking and dirty indeed.

Alice was wondering whom she should approach first when she turned around a hedge and smacked right into a boy she'd had a crush on before she'd started dating Lewis.

"Oh, my!" exclaimed Alice, and her first thought was that he looked as cute as he had back in high school, and her second was that she was totally naked except for her pumps, and her third was that he was naked, too.

"Hello, Alice," he said to her breasts. "It's nice to see you."

Her nipples tingled and tightened under his gaze and her cheeks heated in a blush. "It's nice to see you, too, Dodgson."

His focus skimmed down to her shaved special place, the sparkle of jewelry and shine of moisture visible where her nether lips met. "You sure are looking fine," he said to her crotch, and his member started to lengthen and rise.

Alice was getting very excited now, adding to her embarrassment. She didn't have to wonder why Dodgson was in her fantasy. She'd yearned to have sex with him since puberty, and he'd only been interested in the head cheerleader. But the shock of seeing him here, nude and ready, made her have to catch her breath sharply.

And that made her breasts bounce. She hoped Dodgson noticed.

But he'd dropped his gaze to her blue pumps. "Do you want to have sex with me, Alice?" he asked.

"Very much," Alice answered, her boldness giving her a naughty thrill.

But Dodgson didn't kiss her or touch her breasts or lift his gaze from her shoes. In fact, he didn't respond to her at all.

Alice thought that was strange, but instead of assuming her own fantasy was rejecting her, which would have either been preposterous or an indication of very low self-esteem, she decided to be more specific. "Would you like to sink your wand of passion into my pleasure well?" And to illustrate, she spread her legs a little farther apart.

But still Dodgson didn't react to her offer. Instead he knelt down at her feet.

Another naughty idea popping into her mind, Alice stepped over him, giving him a good clear look at her private area and the glorious upward view of her breasts and erect nipples. She was feeling a little desperate now, and (very!) horny, and she wanted some action. "I want you to plunge your hard cock inside me."

He didn't look up, his gaze still glued to her shoes.

When even her most crude attempt at dirty talk didn't work, Alice knew something was wrong. "Do you want to have sex with me, Dodgson?"

"Yes, Alice."

"Then tell me what you want." she finally said.

"Step on me," he said.

"Excuse me?"

Dodgson dropped down onto his back. "I want you to put your foot on me, Alice."

"With my heels on?"

"At first."

The request was strange, certainly, but since she now had an open mind, she thought what the heck and rested her blue pump on Dodgson's belly, right above his erection.

He moaned.

Alive dug her heel in a bit, twisting it, and he said, "Oh, yes."

Curious at how curious this was, Alice moved her shoe up to Dodgson's face, where he—amazingly—began to suck her spiked heel. Alice was going to comment on how that was probably unsanitary, considering all the dirt paths she'd been on, but Dodgson looked deliriously happy.

"May I sniff inside your shoe, Alice?"

Alice shrugged. "Sure."

He carefully removed the pump, held it to his nose, and took deep, sighing breaths. "May I touch your foot, Alice?" he asked.

"Knock yourself out."

Dodgson ran his hands across her sole, cupping her heel, pressing and kneading. His fingers separated her toes, massaging each one individually.

"May I lick and suck your toes?"

"Might as well."

And he did, and to Alice's surprise, his massaging and licking and sucking felt wonderful. And she watched in fascination as his manhood grew hard as rock.

"Curious," she said, though she didn't mean to say the word out loud.

"Beg pardon?" Dodgson said between licks.

"My feet seem to excite you."

"Your feet are glorious, Alice. Not that I don't appreciate the rest of your charms, but your feet really turn me on."

"Why do you like feet so much?" she asked, truly interested to know.

"I don't know," he said. "I just do. They make me hard. And yours are so beautiful and sexy, they make me want to come right now."

Alice shrugged. She guessed everyone had their kinks. "Would you like me to rub your staff of plenty with my toes?"

Dodgson beamed. "Will you?"

Alice sat on the ground, and she did. And she had to admit, it was kind of fun, too. As she toyed with his stiff manhood, she played with herself, and had an enjoyable time.

"I'm... I'm coming..."

Alice rubbed faster, and soon her toes were covered by his creamy essence, but before she could say anything, he had cleaned her off and was attending to her feet, massaging and sucking, all over again.

This guy would be great to have around after a long day of shopping at the mall, but Alice had other body parts that needed attention. "That was fun Dodgson, but I'm afraid I have to go."

"Don't go, Alice, I'm just getting started."

That may have been so, but after playing with his member and watching him come, Alice was now so horny and dripping wet she wanted some attention paid to her cave of delights, not her feet. "See ya around," she called, and she left her pumps with him, because he seemed to like them more than she did, and then she spotted the Red King.

He had taken off his red robe since she'd last seen him, and he was wearing nothing but his crown and a curious red rubber device that encircled his engorged manhood with one strap and his balls with the other, keeping him high and erect and straining.

"Good day, Alice. I just saw you with Dodgson over there. Quite open-minded of you to cater to his unorthodox needs."

"Did you enjoy watching?" Alice asked. She knew the question was bold, but she was turned on by royalty, as evidenced by all the adventures she'd had to date, and she hadn't quite gotten over her disappointment that the Red King hadn't been able to complete his thrusting into her secret garden back at the Looking Glass House. She believed that sort of thing was called thrustus interruptus.

"I did. It is always exciting to see my favorite movie star in action."

Alice's face crinkled. "Dodgson is a movie star?"

"Not Dodgson, Alice. You. You're the star of *Alice's Sexual Piercing Adventure*, the number one adult film of all time."

"But they just made that movie less than an hour ago. You've seen it?"

"Everyone has seen it. You're the fantasy of everyone here, Alice."

"I am?"

"Indeed. In fact, you are the subject of an unbearably long poem. Would you like to hear it?"

"No, thank you," said Alice, desperate to avoid more stupid poetry.

"Are you sure?"

"Quite sure."

"I could just recite a few dozen stanzas. It will be brief."

"I truly don't want to hear any more poetry, no matter how brief."

Apparently unable to help himself, the King opened his mouth to recite anyway. "The lion and the unicorn were—"

But before he could complete the first line, a brilliant idea popped into Alice's head; the perfect way to avoid more poetry. She dropped to her knees and took the king's straining member into her mouth.

"—fighting... oh, mercy!"

And he forgot all about the poem and began thrusting wildly, sliding on her tongue. Alice grabbed his legs, and settled into his rhythm, sucking and teasing and delighting in the sounds he made. She wasn't sure if she wanted him to shoot his essence into her mouth or shower it all over her breasts or bury himself inside her, but any way he did it, the thought excited her so much, she could feel an orgasm building without any stimulation at all.

The Red King's moans had just reached a fevered pitch, when he suddenly stopped. "No, no, wait. Before I come, there's something I do want, more than anything."

Alice let his hardness slide from her lips and she peered up at him. She couldn't help wondering what kind of kink the Red King was into. "What do you want me to do?"

"Ever since I watched you in that mirror, pleasuring yourself, and then we were interrupted, I've wanted to drill into you from behind again and send your breasts bouncing like that. Is there a chance that..."

"Certainly," Alice said, for she was partial to that position, at least she seemed to be in this particular adventure. And of course, she was always eager to be of use, especially where royalty was concerned.

So she stood up and braced her palms on the refreshment table and spread her legs apart, tilting her bottom upward to fully display the entrance of her love tunnel. And the men gathered to watch. Hatta and Haigha brought their cameras. The wildflowers arrived in a bouquet with the Tweedles and Humpty. And the White Queen joined the party, too.

"Oh me, oh my," said the King. He positioned himself behind her and swirled his rigid head around and around in her wetness. "You are so beautiful and sexy, Alice. And so very, very fresh and eager and heavy with dew. Not at all like the Red Queen."

And Alice thought about what Humpty said about her royalness insisting on boredom and falling asleep on the Jabbercock. And although she wondered if those things were true, she thought it was probably rude to ask at the moment the Red King was getting ready to enter her.

So she didn't, and he did.

He moved slowly at first, gliding inside, then pulling out. Then his strokes grew faster, and soon he was pounding into her, his sack slapping against her hungry nub. Then his fingers were on her as well, teasing and inspiring and grabbing her hips and thrusting.

Pressure built in Alice and her breasts bounced and all the men and women from her fantasies stroked themselves and each other and a full out orgy ensued.

"These positions are not approved!" A screech ripped through the park and frightened the birds in the trees. Everyone looked up at the Red Queen, who stood in the center of the gazebo and had her arm outstretched and finger pointed at the crowd in an accusatory manner.

"All of you are in violation!" she declared. "Knight! Arrest them, and take every last one to the HDO!"

Chapter 8

"It's My Own Invention"

Everyone scattered, like a bunch of people scattering, and Alice ran with them, bumping into Humpty, who was struggling to keep up.

"I thought you were going to warn everyone about the raid!" she scolded.

"Lost track of time. Blowjobs do that to a guy. Run and hide, Alice! Don't let the Knight catch you!"

"I won't!" Alice said. "Never!"

Then the Knight caught her. He galloped by on a great steed and grabbed her arm, yanking her up behind him. The horse was moving at such a quick clip that Alice was forced to throw her arms around him, grasping his armor-plated midsection, holding on for her life as the horse leapt over some hedges and headed down—you guessed it—a path through the woods.

"Let me go!" Alice cried.

"But you're the one holding me," said the Knight.

"That's because you're going so fast. Slow down at once."

"I only take orders from the Red Queen, said the Knight. And she demanded you be taken to the Hall of Denied Orgasms."

A tremor of fear seized Alice. "Please, I don't want to be taken to that dreadful place."

"Okay. We'll go somewhere else then."

"Really?"

"No, of course not, you naive wench. To the HDO with you. The Jabbercocky will tame your firey spirit, that's for sure."

"What do you know of the Jabbercock?" Alice asked, voice quivering.

"It's my own invention. I designed it. Just like the chapter heading said."

"You designed a machine to sexually torment people without allowing them release? What kind of person would do something so terrible?"

"Why, a sadist, of course. But I'm not into the whole beating and dominating scene. I simply prefer to tie up nubile young ladies and tease them until they go insane."

That sounded vaguely familiar. Alice hadn't gotten a look at the Knight's face, because it was hidden under one of those armor helmets with the beaked nose. But even though his voice was hollow and echoey, Alice thought she'd recognized it.

"Gnat? Is that you?"

The Knight turned around, and lifted up his face shield thingy.

"Hello, Alice," said Gnat. "I must say, you were terrific in *Alice's Sexual Piercing Adventure*. And *Alice's Multi-Orgasmic Gangbang in the Park* was even more fantastic. When that Samoan went down on you—pure cinema magic. It is my favorite film of all time. I even liked it more than *Wall-E*."

"Gnat! I thought we were friends!"

"We are, Alice."

"So how can you do this to me?"

"Simple. First I strap you down, so you cannot move no matter how you struggle. Then I switch on the Jabbercock—"

"That isn't what I mean, Gnat. I mean how can you be so cruel to your friend?"

"You heard my sadist comment earlier, right?"

"But I won't be able to stand being teased without release, Gnat! I shall go mad!"

"You'll be fine. Unless you really do go mad, in which case Looking Glass Land has one of the best psychiatric hospitals in the nation. Do you have medical insurance, Alice?"

A sign on the path read HALL OF DENIED ORGASMS JUST AHEAD.

"Please, Gnat. I beg you."

"Sadists like begging, Alice. It turns us on. If I wasn't wearing armor, you could see the evidence."

And then the woods ended and Alice saw it; a dark, stone castle, looking forbidding in the distance.

"Anything but this, Gnat. You can spank me."

"Really?"

"You can tie me down and whip me. Cane me. Force yourself upon me."

"Go on."

"You can have any part of me, Gnat. I'll be your slave. I'll do whatever you ask. But please, don't take me to the Jabbercocky."

"Your begging has given my such a hard-on Alice. It is so arousing that I think I might…"

"Yes?"

"In fact, I know I shall…"

"Shall what, Gnat?"

"I shall pleasure myself while watching the Jabbercocky ravage you. But not for the whole eight hours, of course."

"Eight hours?!"

"I have other things to do today. Maybe I'll come back and check on you a few times, see how the torment is going."

"You're dreadful!"

"Thank you very much," Gnat said, and then they entered the Hall of Denied Orgasms.

Chapter 9

Queen Alice

Gnat the Knight (both the G and K were silent) dismounted the horse and then hefted Alice up on his shoulder and walked into the Hall of Denied Orgasms. As he crossed the moat on the drawbridge and neared the entrance, Alice heard a cacophony of plaintive moans and groans coming from the castle. Sounds of sexual desperation. Begging, groaning, panting, and even some sobbing.

Alice had to admit, terrified as she was, the sounds were pretty arousing.

"Ah, listen to that," Gnat said over the *clank clank clank* of his armored footfalls. "So much frustration. Remember our time in the orchard, Alice? The Jabbercocky is going to make that seem trivial. You're going to be teased for so long, you'll scarcely be human by the time it's over. Just imagine it. Kept on the very threshold or climax, for eight full hours, without release."

"How about when the eight hours end?" Alice said.

"Then you'll come like crazy. I'm a sadist, Alice, not a monster. But even though it will undoubtedly be the biggest orgasm of your life, it won't be worth all the torment leading up to it. The Jabbercock breaks even the most committed masochist and the most diehard submissive. Even those who ache for discipline and humiliation cannot withstand the Jabbercocky's awesome power."

The cries became louder as they crossed the threshold. Alice craned her head up over Gnat's shoulder to see, even though it frightened her to do so. She'd been expecting a dark, dank dungeon, with the suffering hanging on walls by chains, or in rusty iron cages. Instead, the hall was furnished quite tastefully in the Mediterranean style, lots of wood and earth tones, vases boasting lovely fresh bouquets of assorted flowers, soft lighting in the form of candles, oil lamps, and several skylights. It could have been a living room in a well-to-do home in Sicily.

The accused were comfortably seated on chaise lounges, bound to them with matching leather cuffs and buckles. Alice counted seven unfortunates, each moaning and sweating and gyrating without relief as the Jabbercocky tormented their yearning genitals.

The Jabbercocky also fit into the room's decor, in a feng shui sort of way. It occupied the center of the round room, several meters high, surrounded by an assortment of potted ferns. Painted brown in color, this mechanical feat of wizardry was a clinking, whirling collection of gears and pistons and articulated machinations, with spiderlike arms that extended in all directions, attending to the torments of each of the bound victims. It also had a large smiley face painted on it, and under that a sign that read GOOD BEHAVIOR, WELL CHASTIZED.

Gnat placed Alice on her feet and held her firmly around the waist from behind. She was aware of her naked bottom pressing against the metal codpiece of his suit of armor, and Alice fought a desire to rub her growing wetness up against him. If the sexual sounds of the punished weren't arousing enough, the sight of them made her nipples tighten and her throat go dry.

In the first chair, strapped and spread-eagled, was Rose, from the garden. One of the Jabbercock's articulated arms had a buzzing vibrator on the end of it, and it alternated touching her pillowy breasts and the sensitive spot between her legs. Rose was bathed in sweat, straining against her bonds, saying to herself over and over "pleaseohpleaseohplease" while gyrating as much as her restraints allowed. But the Jabbercocky never stimulated her more than a few seconds before pulling away, as if it knew exactly how close she was to orgasm and wouldn't allow it.

"The Jabbercocky knows exactly how close she is to orgasm, but won't allow it," Gnat said. "The chair is monitoring her vitals. Pulse, heart rate, wetness, breathing, muscle contractions. As it stimulates her close to climax, it adjusts to pull away before she is allowed release."

"That's horrible," Alice said.

"Yes. Isn't it a turn on?"

Alice refused to admit it was. But seeing Rose squirm, on the precipice of ecstasy, made Alice's legs weak. She imagined herself in the chair, helpless in the throes of teasing, growing wetter and more crazed with each light touch of the vibrator.

Seated next to Rose was Dodgson, from the park. The Jabbercock had an arm above his head, where a hanging mobile of women's cha cha heels spun close to Dodgson's upturned face. They were of various colors, some of the platform variety, others with plumes of ostrich feathers, others strappy stilettos.

"The shoes have all been worn," Gnat said, "so they have an odor which he finds intoxicating."

Alice noticed that another robotic arm, which had a very realistic-looking rubber foot on it, kept prodding poor Dodgson's bobbing erection. It would rub against him, stroking for a moment as it wiggled articulated female toes that looked exactly like the real thing, and then pull away.

"You're using his kink against him," Alice said. "That's dreadful."

Gnat moved his hands up to Alice's chest, the cold metal of his gauntlets teasing her nipples. "Hello? Sadist. That's the point."

On the other side of Dodgson was poor Humpty, who thrashed in his chair as if he were being beaten. But he wasn't. Instead, the Jabbercock's arm repeatedly pressed a glistening artificial vagina on the head of Humpty's erect chode. But he never penetrated it more than a centimeter.

"It's too small for him," Gnat said, obviously delighted. "So all it does it torment him."

Humpty caught Alice's eye. He looked so desperate, so needy for an orgasm, that it broke Alice's heart. She tried to run to him, but Gnat grabbed her arm.

"Is it too much for your friend?" he asked.

"Yes. Please stop it. I implore you."

"Very well."

Gnat picked up a remote control on the table and pressed a button. The small artificial vagina retracted, and it was replaced by the incredibly realistic rubber head of a famous starlet. She opened her lush lips and descended upon Humpty's chode—

But it still didn't fit. Her lips simply brushed Humpty's straining tip, over and over.

"You're a monster," she told Gnat.

"Yeah. Pretty much. It makes you wet, though," Gnat said. "I can tell. And look how erect your nipples are."

Alice refused to dignify his claim, even though it was true. Though she'd been sated in the park, seeing all of these groaning, writhing bodies was a ferocious turn-on.

"Why not punish these people with multiple orgasms instead?" Alice said, trying to ignore the pulsing between her thighs. "Surely the Jabbercocky could do that."

"Of course. But how is that punishment? People would purposely disobey the Red Queen just to be sentenced here."

"How is that bad?"

"Look, Alice, I don't agree with the Red Queen's missionary-only policy. But I'm her Knight, so it is my job to enforce it. The law is the law."

"It's a dreadful law."

"Just because you don't agree with it, doesn't mean it shouldn't be enforced. Have you met Tweedle Dee and Tweedle Dum?"

Gnat pointed to the duo, who were strapped into complicated harnesses and suspended in a 69 position. Each of their erect, outstretched members was only inches away from the other's mouth. Much as they strained their lips and tongues, and much as their charmingly curved erections bobbed and twitched, they couldn't reach one another. To make the torment even worse, the Jabbercocky's terrible articulated arms teased each of their bottoms with dildos shaped exactly like their respective penises.

"Those poor, annoying dears," Alice said. "They love each other so. This must be horrible for them."

"Watch how it gets worse."

Alice watched as suddenly their harnesses moved closer to one another, allowing them each to greedily suck. But just as quickly, the Jabbercocky separated them, neither having more than a brief taste.

"No!" they yelled in unison, straining for the other. Then they began to weep.

Perhaps Alice's open-mindedness had reached the point where she had embraced her inner sadist, but watching the Tweedles tormented so got her really hot. And seated next to them—

The White Queen, strapped to her lounge chair, tears in her eyes. Her legs were wide open, each of her piercings in place, and there were several articulated Jabbercock arms tormenting her with various toys, one after another. First the Sqweel, lapping against the metal rings and studs in the Queen's femininity, making her screech like a banshee. Then the Eroscillator, going from her nipple rings to her clit. Then a quick insertion of the Drilldo, spinning madly. Then other things Alice hadn't seen before. A rabbit vibrator like her own, but with an extra length to be inserted into the bottom, which made the Queen quake all over as it pumped in and out of her like a lover. A Hitachi wand, with a phallus-shaped attachment on the end that made the Queen moan when inserted. A clear, round shield that Alice realized was some sort of vacuum pump, which sucked at the Queen's nether lips and clit and plumped them up to almost twice their size.

And every time the poor dear seemed close to orgasm, the toy would be removed and replaced by wiggling, robotic fingers that tickled the White Queen until she howled with laughter.

"Tickle torture," Gnat said. "Quite insidious. She'll be a wreck when she finally comes."

"It's awful," Alice said. But she couldn't help thinking about switching places with the Queen, having all of those dreadfully lovely things done to her. The vacuum pump especially seemed interesting. How sensitive would she be while so engorged?

"And yet, you think it's sexy, don't you?" Gnat whispered, catching Alice touching herself.

Alice quickly removed her hand. "Yes. Maybe. But only in consensual play. This is being done as punishment."

"Oh, but everyone here does give their consent, Alice. They each have a choice. The Hall of Denied Orgasms, or banishment. If anyone here decides they can't handle anymore, they can choose to end it and leave Looking Glass Land."

"Then I choose banishment," Alice declared, willing to return home rather than face this torment.

"As you wish. But shouldn't we take a look at the last person being tormented here first?"

"Who is it? Hatta? Haigha? Lily? The Red King? Daisy? It doesn't matter. I want out of this place, and out of Looking Glass Land."

But as she was talking, Alice couldn't help but notice the last prisoner, bound to a chair and wearing a skimpy bra and panties, writhing and moaning with teary eyes.

"Why, it's… Lewis!"

Her ex-boyfriend wore Alice's best underwear, a black lacy set he'd bought for her at Victoria's Secret. Stuffed into his mouth was one of her red satin thongs. Like Humpty, the Jabbercock teased poor Lewis with an artificial female head, which licked and sucked at his stiff member intensely but briefly. What surprised Alice most of all was that the head looked exactly like her. Same haircut. Same vacant expression. It even had a tongue like hers.

"Lewis still loves you," Gnat said. "He feels so terrible that you left him. He wished you never found out about his secret kink."

Alice's heart sank. "I didn't know," she said. "If only I'd been tolerant instead of reacting without thinking."

"Too late now," Gnat said. "The poor sap has been here in Looking Glass Land as long as you have, without any release at all. Look at his poor, throbbing erection."

Alice did, and felt devastated by remorse. "What did the Red Queen accuse him of? Cross-dressing? But that's harmless!"

"He wasn't accused of anything. He came here willingly, to punish himself."

Alice shook her head. "No!"

"Yes. You've shamed him so, he feels unworthy of you. This is how he deals with the emotional pain. He suffers because you couldn't accept him. Let me tell you something, Alice. For all the cruel things I do in this place, I never unfairly judged someone I love."

"Lewis!" Alice cried, trying to reach for him. But Gnat held her back.

"You chose banishment, Alice. Say goodbye to everyone here. I'll take you back to your world."

"But I can't leave him like this!"

"So, you choose to stay?"

Alice nodded.

"Splendid," Gnat said, smiling. "Allow me to show you to your seat."

A moment later Alice was strapped into a lounge chair, legs spread, buckled and straps holding her firmly in place.

"At any moment, if you wish for this to cease, simply tell the Jabbercocky 'I quit.' Then you'll be allowed to climax, and quickly banished. You seem to have a strong will, and I admire your attempts to open your mind. But I tested your limits in the orchard. If you last more than an hour, I'll be very surprised. But eight hours?" Gnat shook his head. "There is simply no way you can handle that."

"I can handle whatever you can dish out," Alice said, defiantly.

Gnat laughed. "Really?"

"Really."

"I accept that challenge." Gnat pointed the remote control at the Jabbercocky. "I was going to take it easy on you at first, but now I'm programming it to give you everything it has got. You don't stand a chance, Alice."

Then Gnat stepped away, and the Jabbercock's articulated arms descended upon poor Alice. She stared, helpless, as a large dildo penetrated her, easing in slowly, filling her up in a most delightful way.

Then it began.

The thrusting was gentle, sensual, at first. Already aroused, it made Alice sigh with pleasure, and she could already feel the first inklings of an orgasm dwelling deep within her.

The strokes became deeper, and faster. Two other arms extended and gently tugged her nipple rings, sending a shiver through Alice's body.

It wasn't terrible at all. In fact, it was just what she needed.

Suddenly, faster than any human being ever could, the Jabbercock began to pound into Alice with alarming speed. It was not only unexpected, it was unlike anything Alice had ever known. She went from an arousal level of five immediately up to an eight, and as she cried out her voice sounded like a yodel, the tremors in Alice's body extending all the way to her voice.

Then, abruptly, all motion stopped.

The abrupt change from near climax to no stimulation at all was jarring. Alice's face was already glistening with perspiration, and she was wetter than she'd ever been. She tried, in vain, to move her hips closer to the dildo, which was only centimeters away, but it retreated an equal distance back.

Her nipple rings were gently stroked, making Alice gasp. But the dildo didn't return.

"It's okay," Alice said to herself. "I can handle it."

She took in a deep breath and let it out slow, trying to ignore the nipple tugging. Then the Jabbercocky extended another arm, this one with a Hitachi wand on it. The Hitachi was a back massager with a large, spongy rubber head, capable of extremely intense vibrations. Alice watched, transfixed, as it lowered to her nether lips and pressed against her.

Alice sighed at the contact. When it turned on, she screamed.

It was too powerful. The pleasure was so intense, it was almost pain. But it wasn't pain. It was exquisite, overbearing stimulation to her most sensitive part, and once again Alice rocketed toward a climax—

—that didn't happen. Just as she came close, the arm retracted, leaving Alice out of breath and dizzy.

"Only seven hours and fifty-eight minutes to go," Gnat said, smiling down at her.

Before Alice was able to brace herself, both the Hitachi and the dildo ravaged her, and between the buzzing and the thrusting Alice felt ready to burst.

Then it stopped.

"Right now, it's simply frustrating," Gnat told her. "But soon, all you'll be able to think about is when the Jabbercock's arms will return. The more you think about it, the more aroused you'll become. The more aroused you become, the longer you'll have to wait. Your body will turn against you, and you'll become a mindless, begging slave to your own needs."

"I will not beg," Alice said.

Gnat smiled. "They all beg."

The Jabbercock's dildo extended again, slowly entering Alice. She ground her teeth, trying not to react, trying to ignore the grunting and screaming and pleading from all around her. Gnat removed his gauntlet, and his codpiece, and he touched himself as the Jabbercock began a slow and easy thrust.

"You're so beautiful right now Alice," Gnat said. "This is so exciting. And I can see how aroused you are."

Alice didn't want to look at him. She really didn't like Gnat very much at that moment, and didn't want to see his member so close, or hear his dirty talk, because it only turned her on even more.

"Do you want the Jabbercock to go faster, Alice?" Gnat asked, furiously abusing himself. "Beg me, and I'll increase the speed."

Alice set her jaw.

"No?" Gnat said.

The Hitachi descended, giving Alice a quick, two second jolt of intense vibrations, provoking a desperate whimper from her. She was so close to coming. If only the dildo went just the slightest bit faster…

"Beg for it, Alice. Beg for the speed to increase."

"No," Alice said through her teeth. "Never."

Gnat pressed another button, and more robotic arms surrounded Alice. A tiny plug went into her bottom and vibrated, illuminating all of her tender nerve endings there. Besides the dildo and the Hitachi, a stream of warm water spurted on Alice's genitals, exactly like the spray from her handheld shower massager, which she used to delightful results even more often than her rabbit vibe. The tiny fingers holding her nipples began to vibrate, and Gnat held his aroused manhood inches away from her mouth as he pumped away.

The sensations overwhelmed Alice. Try as she might to not react, it was simply too much to bear. She squeezed her eyes shut, willing her hips to stay still, fighting to keep from squirming or crying out. But try as she might, the orgasm built and built until—

All movement ceased.

"Seven hours and fifty six minutes left," Gnat said. "Me? I'll be done in about a minute. You can watch, if you like."

Alice's whole being seemed to be enflamed with desire. She wanted so badly to take Gnat in her mouth, and felt awful for wanting that, but the Jabbercock was turning her into a slut without any self-control. She yearned to press against the arms next time they stimulated her, and realized Gnat's prediction was coming true; she was becoming more and more aroused, more and more focused on an orgasm that would only be denied. But Alice was unable to focus on anything else. When she tried to take her mind off of the things being done to her, the arms returned, teasing and stroking and vibrating. The water spurt in quick, rapid bursts, hitting her right on her swollen nubbin. The dildo jack-hammered into her then retreated so quickly Alice was shattered by need.

"Beg me," Gnat said, the cords in his neck beginning to tighten. "Beg me, Alice."

Alice listened to the tormented cries of her friends. The poor White Queen, laughing while moaning. Humpty, begging to penetrate something, anything. Rose, sobbing with need. Dodgson, grunting with frustration. Tweedle Dee and Tweedle

Dum, tortured by their strange love and attraction to one another. And Lewis. Poor, sweet, Lewis. Her true love, made to be ashamed of his desires because of her. The sounds they made, the pleasure they were denied simply because they were different from others, reached right down into Alice's soul and told her what she needed to do.

"I beg you," she said to Gnat, her eyes welling up with need but her voice strong and sure. "Do whatever you will to me. Keep me here for days if you must. But let my friends come."

And then a most curious thing happened. With a terrific burst of light, a golden crown appeared on Alice's head.

"Why, you've become a queen," Gnat said, gawking. "You've finally become tolerant of others and opened your mind."

"Let them climax, Gnat," Alice said.

"But, I can't. The Red Queen says—"

"The Red Queen says whoop-de-do," said the Red Queen, strolling into the Hall. "So, you got yourself a crown. Big deal. I'm the ruler of Looking Glass Land. I'm the one who beat the Jabbercocky."

"Because you fell asleep," Alice said.

The Red Queen frowned. "Sex is overrated. All of you people, with your fantasies and your rutting like animals. You should be ashamed of yourselves. Our genitals were created to make babies, not to abuse. They serve a function. Using them recreationally is a waste of time."

"Why don't you enjoy sex?" Alice asked. Then she yelped, "Oh my!" So much had been happening that Alice had managed to cool down a bit, and the Jabbercocky sensed that and once again penetrated and vibrated her to near climax.

"I enjoy sex just fine," said the Red Queen. "As a way to be intimate with my husband. But I'm not like all of you shameless, wicked heathens, who flaunt your promiscuity like it is some badge of honor."

"You've never had an orgasm, have you?" Alice asked between breaths.

"Who cares if I haven't?" said the Red Queen. "I wouldn't want to look as foolish as you do, in the throes of passion. All the screaming and moaning and gyrating. It's downright degrading."

"An orgasm isn't degrading," Alice said. "It is beautiful." She looked at her friends, still being teased. "It is beautiful, no matter what turns you on or gets you off."

"Poppycock," said the Red Queen. "We'll see how strong willed you are seven hours from now."

"Perhaps you'd like to sit on my face," Alice said to her.

The Red Queen turned even redder. "What did you just say?"

"If I have to, I'll tie you up first. Then I'll slide my tongue between your soft folds and lick you right where you're most sensitive," said Alice. "Slow, fat licks, as I gently ease a finger inside your wet—"

"Shut your slutty mouth," the Red Queen snapped.

"And Gnat, as I devour the Queen's sweet nectar with my lips and tongue, you shall enter me from behind. I'll be wet and ready and yearning for your length. You'll give me slow strokes at first, then pound into me faster and harder."

"I'm in," said Gnat.

The Jabbercock's arms were all retracted, and sensing her building excitement, nothing touched Alice at all. But the images in her head, intensified by the words she was saying, were making her hotter and hotter.

"And perhaps I'll have my rabbit vibrator," Alice said, her juices flowing. "And as you lie there, helpless, Queen, I'll plunge it deep inside you as I slather your sensitive clitoris with my tongue."

"Be silent!" the Red Queen said. "I demand it!"

"And Gnat, you can pull out and make me beg for it," Alice said, catering to Gnat's particular kink. "Make me scream for you to mount me again, for you to thrust into me. Make me beg until I can't take it anymore."

"That's so hot," Gnat said.

It *was* so hot. So hot, in fact, that Alice was on the cusp of a gigantic orgasm without any stimulation at all.

"And right when you do," Alice said, "you'll fill me with your sweet cream, and I'll thrust the rabbit so rapidly into the Queen while licking her that OH MY!"

The climax shuddered through Alice, making her cry out, releasing all the tension that had been building since before she arrived, without any stimulation whatsoever.

In mid-spasm, Alice's shackles opened up, and the Jabbercocky's dildo drooped down and touched the floor. Then two other robotic arms appeared, one with a cigarette, and one with a Zippo. The Jabbercock lit up, brought the cigarette to its smiley mouth in its smiley face, and took a deep puff.

Until the machilit the smoke...

This was followed by another flash of light, and the Red Queen's crown vanished.

"My Queen!" Gnat said, getting on one knee and bowing.

Alice stood up, realizing she was now clothed in a brilliant gold bra and panties. Her tormented friends began to cheer and shout.

"That twas brillig, Alice!"

"You go girl!"

"Callooh! Callay!"

"Someone free my hands so I can jerk off!"

"Arise, Knight," Alice commanded. "Program the Jabbercocky to make all of my friends climax, and then release them." She stared at the shocked former Red Queen, who was on the floor, cowering. "Stand up."

"I'm so sorry, my Golden Queen. Have mercy."

"I shall," Alice said. "Knight, bind her to a chair and let the Jabbercocky ravage her."

"What if she falls asleep again?" Gnat asked.

"She isn't to be teased. Have it give her ten orgasms. Be patient with her, until you find out what turns her on."

"Yes, my Queen."

The former Red Queen was stripped naked and immediately bound to a chair as the hall filled with the screaming and grunting of her friends' orgasms. Alice hurried to Lewis, who was being sucked by the imitation Alice head. She pushed it away and pulled the red thong from his mouth.

"Alice," Lewis said. "I'm so sorry. Please forgive—"

"Shh," she said. Then she removed her new, golden bra and draped it on Lewis's chest then took off her new, golden panties, and tied them around Lewis's throbbing manhood and began to stroke him. "Any time you want to put on my underwear, Lewis, it is okay by me. But there's one condition."

"What?" Lewis croaked.

"You have to let me watch. Because it turned me on something fierce."

Then she took Lewis in her mouth, bobbing her head as his hips bucked. He tasted salty and a little sweet and the feel of him on her tongue was like coming home.

He grabbed Alice's bottom, helping her onto the lounge chair, and buried his face between her wet thighs, devouring her. Alice continued to work his pole, looking all around her as her friends all cried out in delight. Even the former Red Queen was surrounded by Jabbercocky arms, and beginning to moan softly.

Within a few seconds, Lewis began to spasm, and that triggered an enormous surge of pleasure in Alice, taking her to the heights of ecstasy once again…

Chapter 10

Shaking

And her body was shaking. And her body was quaking. And she cried out in a deep throated scream—louder—and longer—and stronger—and—

Chapter 11

Waking

And she was standing in her bedroom, naked in front of the mirror, the rabbit buried deep from behind. And before Alice could figure out why these last two chapters were so short (hint: they are also short in the original version) there in the doorway stood Lewis himself, his eyes big as saucers at a tea party and a bulge growing in his jeans.

Chapter 12

Which Dreamed It?

Alice removed the rabbit and tried to come back to reality, which wasn't easy after so many mind-bending orgasms. She looked at her cats, Creampie still pouncing and Felcher still washing and Snowball still receiving her bath. And lastly, because she was embarrassed, she looked back to Lewis.

He threw up his hands, palms out, as if instead of a vibrator, she held a six shooter. "I'm sorry. I'm so sorry!"

After all Alice had experienced in Looking Glass Land and all she had learned, an apology from Lewis was the last thing she wanted to hear. "Why should you be sorry?"

"I... I walked in on you. I didn't mean to. I just came to return your keys. Your friends said you were going to the party, and I figured you wouldn't be home."

Maybe Alice should have felt a bit put out to be caught by Lewis (of all people) in this compromising position, but she couldn't manage it. There was something far more important on her mind.

"Lewis, please forgive me."

"Forgive you?" Lewis's face turned red. "I was the one who barged in while you were naked and thrusting the rabbit into yourself from behind and making your breasts buck and plunge so deliciously, with your hard nipples and luscious mouth and… so… um… I should apologize to you."

"That was an accident." And as Alice stood naked before him, she realized it was an accident that she really didn't mind at all. "I hurt you on purpose."

Lewis frowned. "I don't understand."

"I never should have been so judgmental, so closed-minded. I should have accepted you for who you were."

"Really?"

"I'm so terribly sorry, Lewis." And Alice started to cry.

Lewis raced to her side and held her in his arms, and ran a hand gently over her hair. "It's okay, Alice."

"But it's not," Alice blubbered. "Because I love you, and yet I didn't accept you. That's never okay. That's wrong."

"You love me?"

"Yes. And I want to say a thousand times that I'm sorry. I know that you're not gay."

"Yeah, I'm really not, Alice. You turn me on more than anything. Watching you just now, I thought I would explode."

"You were watching me?" she asked, and a naughty thrill shimmered over her skin. "For how long?"

"Longer than I should have," he admitted. "I yelled your name and no one answered, so I came in here to leave your apartment key and…"

"You liked what you saw?" Alice could feel the wet heat pooling in her lower region and her special place started to pulse.

"Of course I did, Alice. You're the hottest woman in the world." And to prove it, he pressed against her to show the hard evidence of his arousal.

And that's when Alice came up with a wonderful idea how she could show Lewis how sorry and how tolerant she was, and she could satisfy the aching, wet, hollowness that only Lewis could fill. "I'll be right back," she said, and leaving Lewis standing there, Alice scampered across the room.

She opened a drawer in her bureau and rifled around inside. Realizing Lewis was watching, she opened her legs and leaned forward, as she had on the other side of the looking glass, letting her breasts sway in front of her, and when she found her prize and scampered back, he was rubbing himself through the denim.

"Let's get those pants off you." Alice inched the zipper down over his bulge. She stripped his jeans off, then followed with his boxers, leaving him gloriously naked and his manhood as hard as a bedpost.

"And now let's get these on." She pulled out a pair of her frilliest, laciest, sparkliest golden panties (which is what she'd retrieved from the drawer) and cinched them around his jutting staff, just as she'd done in the Hall of Denied Orgasms.

"You're so pretty now, Lewis."

He stared at her as if he didn't know how to respond, but his erection wasn't so confused, and although Alice hadn't thought Lewis could get harder, somehow he managed.

She touched his shaft, sliding the lace and silk over him. "You're so sexy, too," she said.

"Is this really okay with you, Alice?"

"Yes, it's really okay. It's more than okay. Because I want you to enjoy yourself. I love you just the way you are. And seeing you aroused like this really turns me on."

With that she kissed him, long and passionate and hot. She nipped at his lips and delved her tongue into his mouth and held him and loved him and never wanted to let him go.

Then to prove just how hot she found him (very!), she sat on the futon and took him in her mouth and rubbed his manhood between her breasts and then accepted him into her most intimate place. Alice's nipples begged and her love garden sang, and she rode him like his rod was the Jabbercock itself. After both were spent, and they lay back on the sheets, and Alice was finally satisfied...

...at least for a little while.

Lewis spoke first. "I never want us to be apart again, Alice."

"I don't want to be apart either," she answered, feeling warm and accepted and loved in his arms.

"I love you, Alice. I think I have since we first met."

Once again, tears misted Alice's eyes, but these were the good kind. "I love you too, Lewis."

He smiled a sweet smile. "I was thinking maybe we could go buy some jewelry to help show our love."

"You mean a clit ring? Or something sparkly for my nipples? I've been fantasizing about getting a piercing."

"Wow," Lewis said, and being that he was eighteen years old as well, his member started to revive (already!). "That sounds wonderful, Alice, but I had something else in mind."

"What?" asked Alice.

He folded Alice's hands in his. "An engagement ring," he answered. "I want to marry you, Alice."

Alice smiled and her eyes misted, knowing this is what she had wanted all along. "Even if I can be short sighted and intolerant, and unfair sometimes?"

He grinned and fingered the golden panties. "I think you've learned your lesson."

"I have," Alice said. "I've learned that I love you, Lewis. Exactly the way you are."

"So you'll marry me?"

"Yes!"

Alice squealed, and kissed him all over, and being eighteen, neither one of them had any earthly idea they were too young to marry.

And as Lewis lay back on the futon, Alice kissing his length, he said in a soft voice, "I should probably pinch myself, because this all seems like it's straight from my dream."

Alice smiled, because here all along she thought Lewis had been a player in her fantasies, but maybe, all this time, she'd been a player in his. Then she took him in her mouth and brought him back to life.

"Doesn't this all seem like a dream, Alice?"

"Mmmph," she answered.

And they lived happily ever after, until sometime later when they were kidnapped and taken to the infamous Hellfire Club where all manner of dastardly things were done to them.

But that's another story…

Part 3

Kinky Secrets of Alice at the Hellfire Club

Chapter 1

Alice Begins Her Adventure and Is Kidnapped by Pirates, Sort of…

Lewis rolled off of Alice and plopped onto his side of the bed. He hadn't even been inside her long enough to be out of breath, let alone work up any sort of sweat. Alice had scarcely felt a thing.

That was bad enough, but it got worse. They'd reached the point in their marriage where he didn't even bother to ask how it had been for her, and Alice had long ago stopped pretending she'd enjoyed his lame attempts at lovemaking. During their thirty-second session, Alice hadn't so much as sighed. But Lewis had pumped away just the same, treating her like a vessel to fill instead of the object of his love and desire.

Alice felt like crying. So much had changed in the past few years. Since their fantastic adventures in Wonderland and through the Looking Glass. They'd grown up, lost the imagination, the whimsy, the sense of adventure.

They used to be so into each other. She'd dress up in naughty lingerie and kinky boots. She'd shave her special place and wear his favorite perfume. Lewis would serve her champagne and strawberries in bed. He'd taken extra special effort to please her, making sure she came at least once before the sex began. They used to spend whole weekends laughing, drinking, pleasuring each other.

But a fire that burned so brightly burned out twice as fast.

Alice knew Lewis wasn't the only one to blame. Her parts weren't into it either. Whereas she used to gush and throb, lately Alice felt more like a barren desert. Sex had become mechanical, as perfunctory as brushing your teeth. The romance, the eroticism, the longing… it all had become ethereal, like a dream she couldn't really remember.

Alice gathered the covers around her, fluffed her pillow, then turned her back to her husband, wondering if this was their fate. Doomed to decades of bad sex.

Or worse, no sex at all.

The problem was, she still cared for Lewis. She didn't want to give up their physical relationship, but she wanted to stay with him, even though both knew they were drifting apart. Alice couldn't even remember the last time they'd said, "I love you" to one another. She wasn't sure when it began, but it seemed as if it had been such a long time since she'd heard Lewis utter those words.

That hurt as much as the lack of orgasms.

Could she stay with a man so inattentive and oblivious to her needs? Or were they doomed to drift apart until their love vanished?

Alice wished she knew how to keep it from coming to that.

Coming…

Lewis's snore rippled through their bedroom.

When Alice and Lewis were first dating, back when they were eighteen, their fumbling attempts at sex always left him snoring and her unfulfilled. She hadn't thought about those days for a long time, about what had changed everything for her and for him, at least for a while. But if there was the smallest chance she could change their yawn of a sex life now, it was worth a shot.

Alice slipped out from under the covers, the air cool on her naked skin, and tiptoed to the bureau. She slid open a drawer, and reached inside. Tucked behind a stack of clean panties and her pink lace bra, she found what she was looking for. Something she hadn't seen in more than two years.

The White Rabbit.

Now this wasn't the rabbit from the old stories. This rabbit was long and battery-operated and had the cutest little vibrating ears that hit her just in the right spot.

She pulled the white rabbit from the drawer and climbed back in bed, right next to her sleeping husband. If Alice could get her juices flowing and some of the excitement back, then maybe she could inspire the both of them.

It had worked before.

She flipped the switch and the rabbit purred to life (this was the kind of rabbit that purred). Remembering all the maneuvers that had given her so much pleasure in the past, she started moving the rabbit over her breasts, circling one nipple then the other. A quiet whirr tickled the air. Delicious vibrations trembled over her skin. She pushed the sheet down with her free hand, baring her belly, then lower to expose her special place. Splaying her thighs wide, she let the cool air caress her, then skimmed the rabbit over her most sensitive spot.

As her juices began to flow, her fantasies drifted to the Hellfire Club.

The Hellfire Club was legendary. The most notorious location in Europe. A secret association dedicated to every imaginable form of sexual debauchery. A den of depraved carnality that supposedly catered to the most lascivious lusts of men and women.

In other words, the perfect remedy for her awful sex life.

Many claimed it existed, but only as hearsay. It always came down to someone who knew someone who heard of someone who'd been there. But Alice hadn't settled for rumors. As part of her desperate attempt to fix the problems in her marriage, she had gone on a private quest to prove its existence, and location. After hours of research, having talked to dozens of people, she'd actually found one of the ruling members, a woman of enviable beauty named Madame Bovary. Madame Bovary also was trapped in a lackluster marriage, to a dullard named Charles, and she'd taken some drastic steps to rectify the situation. Meeting with other, likeminded public domain characters and historical figures, they created the Hellfire Club. A place where no fantasy went unfulfilled, no lust unsatisfied.

They also served pretty good chicken wings.

Madame Bovary had offered Alice a Hellfire Club contract; a contract guaranteed to spice up the dullest of marriages.

Alice signed it immediately and had gotten Lewis to as well, though he'd been distracted and dismissive and barely looked the contract over when adding his name.

That had been a week prior. Alice had turned the contract in, along with a substantial payment (money she'd been saving for their summer vacation), but nothing had come of it. Madame Bovary had been vague about when their sexual reawakening was supposed to begin, but Alice assumed it should have happened by now. She suspected Madame Bovary had conned her. Perhaps the Hellfire Club was indeed just a fantasy after all, and Alice had played the trusting rube and given away their vacation savings in a vain attempt to inject some excitement into their married life.

But rather than dwell on what was probably an impetuous mistake, Alice switched the rabbit vibrator to a higher setting and fantasized about what an imaginary Hellfire Club might actually contain.

Did it have orgies? Most certainly. Men and women, joyously, shamelessly copulating in public. Alice pictured a chain of entwined bodies, one connected to the next via mouth or genitals, thrusting and undulating while voyeuristic eyes drank in every naked, sweaty inch, and hungry ears savored the grunts and moans of a dozen or more.

Gang bangs? Alice could imagine four decadent, ravenous rogues making love to her simultaneously. A mouth on each breast. A stiff cock in each hand. Men kissing her and sucking her and teasing her and filling her in every way possible.

Bondage? Alice pictured herself restrained and helpless, as a cruel master forced her to come over and over until she practically went insane. Then, because she was such a bad girl, such an insatiable, naughty whore without any self-control, she would be punished. Perhaps spanked, maybe even with a paddle or riding crop, as unrelenting hands continued to coax orgasm after orgasm from her helpless body as it twitched with every slap and strike.

Or perhaps Alice could be the one in charge, with a group of obedient slaves she could tease and torment. Men begging her for release as she tortured them with slow, soft blowjobs, butterfly kisses that engorged their members but offered no relief. Or maybe she would tease women, helpless and pleading to climax as she slid all manner of vibrating toys into their—

The door burst inward, and Alice jack-knifed in bed, her mouth hanging open in surprise.

"Well, what do we have here, matey?"

The man speaking had an eye patch, and a full, gray beard. He wore a sea captain's hat. His shirt was unbuttoned exposing a hairy chest and cinched only by the wide belt at his waist, a long scabbard hanging beneath. Next to him was a bald Caribbean man, a gold hoop in his ear. Below the waist, he was dressed in the same garb as his companion, but his naked and muscular torso was covered in obscene, sexual tattoos.

Pirates! Her bedroom had been invaded by marauding pirates! What were the odds of that happening?

"She seems to be a'pleasuring herself, Captain," the bald one answered.

"Aye. Look at those ripe breasts, those rosy nipples, and the treasure between 'er legs. Quite a spectacle, ain't it, Queequeg?"

Realizing she was indeed totally naked and splayed in front of two strange men—no, two strange *pirates*—Alice blossomed red with shame. She reached for the blankets to cover herself, but the tattooed pirate drew his sword and slashed the covers right out of her hand, making her gasp.

"We like the look of you, poppet," the captain said. His eyes traveled over every exposed inch of her skin before centering on her exposed special place. "We been at sea a long time."

The tattooed bloke said nothing, but he didn't have to. The hunger in his eyes and the bulge in his pirate breeches said it all.

To Alice's horror, her nipples peaked and hardened, as if begging to be taken into these men's mouths.

"Pick up the rabbit," the captain ordered.

Alice couldn't move; she was too focused on the embarrassing response of her body. Queequeg approached her snoring husband, and placed his cutlass against Lewis's throat.

"Pick up the rabbit and slide it into your cave of riches," the captain said, "Put on a good show for us, my beauty. Lest you want to be a widow."

"Isn't that a bit extreme for humorous erotica?"

The captain waved her comment away. "Just go with it. There's been too much exposition already, and readers want to get to the good stuff."

With a trembling hand, Alice picked up the rabbit vibrator.

"Turn it up on high," the captain said.

She turned the rabbit up to its highest setting, the base rotating quickly and the ears buzzing loud enough for the neighbors to hear.

"Now bury it inside your tight, slippery walls. But don't you dare come without permission. If you do…" The pirate drew a line across his throat, indicating what would happen to Lewis if Alice didn't obey.

Biting her lower lip, Alice moved the vibrating length down her belly and between her thighs. Even though she wasn't touching herself yet, she could feel the tantalizing buzz. Through the air. Through her fingers. Through the stares centered on her.

"Deep inside ye, lass. All the way up against that swollen little nub of yours."

Alice slid the rabbit between her nether lips, then pushed it in inch by inch until the vibrating ears pressed hard against her clitoris. The sensation made her yelp, and she flinched and began to withdraw.

"I said all the way in!" the captain boomed.

"It's too much, too soon," Alice spilled out. "I need to start on a lower setting and work up to—"

"NOW!"

Clenching her teeth, Alice thrust the toy deep inside her, fighting not to withdraw from the incessant, throbbing vibrations, so intense they made her wince.

"Spread those thighs wider, my beauty. And lift up that chin. I want to see your pretty face as you struggle not to come."

Alice did as she was told, and the pleasure between her legs intensified. The rabbit always made masturbation fast and easy, producing results within a few minutes. But in front of horny pirates, forced to put the settings on high, Alice couldn't stop the arousal from overtaking her immediately. Even her nipples betrayed her, sticking straight out, throbbing with want.

"Methinks the girl wants you to tug on her buds."

Queequeg grunted and walked around to her side of the bed, staring at her bare breasts like a starving man might stare at a feast. He reached down for her, and with rough, calloused hands began to roll and pinch her erect nipples.

Alice moaned. The pirate's hands on her, twisting and tweaking, made the vibrations even more intense. Each time he pulled, it was like a shock that went straight to her womb.

"No coming until I say so, lassie. We're not at the Hellfire Club yet."

The Hellfire Club! Of course! This wasn't just a random pirate home invasion, like you read about in the newspapers. These pirates were here to take her and Lewis to the club. Still, this wasn't what Alice had been expecting.

"But the contract says…"

"I know what the contract says, dear Alice." The captain grinned wickedly. "But I mean to have some fun first. Like I said, long time at sea makes a man long for certain pleasures. And there 'tis nothing more pleasurable than a beautiful, naked woman begging for release. Just look at your face now. All tensed up. Jaw clenched. Lips pressed together. The very picture of ecstasy. You're close, aren't you?"

Alice's face burned red. She nodded shamefully and panted, "Yes."

"You want to come?"

"Yes. Oh yes, please."

The captain rubbed his beard, seeming to consider it.

The vibrator continued to ravage her.

The pirate plucked and squeezed.

Alice's hips rose and fell, pressing against the rabbit. Her tender clit was wet and swollen, and her insides churned with pleasure like a dam about to burst.

"No," the captain said.

"But how am I to stop myself?" she cried out in frustration. "I… I can't… I…"

"Distract yourself with other thoughts."

Alice had to squeeze her eyes closed and try to think about something other than the delicious sensations she was feeling. She thought about paying taxes. Doing laundry. Washing the dishes. Being stuck in a business meeting past lunchtime while enduring an endless PowerPoint presentation containing a lot of bar graphs and pie charts. Watching *The View*. But even with her head filled with unsexy thoughts, her body still undulated with the vibrations she was being forced to endure.

Alice thrashed her head back and forth, willing herself not to give in to the pleasure, fighting her body's natural response.

"Queequeg, why don't you help the young lady with her rabbit? Perhaps a bit more vigorous with the motions?"

The pirate took hold of the rabbit's base and began to twist and thrust it, working it in and out of Alice, until all she could do was clench the mattress and bite the side of the pillow to avoid screaming. Queequeg knew what he was doing. He was both gentle and firm, alternately teasing Alice with its length by using slow, shallow strokes, and then entering her hard and pressing it firmly against her G-spot, his thumb on the vibrating ears so the intensity became unbearable.

"I... I need to come!"

"No."

Alice felt the warmth building in her, layer upon layer of pleasure that was quickly starting to peak.

"Please!"

"No."

She tried to retreat from the pirate, to get away from the unrelenting sensations, but he cupped her bottom and held her pinned on the sex toy, lifting her as he plunged it in. Alice began to cry out, somewhere between pleading and sobbing. She just couldn't take anymore.

"Do you want to come now?" the captain asked.

"Yes!"

"Are you certain, love?"

"YES!"

"Good. Now pull it out and set it aside."

Alice felt like wailing as Queequeg withdrew the rabbit, leaving her a quivering jumble of sexual frustration.

"You're... you're so cruel," Alice said.

"We're pirates. We aren't known for our social graces." The captain winked. "But don't you worry. You'll have more than your share at the club. I just wanted you to have a taste of what you signed your poor husband up for. Now let's get moving. Climb into one of these burlap sacks."

Queequeg held one of the items up, ready to pull it down over her head. "See how the sacks are decorated with fine graphics?"

The graphics were indeed fine, especially for being printed on burlap, but Alice made a face. "Is this necessary?"

"I'm afraid it is."

"Can't we just come along with you? Why do we have to get into sacks?"

"Are you kidding? That's why people read these stories. For the graphic sacks."

The pun was almost as awful as the pulsing, wet heat between her legs.

"Hurry now, lassie. We've got quite a night planned for you and your husband both."

Chapter 2

Alice Is Teased and Edged Until She Can't Take it Anymore...

Alice's hands were bound behind her, the graphic burlap covering her head, shoulders and body down to the top of her thighs. Without use of her hands, she hadn't been able to relieve her sexual frustration during the carriage ride.

Lewis was snoring beside her—he could sleep through anything—and Alice tried to focus on something other than the throbbing in her loins. But every time they hit a bump in the cobblestone, it seemed to go right to the center of her womanhood. She'd never been more wet, and to make matters worse, her lower half was exposed, cool air constantly reminding her that her special place was quite bare to the world.

To make matters even worse, the bald pirate Queequeg had taken it upon himself to give Alice the most wonderful foot massage. He began with peppermint oil, rubbing her heels, and the arches of her feet, with strong, expert hands. Alice had always found foot rubs to be sensual, and this callous-handed brute stroked and kneaded her like he was making love to her feet. It did nothing to quell the empty ache in Alice's femininity, and she squirmed as he touched her, trying to find something to rub against to relieve herself, but unable to do anything but hump the air.

Then the pirate began to splay her toes and—

My goodness. He's licking them.

"Such pretty tootsies," he said, low in his throat. Then he took her large toe in his mouth and began to suck.

The sensation was impossible to describe. Somehow her feet had become an erogenous zone, and each lick and stroke brought pleasure as sure as if it had been against her private parts. Alice undulated in her sack, her eyelids fluttering as the pirate's tongue encircled each toe, sucking and nibbling as his hands continued to caress.

"You can have your way with me," Alice whispered, low and throaty.

"I'm fine with what I've got. Always been into feet. And yours are lovely."

He took Alice's entire heel into his mouth and sucked at it as if it were her breast, rolling his tongue around, making the heat between her legs even more unbearable. A pirate with a foot fetish. Who woulda figured?

But then, since so many had peg legs, maybe feet were a novelty.

"Seems as if you like it, dear Alice."

"I do!"

"Seems as if you'd like me to lick and stroke more than just your feet."

"Yes."

"How about I lick slowly up your leg and then slide my tongue between yer thighs? Would ye like that?"

"Oh, yes." Alice rolled her hips. Although she knew what she was doing was more than naughty, cavorting with a pirate while her husband was lying next to her, she couldn't help herself. She was so hot, so wet, Alice could hardly think. She needed relief so badly. Alice tried to arch her pelvis so he had easy access.

"Bet you'd like my cock in your mouth, too."

Alice moved her tongue over her lips, almost able to feel his shaft slip between them, almost able to taste his essence.

"My cock? You like that idea?"

She buried her face shamefully in the sack, but admitted, "Yes."

Queequeg shrugged. "Sorry. The captain won't allow it. You can't come until we get to the Hellfire Club. And I reckon you'll have plenty of hard cocks to savor then. But he said I can touch your feet all I like, and recite my pirate poetry. Would you like to hear a poem?"

This wasn't the time for poetry.

Come to think of it, was there ever a time for poetry? Did anyone actually like poems other than the needy poets who penned them?

"No. I really wouldn't," she answered honestly.

Queequeg began to recite anyway.

"I love to be a pirate,
And sail the seven seas,
I also love lasagna,
With extra feta cheese."

"That's... awful," Alice said.

"Awful? But it rhymes."

"Just because it rhymes it doesn't mean it's good."

"Sure it does. Would you like to hear another?"

"Absolutely not." She wanted to go back to imagining his tongue lapping at her, his hard manhood penetrating her lips.

But Queequeg cleared his throat and began again.

"I searched for better cheddar,
But I could only find pretty gouda."

"Abysmal," Alice said.

"It's blank verse. That's why this one doesn't rhyme."

"I picked up on that. You should have left it completely blank."

"That's a bit rude."

"Why the fixation with cheese?"

"I like cheese. It's my second favorite thing."

"Is your first favorite ravaging extremely horny women?" Alice asked, hopeful.

"No. It is cheese-flavored snacks. Ravaging women is third. But Captain Blackbeard said I'm not to ravage you. And you don't seem very cheesy anyway, although this story certainly is."

"That's the famous Captain Blackbeard?" That she and Lewis had been abducted by a famous pirate hadn't occurred to her. "But his beard is mostly gray."

"Can't a man get older? Got hisself a catchy nickname, so he has to resort to coloring products to keep up with his image? You expect the most feared pirate on the seven seas to touch up his gray with Miss Clairol?"

Alice arched up and opened her legs wider, hoping the sight of her bareness would be enough to move ravishing horny women to the top of the pirate's list. "Hang the rules. Have your way with me. I beg of you. The captain won't know."

"Aye, you're a saucy one, ain't ya?"

"Don't I arouse you?"

"Indeed you do."

Alice took the foot he wasn't orally copulating with and lowered it to below his belt, groping with her toes until she found something very long and very hard.

"Why, you're enormous!"

"That's the hilt of my cutlass, lass. But since you're curious…"

The pirate grabbed her ankle. Shuffling aside fabric, he pressed her foot against something not as long or hard, but definitely warm and male. She rubbed her toes up his length and he moaned.

"Oh, please," Alice said. "I must have it inside me."

"My willy or the handle of my sword?"

Alice sighed. "At this point I'll take anything."

"Anything? Well I have this poem..."

Was he kidding? "Anything other than poetry. Please, I need to come."

"You know what's in store for you at the Hellfire Club. You signed the contract. It's bound to be downright exhausting."

"I don't care. If I don't come soon I fear I'll go insane. I'll do anything you ask. Want me to pretend to be a big wedge of provolone?"

"Intriguing, but I don't think so."

She was getting truly desperate. "What if I also recite bad cheese poetry?"

"What do you mean by *bad*? My dear mother loves my poetry. Said my limburger iambic pentameter was so lyrical she could smell the funky stink."

Alice began her verse.

> *"Eat me like your Roquefort,*
> *Lick me like your parmesan,*
> *Treat me like your cream cheese tort,*
> *I don't have my panties on."*

She tried to gauge his reaction, but Queequeg seemed unimpressed. Alice wondered if she should have gone with her first idea, something to do with *mozzarella* and *blow a fella*. What man could resist that?

"I think I'll go back to sucking your toes," he said.

"Is that all you do?" she asked, petulant. "Cheese poems and foot fetishism?"

275

"I'm also carving my own coffin. I have a feeling I'll be needin' it when the Pequod ships out in a few days. That's what Ismael says."

"Ismael?"

"They call him Ismael."

Alice tried to think of some Moby Dick pun, but Queequeg once again began fellating her toes, ruining her concentration, making her squirm and whimper. She didn't even notice the carriage had stopped until she heard Blackbeard's voice.

"She been begging for it?" he asked.

"Aye, Captain. Quite a case of the hornies, this one has."

"Didn't I say you weren't allowed to come until we reached the Hellfire Club?

"I don't care what you said," Alice spat, defiantly.

"Perhaps I should punish you before we enter the club," the captain said.

"Yes, punish me," Alice said. "I insist." She was so close to orgasm that a few spanks on her bottom would be more than enough to send her over the edge.

"Tie her to the floor of the carriage. I'll give her the Blackbeard special."

Queequeg's eyes got big. "But Captain! That's too cruel!"

"Her insolence warrants it. Bind her."

Soon Alice was happily free of the burlap bag and bound, naked and deliciously spread-eagled, onto the floor of the carriage. Whereas she'd felt so self-conscious when the pirates had first burst in on her while she masturbated, Alice was now completely wanton. Lewis was still sleeping, now heaped on the top of the carriage with the luggage, but she hardly gave a thought to her husband. She could focus only on the exquisite release that was to come. Whatever happened next would no doubt be wonderful.

"Do your worst," she challenged Blackbeard, her skin tingly all over.

The captain got down on his knees and nestled his face between her legs.

Alice felt his hot breath on her thighs, and his long beard tickle her most sensitive spot. She began to thrash her head back and forth, her hips squirming. "God, yes!"

She pressed her pelvis up against his mouth, but Blackbeard pulled away.

"Tie her hips down, too."

When her hips were suitably secured, the captain once again tickled her nether regions with his beard. It was such a light, soft touch, Alice could barely feel it. But each stroke of his whiskers heightened her sensitivity a fraction. She squeezed her eyes closed and tried to focus on his beard, on it gently brushing her engorged clit, back and forth.

Just a little more, and I'll come. Just a little bit more and…

The captain moved his beard away.

Alice clenched her fists and yelled. "No! You… you scoundrel!"

Blackbeard laughed, hard enough for his whole body to shake.

"So this is how you punish me? By making it even worse?"

Queequeg rubbed the bulge in his pants. "I seen the captain do this to one lass for two whole days without letting her come. Poor thing was in tears by the end of it."

"That's inhuman!"

Blackbeard stroked his facial hair, slick with her juices. "It's called edging, dear Alice. Bringing you close, then stopping. It's a form of orgasm denial, and it's what will be done to your poor husband. What's good for the gander is good for the goose. He's to be edged until his balls ache."

Alice felt a pang of pity for Lewis, but then the beard was back, brushing against her as soft as a spider's web. She fought against the ropes. All she needed was a tiny bit more pressure. His lips or tongue on her. Even his chin. Something to rub against so she could relieve the insufferable heat.

But Blackbeard simply continued to stroke, back and forth, up and down, light as a feather. She had never felt so close to coming, but the brute knew just when to stop before allowing it.

"Bet you wish you still had that rabbit," Queequeg said.

Alice's voice was dry and cracked but she said, "Please. I have money."

"And what do you mean to pay us for?' Stroke stroke stroke.

"Lick me."

Stroke stroke. "Lick you where?"

"Between my legs."

"Call me crude, but I prefer it when women talk dirty."

"My pussy." Alice blurted out, feeling both emboldened and ashamed by the vulgarity. "Lick my pussy. I'll pay you to lick my pussy."

Stroke stroke stroke. "I could lick you and put a finger inside at the same time."

"Yes... oh yes... finger fuck me while licking my pussy."

"And maybe you'd like Queequeg to put his cock in your mouth." Stroke stroke.

Alice remembered the feel of his stiff member against her toes. The thought of him in her mouth while the captain licked and fingered was so exciting it brought Alice to the very brink of orgasm. "Yes! I want to suck his cock. I want to suck both of your cocks until you come all over my tits."

She wasn't sure where the idea came from, perhaps faded memories of another adventure, but as the words left her lips, she realized that was exactly what she wanted. She wanted it so badly, she was panting.

"Admit you're a horny little slut."

"Yes," Alice gasped, the words arousing her even more. "Yes, I'm a horny little slut."

"Well, do you know what horny little sluts like you get?"

Alice knew. And she craved it.

"Horny sluts like me get fucked," she said. "Please fuck me. Both of you at once."

"Actually... what you get is this."

Stroke stroke stroke stroke.

Alice screamed in rage and frustration. The two pirates laughed at her agony, and the damnable beard continued to tease her. She was almost ready to die of sexual frustration when the carriage door opened.

The trio looked up to see Madame Bovary, being helped into the carriage by a gentleman companion. The Madame wore a fashionable petticoat dress with ruffles, a black hat, and black, high heeled boots. The fellow wore a tailored black suit. He was swarthy, handsome, perhaps with some gypsy blood in him, and he had a glint in his eye that was either mischievous or cruel.

"Has she come yet?" Madame Bovary asked, looking directly at Alice.

"No, Madame."

"And her husband?"

"Still asleep."

Madame Bovary hiked up her dress and squatted next to Alice. The woman wore no undergarments, and was shaved down there.

"You're suffering now, Alice, pleading for release, aren't you?" she asked.

Alice nodded and stared at the woman's uncovered femininity, which somehow aroused her even more. "Yes. Please help me. I beg you."

"I know how you must feel. The longing. The lusting. Blackbeard certainly knows how to edge. He's so good at orgasm denial it is practically criminal."

Blackbeard tipped his hat. "I could continue for a few more hours, if Madame desires."

"No!" Alice begged. "The contract I signed, it says I'm not to be denied my pleasure."

"I know. It's your husband who is to be edged and denied. I'll be orchestrating that. But you've consigned yourself to something even crueler."

"Nothing can be crueler," Alice said biting her lower lip and shivering as Blackbeard resumed his incessant stroking.

Madame Bovary glanced up at the handsome man whose black eyes were roaming Alice's naked breasts. "This is Mr. Heathcliff. He is one of our experts here at the Hellfire Club. He specializes in orgasm torture."

Heathcliff squatted next to Madame Bovary and smiled pleasantly at Alice. "I'm going to make you come, over and over again."

"That sounds wonderful," Alice moaned.

"You would think so." Heathcliff said mysteriously. "We'll see how you feel after a full day. Release her, bring her to the Swing Room."

Blackbeard finally stopped torturing Alice with his facial hair, and the pirates undid her bonds. Alice quickly reached for her special place to give herself release, but Heathcliff caught her wrists.

"Right now, all you can think about is coming. Very soon, you'll be begging me to stop."

Alice stuck out her chin, defiant. "I welcome that challenge."

Heathcliff smiled. "We shall see. We shall see."

Chapter 3

Alice Begs Heathcliff to Stop Making Her Come...

The rafters in the Swing Room had all manner of hinges, ropes, and pulleys attached to them. Alice was strapped into a leather harness and she was hung two feet above the floor. It supported her weight comfortably, and her legs were in stirrups that kept them wide apart. Her wrists were fastened to the rope above her head.

"So beautiful. So defiant." Heathcliff smiled. "I'm going to have fun breaking you. Taking you to wuthering heights."

"Ugh." Alice wasn't sure what was worse, her unquenched lust, or the stuff that passed for humor in this story.

"Would you like some tea first? I have a special kind."

"Let me guess," Alice said. "Is it Bronte?"

"Three kinds, in fact."

"Can we skip the terrible puns and get to the orgasm torture?" Alice demanded, trying to sound as defiant as he seemed to think she was. In truth, she was a little frightened. She'd been in a swing like this before, back in Wonderland, and the experience had been naughtily divine. But Heathcliff was so mysterious and sexy, that Alice wasn't sure if being at his mercy was more on the frightening side or on the delicious side.

Alice settled on deliciously frightening.

"So are you going to make me come now?"

"So eager." Heathcliff laughed and then knelt between her legs. "But within ten minutes, you'll be begging me to stop. Pleading to rest and recover."

She gave a little shiver, and clenched her bottom in anticipation. "What do you intend to do to me?"

"I'm going to start by eating you out, Alice. I have a particularly large tongue, and I'm quite good at using it. Many a lady in your current position has gone hoarse, screaming for mercy. No doubt you'll soon wake your sleeping husband, and he'll be able to watch your ordeal."

The very thought of it was so electrifying that Alice almost came right then, but the mention of her husband made her curiosity pique. "Where is Lewis?"

"Just beyond that curtain," Heathcliff indicated the partition hanging on the far side of the room. "Madame Bovary will be pleasuring him, but she won't let him come."

"She won't?" Alice remembered the exquisite torture of Blackbeard's gray beard, and the orgasm that still eluded her. She'd signed the contract, but now the idea of putting Lewis through what she'd experienced felt cruel.

"That's what you want, isn't it? For Lewis to last longer? To consider your pleasure rather than selfishly caring only for his own?"

"Yes." He had a point. She wanted their sex life to get better, didn't she? And she was sure Lewis would want that, too. And when it came down to it, her arousal had engorged her nether regions and made her so wet that what pleasures awaited her were all she could really think about. She raised her feminine parts and tried to swing in Heathcliff's direction. "That's why I signed the contract. That, and the hundred orgasms I've been promised."

Heathcliff laughed, deep and heartily. "Only a hundred?"

Alice pursed her lips. "You think me greedy?"

"Of course not. You deserve more than a hundred. And you're about to get them."

"More than a hundred?"

"Dear girl, you must not have read the contract's fine print. You'll be freed when you have a hundred orgasms, but only if your husband doesn't come. If he does, your number is reset and you start over from zero. You might be here for weeks until he learns to control himself."

Before Alice could overcome her shock at the pronouncement, Heathcliff buried his face between her legs. His tongue touched her swollen clitoris and hadn't even begun to lick when Alice's orgasm overwhelmed her.

She gasped and shuddered as she came, her whole body clenching in glorious release. It was one of the most powerful climaxes she'd ever experienced—no doubt because of all the previous edging—and after the contractions ended Alice felt herself on the verge of a second.

Heathcliff slathered her with a slow, fat lick, and another wave of sensation flooded her. It was even more intense, and he buried his long tongue inside her and held her buttocks, bouncing her on the swing as Alice cried out in ecstasy.

Weeks? Alice would gratefully stay here forever! Within a minute Heathcliff had eradicated years of mediocre marital sex. Hopefully he would teach Lewis his tricks so her husband would be equally adept with his mouth.

Alice let her head fall back as Heathcliff expertly went to work, bathing her privates with long, languid licks punctuated by short, stiff jabs inside her. It was so marvelous, so wonderful, that Alice wondered if it was all just a fantasy, because no woman could ever be so fulfilled.

A third orgasm shook Alice, leaving her out of breath.

It was amazing, wonderful, yet when the spasms subsided, she felt another need yawning deep inside, and more than anything, she wanted to be filled. "Make love to me, Heathcliff. Please. I need you inside me."

Heathcliff didn't answer. Nor did he strip off his clothes and fill her with his manhood. Instead, he merely continued to lick, his tongue seemingly insatiable. He pressed her hard against his mouth, focusing entirely on her clit, and a fourth climax overtook her.

Alice tried to close her legs—a reflex reaction because the multiple orgasms had made her sensitive down there. But the ropes and harness kept them wide open, and Heathcliff continued his oral assault.

She grunted, low in her throat. "I want... I want your... I want your cock..."

He coaxed another orgasm from her, and Alice shook in the ropes and tried to swing away from him. His probing, darting tongue had made her so sensitive that it was almost painful. She needed a minute or two to recover, to reset.

But Heathcliff gave her no mercy. If anything, his ravenous tongue increased in speed, forcing Alice to come once again, even though she required a rest.

"Please," Alice said, trying to squirm away from his probing mouth. "I'm too sensitive. I need a moment."

"Five down, ninety-five to go," Heathcliff said between licks.

"I can't... I..."

Once again, an orgasm crashed through Alice, gripping her whole body. Alice screamed again, Heathcliff forcing it out of her even though she fought against her bonds and his tongue.

It was both delirious pleasure and merciless torture at the same time. Alice no longer had any control over her body. It was as if she was an instrument Heathcliff was sadistically playing. He would make her come, she would beg for rest and try to get away, his licking painful on her sensitive bud, but he would keep at it until the pain became intense ecstasy once again.

"Too much... it's too much..."

"We've only just begun."

Alice squeezed her eyes shut. This *was* worse than the edging Blackbeard had made her endure. When orgasms were separated by a few seconds or minutes, Alice could have them all day long. But being made to come over and over again, without any respite, had turned orgasms into some kind of exquisite punishment. She didn't think her body could handle any more stimulation, but Heathcliff wouldn't let up. After she came, when her female parts were most tender, he would increase his speed and pressure, causing her body to clench and shake in an effort to get away from him.

But Alice couldn't get away. She was his helpless prisoner, forced to endure climax after climax even as she pleaded for mercy.

"I can't take anymore... I can't... please..."

He took her sensitive clit in his mouth and sucked upon it, hard, while furiously assaulting it with his tongue.

"I beg you," Alice begged, coming for the tenth time.

Heathcliff looked up at her, rubbing her sore, swollen clit with his thumb. "No mercy, dear Alice."

"Don't I have a safe word?" she moaned. "Something I can do to make this stop?"

"There are no safe words in the Swing Room, Alice. I will continue to force you to have orgasms until you reach a hundred, or until you pass out. How many have you had so far?"

"Eleven."

"From now on, you're to count them aloud." He began to lick her again, with increased intensity. "Welcome to the Hellfire Club."

Chapter 4

Lewis Learns a Lesson In Orgasm Denial...

Lewis awoke to the sound of a woman screaming, somewhere close by. A sound he knew intimately well.

Alice.

Even though his head was still fuzzy from sleep, he recognized this kind of screaming from earlier in their relationship, before their sex life had become perfunctory and routine. Alice was coming. Hard. And from the intensity of her cries, Lewis knew whomever was making her come was doing a very good job.

He wanted to be that person.

Lewis opened his eyes and tried to sit up. Couldn't. He was tied to a padded, leather table, his arms stretched out over his head. He strained against his bonds and found them to be strong and tight. Then he looked down and saw he was naked.

Where the hell were they?

Alice screamed again, ecstasy dripping from the sound. "Please! No more! I can't take another! I beg you to stop!"

Lewis followed her pleas, realizing they came from behind a curtain on the far end of the room.

Then his wife began to moan again, low in her throat, then rising in pitch.

He tried to remember where they were, how they'd gotten here, but the last thing he recalled was falling asleep after some mediocre sex with Alice. So what happened? Had they been kidnapped?

The seriousness of the situation should have hit him hard, but instead his wife's cries had a different effect. His cock grew long and stiff, stretching upward along his belly.

Alice was being ravaged, just beyond the curtain, and all Lewis could think about was how turned-on he was.

"You did this to her," a female voice from behind him said.

Lewis craned his neck to see who was speaking. It was a woman dressed in thigh-high boots as black as her hair. She wore a leather corset that pushed her bare breasts out, nipples hard and pointing toward him. He skimmed his eyes lower, and realized she wore no additional undergarments, and her feminine parts were shaved and smooth. In her hand she held a black riding crop.

"Who are you? Where are we?"

"This is the Hellfire Club. I am Madame Bovary." She skimmed her riding crop over her breasts and rested its leather tongue against one protruding nipple.

"I demand you release us immediately."

Madame Bovary smiled in a way that was quite cruel. "You signed the contract. You paid for your stay here. You cannot leave until the contract is honored."

Behind the curtain, Alice moaned, "Yes, I'm a dirty little slut! I'm a dirty little slut! Now please, stop!"

"What contract?" Lewis asked, but his attention was mostly focused on his wife's moans and this stranger's nipples.

Madame Bovary produced a piece of parchment covered in ornate script. At the bottom were his and Alice's signatures. Lewis vaguely recalled signing it after dinner several days ago. Alice had brought it to him when he'd been tipsy with mead and half-asleep, saying something about how it would improve their marriage.

"What did I sign?" he asked, suddenly fearful. Had he unknowingly conscripted them to sexual slavery?

"You and Alice are to stay at the Hellfire Club until the terms of the contract have been fulfilled."

"What terms?"

"Alice must have one hundred orgasms before being allowed to leave."

Lewis blew out a sigh of relief. Though he'd been an inattentive and selfish lover these past few years, he knew full well his wife's capacity and appetite for sex. Alice would enjoy herself; she was clearly enjoying herself right now. A hundred orgasms shouldn't take more than a day or two.

"How many has she had already?"

"A dozen at least, I'd guess from her cries. Heathcliff is quite gifted at making women come. Even when they are completely exhausted. But while your Alice is being forced to orgasm, you shall be allowed none." Madame Bovary raised an eyebrow. "Which seems fair, considering how many you've had during your marriage at the expense of your poor, long suffering wife."

Ouch. That hurt. "She... told you that?"

"She did. It's the main reason she came to us."

"I know I haven't been a very good lover. But when, when we're... *together*..."

"You mean when you're fucking?"

Madame Bovary ran the end of the crop up Lewis's bare thigh, making his erect cock twitch.

"Yes, well, when we are, Alice enjoys it as much as I do."

"Is that what you believe? That all she needs is a kiss on the cheek and thirty seconds of your pathetic thrusting? You think that satisfies her?"

Lewis felt his face redden.

"Did you ever ask her if she was happy with your sex life?"

"We... never talked about it."

"She never tried to talk about it with you?"

Lewis swallowed. He recalled the many times Alice had broached the subject of lovemaking, and he'd always brushed her off. It wasn't that he didn't love Alice, or care about her needs. But work was stressful, and he was often tired at the end of the day. Every other part of their relationship was perfect. So, the sex was mediocre. If that was all that was wrong with their marriage, Lewis happily accepted it.

"I admit I avoided that particular subject," he said. "But I fail to see how this remedies anything. I have to lay here and listen to my wife have orgasms, while I can't have any. Is that supposed to even the score?"

"Alice is a loving, generous, gracious woman. She didn't come here to even any scores, or punish you for being a poor lover." Madame Bovary leaned over, slinging her breasts forward, her stiff nipples brushing against Lewis's neck as she whispered, "Though I may do a bit of punishing of my own accord."

The riding crop flicked against Lewis's stiff rod with a *thwack*, and he cried out.

"Then why are we here?" Lewis said, somewhat hoarsely.

"Training. Alice will be trained to come faster, so even your poorest attempts at lovemaking will satisfy her. And you..." Madame Bovary reached down and gripped Lewis's manhood. She began to pump it vigorously. "You will be trained to last longer."

"Uhhhnn," Lewis answered.

"Every time you come, Alice must start again from zero."

"Say what?"

"If you ejaculate, Alice will be forced to endure another hundred orgasms."

"But... you're stroking me!"

"And your hips are bucking, rising to meet my hand. You're a selfish lover, Lewis. Eager for your own satisfaction while caring not of poor Alice's needs. But we shall teach you self- control."

Lewis squeezed his eyes closed and forced himself to remain still, but Madame Bovary continued to pleasure him. She went from long, languorous strokes to hard, fast ones.

"Look at how quick you are," she said. "A drop of your essence has already leaked from your tip."

Lewis felt a tongue slowly swirl across his glans, and he shuddered with pleasure.

"This isn't fair!"

"Were all of your marital quickies fair?" Madame Bovary said as she returned to pumping him, the moisture from her mouth lubricating her fist. She had switched her grip so her thumb rubbed under the ridge of his head every time she moved her hand up.

"No," Lewis admitted, though it came out more like a moan.

"Would you like to see what Heathcliff is doing to Alice right now?"

Lewis did want to see. Alice was now alternating between pants and whimpers, and it turned him on tremendously to see her in the throes of pleasure. But if he were any more turned on, he'd be past the point of no return and spurt all over Madame Bovary's knuckles.

"I'd like to see," Lewis said, "but only if you stop what you're doing with your hand."

"Fair enough."

Madame Bovary released Lewis and walked over to the velvet curtain. With a lascivious grin she tugged the partition back, revealing the debauchery in the adjacent room.

Alice—sweet, dear Alice—was totally naked and hanging from the ceiling on some sort of swing, several feet off the floor. Her legs were in stirrups, spread wide, and like Lewis her hands were bound above her head.

Kneeling between her legs was a dark-haired man Lewis presumed was Heathcliff. His head was buried there, shaking back and forth aggressively, as Alice cried out in her throat. Heathcliff was shirtless, broad-shouldered and muscular, his hands cupping Alice's bottom as his thumbs parted her womanhood wider.

Lewis felt himself very close to coming, and his prick jerked and twitched at the sight of his wife being so vigorously licked.

"How many orgasms have you had so far, Alice?" Madame Bovary asked.

"Fifteen," Alice moaned. "Please let me rest. I can't take any more."

"Describe to your husband what Heathcliff is doing to you."

Alice's eyes widened when she saw Lewis. "Lewis! You must be… appalled… seeing me like this."

Lewis tried to swallow. "You're so beautiful, Alice. I wish it were me with you right now."

"Describe it," Madame Bovary demanded, her voice deep and stern.

"He's torturing me with orgasms. Licking me. Nipping me. Swirling his tongue all over me. My clit feels as if it is aflame, and he… ooohhhhh!" Alice shuddered. "Sixteen! He keeps punishing me with his terrible tongue. He won't let me rest, even for a moment. I can't take any more. I'll go insane."

"Has he penetrated you yet?"

"No. I wish he would. Anything to stop his licking."

"Be careful what you wish for, Alice," Madame Bovary said. "Heathcliff can do things far more intense to you than the tongue lashing you're currently receiving. He hasn't even taken out his toys yet. Sixteen orgasms is only the beginning."

Lewis was amazed. Sixteen orgasms, all through oral stimulation? The most he'd ever given Alice was two. He watched as Alice thrashed on the swing and then mumbled, "Seventeen."

Then his attention was drawn by Madame Bovary, who had substituted her riding crop with a long, black, raven's feather. She began to stroke it along his shaft. It was a wonderfully sublime sensation, and Lewis's cock seemed to grow even stiffer.

"See how she handles one finger, Heathcliff."

Heathcliff turned and smiled, his handsome face slick with Alice's juices. Then Lewis watched as he slowly inserted his index finger into Alice.

"Oh, my!" Alice gasped. "Eight… eighteen…"

Heathcliff began to work his finger in and out, and with the same rhythm Madame Bovary teased Lewis's cock with the feather.

"Describe what he's doing to you, Alice."

"He has… his finger… unnnhhhh… inside me…"

"What's he doing with his finger?"

Heathcliff began to move so quickly, his hand was a blur. Alice screamed.

"Fucking me! He's finger fucking me!" Alice grimaced and threw her head back, her bare breasts bobbing with the rhythm of Heathcliff's penetration. "Oh… nineteen!"

Madame Bovary tickled the head of Lewis's cock with the raven feather, and Lewis was so turned on he was moments away from spurting all over.

"Please stop…" Lewis said. "I'm going to come."

"Don't come, Lewis!" Alice screamed. "I can't bear to start over!"

Lewis closed his eyes, trying to blot out the sight of Alice naked and in ecstasy, trying to tune out her moans, trying not to feel the gentle stroking of his manhood with that awful feather.

"Keep your eyes open or I'll oil up my hand and finish you off," Madame Bovary said. "And after you come, I'll continue to stroke you."

"That's cruel. It's too sensitive after I come."

"That's what your poor wife is enduring right now."

Lewis opened his eyes. He watched as Heathcliff slipped a second finger inside Alice.

"Describe what he's doing, Alice."

"His… oh God… his fingers are rubbing my G-spot. I'm going to… I'm going to… twenty!"

"Please," Lewis said, his whole body shuddering. "I can't bear to watch."

"But watch you must. Look closely as Heathcliff uses his fingers and tongue at the same time."

Heathcliff did as Madame Bovary said, going down on Alice as he thrust his digits inside her, and Lewis's wife made a sound he'd never heard before. It was like the growl of a bear, and she thrashed back and forth with an intensity Lewis didn't even think was possible.

It was too arousing, too erotic, for him to handle. And as his wife shook with orgasm, Lewis's prick jerked and he spurted all over his belly. With so little stimulation, his orgasm was a poor one.

"Oh, Lewis!" Alice cried. "No!"

"I warned you," Madame Bovary said. She went to the chest and removed a bottle of oil, pouring it on Lewis's still-twitching manhood. Then she began to stroke him.

Lewis cried out. His cock was too sensitive, and her touch was painful. But she continued to pull on him as he struggled in vain to get away.

"This is what bad husbands get for coming too soon," Madame Bovary said, torturing him with tugs.

Lewis groaned in agony. It was worse than tickling. Worse even than pain.

"Do you wish me to stop?" Madame Bovary said.

"Yes! Please!"

"Then make me come."

She climbed atop Lewis, straddling his face, her bare sex pressed against his lips. Lewis began to lick her, desperately wanting her to stop tormenting his poor, sensitive penis.

"Do you like seeing me sit on your husband's face, Alice?" Madame Bovary said. "When was the last time you did? Answer me."

"Years," Alice moaned.

Years? Had it really been that long? Lewis closed his eyes, despising himself as Madame Bovary continued to torment him. He deserved this, and more, for taking Alice for granted.

"One!" Alice yelled.

"Lick harder," Madame Bovary commanded. "We'll make a lover out of you yet, Lewis."

Chapter 5

Alice Gets to Thirty
(Which Was Really Many More but
She Had to Start over Because of Lewis)…

Heathcliff was just as devious with his fingers as he was with his tongue, and he ripped climax after climax out of Alice until she felt ready to collapse. Even worse, watching Madame Bovary torture Lewis turned Alice on something fierce. She rode his face while teasing his soft manhood, crying out in orgasm as her husband whimpered in agony. But, incredibly, Bovary's expert hands were able to reinvigorate Lewis's arousal. Alice couldn't remember the last time he'd gotten it up twice in one day, let alone twice within ten minutes. Watching it made Heathcliff's orgasm torture even more unbearable.

Madame Bovary came a second time, then crawled off of Lewis's face and impaled herself on his cock, reverse-cowgirl.

It was Lewis's favorite position. He always loved to watch his shaft disappear inside Alice as she bobbed up and down. And Madame Bovary was good at it, making her strokes slow and sensual, her breasts swinging with each plunge. Alice groaned inwardly, and then outwardly. Her husband wouldn't last long.

As Madame Bovary humped Lewis, she said, "Get your toys, Heathcliff. And get the wordsmith to help you."

Mercifully, Heathcliff stopped his oral assault, and Alice was left hanging there, open and exposed, dripping with arousal, watching a beautiful woman ride her husband. She caught Lewis's eyes, and his were intense with passion.

"I will try to hold out for you, sweet Alice," he said.

Then Madame Bovary reached down and began to knead his balls as she rode him. He moaned.

Alice continued to watch the coupling. She'd never really gotten into pornography, but this was different. She wasn't watching some well-hung actor. She was watching her husband, his shaft hard and ready, his eyes electric with lust. And Madame Bovary was so beautiful, wild and aggressive, her breasts buckling with each thrust. Alice could hear every moan, every slap as the woman sheathed Lewis's full length. She could smell the tangy scent of sweat and arousal, Lewis's, Madame Bovary's, and her own.

The more she experienced the scene, sitting in the swing, drenched and open, the more electric she felt. In under a minute she'd gone from begging Heathcliff for mercy to wondering what was taking him so long to get back to her. Thinking about him, between her legs, entering her with his fingers, maybe even his cock, made Alice squirm in her harness.

"I see I haven't broken you yet," Heathcliff said, his eyes gleaming. "No worries. I've got a friend who can assist."

A stern, brooding man with a long goatee walked into the Swing Room. He was at least twice Alice's age, and wore a vintage tuxedo.

"Alice, allow me to introduce bestselling author Charles Dickens."

Alice frowned at the new arrival, her ardor cooling, at least a little. "I'm familiar with Mr. Dickens. He screwed me many years ago."

"He did?" Heathcliff asked.

Alice nodded. "In high school. I had to read Little Dorrit and got a D on the book report."

"I'm sorry to hear that," Dickens said. "Hopefully I can make up for it."

"I don't see how."

"Well," Dickens smiled politely, "I have great expectations."

Lewis groaned. It may have been from Madame Bovary's undulations, but Alice leaned toward it being the bad Dickens joke.

No doubt there would be more, as well.

"Can we get the Tale of Two Titties pun out of the way before we get started?" Alice asked.

"My, she's a saucy one, Heathcliff." Dickens focused on her naked titties and grinned. "What are we using on her?"

"I'm going to use the Hitachi wand on her bare clitoris, while you work on her with the dildo stick."

"That should temper her literary criticism for a bit."

"I suspect there will be a *Hard Times* reference as well," Alice said.

"Perhaps a ball gag, too," Dickens suggested.

"Good idea."

Alice abhorred ball gags. When she could no longer talk she felt depersonalized. Just a mindless animal, acting on instinct while strange, mysterious men played with her helpless body. Like cruel children with a toy.

The very idea made her shiver in anticipation, and when Heathcliff strapped the gag in her mouth Alice had a small orgasm.

"Eimm," she mumbled.

"I think she said *eight*," Dickens said.

"I'm making her count her orgasms," Heathcliff said. He was holding a stick the width and length of a broom. But rather than straw bristles on the end, instead there was a large, black dildo. Alice's eyes widened at the sight.

"Never seen one before?" Heathcliff asked.

Alice shook her head, feeling her breath catch.

"I picked it up at the old curiosity shop," Dickens said. "Right next to the Pickwick Club."

"Charles, would you like to show the lady how it works?"

"With pleasure." Dickens took the stick and rubbed the tip against Alice's opening. "The long handle allows for much greater control. One can do things with this that are impossible with a regular dildo. For example..."

Dickens eased the rubber shaft into Alice. She was quite wet from all the earlier activities, and she stretched wonderfully open to accommodate its width. It felt otherworldly, and she moaned.

He started by plunging languorously in and out. Each time he sank the full length into her, Alice gasped for air, sensations building.

"Now watch how fast I can go."

With short, three inch strokes, Dickens caused Alice to scream in her throat. It was much faster than she could ever do to herself with her rabbit. It was even faster than a man could make love to her.

"And I can also use a turning, churning motion," Dickens said. "I like to call this the Oliver twist."

As he pushed in and out of her, Dickens twisted the rubber cock like a turn of the screw (even though that was written by Henry James, not Dickens). The sensation was so magnificent, so overpowering, Alice couldn't draw a breath. When she was finally able to fill her lungs she mumbled, "Enn."

"That's ten, Charles," Heathcliff said. "You've given her two."

Then her bottom was being cupped, and Alice's clitoris ignited. Heathcliff was holding the world's strongest back massager—a Hitachi wand vibrator—against her as Dickens continued his thrusting.

The combination of both at once was mind-blowing. Alice went into orgasm overload. She couldn't think, had no control over herself, and lost her mind to the intensity of the experience. It was less like a climax and more like convulsions, taking her to a place she'd never been before.

Not even in her previous fantasies.

Alice was vaguely aware of Lewis crying out, so loud that Charles dropped the dildo stick.

"I do believe that Lewis scared the dickens out of her," Heathcliff said.

"He came again," Madame Bovary said. "Restart her count."

"Not a problem," Dickens said, entering Alice again. "Now let's change the angle and give that g-spot a workout."

As Lewis yelled again, Madame Bovary tugging on his spent cock, Alice gave in fully to the seemingly endless multiple orgasms, one peak crashing into the next until she lost herself completely. She was vaguely aware of Heathcliff licking her neck and her nipples as her body contorted and she was rocked with never ending pleasure.

Also, she decided that maybe Little Dorrit wasn't that bad after all.

It went on and on and on. Dickens kept changing positions and angles, coaxing new sensations from her. Heathcliff fingered her labia open and pressed the Hitachi firmly against her exposed, swollen clitoris, keeping it there even as she thrashed and shook.

When she reached an uncountable number of climaxes, Alice hung there, limp and exhausted, momentarily confused as to why the gentlemen had stopped. A moment later she was being lowered gently to the floor, Heathcliff rubbing her wrists, Dickens removing the gag and handing her a delicious glass of cold orange juice. It took her a few minutes to remember where she was, and when she looked for Lewis in the other room she noted he was gone.

"Where's my husband?" she asked lazily, surprised by how little she cared.

"Poor chap was having some difficulty maintaining his fifth erection." Dickens said. "Madame Bovary took him to get a Viagra shot."

"Five?" Alice asked. "I only noticed the two."

"That's common during orgasm torture," Heathcliff said. "The experience is so intense you lose track of time."

"How many did I have?"

"Altogether? Well over a hundred and fifty. But because of Lewis's poor performance, we can only credit you with thirty."

Alice stretched and yawned. "I feel wonderful. Almost drunk."

"I'm sorry we had to stop. You were really into it."

Alice sipped more juice. "So… while we're waiting… perhaps the two of you would like to…" She stared at the bulges in each man's trousers, imagining one in her mouth and one gloriously fucking her.

"Speaking for us both, we'd love to, Alice." Heathcliff smiled, but his eyes were sad. "But Madame Bovary said, as soon as you're able, we're to take you to the baths."

"What happens in the baths?" Alice asked.

Dickens shrugged. "Baths, of course. Oh, and degenerate sex. Same as every room at the Hellfire Club."

"Will you two be joining me?" she asked. She'd grown fond of them and could imagine lounging in warm water, a stiff cock in each hand.

"That would be lovely," Dickens said. "But we have to stay here and work on a woman named Jezebel. She fell off a beanstalk or some such silliness. We're supposed to take her mind off of things."

"Oh. Well, I can't say that I'm not disappointed. You both were quite extraordinary, and I haven't come that many times in, well, *ever*. I'd really love to have the opportunity to pay you back."

"Your pleasure is our payment," Heathcliff said.

"Maybe next time?" she said.

"You can count on it."

Alice tried to stand up, but found she was still a bit dizzy and her knees were weak. Heathcliff wrapped her in a white silk kimono and scooped her up in his strong arms.

He carried her through the Hellfire Club, and Alice feasted her eyes on some tasteful interior decorating, along with many fascinating acts of debauchery.

The first room they passed held a large, wooden pillory. The device was clamped around the head and neck of a woman, forcing her to stand bent at the waist, legs locked in a splayed position. A line of men stood behind and in front, waiting their turns to enter her in a variety of ways, sending her full breasts bounding with their thrusts. Each time one man finished, grunting his satisfaction, the woman yelled, "Bring on the next hard cock!" And so her wish was granted, a ready shaft being pushed into her mouth or between her open nether lips.

If Alice wasn't luxuriously exhausted, she might be ready to try something like that.

The next room was abuzz with electricity… literally. Couples lounged on simple couches and braced themselves against walls. Some were bound, some not, but all of them were experimenting with some kind of electric devices, many causing visible electric arcs and zapping sounds.

"What are they using?" Alice asked Heathcliff.

"They're stimulating various erogenous zones with violet wands and TENS units."

"What are those?"

"Violet wands deliver an electric charge, like a shock. It can be quite stimulating."

"Ooo," Alice said, thinking of how much fun she could have with that, depending on the region zapped. "And TENS units?"

"They connect to electrodes that are either adhered to the skin or inserted inside."

"Inserted inside?" Alice could almost imagine how that would feel. "Like an electric shock dildo?"

"Or a butt plug, yes. But those don't feel like shocks. The electricity causes the muscles to contract. The sensation is similar to the contractions of an orgasm."

Now *that* Alice could imagine. "Maybe we could go back there?"

"Maybe, dear Alice." He kept moving down the hall.

The next area they passed smelled good enough to make Alice's stomach rumble. But the scene itself wasn't just about eating. It was a vegan orgy where fruits and veggies were being used in a much more erotic way. Bananas appeared to be popular, as did carrots, and grapes. One adventurous woman, surrounded by a semi-circle of appreciative onlookers, was doing something mind-boggling to an enormous butternut squash. And a lone man was having what appeared to be an intense argument with a pineapple as he fingered a tomato, neither of those euphemisms.

Saying goodbye to the fruits and veggies, they moved on to a very curious room. Divided by a thin wall, men lined one side, women the other. Between the two were holes at genital level. Many of the men thrust their hard members through the holes, the women on the other side doing whatever they liked with mouth and pussy and breasts. Alice had heard about these—glory holes they were called—and she always thought it would be wicked fun to have sex with a totally anonymous cock in that way.

The next room wasn't a room at all but a small amphitheater. Grandstands of seats surrounded the stage where a woman was chained to some sort of vibrating saddle device while being spanked by a handsome man dressed in a leather cape. She thrashed wildly, and the sounds she made rivaled Alice's in the Swing Room.

Next was an oral sex daisy chain, twelve people in a circle, each sucking and licking while being sucked and licked. It seemed like a perfect example of cooperation.

Next, a man in a latex vacuum bed, who breathed through a tube while women rubbed oil and themselves over his vacuum-encased body. It looked more odd than stimulating, but to each their own.

Next, a wrestling mat, where female combatants wore strap-ons. Alice wasn't sure what determined wins and losses, but perhaps that wasn't the point. After watching for a moment, she realized that everyone was a winner.

A foot worship area was after that, where Alice found Queequeg, who was dividing his time between licking a pretty girl's toes and licking a large wedge of brie. He gave her a wave.

"Hello, Alice. Would you like to hear more poetry?"

"How can I phrase this nicely?" Alice asked. "I'd rather be stabbed to death with rusty forks and my body thrown to wolves."

"A quick one then." Queequeg cleared his throat and said:

"Cheeze Whiz, Cheese Whiz
All I see is Cheese Whiz
It's in my pants
It's in my hair
It's up my ass
It's everywhere."

"Dreadful," Alice said.
"Perhaps another, then."
"Please, no."
"It's a short one."
"I still couldn't bear it."
Queequeg recited anyway.

*"I ate some bad cheese,
And I got a disease."*

"Deplorable," Alice told him. "I want those three seconds of my life back."

Queequeg laughed, waved her off, then went back to his toe and brie sucking. Heathcliff continued the tour.

They passed a bound man who was having hot candle wax poured onto his body as he whimpered. To Alice it seemed unpleasant, but the man's enormous, twitching erection told a different story.

And then, a room filled with people eating hot wings. Nothing erotic about it at all, but they smelled pretty good.

They also passed a room with a lot of semi-clothed people going to the bathroom.

"Call me a prude," Alice said, "but I never understood how people could get aroused by bodily functions. Especially enough to dedicate a whole room to it."

"That's the restroom," Heathcliff said.

"Oh. Nevermind, then."

"Even so, Alice, nothing is morally wrong if two adults consent to it. One person's turn-off could be another person's kink. There's a character here who walks around wearing a diaper and acting immature."

"Really? Who?"

"A Danish Prince named Hamlet. He's always moping about, asking 'to pee or not to pee'."

"Why does he do that?"

"That is the question."

Eventually they came to a room which seemed straight out of ancient Rome, complete with Doric columns, a large pool of steaming water, and various naked statues. Chained to one of them, sporting a lovely hard-on, was—

"Lewis!"

Heathcliff set Alice on her feet, and she ran to her husband, feeling a sudden urge of affection for him. She kissed him on the mouth, but he demurred.

"Lewis, what's wrong?"

"Oh, Alice. I've let you down."

What could she say? In the bedroom, he had. In their marriage, he had. And that one time they spent three hours driving around Pittsburgh because he refused to stop and ask for directions, he had.

"That's why we're here, sweetheart. We're going to change that. This whole thing is about improving our marriage."

"I don't know…"

"Lewis?" Alice hadn't planned for this. Lewis had always liked sex, but what if by signing them up for the Hellfire Club, Alice had gone too far? What if she'd endangered their marriage?

"I know it may not be fun for you to see me having sex with all these other men…"

"It's not that, Alice. Honestly. That's a gigantic turn-on. You're so incredibly sexy."

"Then what is it, Lewis? You're scaring me."

He hung his head, and everything about him seemed to droop in defeat. Everything except for his magnificently hard phallus, that is.

Alice reached for it. "I only really want you, Lewis. You have to know that." She curled her fingers around his base, right above his soft sack.

"No, Alice. Don't."

"I would give up all of it, even orgasms for the rest of my life, to be married to you." She stroked her hand up his length, wanting to throw off the silk robe to rub herself all over him and then pull him deep inside.

"Alice, no. Don't touch me."

She pulled her hand back. Mouth open, mind refusing to absorb what he'd just said. "You can't mean that."

"I do."

Tears turned her vision into a Roman bath. "What are you trying to tell me? That it's over?"

"Over?" he said, as if he wasn't following.

"Our marriage. You want a di—" She couldn't say the word.

He shook his head, violently. "No! Of course not! Oh, Alice…"

She reached for him again.

"But you can't touch me. Please. You're so sexy, so beautiful, that your touch will make me come for sure."

Alice glanced down at his erection. "Oh, I hadn't thought of that. Sorry."

"But that's not all, Alice. Sometimes I do wonder…"

"Wonder what?" From the corner of her eye, Alice could see a woman on the edge of the bath. Dark hair to her waist, small gold band encircling her head, she was totally naked otherwise. Small shapely breasts turned up in a dusky nipple. The hair around her special place shaved into the shape of a cat's head. Was she here for Lewis?

"Are you listening to me, Alice?"

"Oh, sorry. Sometimes you wonder what?"

"Why you ever married me."

Alice brought her full attention back to her husband. "I chose you, Lewis."

"But why? I don't deserve you."

"Don't say that."

"Why not? It's true. I've never known how to please you like Heathcliff and Dickens did. Like you please me. I took you for granted…"

"We're going to fix that, remember?"

He let out a sigh.

"Do you want to fix it, Lewis?"

"More than anything."

"Okay, then try."

He nodded.

"I mean really try," she said with emphasis. "When the pirate was using the rabbit on me, he suggested—"

"The Pirate? A rabbit? You mean the rabbit I bought you when we were dating?"

"Never mind that. But I wasn't supposed to come, and he suggested I distract myself with my thoughts. So I concentrated on the most unsexy things I could think of. Can you do that?"

"While seeing you naked and writhing in ecstasy? I don't know. It will be hard, and by hard, I mean like this." He looked down at his hardness which was indeed hard.

And she wasn't even naked at the moment.

Or writhing.

"Do your best, Lewis. Try." She almost said *try hard*, but figured that might be a little repetitive.

Lewis raised his chin bravely and looked into her eyes. "I will, Alice. For you."

Chapter 6

Lewis Watches Alice Get a Taste of Good Clean Fun. And by Good Clean Fun, We Mean a Sexy Bath. And by Taste… Oh, You Figure It Out…

Lewis was so busy watching the shapely curves of his wife's body under that silken robe that he jumped in surprise when he heard the sexy tones of a strange female voice.

"I'm here to make you feel beautiful, Alice," she said. Black hair poured down her back, glossy and smooth. A gold band encircled her head like a crown, the front turned up in an ornament that resembled a snake with ruby eyes. And her clothing…

Er, she wasn't wearing any.

He felt the sight of her naked, upturned breasts, mocha skin, shapely hips, and bare lips (the *other* kind of lips) add to the torturous want he was already feeling at the sight of his wife.

Where Madame Bovary had been sexy, the surprise of finding himself naked and tied while a rogue of a man licked and finger fucked and used all manner of sex toys on his wife had tempered his desire.

At least a very tiny bit.

But this woman's beauty, and the way she stared at Alice and spoke her name... Lewis worried he'd have even more trouble distracting himself than he'd anticipated.

But he had to do it. For Alice.

The woman reached the edge of the steaming Roman bath. She skimmed hands over Alice's shoulders and began kneading her muscles with strong fingers.

"Oh, that feels so good," Alice said.

"Sex is about feeling good, my dear." She smiled. "It's about feeling beautiful, feeling desirable, feeling powerful."

Alice drew in a shuddering breath. "Yes. Powerful. Irresistible."

"And does your husband make you feel that way?"

Lewis tensed, wishing for the answer he knew Alice could only give if she were telling a lie.

Alice opted for the truth. "No, he doesn't."

The woman stared at him, but her gaze wasn't reproachful. The message in her eyes was worse.

Pity.

"You will pay close attention? I will show you how to make a woman feel beautiful, powerful, irresistible. I will teach you."

Lewis nodded, eager to learn. "Thank you... I'm sorry, I don't know your name."

"Cleopatra," the woman said.

"Cleopatra? The Queen of the Nile?"

She shook her head. "No, that would be Madame Bovary."

"Madam Bovary?" Alice asked.

"Yes. As Lewis knows, she's the true queen of denial." Cleopatra winked. "And by the time we are finished, Alice will feel like a queen as well."

Lewis smiled. Alice was fond of royalty. She was sure to enjoy this.

And enjoy she did. Cleopatra smoothed her hands down Alice's arms, pulling the robe off on the way and letting it pool onto the marble floor. Then she skimmed her hands back up Alice's sides and cupped her perfect breasts, teasing the nipples with her fingers.

Alice closed her eyes, her head slightly back and let out a moan. Then she moved her own hands behind her grasping Cleopatra's buttocks and pulling her tight against her back.

They just stood like that for a long time, both women cupping and caressing, grabbing and grinding. Blatantly naked in front of him.

"You see, Lewis? I am appreciating Alice's body, and in turn, she is appreciating mine."

"And I'm appreciating the appreciating," he said. He couldn't get any harder, but the inspiring scenery in front of him was beginning to make him ache.

"I am worshipping her with my touch," Cleopatra continued, running one hand over Alice's belly and dipping between her thighs. "Not just telling her she's beautiful, but showing her, seducing her."

Alice moaned.

Lewis's manhood twitched in response. Watching Cleopatra, he could imagine her hands were his, the softness of Alice's back and breasts as he held her close, his cock nudging between her legs from behind, the vibration of her moan registering in his chest.

And when a man cleared his throat on the other side of the naked statue Lewis was bound to, Lewis jumped again, sending his painfully hard erection bouncing.

"Beautiful, aren't they?" the man said.

Lewis reluctantly ripped his eyes from the swaying women to look at the new addition. Like the woman, he was a fine specimen. Dressed in armor that covered his chest and shoulders, he was bare from the waist down except for the sandals strapped to his feet. Dark hair sprinkled his legs and peeked out under the armor spanning his broad chest, but his package was nearly hair free.

But that wasn't what Lewis found remarkable.

The man's penis was huge; thick as Lewis's wrist. It reached up like a sword, tight to his belly, veins cording under soft skin. And at the head, a barbell piercing that went sideways through the glans. It looked like someone had stuck a gold nail through the top of a long potato.

"Wow," Lewis said before he could stop himself.

"I'm Marc Antony," he said, tilting his hips forward as if saluting Lewis with his stiff cock.

"Are you here… for me?" Lewis said, a little worried about the answer.

Okay, a lot worried.

"Do you want me to be?" Marc said.

"No."

"Then I'm not. At least for now."

That sounded a little threatening to Lewis, and he held on to that thought, figuring it might help him keep his passion under control. A distraction, as Alice said.

Alice…

He turned back to her. The women were facing each other, breast rubbing breast. Cleopatra reached up and stroked Alice's blond hair. She cradled the back of Alice's neck and drew her close, kissing her mouth.

As Cleopatra had worshiped Alice's body with her hands, now she worshiped with her lips. First lightly, pulling away to brush Alice's cheeks, chin, neck. Then stronger, harder, claiming Alice, exploring her with her tongue, nipping at her lips.

Doing to Alice's mouth what Heathcliff had done to her *other* lips.

It was tortuous to see. Two beautiful, sensual women, kissing each other, just out of his reach.

Just when Lewis thought he might not be able to take any more, the Egyptian Queen gave Alice one more very deep, very intimate kiss, then looked at Lewis. "Are you wet, Alice?"

"Yes," Alice said on a puff of breath.

"How wet? Touch yourself."

Alice skimmed a hand over her belly and dipped her fingers between her thighs. She tilted her head back and groaned. "Very wet. Your kisses, they're divine." She pulled her fingers free, just as Cleopatra claimed Alice in another kiss.

Lewis watched his sweaty wife shudder. "Thirty-one."

Cleo (Lewis figured he could call her that since she was having her way with his wife) again turned her focus on him. "But Alice, you came when you weren't even touching yourself."

"I was... I was so close. And your kiss..."

The women resumed kissing, and Lewis had to glance away.

"Can't take the heat, eh?" Marc Antony said as watched the women and stroked his powerful length. "That's part of mastering control. Married to such a vivacious woman, you're no doubt constantly stimulated. But you need to take your time. There's no rush. If things get too intense too fast, slow down. It doesn't have to be a race to orgasm. Enjoy the whole voyage."

Feeling totally inadequate, Lewis forced himself to look back to his wife, determined to be as strong as the conqueror beside him.

The women had untangled from one another now and were descending the steps into the steaming water. Something scented wafted up from the bath, roses... no peonies. It smelled heavenly. Beautiful, like Alice.

"Are you jealous?" Marc Antony asked.

Lewis shook his head. "Envious. I want to be with them in that fragrant water."

"I get it. Peonies envy."

Alice dipped herself into the water, her breasts buoyed a little, high and full. She paddled around a little, laughing and smiling at Lewis. Then Cleopatra joined her, one of those scrubby things in her hand. Alice stood, and Cleo washed Alice's shoulders, her arms, her breasts. She swirled it around Alice's pink nipples eliciting a moan from deep in her throat. Then Cleopatra moved the scrubby lower, between Alice's legs.

Lewis groaned. "How do you do it, Marc?"

"Do what?"

"Control yourself while watching that? I mean right now I'd give about anything to go over there and fuck my wife's brains out."

"Why now? Here? From what I've been told, you didn't do that at home when you had plenty of chances."

Lewis thought about that, but an answer didn't come.

Alice did, though. Grinding against Cleo's hand, she groaned and moaned, and let out a little yip. "Thirty-two!"

"And you're not clean yet, my dear." Cleopatra knelt down in the water, moving her hands between Alice's legs and then following with her mouth.

Alice stood still, legs spread, breasts glistening with fragrant soap, nipples protruding through the bubbles. She shuddered, coming again. Then again.

Lewis's hips began to move of their own accord, and it took him a full twenty seconds of envisioning himself washing bird poop off windows before he could bring them back under control.

"Thirty-five!" Alice said.

Next Cleopatra brought out shaving cream and a razor. She started with Alice's calves, lathering her up, her fingers moving over Alice in a massaging motion. Then she skimmed the razor in small strokes. After finishing both legs from feet to thigh, Cleopatra kneeled down in front of her again, her face again at the level of Alice's crotch.

Lewis couldn't look away.

Kneeling in front of Alice, Cleo lathered up every square inch of skin around Alice's privates and started to shave.

Alice groaned, moving her legs apart, giving Cleopatra room. Lewis watched as Cleo spent more time rubbing and stroking than shaving, pulling the razor away each time his wife shook in climax. Then, when she was completely hairless, Cleo put her face close and blew a steady puff of air at Alice.

Alice gasped, "Oh my goodness!"

"It's a menthol shaving cream," Marc Antony explained. "Right now your wife is tingling mightily."

Cleopatra licked Alice, then blew air again. Lick and blow. Lick and blow. Alice's legs began to tremble, and she grasped the queen's hair and pressed her close, croaking, "Thirty-nine."

Lewis whimpered.

"Having a hard time of it, huh?" Marc Antony said.

"I want to feel how smooth she is," he said, knowing Alice could hear, wanting her to. "I want to rub my cheek against her, my tongue, my cock."

"Careful," Marc Antony warned.

Lewis took a full minute this time, remembering the pony play he'd seen on the way to the baths. Crawling around on hands and knees with a bit in his mouth was so not his thing, so it was a good image to temper his ardor. "How do you do it?" he asked again, afraid to look back at Alice and Cleo.

"I don't know, man. Your wife is so hot. And seeing her with Cleopatra, rubbing their soap-slick breasts up against each other, their hard nipples sliding over slippery skin, it really does make me want to go over there, drape them on their bellies on the pool deck, and fuck them both from behind, one after the other."

"Please stop," Lewis said. It sounded too good. He could imagine it too clearly. Pounding into Alice, making her come, her pussy muscles tightening around him, squeezing him. Then when she'd had all she could take, he'd pull out and plunge into the Queen of the Nile. "Just tell me how you handle not doing that right now."

Marc stared at him, then one side of his mouth tilted upward in a smile. "I don't know. I really don't. But then I don't have to. I think I'll walk over there right now and see if they'll go for my idea." He turned away from Lewis, detached his red cape and slung it off his shoulders. "You know what you need, Lewis?"

"What? Tell me."

"Some confidence."

Lewis knew he was right. But as lovely as his wife was, and as much as she told him she wanted him, he couldn't quite make himself believe she was his. How did he get so lucky? How could he ever hope to deserve a woman this smart, this beautiful, this alive?

Marc Antony continued. "Take my wife, she's a seductress, a powerful queen. You know that she invented the vibrator? Put live bees in a dried gourd. Shook it up, it buzzed. True story. And me? I'm a conqueror. I'd have to be with a woman that beautiful and smart. So it's a perfect match, really. If you want to conquer Alice, to know deep down that you've won her love..."

"Yes?"

"I'd suggest you battle a rival."

"What do you mean?"

"Kill someone. In front of her. Women love that."

Lewis didn't think Alice would like that. He certainly wouldn't like it, either.

"If you want, I can cut your bindings and we can have a go at it right now."

"Uh..."

"Swords, if you like. Or daggers. There's nothing quite like feeling the blade go into your enemy's belly, up to the hilt as the blood spills out."

"As wonderful as that sounds, I'm afraid I'll have to decline."

"How about those big wooden clubs with spikes on them?"

"No."

"Longbow? We stand across the room and shoot poison tipped arrows at one another."

"Hell no. I don't want to fight you to the death. I don't want to fight you at all."

"Fair enough. In that case, I'm just going to go over there and fuck your wife until she squeals." Then he started taking off the armor and unstrapping those strappy sandals.

Great. Now Lewis had to find some way to endure watching Alice make it with a gorgeous woman *and* one of the biggest cocks he'd ever seen.

He glanced back at Alice, beautiful Alice, just in time to see that Cleopatra now sat on the edge of the pool, Alice's mouth between her open thighs, his sweet wife putting more effort and joy into pleasuring this stranger than he'd ever managed in pleasuring her.

At first, Lewis felt self-pity. But then he became angry with himself.

Alice was *his* wife. He'd let her down.

But they were here for Lewis to learn, not to be punished.

This was an opportunity. And Lewis decided, for the sake of their marriage and the woman he loved, to take all he could from this experience, and use it to make Alice happy.

Then he watched Marc Antony walk up to Alice, his cock swinging like a third leg, and he fell right back into self-pity.

Chapter 7

Alice Meets an English Woman and Is Wooed by Some French Guys Who Speak English…

When Alice was finished with her bath and dried in thick Egyptian cotton towels (of course they were Egyptian), she was so relaxed, so smooth, and smelled so good, she could have died a happy woman right there and then.

Add that to the fact that Lewis made it through the whole thing with a spectacular hard-on and no spewage, and Alice had no cause to be wistful.

Strangely, she was.

When she'd seen Marc Antony stride into the baths in his cape and armor and really cute gladiator sandals (and so in style right now), she'd been hoping to feel the warmth of some really hot, really live, really hard man flesh between her lips… *both* types of lips. Unfortunately, Cleopatra turned out to be a tad jealous. Something about Marc going off to marry some other woman, yada, yada. So while she'd enjoyed Alice thoroughly, and had given her a great bath, a smooth shave, and many orgasms, she wouldn't allow her husband to enjoy her as well.

Cleopatra held out the silken robe. "Come, Alice."

"Again? Okay." Alice slipped her hand between her legs.

"No, I mean come with me. Now that you've had your bath, it's time to get dressed."

"But I'm having such a fine time naked." Alice pouted. "The robe is lovely, but I don't see why I can't run around the halls nude. Everyone else seems to."

"I'm not talking about the robe. It's time for you to dress for dinner."

"Oh." Alice was getting a little hungry, although she still wasn't sure why she couldn't dine *au naturale*. "Will Lewis be at dinner, too?"

Cleopatra merely smiled. "Come now."

The female pharaoh seemed to be very set about ushering Alice out of the bath, so being curious about her next adventure, and hoping her dinner would include eating a nice tube steak (it was her favorite), Alice slipped into the robe and followed her down the hall.

Growing curiouser and curiouser about seeing more of the rooms in the Hellfire Club, Alice was a little disappointed when the queen ushered her through the very next door and into a tiny room furnished with nothing but some mirrors and a dressing table.

"Have a lovely time, Alice," she said and closed the door.

Alice almost didn't notice the mousey little woman wearing a long green dress standing in the corner. The woman's hair—an average brown color—was pulled back in a very conservative, somewhat severe twist at her nape. Although Alice was slim and not terribly tall, she was at least four inches taller.

"Hello," Alice said politely. She thought about adding a curtsy, but wasn't sure she still remembered how.

"Hello," the woman said, her eyes carefully downcast.

"Are you a maid?"

"No, I'm a governess. My name is Jane Eyre."

In that case, Alice certainly should have at least attempted a curtsy. "Glad to meet you, Jane. But I don't understand why you're here. I finished my schooling years ago."

"Not all your schooling. Our entire lives are learning experiences, dear Alice. One can never know too much."

"A good point. Are you to teach me a new way to reach orgasm?" Alice felt one could never know too much about that.

"No. I'm not here to teach you. I have a different pupil. Your husband."

Alice glanced around the closet-size room. "Lewis? Where is he?"

"We will both see him soon. But first, you must dress for dinner."

Jane held up a garment and helped Alice into it. Made of luxurious pale pink silk, the corset stretched from Alice's hips to the base of her breasts. Above she wore a sheer white lace blouse, and the skirt below was of the same sheer lace.

Jane yanked the laces running up Alice's back, mounding her breasts nearly to her chin. Then she motioned to one of the long mirrors. "Look how beautiful you are."

"Oh my," Alice said. "My breasts look three cup sizes bigger."

And not only were they bigger, but with only the sheer blouse covering them, they were essentially bare. She gave the skirt a swirl. Completely see-through as well, the lace called attention to her smooth-shaven feminine parts and curvy bottom rather than covering them. And Alice had to admit, as lurid as her nipples looked, pushing eagerly through the lace, the outfit made her look, somehow, classy.

"Now to do your hair and makeup," Jane said, ushering her to the dressing table.

To Alice's relief, Jane didn't fix Alice's hair as she had her own. Instead, she brushed it until it was silky smooth and held it back with a white lace ribbon. And the makeup was just enough to bring out Alice's big blue eyes.

"I feel lovelier than I have in a very long time," Alice said, looking at her reflection.

"You should. You are lovely, Alice. I am plain and small, but you are as beautiful as a queen."

Alice wanted to tell her she wasn't plain and small, but since she kind of was and seemed to insist upon it, Alice decided to just let it go. "Why don't you wear some makeup and do your hair like you do mine? You obviously know how. You could make yourself beautiful and confident, too."

"I'm afraid it doesn't work that way, Alice."

"I don't understand."

"You were beautiful and confident before you walked into this room. Seeing yourself this way is fun, but if the confidence isn't there, then clothing and hair products and makeup are just clothing, hair products, and makeup."

Alice thought about that for a moment.

"When you feel sexy, you are sexy," Jane said. "I don't use makeup or brush out my hair, because that's not what makes me confident. I feel sexy and powerful when I'm doing good. Teaching. Helping others."

"Oh," Alice said. She'd never considered those things to be sexy. "I guess anything can be sexy then."

"Your biggest erogenous zone is your mind. Sex is all in your brain. If the brain gives into the fantasy, the body will follow."

Alice remembered what Jane had said earlier. "You're going to be teaching Lewis."

"That is the idea, yes."

Alice wasn't sure Lewis really needed to learn to turn himself on with his thoughts. He'd never had problems like that. In fact, he was a little too efficient when it came to his own arousal. But there was something she'd like Lewis to learn. "Can you make him understand that I love him?"

"Doesn't he know that?"

Alice lowered her head. "We... we haven't said it in a long time. He doesn't seem to think he deserves me. At least that's what he said."

"I can teach him some things, Alice. But many a person must learn for themselves." She motioned to another door hidden behind one of the mirrors. "Now follow me, Alice. You have suitors waiting, and I must see to my pupil."

Alice followed Jane into a large, dining hall with tapestries hanging on the walls and stone floors under foot. Candles twinkled from ornate candelabra around the room, and in one corner there was a table set with the most glorious silver goblets and beautiful china.

"Is this a castle?" Alice said, giving a little shiver. Castles always went with royalty, and being polite to royals never ceased to turn her on. Especially when being polite entailed having sex with them.

"Of course, it is."

"Will I be on top of the round table, ravaged by King Arthur and his knights?"

"No. This castle is from the seventeenth century, Alice. Not the middle ages. I thought you said you completed your schooling."

Alice would have been cross with Jane for being such a know-it-all, but she had better things to do. Besides, after having racked up a total of forty-five orgasms, she couldn't manage being cross with anyone. "Seventeenth century... hmm..."

"Paris," a heavily accented voice said from the shadows. He pronounced it 'pah-ree'.

"Who is there?"

A man stepped forward. Dressed in a leather doublet, white linen shirt, suede breeches, and knee high boots, the man had a sword and scabbard strapped to his waist, and on his head was a wide-brimmed hat that sported a fluffy feather. His hair curled to his collar and his face was handsome and strong, his mustache and goatee making Alice tingle with anticipation.

He took off the hat and with a flourish, bowed deeply. "Athos at your service. So pleased to meet you, milady."

Alice frowned, but she managed a curtsey. "You're so... dressed."

"I beg your pardon?"

"Dressed. Like wearing clothing. A lot of clothing. And here I'm almost naked."

"I'm afraid I don't understand." His gaze traveled over her. "You are wearing clothes."

"But you can see right through this lace."

"Really?" he said.

"Of course," Alice insisted. Couldn't he see? "I mean look here, at my breasts. You can see my nipples."

As he studied her nipples, they tingled and hardened, trying to poke through the loose lace. "You're correct. I can see your delicious-looking nipples."

"And my..." Alice twirled a little, the lace swishing around her. At first, when she saw he was fully dressed, she'd been a little embarrassed at being so nude, ridiculous after all she'd done since she'd arrived at the Hellfire Club. But now, the way Athos was looking at her, she wanted to be bold. She wanted to be naughty. "My pussy. See? You can see my shaved pussy right through the lace."

His gaze moved down there, and she could see a bulge building in his breeches.

"I do see it. Like a halved peach, and every bit as sweet, no doubt."

"Why don't you take off your pants?" she asked.

"I beg your pardon, milady, but champagne awaits us."

Alice would have been disappointed, except she was thirsty. And she couldn't wait to see what Athos might do when he got a little bubbly in him. She'd loved her time with Cleopatra, but she had a craving for a man. She swished in the direction he directed.

There was indeed a champagne bucket standing next to a silk upholstered bench, more modern day than 17th century, but Alice wasn't going to quibble. Alice perched on the bench, ankles crossed like a perfect lady. Of course, she was a lady who happened to be exposing all her feminine parts to the world.

She had to admit it was very exciting.

Athos reached behind the bench and pulled out a bouquet of roses.

Alice smiled, accepted the flowers, and held them to her chest and sniffed deep, the rough stems brushing her nipples.

Athos picked up the champagne, opening it with only a slight pop. He offered her a glass. "For you, milady."

She took a sip, sneezing a little from the bubbles. Alice felt very much like a fairy tale princess.

Well, a slutty fairy tale princess who really needed a cock inside her. Maybe even more than one. She wondered if Snow White ever got this horny. She must. Why else live with seven little men?

"You are a vision, milady," Athos said, bowing deep.

Alice looked at the gorgeous Athos. She looked at the champagne and the flowers. It made her feel wanted, and special, and was a nice breather from all the orgasms.

And, strangely, it made her want more orgasms.

"You're very polite, Athos, and very attractive. A perfect gentlemen. Are we going to get to something physical anytime soon?"

"Soon, milady."

Then a door into the chamber opened, and Lewis walked in, Jane Eyre at his side. He was still completely naked, his erection bobbing as he walked. But this time, something was different.

"They shaved you!" Alice observed. "You look at least two inches bigger!"

"And you look so beautiful, Alice. So sexy I can hardly bear it." He gave Alice a little smile that she could feel all the way to her toes, and he skimmed her barely hidden breasts and crotch with his gaze.

"Steady, Lewis," Jane said. "We haven't even begun the lesson."

Lewis swallowed hard, and nodded. "What is the lesson about this time?"

Jane made him sit on a bench and chained his arms to the column above. "Respect."

"Respect?" Lewis made a face. "People don't seem very respectful around here with all the tying and teasing and forcing of orgasms."

"All healthy sex includes respect, Lewis."

"But Alice was begging to stop and no one listened. That didn't seem respectful."

"And that was part of the game, part of what she signed up for here at the Hellfire Club. Even the edging by Blackbeard and the orgasm torture in the Swing Room were about consent, trust, and empowerment. Heathcliff, Dickens, and Blackbeard were only doing what she chose, playing out her fantasies. Weren't they, Alice?"

Alice nodded. She'd been through a lot, and at moments she'd wondered if she could take it all. But it was exactly what she'd signed up for.

"And now on to the lesson." Jane grasped the collar of her very proper dress with the row of buttons running down the front and gave it a pull. One by one, the buttons popped free, and a voluptuous pair of naked breasts spilled from the opening.

Oh, my.

Jane let the dress fall to the floor, baring the rest of her surprisingly shapely body (that proper, governess dress hid a lot!), and then she turned to Lewis. "I want you to pay close attention to what I do and say. First I'd like you to notice how Athos is wooing Alice. Flowers, champagne, treating her like a lady. Not pawing her. Not taking advantage. Not only thinking of his own pleasure. He's treating her like the special woman she is."

Lewis nodded, and gave Alice another little smile.

Jane went on, pulling on her nipples as she talked. "Besides being the trappings of romance and showing a woman she's special, the scent of flowers, a little bubbly, it all stimulates the senses, lowers inhibitions, and can arouse desire."

Alice had to agree with that. And the dashing Athos only added to the picture.

"And while you think about how you will romance Alice, I'm going to suck your rochester." She knelt down between Lewis's thighs. As it turned out, Lewis's rochester ended up being his cock, and Jane sucked as she'd promised, starting with a swirl of the tongue, then taking him fully into her mouth.

Alice sipped her champagne. Delicious. She smelled the flowers. Divine. She watched Jane pleasure her husband, then feasted her eyes on the dashing Athos, still bowing his apology, his eyes glued to Alice as if the spectacularly nude Jane wasn't even there.

So Lewis would learn from Jane and Alice would have her fun with Athos. She couldn't wait to get started. "So perhaps it is time for my lesson?" she asked her dashing suitor, hoping that would inspire him to strip like Jane had.

"Of course it is time! I have arrived!" Another man strode into the dining hall his riding boots clicking on the stone. His hair was shorter, and beard and mustache slightly more full. Dressed similarly to Athos, he held a tray heaped with food. "I'm Porthos, and I can tell Athos has left you hungry, both for food and romance."

Athos grunted.

But before Alice could comment, both men were feeding her. The freshest nectarines, the most succulent strawberries, and the sweetest cherries, nectar dripping to her chin.

"Certain foods can be very sexy, too," Jane said, coming up for a breather. "The whole ritual of feeding each other can be a real turn-on."

"I can't get any more turned-on," Lewis said, beginning to sound a little desperate.

"May I have a nectarine, Athos?"

"Pardon me for a moment, Alice." Athos rose and brought Jane a piece of fruit. "Would the governess like it sliced in half?"

"If you please."

Athos tossed the nectarine into the air, unsheathed his sword, and deftly cut it in half. Just as deftly, Jane caught one of the halves and began to rub it along the length of Lewis's cock.

"Thank you, Athos."

Athos bowed, and returned to feeding Alice, as Jane alternated licking the juice from her husband and applying more. Lewis's face pinched, and he began to pant.

As much as she was enjoying herself, Alice had to admit she was getting a bit tired. The whole day had been an endless wave of orgasms. If Lewis couldn't hold out, if she had to start over...

"Please hold out, Lewis," she said, catching his eye. "For me."

"I'm trying, Alice. I'm really trying."

"Think unsexy thoughts, Lewis," Jane said. This time she took his manhood in both hands, one fist on top of the other, and started to twist in opposite directions. She worked up the length of his shaft, and when she started twisting her way back down, she took his tip into her mouth.

"This isn't fair," Lewis sputtered. He clenched his eyes shut and started babbling lyrics to Broadway musicals. Weren't many things unsexier than that, except maybe death metal.

"It looks as though I have arrived just in time!"

Alice looked toward the voice, and yet another man entered the room, same garb, yet with long, dark hair, a wickedly pleasurable looking mustache and only a hint of beard.

"Aramis at your service, milady!" He took her hand and kissed it, then guided her out of her chair. Just like that, music began to play, a passionate tango, and Aramis took her in his arms and started dancing.

Alice whirled around the floor. Some steps in the dance were smooth and romantic, some staccato and sharp, but every spot she placed her feet seemed to be right, as if she'd spent the last ten weeks on *Dancing With The Stars*. And Aramis looked down at her face, her breasts, as if he was thinking of much more than dance.

Her fatigue forgotten, Alice felt stimulated, alive, and she hoped they moved to the *much more* stage soon.

"Dancing is also very sexy, Lewis. Look at how their bodies move in rhythm with one another. How Aramis takes the lead. How Alice matches him step for step as his equal. You can tell they want to fuck each other, and yet they are still restrained."

Alice continued dancing, only getting glimpses of Jane tucking Lewis between her generous breasts and sliding up and down. She looked at Aramis, so handsome, so dashing, and thought about what it might feel like to try the same thing with him. "Aren't you hot from dancing? All three of you seem so overdressed."

"Anticipation, Lewis," Jane said, still moving while she cupped her soft flesh around him. "That's part of the fun of flowers and romantic dinners and dancing. Alice is anticipating the sex to come."

"And come she will!" A fourth man strode toward Alice. Around Alice's age and a bit younger than the other three, he wore the same boots and breeches as the other men, but instead of the leather doublet, he sported only the white shirt, unbuttoned to his navel. His chest was as smooth as his face, and his wavy hair reached to his shoulders. "I'm d'Artangan, and I'm here for the sword fight."

Now, Alice had fantasized before about a sword fight, and the thought of these four handsome and dashing men engaged in rubbing their hard shafts together made her knees feel a little weak. She stopped dancing, sagging a little in Aramis's arms.

"I'd love to watch the four of you sword fight," she said on a puff of air.

"Oh, you're not going to watch, Alice. We are going to sword fight. You and me."

"I'd love to. But I don't have an… um… sword."

Athos looked from one musketeer to the other. "I don't know about the three of you, but I'm a little relieved to hear that."

"I agree," Porthos said. "We already have four. Seems we have the sword thing covered."

"Besides," Aramis chimed in. "We would have to be blind not to notice. That lace skirt really hides nothing. Looks like half of a nectarine."

"I observed the same," Athos offered. "Except I said a peach."

"Are a peach and a nectarine the same thing?" Aramis asked.

"A peach has velvety fuzz," Jane said between licks. "A nectarine is smooth. The comparison of Alice to a nectarine is apt, because she is freshly shaven."

Alice cared little about whether she looked more like a peach or a nectarine, but she was more interested in the proposed sword fight. "Can we hurry this process along somehow?"

Athos, Porthos, and Aramis gathered around, and Porthos handed her his sword. To Alice's extreme disappointment, it was the sharp kind of sword, made from steel. "Use this."

"Really? This is what you meant by swordfighting? Actually swordfighting?"

She'd barely figured out how the thing fit in her hand when d'Artagnan drew his own sword.

"Ready?"

"But I don't know how—"

"I'll teach you. It's like dancing."

"Dancing usually ends with a dip, not a laceration."

"I know you'll do fine. Now hold your sword in front of you and watch my feet." He took a few steps forward, tapping her blade lightly, then a few steps back.

Alice had to laugh. It *was* like dancing. And her heart was racing with each swish of his blade.

"You try."

She did. And like with the dancing, her feet seemed to move flawlessly of their own accord.

"Now together."

He lunged. *Tap-tap-tap.*

Alice held out her blade and somehow managed to parry. Then it was her turn to attack. *Tap-tap-tap.*

Jane raised her head from Lewis's lap. "Fear is one of the most powerful aphrodisiacs."

d'Artagnan shifted to the side, moving so fast it was hard for Alice to follow, but somehow, she did.

"Of course, you don't have to risk your life, like Alice is doing now," Jane continued. "You could just do something a little out of your normal rut. Go skiing. Travel somewhere adventurous. Read some edgy erotica. Stream a scary movie through Amazon Prime. Or take a trip to the Hellfire Club."

A little lunge, a perfectly good parry, and Alice backed into a wall, d'Artagnan's blade at her throat. "My goodness. That's quite frightening, being on the end of a blade."

"I'm not going to hurt you, Alice."

"What do you want?"

"Your nipples are very hard, Alice," d'Artagnan said. "Very excited."

"Y-y-yes."

"I'd like to see them better."

She reached up to her cleavage, ready to pull the lace down.

"Don't move!" he said. "Stand very still."

Alice did her best to freeze, but her heart was pounding and her breasts rose and fell with her panting breaths.

Three swishes of his sword, and the lace blouse fell to the floor, fully exposing her breasts.

"There. How do you feel, Alice?"

"Hot." She felt more than hot. She felt wicked.

"Just one more thing, Alice. Hold still for me again." Three more slashes and her lace skirt lay on the stone, leaving her naked except for the corset.

"Will you spread your legs for me? Just a little so I can see you better?"

Alice did, cool air caressing her swollen and very wet sex. She glanced behind d'Artagnan, looking for the other musketeers, wanting all of them to see her like this. Hot. Naked. Ready.

"I can confirm the tangerine metaphor."

"It's a simile," Jane said, her mouth full of cock.

The other three musketeers filed back into the room. They were nude now, except for black rings encircling each of their shafts and balls, and their magnificent swords (yeah, *that* kind of sword) surged toward Alice.

After all her orgasms and dancing and fencing, Alice's knees wobbled, her thighs weak. At the sight of three hard cocks attached to three dashing men—no, make that four, since d'Artagnan had now removed his clothing as well—her legs folded, and she kneeled on the floor, taking them all in at eye-level.

Athos had a large head and prominent ridge. He curved to the right a little and bounced as he walked.

Porthos curved to the left and was the smallest of the group, but his balls were huge, and Alice could imagine taking their soft bounty in her mouth, heavy on her tongue, or having them slap against her as he thrust into her from behind.

Aramis curved upward, his shaft thick and veined, and she could imagine him filling her, his head massaging her G-spot. Hair covered his chest, tapering down his belly, as if he was half animal, and she longed to feel the rasp on her nipples.

And last but not least, d'Artagnan shot straight up along his belly, as if gravity had no power over the surge of his manhood. He was the only one of the three who wasn't wearing a cock ring.

The men gathered around her and tilted their erections into the air, tips touching.

"All for one, and one for all!" Alice said.

The men stared at her, blank looks on their faces.

"Where did that come from?" Athos asked.

Alice stared at him. "You're the three musketeers, aren't you?"

"But there are four of us," d'Artagnan said, counting stiff rods.

"I know," she explained. "But that's because you just joined them. There were only three musketeers at the beginning."

"There have been hundreds of musketeers, milady," said Porthos.

"And what is this all-for-one-for business?" Aramis asked.

"It's what you say. The three of you and d'Artagnan. Before you go into battle or whatever."

Porthos shook his head. "Doesn't ring a bell. If you like that sort of thing, maybe you should check out the Knights of the Round Table. They're over in the medieval room. That Lancelot… he sure can lance a lot."

"Never mind," Alice said. These four might not know their story very well, but at least they hadn't started reciting bad poetry. And instead of giving them the chance to start, she took a shaft in each hand and caressed the soft skin.

Athos and Aramis moaned.

Alice leaned forward and flicked Porthos and d'Artagnan with the tip of her tongue, then swirled over and around one prominent head then the other, the way she'd seen Jane do to Lewis.

Both grunted their appreciation, and she shared her tongue with the two in her fists. They each tasted different, one sweeter than the next. She took one between her lips, caressing his underside with her tongue. Then the next. Then the next. When her mouth was filled with one, the others rubbed her cheek, as if waiting his turn.

"I feel like all four of your cocks are worshipping me."

"And why wouldn't they?" said Aramis. "Your tongue is so skilled, Alice. And I want to rub myself all over your body."

The other's agreed, and Alice was so flattered, she took Athos and Porthos into her mouth at the same time, feeling them rubbing together. Then Aramis slipped in as well, and she had a mouthful of Three Musketeers, although these had fewer calories and no chocolatey nougat center. And they weren't the puny, fun-sized bars you got at Halloween, either. How could something an inch long be considered fun-sized anyway?

"So you're not going over to the medieval room?" d'Artagnan asked encircling one of her nipples with his hard tool.

When she'd arrived, she'd been fantasizing about taking on all of King Arthur's knights, but after the romancing and dancing and recovering from her fear, she really wanted to experience all the fancy sword play these musketeers had to offer. "I have plenty to keep me busy here."

"Glad to hear it, Alice," Athos said. "Because we have much more in store for you."

Chapter 8

The Four Musketeers and Alice Have a Sword Fight...

Athos scooped Alice into his arms and carried her to a large tapestry hanging on the wall closest to Lewis. Porthos pulled a tassel, and the ornate hanging pulled back like a curtain, exposing a small cove totally filled with a gold silk-covered bed and festooned with purple and green pillows.

Alice glanced over to Lewis.

Jane was lying on the floor beneath him now, her naked body outstretched, her mouth filled with his balls. Eyes glazed, Lewis gave Alice a wobbly smile. "You're so beautiful, Alice."

"Careful," snapped Jane, her voice stern. "I think seeing all those cocks revering Alice is close to sending you over the edge."

"It is spectacular, Alice. Reverence is what you truly deserve."

If Alice wasn't mistaken, Lewis sounded a little sad. And she would have asked if he was okay, but Jane reached up and pinched the tip of his cock, and he let out a surprised yelp.

"Watch closely, Lewis. I'm gently squeezing your frenulum, that's this area along the underside of your penis stretching from the shaft to the glans. It's really sensitive to stimulation, but a small squeeze can reduce your urge to come."

"It did!" Lewis looked up at Alice, beaming. "It really worked."

Jane cupped his balls in one hand. "There's a muscle right behind your testicles that you can learn to squeeze, too. It's the one you use to stop and start urinating. Like a woman does Kegel exercises. Then you can control your ejaculation without even touching yourself." She lowered her mouth to him again, and Lewis appeared to clench.

"What about the cock rings?" Alice asked, bringing her attention back to the four examples of manhood waiting for her attention. "Don't they help you last?"

"They do," Aramis said with a wink. "And they have another fun feature, too."

"What?" She skimmed her hand along his fat head.

He stepped close to her, his chest hair grazing her nipples. "You'll see."

Porthos and Aramis helped her onto the bed and climbed on beside her. Aramis opened a panel in the wall, took out a beautifully curved sapphire bottle.

"What is that?" Alice asked.

"Massage oil, milady. We are going to start by rubbing our hands all over you."

Aramis grinned wickedly and poured oil into Porthos's hand and then his own. The scent of jasmine filled the air. Alice lay back against the pillows and the men skimmed their hands over her skin. Their touch was light at first, just the barest whisper.

"It's warm, and getting warmer."

"It heats up as friction is applied."

Their fingers became more demanding, kneading, claiming her body as their own.

Athos and d'Artagnan took oil of their own and started on her feet, playing with her toes, working their way over her ankles, up her calves to her knees, and finally reaching her thighs. She spread her legs, willing them to touch her most sensitive spot. But while they kept their hands moving, manipulating her muscles, coming close to her center but not touching, neither gave her the release she sought.

She wriggled her butt on the silk.

"Patience, milady," Athos said.

"You're not planning to edge me, are you?" Alice asked. With four ready cocks bobbing just inches from her mouth, her pussy, the thought of not being allowed to come and come and come was too much for her to bear.

"You will feel everything. Things you can't even imagine. But most of all you will come."

"A lot?" she asked hopefully.

"A lot."

Porthos leaned down and kissed her lips. He was gentle, long caresses with his tongue and feather nips, and Alice swore as wispy as the sensations were, she could feel them all the way to her toes.

Aramis was next, littering kisses over her cheek, her ears, her neck, and her collarbone. She arched her back, wanting to feel his hot mouth on her nipple, his teeth teasing, but he took his good sweet time. Kissing down her arm and back up, circling under the weight of her breast, along her breastbone, but finally he reached the spot she longed for, circling the tight nub with his tongue, then flicking it before suckling.

Chills stormed over her skin.

Then Porthos was moving too, leaving her mouth and taking a similar circuitous route on his way to her other breast. And starting with her toes, Athos and d'Artagnan moved up her legs, feathering kisses and licks, on their way to her center.

She tried to open her knees wider, tip her hips up to greet them, but they wouldn't let her move, taking their time, driving her mad with passion..

Athos reached her womanhood first, dancing around it with his tongue. Then d'Artagnan joined, two tongues, circling but not yet giving her what she wanted, what she needed.

"Please," she said.

But they didn't listen. Two sucking her nipples, fondling her breasts. Two driving her mad, making her feel so empty, so crazy with desire.

"Please," she said again, louder this time. "I need you to touch me, to enter me."

"To touch you where?" Athos asked. "Tell me where. Turn me on."

"My pussy," she said on a puff of breath.

"And what do you want me to touch you with, Alice?"

"Your hard cock." It was crude and rude and so delicious, Alice felt a shiver. She watched Athos's face, the lust there, then noticed his erection stir. She went on. "I want you to thrust it into me. To fill my pussy with your big cock. To plunge in and out."

And just like that, Athos moved up her body, positioned his fat head at her opening, and sank inside.

He filled her, stretched her, and then started to move his hips, driving into her. It felt so good to be entered by a man again, her first since arriving. And an orgasm swept over Alice, more powerful for the wanting, the waiting.

Then d'Artagnan's mouth was on her clitoris, right above Athos's thrusts. Teasing, nibbling, prolonging and intensifying what she was feeling, and then sending her over the edge again.

"Forty-six-forty-seven-forty-eight!" she moaned as her multiple orgasms overtook her.

She reached out for Porthos and Aramis, taking one in each fist and holding on. They were so solid under her fingers, and she could feel them pulse with want as they watched Athos plunder her, as they watched another shudder claim her.

When she finally was able to take a breath, Aramis brought his large, veined length to her lips. She didn't bother circling with her tongue or teasing with tiny flicks. This time, she just took him full on and started sucking as yet another orgasm hit.

"Mmphmmph," she said.

"That was number forty-nine, I'm guessing" interpreted Jane.

Alice was worried she was again on her way to orgasm overload, when Athos pulled out, his member glistening with her juices. "We are all going to fuck you, Alice."

The words were so crude and Alice almost felt embarrassed by the flush of heat that flooded her. "I want you to. All of you."

"You want us to do what?"

"To fuck me with those hard cocks."

"And do you want to suck us too, Alice?" Aramis said, his manhood swaying an inch from her lips.

She licked her lips. "Oh, yes."

The musketeers guided her to a new position. This time d'Artagnan lay back on the pillows. "Climb on top of me, Alice."

Alice eyed his gravity-defying erection. "You're not going to stick your big tool in my bottom, are you?"

He grinned. "Not my big tool."

Since here at the Hellfire Club that was a perfectly acceptable answer, Alice did what he said, lying back on his warm body, her nipples pointing in the air. "Now what," she asked, eager to hear the answer.

"You seemed to take to swordfighting," d'Artagnan said, nibbling her ear.

"That was fun," she breathed.

"So let's do more."

Alice hesitated. "This swordfighting doesn't include the sharp steel kind, does it?"

"No, it doesn't." d'Artagnan teased her lobe with his tongue, his breath hot on her cheek.

"Well, if these swords you're talking about are commonly called cocks, then I'm all for it."

"That's what we wanted to hear," Aramis said, grinning at her from the bottom of the bed.

"Alice is now going to have all four men at once," Jane explained. "And I am going to show you the right way to nibble corn-on-the-cob."

"Nunghgnmm," Lewis replied.

"How are you doing, Lewis?" Alice asked, because as much as she was enjoying these four men, she wasn't sure she could take another hundred orgasms, not now that they'd gotten so far.

"I'm okay, Alice. Jane is a good teacher! You enjoy those swords!"

And Alice was determined to do just that. She gave the three a smile and opened her legs as wide as she could. "I want to take all four of you. All at once."

Athos and Porthos climbed onto the bed and knelt on either side of her, each playing with her nipples, their hardness reaching toward her.

Aramis knelt at her feet, his focus riveted between her open thighs. He stroked his length, as if imagining drilling into her.

"I'm going to enter you now, milady," d'Artagnan whispered in her ear.

He moved his hips, and she could feel his tip probe her opening. Then Aramis guided him into her, and d'Artagnan rocked his hips, moving smoothly in and out, her juices flowing like they'd never flowed before.

"Now I'm going to thrust my cock inside you, too," said Aramis, his voice gruff. He moved over her, his hands on either side of her hips.

She could feel his head touching her, sliding over her sensitive nub, teasing at the entrance already occupied by d'Artagnan. "How will you fit?" she asked, a shiver of fear skittering over her skin and making her even more wet, more excited.

"I'll take it slow," Aramis promised. "It will be intense at first with both cocks in you, but we won't hurt you. Do you trust us, Alice?"

"Yes." The word slipped out before she even thought about it, but she realized it was true. She didn't know these men, had never met then until an hour before, but she still trusted them. They wouldn't hurt her. And she wanted to feel what it would be like to take them both inside.

Aramis pushed his slick manhood to the opening that d'Artagnan already occupied and eased his large member inside.

She stretched and stretched, her perimeter burning. And just when she thought it was too much, the men settled into a rhythm, building off each other.

"Ohhhhh," she moaned.

"Are you all right, Alice?" d'Artagnan whispered in her ear.

"I… I think so… yes." She felt full. She felt stretched. Really stretched. But as they rocked, and as her nectar surrounded them, the discomfort turned to pleasure, and worry turned to heat.

Athos and Porthos moved closer, their soft yet firm heads rubbing her cheeks on either side.

She turned her head one way and took Porthos into her mouth, tonguing his left curve, feeling his large balls tap against her chin and cheek.

Then she turned the other way, swallowing Athos's bulbous head. She could taste herself on him, and her tongue playing incessantly with his prominent ridge and the spot Jane called the frenulum.

"Both of us, Alice," Athos said. "At the same time. Just like d'Artagnan and Aramis. A sword fight in the mouth and another in the puss."

Alice had been told she had a big mouth before, but the only place it seemed to be fully appreciated was in her fantasies. She opened her lips and accepted both cocks, sliding their heads together, watching the men's expressions as cock rubbed cock, her tongue in the mix.

Aramis moved his hand to her clit, caressing, massaging, out-and-out rubbing.

"Ahhhahhhahhhhahhhhhhha!" Alice exclaimed as ecstasy claimed her. "Fibby!"

Tough to say "ft" with two dicks in your mouth.

She was so full. So wet that she could feel the moisture dripping over her bottom. So hot and stretched and relaxed she felt like she could take a whole football team inside.

Athos threw his head back and moaned. "Time to take it up a notch, Aramis," he said.

Before Alice could ask what he was referring to, they doubled the speed of their thrusts and...

Their cocks were actually vibrating!

It was the cock rings they wore. Apparently they were battery powered and fitted with powerful stimulators.

As another wave took her, Alice cried out again. "Fibby-ub!"

She came one more time, sucking hard on the two cocks in her mouth, before one of the musketeers had to take a break, and it wasn't because she asked.

"Alice, you are so hot that I almost came in your mouth," Porthos said. "Would you mind if I licked your clit while I get back under control?"

Since she still had Athos deep in her throat, Alice answered by opening her thighs a little more.

Porthos added his tongue to the buzz of Aramis's cock ring, licking in circular motions. Fast. Faster. The sensation was overwhelming, and Alice soared, fell, and soared again.

"You are so sexy, Alice!" Lewis called to her.

Alice came again, her body clenching around two shafts. "Fibby-ooh!" she screamed, not sure if she could take any more.

"Stop, stop," Aramis said, and all the thrusting and licking and buzzing stopped. "I think Alice needs a breather."

Athos withdrew from her mouth, the other two men pulled out as well.

"Thank you," she told Aramis. "I didn't want it to end, but…"

"It won't end, milady, unless you want it to."

"No, no."

"Very well. Just stretch out and let us take care of you."

So Alice did, lounging on the bed, the four men massaging her tenderly and offering her sips of champagne, the fragrance of jasmine teasing the air.

"This is amazing," Alice finally said.

"Do you feel good, milady?" Athos asked.

"I do. In fact, I feel so good, I'd like to try more. But I'm not sure what."

"Leave that to us." Athos lounged on the bed and guided Alice on top of him. He kissed her and nibbled her lips, and astoundingly, she felt desire once again yawning inside her. As if reading her mind, he teased her opening with his tip, then eased his length inside. He had just begun to move, rocking her softly, when she felt a warm, slick caress on her bottom.

Porthos kneaded her buttocks, then moved his fingers, stroking between her crack, and then massaging and stretching her deeper. "I'm massaging you with a water-based anal lube, Alice. How does that feel?"

She had to admit, it felt pretty good. "Good. Relaxing, I guess. But hot."

"Have you ever tried it before?" Porthos asked.

"You mean, in my nether opening?"

"Yes."

"Once."

"Did you like it?"

She thought about the first time, in Wonderland. She'd tried all manner of things in that adventure, but the tea party had been something she'd cherish forever. "Yes."

"Would you like to try it again?" Porthos said, sounding eager.

She hesitated, but only for a second. Porthos was the smallest of the four, and she'd already had two men inside one opening. "If it hurts, will you stop?"

"Immediately, milady."

"Okay, then I'd like to try it very much."

"Very well. Don't worry, I'll make sure you're very ready before I ease inside."

While Porthos continued massaging her, she sat up on Athos. Arching her back, she rode him, her breasts bucking with each thrust. The other two musketeers moved on either side, and she grasped one in each hand and took turns licking. Then they both pushed into her mouth, the salty taste of their pre-cum on her tongue. Athos pinched her nipples, and when he turned on his vibrating cock ring, she crashed into her fifty-third orgasm.

"I think you're ready now, Alice," Porthos finally said. "I want to enter you."

She shivered a little and leaned forward. "Okay."

He took it slowly, sliding in, stretching her, filling her. He'd kept his promise, making her relaxed and ready before entering, but she still felt an overwhelming pressure, and it wasn't until her body seized in another orgasm, that she recognized the cause.

"You're so tight, milady," Porthos said. "I feel like I'm going to come, and I haven't even started moving."

Unable to speak, Alice rocked her hips a little, working the two shafts deeper into her body. Taking the hint, Porthos started to move, slowly at first, gently. Then his thrusts built, and she could feel his soft sack slap against her.

They rocked and she sucked and her juices flowed. With each rock and thrust the friction built and built and another wave of orgasms overtook her, then another, until one was indistinguishable from the next.

"I don't know what my count is," she said, after she caught her breath.

"I counted five," Jane shouted. "Which brings your total to fifty-eight." Although from her distance and with Lewis's shaft down her throat, Alice couldn't guess how she could possibly know.

They tried countless combinations. Alice on her back, Alice on her front, Alice on one lap, Alice doing a back bend. Alice on her head. And all Alice could think about at the end, besides how much fun she'd had and how many orgasms she'd racked up, was how grateful she was that she'd been on the gymnastics team in high school.

And how much she wanted to be home with Lewis so they could try out all they'd learned.

Chapter 9

Lewis Decides He Must Duel to Win Alice, but Can't Decide How, so Seriously Considers Belching…

L ewis watched The Four Musketeers come, one by one, all over Alice's luscious tits. As they rubbed their lengths against her nipples, she giggled, shuddered through yet another orgasm, then giggled again.

"I'm so glad we've pleased you, milady," Athos said, all four sweeping down in a dramatic bow.

Lewis did not come. And for that he was grateful, especially seeing that he had to endure Jane's mouth in addition to watching his lovely wife soak up all the pleasure she so richly deserved.

Pleasure he hadn't given her. She was up to sixty-five orgasms.

"She belongs with men like that," he muttered.

Buttoning up her prim dress, Jane frowned. "Maybe. She certainly enjoyed herself with them, but she married you."

"Sometimes I wonder why."

"I'm sure she had her reasons. Have you asked her?"

"I did once. A long time ago."

"And?"

"She said she loved me."

"So there's your answer," Jane said matter-of-factly, as if that settled it.

But to Lewis that answer seemed less and less adequate the more orgasms Alice experienced at the hands, mouths, cocks, and various devices of those at the Hellfire Club. "Marc Antony said I should fight for her, win her."

"Maybe he's right. But don't fight him. You wouldn't stand a chance. He does this thing, with poison arrows. You'd be dead in seconds."

Lewis watched Aramis spurt into Alice's open mouth. "How about the musketeers?"

"Are you kidding me?" Jane shook her head so hard her breasts jiggled free, and she had to redo the buttons on her dress. "They'd lop off your limbs before you took your first swing."

"This Blackbeard you spoke of?"

"He's a pirate. He wouldn't fight fair. Besides probably killing you with one swipe of his cutlass."

Lewis was running out of options. "Heathcliff?"

"Do you know how ruthless that man is? Besides, I won't stand for it. You could say he's like family to me."

"Cleopatra?"

"You know her history, right? She's more dangerous than all the rest combined."

"Then whom?" Madame Bovary scared him. And he'd grown fond of his teacher, Jane. "It's hopeless."

"For you to win her in mortal combat? Yes. It's also stupid. Alice doesn't want you to kill for her."

She was right. Alice was gentle and kind. She would hate bloodshed in her name. "Then how can I possibly win her?"

"Fight in an arena where you excel. What are you good at, Lewis?"

Lewis considered it. "Well, I'm pretty good at cooking omelets. The trick is to use olive oil, and not get the pan too hot."

"A useful skill, but probably not a way to win a woman's heart."

"Back in college I could hacky sack."

"Oh, yes. That drives the ladies mad."

"Really?" Lewis entertained a glimmer of hope.

"Of course not, Lewis. Don't be daft. A bunch of unwashed slackers skipping Civics class to smoke pot and kick around a little leather ball is about the worst way to impress a girl."

"I can do a pretty good Sean Connery impersonation." Lewis lowered his voice. "The name is Carroll. Lewis Carroll."

"That was awful. Very awful."

"So what, then? Pottery? Belching the alphabet? Making fart sounds with my armpit?"

"How did you ever get laid, let alone married?"

"I'm hopeless!" Lewis moaned. "There's nothing I can do that will woo Alice."

"You write, don't you? Nonsensical yet whimsical children's stories filled with bad poetry?"

"You could say that. Wait… *bad*?"

"So that's how you compete for Alice. By being yourself. Doing what you do best."

"The belching thing?" Lewis burped the letter A.

"Poetry, Lewis. My God, you're thick. Give me a moment, and I'll take care of everything." And with that, Jane left the chamber.

Lewis watched as the younger d'Artagnan came for a second time to Alice's glee and pondered what he'd just gotten himself into. He supposed writing was better than fighting to the death, at least some days. And while mortal combat with all these dashing figures would no doubt leave him dead, he could probably come up with better poetry. By the time Jane returned, Lewis was downright hopeful.

"I have it all arranged," Jane announced. "Lewis will now duel to win his wife's favor."

"Duel?" echoed Alice. Her expression horrified, she held a hand to her cum-slick breast.

Athos, Porthos, Aramis, and d'Artagnan grinned and stroked their swords. "We're ready," they said in unison.

"Not so fast," Jane said. "It will be a literary duel."

"A literary duel?" Athos looked stricken.

Jane nodded. "Also known as a poetry slam."

The musketeers grins faded, and Lewis came up with a smug smile of his own. Now he had them. No matter how much he doubted that he truly deserved sweet, beautiful Alice, he was sure he could write better than a collection of swordsmen, pirates, a Roman general, an Egyptian queen, or an orphan found wandering the moor.

"And he will be dueling," Jane continued, drawing out the moment "Some of the most famous love poets who ever lived!"

Lewis's smug smile faded, and he thought to himself, *Aw, shit.*

Chapter 10

Alice Blows Some of the Most Famous Love Poets Who Ever Lived...

By the time Alice had another bath, her skin now silky soft from cum and massage oil and jasmine-scented soaps, Jane said the dueling arena was ready. Back in her silk robe, Alice followed the governess through the club to a room she'd never seen before. The space itself was the width of a very narrow, dead end hallway. But the walls weren't walls exactly, they were mirrors.

"One way mirrors," Jane explained. "The duelers can see you, but you can't see them."

"So I stand in the middle of the mirrors and they recite poetry?"

"You don't just stand, dear. You choose the verse you like. You are the one and only judge."

"Do I fill out some kind of score sheet?"

Jane gave her a disappointed look and shook her head. "Where's the fun in a score sheet? This is a book of fantasy erotica, not a newspaper sports page."

"So what do I do when I like a verse?"

"You show your appreciation, of course." And as if Jane's words were magic, eight small holes slid open along the mirrored walls four on each side. A few feet off the ground, the holes were right at the level of…

"They're glory holes!" exclaimed Alice, remembering the other glory hole room she'd seen on her way to the bath. "This is just a fancy set up for glory holes."

Jane nodded her approval, and Alice felt the proud flush that came with being a good student.

"The poets will read, and you will be the judge. You can reward them or not, however you like. It's all up to you. But in the end, there will be one cock standing."

"Lewis's!"

"That depends, Alice," Jane cautioned. "All voices will be disguised. You'll only have the words and the genitals on which to make your decision."

"But won't I recognize my husband's member?"

"If this story were anchored in realism, you probably would. But you just fucked the four musketeers. So you'll just have to try them all out."

"That sounds delightful!" Alice eyed the mirrors. "And they can see me?"

"They can see everything."

Alice took a moment to imagine all those eyes on her body, watching her do all manner of naughty things, and excitement shivered over her skin. She had always been a shy person, modest, a good girl. But being naked in front of strangers, while terrifying, also made her feel desirable, powerful. "So when I like a poem, I can do whatever I want to them?"

"Yes. But don't show your appreciation too much."

"Why is that?"

"Well, the publishing industry has a tradition of mistreating most authors, so good treatment tends to confuse them. But in the case of our competition…"

"The last cock standing wins." Alice finished.

"That's right. Lewis comes, he loses."

"And my count starts over." Alice was at sixty-six—she'd had a tiny one during her second bath—and didn't want to start over again. The very thought of it exhausted her. "Okay, so the poets I like get a few licks, but I don't allow them to come."

"Right."

"And the others?"

"Do with them what you will." Jane smiled. "Ready to begin?"

Alice nodded. She stepped into the mirrored hall and let the silk slide off her body. Her nipples tightened and tingled, protruding so luridly they cast shadows. She could almost feel eight sets of eyes on her, moving over her breasts like eager hands, venturing between her wet folds, wanting her. Movement stirred in the holes, cocks rising, cocks poking through, a regular candy store of cocks, all hungry for her.

"May the first poet begin!" Jane called.

> *Wine comes in at the mouth*
> *And love leaks out at the prick;*
> *That's all we shall know for truth*
> *Before we grow old and sick.*
> *I lift the glass to my mouth,*
> *Now quickly suck my dick.*

"Hmm," said Alice. She studied the rod that went with the poem. It was nice enough, long and smooth, the ridge prominent enough to make sucking it fun. But there was something missing. She wasn't sure what. "I really think the word cock is a lot hotter."

"Picky, picky, suck my dicky," came the poet's answer.

Alice shook her head. Some writers just couldn't take constructive criticism. "Sorry. I'm not turned on at all."

"Yeats? You're eliminated!" Jane declared.

"But she didn't so much as touch me!" W.B. Yeats declared. "How am I supposed to work on my Second Coming?"

"You know the rules, Yeats. And that joke was so obscure only lit majors and those who Google it will understand it."

"Well, you both can kiss my widening gyre." The cock withdrew from its hole.

Alice looked at the remaining seven holes. She hadn't counted on eliminating a poet so fast, but as soon as he'd brushed off her opinion as if it didn't matter, she just couldn't muster the enthusiasm.

"Number two," Jane called out. "You're up!"

A grunt sounded behind the wall.

"Not *that* number two. Read the poem."

O my Luve's like a red, red rose,
That's newly sprung in May:
O my Luve's like a hairdresser,
Because I think I'm gay.

"What?" Alice said to the penis. "If you're gay, then why are you competing to win my favor?"

"I don't know. You seem perfectly nice, but I don't really want to win your favor. It just seemed like a good opportunity to read my poetry."

"Robert Burns, you're eliminated!" Jane declared. "Sorry about that, Alice. But that's the type of thing you get with an open poetry slam."

"Oh my." Alice put her hands on her naked hips. "So far, this has been somewhat disappointing. That Burns fellow wasn't good at all. I also think he was trying to poop."

"I had too many chicken wings!" Burns declared. "I can feel the Battle of Sherramuir raging in my bowels."

Alice wondered how many more little known literary references she'd have to endure before this was over. It wasn't erotic in the least. And it couldn't have been funny for more than one person out of ten thousand.

Jane nodded sympathetically. "It will get better. It almost has to or this book will get terrible reviews. May we have the next poem, please?"

> *Love at the lips was touch*
> *As sweet as I could bear;*
> *And once that seemed too much;*
> *Nice titties, quite a pair!*

"You like them?" Alice asked. She skimmed her hands up her sides, catching her breasts and lifting, fluffing them up like the corset had.

"Very much," said the poet. "Will you pinch your nipples for me? Make them really stiff?"

Now this was more like it! She rolled her nipples between her fingertips, until they jutted out as if begging to be sucked. Then she lowered herself to her knees in front of the hole.

The manhood pushing through was long, and very hard, the head the rich red of a cherry popsicle. Alice couldn't wait to taste. She swirled her tongue over him, tracing the ridge, then teasing at the frenulum underneath. Then she fit her mouth over him and took his whole length deep into her throat.

"Please, Alice," the poet said. "Those tits. Can I feel them?"

"Of course." Alice brought her hands on either side of her soft mounds. Moving closer to the wall, she slipped his member into her cleavage. He was still wet from her mouth, and when she started to move, he slid, slick and easy.

She moved up, the reddish head disappearing between her voluptuousness. Then she slid down, and he burst free, thrusting up toward her mouth like a spear. Down. Up. Down. Up.

"I'm going to lose it, Alice. I'm going to come all over those luscious tits of yours."

Alice liked that idea. She liked it a lot. But she'd also liked his poem. She let his hardness slip free. "I'm sorry. But I want you to continue to the next round."

"Thank you," he said, but she couldn't help note that he sounded disappointed.

Alice couldn't help note she was a little disappointed, too. And really ready to see what she could do with the next cock that recited a poem she liked.

"All right," Jane said. "We have one poet moving to the next round. "Will the next poet please read?"

Those other poets
Rhyme like newbies
Now I want to
Suck your boobies

"Sort of charming, I guess. At least it conveys the spirit of the competition." Alice actually thought it was terrible, but she felt like sucking some cock, so she'd let that slide. She eyed the glory hole, but could see nothing but the smallest hint of a tip. She knelt down for a better look, then realized the problem.

This poet's penis was too fat to fit through the hole. In fact, its girth was much larger than its length, and the shape reminded Alice of a fire hydrant. It also reminded her of something else.

Well, not something, actually. *Someone.*

"Humpty? Is that you?"

"Miss me, Alice?"

She had. The old egg was obnoxious at times and totally inappropriate and kind of annoying, but he had the warmest hugs, and Alice considered him an old friend. "It's so good to see you!"

"At least it's good to see the chode, eh?" He said, wiggling the head around a little.

"Actually, yes. But I can't fit you in my mouth, Humpty. You're wider than you are long."

"That's okay. I can't even fit it through the hole. But even so, it was worth taking a trip to this side of the looking glass just to see you naked again."

Alice bent down and gave him a couple of licks just for being such a sweetheart.

"I'm sorry," Jane intervened. "This is nice and all, but we promised poetry and hot blowjobs in this scene, so you'd better get back at it, Alice. Humpty Dumpty is eliminated. Next!"

She walks in beauty, like the night
Of cloudless climes and starry skies;
And all that's best of dark and bright
I'll stick my cock betwixt your thighs.

And since Alice was feeling a little hungry again between her thighs, she squealed in delight. But when she bent down to give a nice, medium-sized cock with an upward slanting glans a big kiss for a reward, he spurted before she even touched him with her lips.

"Lewis? Oh no, that's not you, is it Lewis?"

"I'm sorry," the disguised voice said. "I haven't been here at the Hellfire Club very long, and you were just so hot I couldn't control myself."

"Oh, no. Lewis?" Alice was really getting worried now.

"No. I am Lord Tennyson."

A member of the aristocracy! Alice was mortified. She bowed her head and curtseyed, possibly a ridiculous thing to do while she was totally naked. "I'm so sorry, Lord Tennyson, sir."

"No. I enjoyed it. 'Tis better to have come and lost than never to have come at all."

"Alfred Lord Tennyson is eliminated. Next!" Jane called.

How do I love thee? Let me count the positions.

"Short and sweet. I like that." Alice glanced down to examine the poet, but to her surprise, there was no cock sticking out of the glory hole. "Will you thrust yourself through? I want to take you in my mouth."

"Look closer," said the voice.

Wondering if this was some kind of trick, or that Humpty had tricked Jane and found his way to another glory hole, Alice bent forward at the waist, her breasts swinging forward. The poet on the other side of the hall probed between her legs with his long tool.

"I still don't see anything."

"Look closer."

So Alice did, and then she saw it. But it wasn't a cock. There in the glory hole was a beautiful flower of a vagina, the poet pressed back against the wall to give her access.

Sticking out her tongue, Alice reached it through the hole and gave a lick. Then another. And soon she was swirling her tongue over the poet's clit, then plunging into her opening. Swirling and plunging. Swirling and plunging.

"Ahhhhh," the poet moaned.

As Alice worked, the stiff shaft behind her worked as well, swirling his tip over Alice's clit, then dipping into her wetness.

"Ahhhh," Alice moaned.

She pressed back against the poet behind her, impaling herself on his length, feeling him stretch her as he sank deep, then she moved forward, sinking her own tongue into the poet in front. And with each rock forward and back, her breasts swayed, heavy and ripe.

"That is so hot," said one of the other poets.

"I wish I could be part of that," said yet another.

"Oh my God!" cried the poet Alice was mouthing.

Alice moved her tongue faster, feeling the muscles in the poet's pleasure cave pulse around her tongue. Finally the pussy moved away from the glory hole and out of her reach.

"I'm afraid Elizabeth Barrett Browning will have to be eliminated," Jane said.

"Why?" Alice asked. She hadn't expected a woman to be part of the duel, but once she'd gotten over the surprise, they'd had such a lovely time.

Jane shook her head. "First of all, you made her come. Secondly it's stated very clearly in the rules that the last cock standing wins. And since the next cock to read—er, I mean poet—is already penetrating you forcefully from behind, let's just get on with the verse, shall we?"

> *Shall I compare thee to a summer's day?*
> *Thou art more lovely and more temperate:*
> *Rough winds do shake the darling buds of May,*
> *It makes me want to masturbate.*

"Why don't you forget masturbating and just keep shaking my buds like a rough, rough wind?" Alice said, bracing her hands on the mirror in front of her and pushing her bottom against the mirror behind.

And shake he did. His shaft sank deep, then pulled out, so just the tip was still inside, then plunged again, moving in long, hard strokes. And as he pumped, his swinging balls slapped against her most sensitive bud.

Tension built, low in her belly, then an orgasm gripped her, shuddered through her, clenching her muscles and making her knees weak. She couldn't even manage to count out loud when another claimed her, then another. "Sixty-nine!" she finally cried out.

"We have one more poet to read," Jane said. "And in the interest of preserving this hot scene, he will take Elizabeth Barrett Browning's place."

And just like that, a beautiful, erect cock slid out of the wall in front of Alice. It was the perfect size and boasted a charming, upward curve. Just the sight made Alice all shivery. She took it in her mouth before the poem even began, licking and swirling and sucking hard.

> *Urgh... I mean*
> *I am your helpless love toy*
> *How my loins sweat for you*

I'm so hot for your body
I don't know what to do
I'll take you in my arms
And take off all your clothes
And lick your little nose
And smell your pantyhose

Alice let the cock slip from her mouth. She'd almost gotten carried away, sucked that last poet off before he'd even finished his poem. "That was so sweet."

"We have three finalists," Jane announced. "And now you'll move to the end of the room."

The poet behind her pulled out, leaving her dripping, her pussy gripping nothing but air.

But being a good girl who liked following rules, Alice positioned herself at the dead end, and to her delight, a glory hole opened on each wall, forming a horseshoe around her, and three cocks poked through.

Alice paused, savoring the splendor in front of her, men who could spin words, ridiculous as they were, and yet were also flesh and blood, wanting her, longing for her.

"Poem!" demanded Jane.

She is as in a field a silken tent
At midday when the sunny summer breeze
Has dried the dew and all its ropes relent,
And then I'll tap that ass with ease.

She gripped his member, stroking her fist up and down his length as the next began.

Love is not love,
Which alters when it alteration finds,
Or bends with the remover to remove.
Oh, no! it is an ever-fixed mark
Your labia reminds me of a baloney sandwich.

Not a very good last line, but she took this one into her mouth anyway. The longest of the three, this bard tasted of her juices and she realized he was the one who'd been buried hilt deep in her before.

> *You have a perfect ass*
> *You have a perfect ass*
> *You have a perfect ass*
> *That's why I come so fass*

The poem was bad—almost Queequeg bad—but Poet 3 liked her ass, and at that moment, that was all Alice really cared about. She spread her thighs apart, giving him a good look, then she pressed back, taking his length into her body.

She took Poet 1 in her mouth then and Poet 2 in her hand. Licking, sucking, pumping.

The sensations built again, making her feel dizzy, intoxicated, maybe even a little insane. She moved her head back and forth, back to sucking Poet One, then Poet Two, then One again, her tongue deft in its movements, more skilled than she'd never felt before.

"Oh, Alice. You're so skilled. Like I've never felt before." Poet One muttered.

"Alice," said Poet Two. "Such heavenly touches ne'er touched earthly cocks."

Alice felt a rush of heat to her nether regions. Both were so nice, so appreciative, so grateful, although she had to admit, Poet One was a little more accessible.

She slathered her tongue over his soft pouch, the hard nuggets inside teasing her, tantalizing her, begging her. His length bobbed against her cheek, hot and stiff, and when she took one of his balls in her mouth and sucked, the head jerked against her cheekbone.

"Oh, yesssssss," Poet One ground out.

She turned her cheek just in time and captured his hot essence with her mouth, sucking it in, savoring the bath of salty heat. It dribbled down her chin, and she looked up into the mirror, imagining him watching, and licked it off.

"Robert Frost is eliminated!" Jane declared.

A thrust from behind, brought Alice's mind back to the present and off the warrior fallen in battle. She grasped the solid cock in front of her, the longest of the three. Opening her mouth, she let his manhood skate down her tongue. Then hugging her lips around him, she moved her tongue over his soft skin, teasing his ridge, savoring the taste of him, salty and sweet. She breathed deeply, taking in his scent, hot and strong and male.

Another strong thrust came from behind, stealing her breath, stirring something dark deep inside her, something ravenous.

Alice wanted them both, everything they had to give. Her vision closed in, focusing on the cock in front of her, as if the texture of his skin, the scent of his body, the taste of the pre cum on his tip was the only thing in the world. She sucked and teased, her movements both tender and fierce.

Another thrust from behind, and she was coming again. She soared... floating... falling... never wanting it to end. Grasping the shaft in her mouth, sucking him with the force of her yearning.

Salt flooded her mouth, dripping out the corner and dribbling down her chin.

"William Shakespeare has been eliminated!" Jane yelled out.

"O, how bitter a thing it is to look into horniness through another man's cock."

"Come on," Jane said crossly. "You lost. Now take your willy out of here."

"I like to call it The Bard."

The Bard withdrew The Bard from Alice's mouth and the glory hole.

Jane cleared her throat. "Poet Three, read your last poem!

Reluctantly, Alice stepped forward, letting the victor's stiff manhood slide from her entrance. Then she turned to face it, a tremulous breath escaping her parted lips. "I'm yours. Please. Grace me with your brilliant verse."

*I am not Colin Farrell,
But blow me at your peril,
For I am far from sterile,
My name is...*

"Lewis Carroll!" Alice exclaimed "I knew it was you! You haven't come yet!"

"It was quite frustrating, but I'm doing it for you. Maybe I can't make up for all those years of bad sex, but I'm trying, Alice."

"Try you may, but you shall fail."

A man entered. Regal, aristocratic, wearing a dark suit and a black leather cape.

"Neither of you will escape the Hellfire Club. I shall make sure Lewis comes, and Alice's count goes back to zero, or my name is not the Marquis Donatien Alphonse François de Sade."

"So what is your name?" Lewis asked.

"It's the Marquis Donatien Alphonse François de Sade. I just said that."

"The Marquis de Sade?" Alice said. "Oh... my."

Chapter 11

Alice Does a Sybian Show with the Marquis de Sade and Everyone Watching...

A lice was led out of the room by a leash attached to the leather collar around her neck. She was naked, except for the fur-lined handcuffs she wore behind her back and the black, leather boots with the platform heels that were difficult to walk in but made her legs and ass look fantastic—something she noticed when they passed a mirror.

The Marquis held her leash in one hand, and Lewis's in the other. Her poor husband still maintained his erection, which bounced as he walked.

"After all the times I came at the poetry slam, I'm at eighty," Alice said to him, grateful that Jane had been keeping track, since she certainly hadn't. "Do you think you can hold out?"

"I'm trying, honey. It's so hard."

"I can see that," she said, glancing at his cock and trying not to smirk.

"I mean it's hard not to come. Watching all the things being done to you—all the things you're doing—it's a terrible turn-on. And then when I'm stimulated at the same time... I feel like I'm going to explode."

"I don't know what de Sade has planned, but if I can get twenty more, you can have your release, dear husband."

"You must be exhausted." She saw pity in Lewis's eyes. She saw something else there, too. Something she hadn't recognized in quite a while. Confidence.

"A woman's got to do what a woman's got to do. If I must endure twenty more orgasms for you, I'll try to be brave about it."

Alice was only half-serious, but Lewis's expression was full of concern.

"Maybe we should work together," he said.

"Together? How?"

"Could you... try to tone down your reaction?" he asked.

"How do you mean?"

"I love it when you lose all inhibitions, Alice. When you go wild and give yourself fully to pleasure. But seeing you in ecstasy is my biggest weakness. I get so excited I have trouble keeping myself from coming."

"So you want me to control myself?"

"If you could, perhaps, not scream so much. Or thrash around, with your beautiful breasts bobbing up and down."

Alice could see how that would arouse Lewis, and she counted herself lucky that she married a man who was so turned on by her excitement. Hopefully, when they were able to leave the Hellfire Club, he would remember these lessons and devote himself to exciting her.

Make that *if* they were able to leave the Hellfire Club. If Lewis blew his load, her count would be reset, and goodness knows how long they would be there. Much as Alice was enjoying herself, she really was exhausted.

"Is there anything else I shouldn't do?" she asked gently.

"Try not to grunt. Or moan. Or make that face."

"Which face?"

Lewis bit his lower lip and squeezed his eyes closed, apparently doing an impression of Alice in the throes of orgasm.

"That's what I look like?" she asked. "You keep your eyes and mouth open and sort of stare off into the distance as you groan."

"Please don't groan either."

"I'll try, Lewis. I'll really try."

"And how can I help you?" he asked.

Alice paused. She hadn't thought about that. But that was, after all, what working together was all about, helping each other reach their goals. "Well, I really like to feel you watching me, Lewis, and getting turned on. But that might be counter-productive."

"Yeah. Not sure that's a good idea."

"So I guess I don't know what to tell you."

"Don't worry, Alice dear, I'll figure something out."

That confidence was in his voice again, and it made Alice feel safe. Hopeful. "I'm sure you will. We're going to do this, Lewis. You and me. And then we'll be able to go home. Right?"

"Right."

They came to a closed door and stopped. Alice remembered it as the entrance to the amphitheater from her first walk through the club. De Sade turned and faced them.

"You are to obey my commands," he said. "If you don't, you'll be paddled. Of course, I may also paddle you if you do obey. No good deed should go unpunished."

"That's sadistic," Alice said.

The Marquis rolled his eyes. "Well, no kidding. I'm de Sade. That's where the term comes from."

Alice cast a worried eye at Lewis. A few times, early in their marriage, they'd spanked each other while role-playing in bed. The naughty schoolboy. The stern boss. They'd both enjoyed the experiences, but Lewis more so. Alice feared, if he was paddled, he'd squirt everywhere like a Super Soaker.

"You shall also," de Sade said, "continue to count your orgasms aloud, Alice. And do so loudly, as there is a large audience."

"An audience?" Alice shivered, although this time she wasn't sure if it was from excitement or fear.

"Everyone at the Hellfire Club has turned out for this event. More than a hundred people will be watching."

Alice felt herself redden at the thought of so many eyes on her. Staring at her breasts. Noting the lurid way her nipples poked out. Seeing the glistening wetness between her thighs.

"What exactly is the event?" Lewis asked.

"Alice will ride a Sybian in the center of the arena."

Lewis raised an eyebrow. "What's a Sybian?"

"A Sybian is a mechanical device, the size of a saddle, with a dildo in the center. Alice will sit upon the dildo, letting it impale her, working it deep inside, and she'll be tied into position so she cannot get off. The Sybian has a remote control box that rotates the dildo, like so." De Sade raised his index finger and turned it in a circle. "It also has controls for the vibration intensity. At 1/3 horsepower, it is the most powerful vibrator in the world."

"More powerful than the Hitachi wand?" Alice asked, her voice barely a squeak.

De Sade smiled. "It makes the Hitachi look like a child's toy."

Alice was immediately overwhelmed by a wave of fear. She remembered the woman in the amphitheater she'd seen earlier, shaking and screaming as she rode the Sybian. While Alice wouldn't have any trouble hitting twenty orgasms on such a powerful device, she wasn't sure how she would be able to contain her own excitement. Which meant Lewis would no doubt explode before Alice could finish.

"Lewis will be working the controls, while masturbating," the Marquis continued, "with arousal gel. It will make your manhood more sensitive."

Alice's hopes sunk even lower. Lewis was learning to have more sensitivity concerning Alice's needs, but he didn't need help concerning his own. Arousal gel for Lewis would be like throwing gasoline on a brush fire. As the Marquis led them into the amphitheater to the applause and catcalls of the crowd, Alice felt as if they'd already failed.

The disappointment became fear once again when she noticed the Sybian. On a stand in the middle of the room, a curved, padded, black saddle with a flesh-colored dildo mounted on top. A dildo, with length and girth considerably larger than Lewis. In fact, it approached that of Marc Antony's proud staff.

"Make way, make way!" a voice cried out. "Camera crew here! We need to capture this for all time!"

Alice turned in the direction of the voice, and there running toward them were a handsome man wearing breeches and a movie director's beret and another man toting a camera and donning the upper half of a bunny costume. "Hatta and Haigha!" she cried.

"That's Hatter and Hare," they corrected in unison.

And even though the way they changed the pronunciations of their names constantly was annoying, Alice was truly glad to see them. They were old friends from previous adventures, and their presence made her current predicament not as scary.

The Hatter ran his eyes over her body, the bulge in his breeches growing. "You are nakedly superb as always, Alice."

"And superbly naked!" the Hare added, focusing his lens on her, and since he was wearing no pants, his appreciation was obvious.

"Enough!" the Marquis yelled. He raised a hand, and the crowd went immediately silent.

"Good eventide, everyone. Tonight's entertainment should be most exciting. In order to fulfill their Hellfire Club

Contract terms, sweet, beautiful Alice must have twenty orgasms before her husband Lewis has one."

The crowd murmured to itself, and Alice watched some money change hands. They were betting on the outcome.

"To make things even more interesting, they'll both be slicked up with arousal lubricant, and I will be giving them commands. If they fail to follow my commands..." The Marquis picked up a long, wooden paddle, which was resting against the Sybian stand. "...then they will be punished."

Applause and cheers.

"And if Lewis comes before Alice is finished, they'll be put in the pillories, and every one of you will be able to use them as you see fit."

More cheering, especially from Hatter and Hare. Alice looked over the huge crowd. She recognized the pirates, Antony and Cleopatra, the musketeers, several famous poets, the Knights of the Round Table, Dickens, and so many others. After the exhausting day she'd had, Alice didn't think she'd be able to handle sex with several dozen more people. If she had to, she would. But she was getting rather sore and worn out.

Perhaps that was why this place was called The Hellfire Club, and not the Warm Fuzzy Club.

De Sade snapped his fingers, and a naked couple quickly approached. Heathcliff and Jane Eyre.

"Hello again, dear Alice," Heathcliff said. "Been having a nice time?"

"It's been an epic fantasy. Like being the heroine in an erotica story."

"Imagine that."

Heathcliff smiled pleasantly as he applied a gel to Alice's womanhood. Where he touched her immediately began to tingle. Not like the shaving cream Cleopatra had used, or the oil the musketeers preferred. This gel made her clitoris swell to almost twice its size, every nerve in it igniting. A liberal amount was also rubbed onto her breasts, and the sensation made her nipples stick out more luridly than ever before. She watched as Lewis endured similar treatment under Jane Eyre's skillful hands, his eyes closed and his hips bucking on their own accord.

"To the Sybian!" the Marquis ordered.

Heathcliff took Alice's leash and led her to the center of the room. She stood over the dildo, straddling the device. It was so big, she wondered if it would even fit inside her. He rubbed it with more arousal gel, and then held her hips.

"It's so big," she said under her breath.

"You can handle it," he whispered, then winked. "I did."

"You fit that," Alice pointed, "in your bottom?"

"You're going to love it. Nothing at the Hellfire Club comes close to the Sybian."

He pressed down on her hips, and the tip of the dildo rested against Alice's opening. She hadn't needed any lubricant—Alice was already very wet. But the arousal gel seemed to make her warmer than she ever felt. Warmer, and hornier. Alice began to shiver.

"The gel brings blood to the surface of your skin and stimulates nerve endings," Heathcliff said. "You're never going to want to get off."

"But I do want to get off," Alice said. "Twenty more times."

"That's the spirit," he said.

Slowly, she lowered herself, the dildo stretching and filling her in such a delicious way she felt very close to coming. When she finally took in its full length, she was comfortably seated on the rounded, leather saddle. Heathcliff cuffed her ankles to either side of the device, smiled at her, and left.

Lewis was only a meter away, holding his cock in one hand, a small black box in the other.

"I'm worried, Alice. I don't think I'm going to make it," Lewis said, shaking all over. "We're going to the pillories for sure."

"Stop being so negative." Alice adjusted her position, and the movement made her moan. She'd never felt so *full*, and the feeling was incredible.

"You're moaning," Lewis moaned. "I'm going to shoot all over. This arousal gel is driving me insane."

"Lewis, look at me."

"I am. You're the sexiest thing I've ever seen."

"My eyes, Lewis. Look me in the eyes."

He did. Alice saw fear there, but also love.

"All we can do is try our best. That's what marriage is. Sometimes we fall short. Sometimes we screw up. Sometimes we take each other for granted. But as long as we both keep trying, it's all going to work out."

She watched his confidence return, and it was sexy as hell. "I swear, if we get through this, I'll make sure you're always satisfied in bed, Alice. No more thirty second quickies. I'll be the lover you deserve."

"You won me, Lewis, fair and square. I'm all yours." Alice smiled. "And I'll hold you to that promise."

"And I'll come up with some way to help you get those twenty orgasms, Alice. I will. Even if it kills me." Lewis filled his lungs, and blew out a big breath. Then he winked. "Just try not to scream."

"I'll try."

"Lewis," the Marquis commanded. "Set the rotation on the Sybian to level 1."

Lewis turned a knob on the black control box. The dildo inside Alice began to churn in a tight circle, pressing against her g-spot, and Alice immediately began to scream.

"Sorry!" she blurted to Lewis. But the sensation was so extraordinary she couldn't stop herself. It wasn't like the thrust of sword fighting musketeers, or like what Dickens had done to her with the dildo pole. This felt like her feminine parts were on some crazy, sexy carnival ride. She rocked slowly, moving with the rotation, and felt her first orgasm already starting to build.

"Begin to stroke yourself, Lewis." The Marquis demanded.

Lewis, his face stoic, began to run a hand along the length of his shaft, from his balls to the tip, slowly. Watching him was a huge turn-on, and Alice felt a pang of pity. She was allowed to climax watching him, but he was being denied.

The pity quickly vanished as the waves of orgasm overtook her. She bit her lower lip, tried not to scream, and grumbled "eighty-one" low in her throat.

The crowd cheered. Alice stared at them, saw the pirates had their pricks out and were touching themselves like Lewis. Several couples were also making love as they watched, including Cleopatra and Marc Antony. Alice's body flushed in embarrassment at being the object of such intense scrutiny, like she has a circus animal performing for their amusement.

It was so damn hot.

"Turn the vibration on the Sybian to level 1," the Marquis ordered.

Lewis, his jaw clenched tight and the muscles in his neck bulging, turned the second knob.

The dildo, and the area at the dildo's base that pressed against Alice's clitoris, began to buzz.

Oh my!

It wasn't quite as powerful as the Hitachi, but it was more than enough to get the job done. Combined with the arousal gel, and the rotation, Alice would easily get nineteen more orgasms. The only trick would be to control her passion, so she didn't excite Lewis to the point of no return.

Tensing her entire body, trying to remain still, Alice trembled with her second orgasm but managed to stay quiet. She breathed out, "eighty-two" and glanced at Lewis, whose stroking had slowed down. His face was pinched as if he was struggling to use what Jane had taught him, and he was obviously very close to coming.

Then there was a *whack!* and Lewis almost fell forward. Behind him, the Marquis De Sade wielded his long paddle, and he'd given Lewis a hard one.

"Faster," De Sade said.

Lewis twisted both knobs, and Alice screamed. The vibration went *waaaaaaay* beyond the Hitachi, and the rotation was now five times as fast.

"Eighty-three!" she yelled, her toes curling and her entire body wracked with unbearable pleasure.

"I meant stroke yourself faster," the Marquis whacked Lewis again, and seeing him spanked caused Alice's single orgasm to lead into another.

"Eighty-four!"

Lewis's erection seemed to have grown after de Sade's paddling, and he increased his stroking speed while grunting at Alice, "Hurry, Alice!"

Alice needn't any coaxing. The Sybian was truly the most magnificent device ever invented. She quickly climaxed four more times, the last one squirting all over the saddle.

The crowd cheered.

Alice threw her head back and began to hump the device as it ravaged her, and De Sade approached and began to stroke and pinch her breasts. Normally, she would have protested his rough treatment, but as aroused as she was Alice wanted him to squeeze even harder.

Her fantasies were answered as he placed a nipple clamp on her right breast, and then her left. To these he added hanging weights, which pulled on Alice as they squeezed.

Hatter and Hare circled around her, recording the whole thing.

"I do believe she's enjoying herself," Hare said.

"We should ask." Hatter stuck a microphone near Alice's mouth. "Are you enjoying yourself, Alice?"

"Eighty-nine!" she screamed, louder than she had at any time previously that day.

"I think we can interpret that as a yes," Hatter said.

Lewis had his eyes closed—no doubt he'd be paddled for that—but de Sade was presently occupied with Alice, stepping behind her.

"Raise up that luscious bottom of yours."

Alice did, and in lifting her bottom it pressed her throbbing clitoris harder against the vibrator.

The first spank made Alice scream again.

The second made her scream even louder. The sensations of pain and pleasure were intermingling, until it seemed like every nerve in her body was on fire.

The third spank made her come again.

"Ninety!"

Halfway there. She looked up at Lewis, and saw he was completely frozen. He'd ceased stroking himself, and his eyes were wide with both love and lust, his mouth hanging open. Alice had seen her husband look at her like that before, but now, in front of the crowd, with Lewis trying so desperately not to come, she felt more affection for him than she'd had in years.

"Turn both dials up all the way," the Marquis said.

All the way? Hadn't they already been up all the way? How much more powerful could the Sybian...

"OH MY GOD!"

Alice went into orgasm overload, as she had in the Swing Room. Except this was more intense, more relentless. Her entire body felt like electrified pleasure. She screamed and thrashed and bucked so hard that everyone else in the room seemed to disappear. One of her nipple clamps fell off, and the blood returning was more painful than the clamp itself, but that just added to the overall body orgasm. And it went on and on and on.

Alice was so lost in the rapture that she'd forgotten to count, and she managed to rattle off numbers up to ninety-seven.

"Turn the Sybian off!" the Marquis shouted above Alice's cries and the cheers of the crowd.

Alice managed to call out, "Ninety-eight!" just as the vibration and rotation ceased. She was panting, her whole body flushed and sweaty, her hair in her face, and she looked around to see what would happen next.

"This movie will be magnificent!" Hatter declared. "Stupendous! A blockbuster! It will enthrall people like nothing that came before!"

"I left the lens cap on," the March Hare said.

"Okay, let's take it all again from the top," Hatter said.

"Let's not," the Marquis replied, pushing between them. "Jane! Heathcliff! Make Lewis come."

Jane walked over to Lewis and took the Sybian control box from his hands, tossing it to the side. She immediately dropped to her knees and deep throated his cock.

Heathcliff, lubing up his sizeable erection positioned himself behind Lewis and grabbed his shoulders.

When Lewis was penetrated, he cried out in such a way that Alice was sure he'd just climaxed.

But Jane didn't seem to acknowledge it. Her head continued to bob, and Lewis placed his hands on her hair.

"Alice!" her husband yelled. "Hurry!"

Alice began to fuck the dildo, riding it as much as she was able to with her legs bound. She was starting to get the rhythm right when *whack!* the paddle once again slapped against her bottom.

With the Sybian off, the paddle hurt a lot more.

Alice concentrated, trying to get the motion right, but the spanking didn't cease.

Whack!

Whack!

Whack!

Alice began to lose her desire. The spanking had gone from erotic to painful.

She glanced at Lewis, desperate, and saw him in the throes of absolute ecstasy. Alice had stuck her fingers into his bottom a few times during their marriage, rubbing his prostate, and it had always given Lewis violent orgasms. She couldn't imagine how much his prostate was being stimulated with Heathcliff's big cock rubbing against it.

And she watched how that slut, Jane, greedily sucked on Lewis's cock. With all the perverts in the crowd fucking themselves or each other.

The dirty thoughts, and dirty words, began to turn Alice on.

"Do you like having your cock sucked, Lewis?" she called. "Do you like that slut taking it deep in her mouth, and pulling on your balls?"

"Unnghh," Lewis said.

Alice continued to grind against the dildo.

"Do you like being fucked up the ass? That thick cock up your ass feels good, doesn't it?"

"Unnnghg.... yesssss," Lewis managed to squeak out, trying his best to work with her.

"And do you like watching the Marquis de Sade spank my ass with his cruel paddle?"

Lewis nodded just as the paddle smacked against Alice's red bottom once again, but this time her own vulgar words were enough to turn the pain back into pleasure, and she shook with a wonderful orgasm.

"Ninety-nine!" she triumphantly declared.

And then, suddenly, her legs were being untied and the Marquis was lifting her off of the delicious Sybian.

"And that's all you shall have, dear Alice. Now you can watch as your husband comes, and your count is reset to zero."

"That's cruel!"

The Marquis rolled his eyes. "Duh. I'm the Marquis De Sade, remember?"

373

Alice didn't know what to do. With her hands cuffed behind her, she couldn't touch herself. And the Marquis firmly held her by the arm, so she couldn't try to get back on the Sybian, or run into the crowd and let one of them have their way with her.

Her eyes scanned the onlookers and she saw the four Musketeers, all with their cocks out and stroking furiously. "Athos! Porthos! Come down here and fuck me! Please!"

They laughed, but didn't move.

Alice saw Marc Antony impaling his queen from behind. "A little help here?" she asked.

For a second, she thought the Roman general would oblige, then Shakespeare moved up behind him, adding to the daisy chain and destroying her hopes.

"Hatta? Haigha?"

But they hadn't even heard her, still trying to get the lens cap off their camera.

Alice wasn't sure what do. Poor Lewis was almost whimpering, trying to hold his orgasm back. It was pitiable. It was pathetic.

It was a turn-on.

In fact, everywhere Alice looked, something erotic was happening. The three-way Lewis sandwich. The musketeers. The crowd fucking and sucking and masturbating.

Alice recalled what Jane had taught her.

Your biggest erogenous zone is your mind. Sex is all in your brain. If the brain gives into the fantasy, the body will follow.

Alice drank in all the debauchery around her, clenching her buttocks, flexing and releasing her Kegel muscles. She thought about all of the unbearably erotic things that had happened to her today. Blackbeard edging her. Queequeg's foot massage. Heathcliff's orgasm torture. Madame Bovary's orgasm denial with Lewis. Cleopatra's bath. The musketeers swordfights. Being slammed at the poetry slam. The power of the Sybian.

"What are you doing?" De Sade said, noticing Alice had begun to tremble. "Bend over at once, you naughty girl!"

Alice willingly did, and as the Marquis smacked her tender bottom with his paddle, the fantasies in her head took over and she moaned. So close… so close… All she needed was just a little push.

"Alice!"

She glanced up at her husband, his face the picture of determination.

"I love you, Alice!" Lewis yelled. "I love you so much! I always have, and I always will, and I'll hold out forever if I have to!"

And the sound of her husband's voice, yelling the words they'd neglected to say to one another for far too long, telling her how he truly felt, pushed her over the edge, and an orgasm seized her, shuddering to her toes.

"One hundred!" she yelled, triumphantly.

The Marquis raised his hand. "Jane! Heathcliff! Stop immediately!"

The naked duo withdrew from Lewis, and he let out an anguished cry and his erection bobbed free—

—still nice and hard.

"Has he come?" the Marquis asked.

"No, sir," Jane answered, beaming proudly.

The whole crowd erupted into cheers and applause, and Alice's hands were suddenly free. Their contract had been fulfilled. The Hellfire Club ordeal was over. She immediately ran to Lewis, hugging him, kissing him, and reaching for his beautiful erect cock…

Chapter 12

For Those Who Didn't Get It, This Entire Book Was All a Fantasy. All Three Alice Adventures Were All Fantasies Alice Had While Masturbating…

And fantasy is healthy, normal, and part of any good sex life. But Alice now looked at her rabbit vibrator, which she'd used to climax countless times while her husband lay snoring beside her, and realized that if she waited for him to repair their marriage, she might have to wait forever.

But she knew Lewis loved her. And she loved him.

Fantasy was all well and good, but someone needed to save their marriage, and if Alice had to be the one to step up, so be it.

In one, easy movement she straddled his face, pressing her wetness to his lips.

Lewis's eyes opened in surprise, and when he tried to speak, she rubbed herself against him.

"No more quickie marriage sex where I'm unfulfilled," Alice said. "You're not allowed to come until I come three times. Now get going, dear husband. You have a lot of catching up to do."

Lewis gripped her hips, and began to lick.

The rabbit was nice, but it wasn't a substitute for a warm, eager tongue. Alice rolled her hips, guiding him with her movements. When she wanted more stimulation, she pressed down. When it became too sensitive, she pulled away. He found the rhythm she liked, and Alice felt the slow, sensual build, starting in her loins, spreading up through her taut nipples, making her tingle all over. His tongue darted in and out of her, like Heathcliff's had in her fantasy, but the real thing felt sooooo much better.

She gripped the head of the bed and rubbed herself shamelessly over his face, and Lewis held her thighs and lapped at her, ravenously, like he'd been starving for years.

"Oh… oh god… oh god, Lewis… yes… yes…"

And then, abruptly, he stopped.

Alice's eyes flipped open like window shades, and she ceased her gyrations.

What had happened? Why had he quit?

Had she done something? Was he not enjoying it?

What was wrong?

"Lewis?" she asked, still shaking with arousal, but fearful of his response.

"Beg for it," he said.

"What?"

"Beg me."

His dirty talk and take-charge stance made Alice's whole body tense up with vibrant need. What a delightfully wicked thing to say.

"Lick my pussy," she said, feeling both ashamed and unabashedly sexual. "Please lick me."

Lewis reached up, pulling on her erect nipples as he took her in his mouth, using his lips and tongue to bathe her in delicious sensation. Alice moaned, bucking on his face, and once again she felt the wave well up in her, threatening to take her over the precipice.

And once again he stopped.

"Don't stop!" she pleaded. "Please don't stop! Lick me fuck me use me please!"

"Alice…"

"Please, Lewis! I'm so close!"

"I love you, Alice."

Alice looked down at him, saw his feelings for her in his eyes. The lust. The longing. The intensity. The love.

Her husband was back.

"Oh, Lewis, I love…"

But she didn't get to finish, because his mouth devoured her.

THE END
And, naturally, they lived happily ever after.

Peterson & Konrath Bibliographies

EROTICA
(Konrath & Peterson writing as Melinda Duchamp)

Make Me Blush series
KINKY SECRETS OF MISTER KINK (Book 1)
THE KINKY SECRETS OF WITCHES (Book 2)
KINKY SECRETS OF SIX AND CANDY (Book 3)

Alice series
KINKY SECRETS OF ALICE IN WONDERLAND (Book 1)
KINKY SECRETS OF ALICE THROUGH THE LOOKING GLASS (Book 2)
KINKY SECRETS OF ALICE AT THE HELLFIRE CLUB (Book 3)
KINKY SECRETS OF ALICE VS DRACULA (Book 4)
KINKY SECRETS OF ALICE VS DR. JEKYLL & MR. HYDE (Book 5)
KINKY SECRETS OF ALICE VS FRANKENSTEIN (Book 6)

Jezebel series
KINKY SECRETS OF JEZEBEL AND THE BEANSTALK (Book 1)
KINKY SECRETS OF PUSS IN BOOTS (Book 2)
KINKY SECRETS OF GOLDILOCKS (Book 3)

Sexperts series
THE SEXPERTS – KINKY GRADES OF SHAY (Book 1)
THE SEXPERTS – KINKY SECRETS OF THE PEARL NECKLACE (Book 2)
THE SEXPERTS – KINKY SECRETS OF THE ALIEN (Book 3)

CODENAME: CHANDLER
(Ann Voss Peterson & J.A. Konrath)

FLEE (Book 1)
SPREE (Book 2)
THREE (Book 3)
HIT (Book 4)
EXPOSED (Book 5)
NAUGHTY (Book 6)
FIX with F. Paul Wilson (Book 7)
RESCUE (Book 8)

Ann Voss Peterson Bibliography

VAL RYKER THRILLERS
PUSHED TOO FAR (Book 1)
BURNED TOO HOT (Book 2)
DEAD TOO SOON (Book 3)
WATCHED TOO LONG with J.A. Konrath (Book 4)
BURIED TOO DEEP (Book 5)

SMALL TOWN SECRETS: SINS
LETHAL (Book 1)
CAPTIVE (Book 2)
FRANTIC (Book 3)
VICIOUS (Book 4)

SMALL TOWN SECRETS: SCANDALS
WITNESS (Book 1)
STOLEN (Book 2)
MALICE (Book 3)
GUILTY (Book 4)
FORBIDDEN (Book 5)
KIDNAPPED (Book 6)
THE SCHOOL (Book 3.5)

ROCKY MOUNTAIN THRILLERS
MANHUNT (Book 1)
FUGITIVE (Book 2)
JUSTICE (Book 3)
MAVERICK (Book 4)
RENEGADE (Book 5)

PARANORMAL ROMANTIC SUSPENSE

Return to Jenkins Cove
CHRISTMAS SPIRIT by Rebecca York (Book 1)
CHRISTMAS AWAKENING by Ann Voss Peterson (Book 2)
CHRISTMAS DELIVERY by Patricia Rosemoor (Book 3)

Security Breach
CHAIN REACTION by Rebecca York (Book 1)
CRITICAL EXPOSURE by Ann Voss Peterson (Book 2)
TRIGGERED RESPONSE by Patricia Rosemoor (Book 3)

Gypsy Magic
WYATT (Justice is Blind) by Rebecca York (Part 1)
GARNER (Love is Death) by Ann Voss Peterson (Part 2)
ANDREI (The Law is Impotent) by Patricia Rosemoor (Part 3)

Renegade Magic
LUKE by Rebecca York (Part 1)
TOM by Ann Voss Peterson (Part 2)
RICO by Patricia Rosemoor (Part 3)

New Orleans Magic
JORDAN by Rebecca York (Part 1)
LIAM by Ann Voss Peterson (Part 2)
ZACHARY by Patricia Rosemoor (Part 3)

J.A. Konrath Bibliography

JACQUELINE "JACK" DANIELS THRILLERS
WHISKEY SOUR (Book 1)
BLOODY MARY (Book 2)
RUSTY NAIL (Book 3)
DIRTY MARTINI (Book 4)
FUZZY NAVEL (Book 5)
CHERRY BOMB (Book 6)
SHAKEN (Book 7)
STIRRED with Blake Crouch (Book 8)
RUM RUNNER (Book 9)
LAST CALL (Book 10)
WHITE RUSSIAN (Book 11)
SHOT GIRL (Book 12)
CHASER (Book 13)
OLD FASHIONED (BOOK 14)
BITE FORCE (BOOK 15)
JACK ROSE (BOOK 16)
LADY 52 with Jude Hardin (Book 2.5)

JACK DANIELS AND ASSOCIATES MYSTERIES
DEAD ON MY FEET (Book 1)
JACK DANIELS STORIES VOL. 1 (Book 2)
SHOT OF TEQUILA (Book 3)
JACK DANIELS STORIES VOL. 2 (Book 4)
DYING BREATH (Book 5)
SERIAL KILLERS UNCUT with Blake Crouch (Book 6)
JACK DANIELS STORIES VOL. 3 (Book 7)
EVERYBODY DIES (Book 8)
JACK DANIELS STORIES VOL. 4 (Book 9)
BANANA HAMMOCK (Book 10)

THE KONRATH DARK THRILLER COLLECTIVE

THE LIST (Book 1)
ORIGIN (Book 2)
AFRAID (Book 3)
TRAPPED (Book 4)
ENDURANCE (Book 5)
HAUNTED HOUSE (Book 6)
WEBCAM (Book 7)
DISTURB (Book 8)
WHAT HAPPENED TO LORI (Book 9)
THE NINE (Book 10)
SECOND COMING (Book 11)
CLOSE YOUR EYES (Book 12)
HOLES IN THE GROUND with Iain Rob Wright (Book 4.5)
DRACULAS with Blake Crouch, Jeff Strand, F. Paul Wilson (Book 5.5)
GRANDMA? with Talon Konrath (Book 6.5)

TIMECASTER

TIMECASTER (Book 1)
TIMECASTER SUPERSYMMETRY (Book 2)
TIMECASTER STEAMPUNK (Book 3)

STOP A MURDER PUZZLE BOOKS

HOW: PUZZLES 1-12 (Book 1)
WHERE: PUZZLES 13-24 (Book 2)
WHY: PUZZLES 25-36 (Book 3)
WHO: PUZZLES 37-48 (Book 4)
WHEN: PUZZLES 49-60 (Book 5)
ANSWERS (Book 6)
STOP A MURDER COMPLETE CASES (Books 1-5)

MISCELLANEOUS

65 PROOF – COLLECTED SHORT STORIES
THE GLOBS OF USE-A-LOT 3 with Dan Maderak
A NEWBIES GUIDE TO PUBLISHING

KINKY SECRETS OF MISTER KINK

Carla thought she had it all together.

Then Jake moved in next door.

She never expected to fall for someone half her age. Especially Jake, an escort who specialized in very kinky sex.

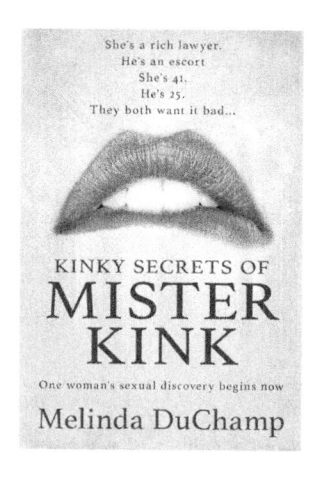

But Carla was curious. And rich. And when Jake accepts her as a client, they each may have gotten more than they'd bargained for…

KINKY SECRETS OF MISTER KINK mixes erotic romance with laugh-out-loud humor. Sexy, funny, and outrageous, this is the book you've always wanted to read. A smart, older woman goes on a journey of sexual discovery, and somewhere along the way finds love. Or at least something equally as tasty.

KINKY SECRETS OF MISTER KINK
It begins where FIFTY SHADES OF GREY left off…

KINKY SECRETS OF MISTER KINK is a 64,000 word contemporary romance by bestselling author Melinda DuChamp. It's hot. It's playful. It's more fun than the last ten books you've read.

Try KINKY SECRETS OF MISTER KINK. You won't be disappointed.

THE KONRATH DARK THRILLER COLLECTIVE
THE LIST (Book 1)
ORIGIN (Book 2)
AFRAID (Book 3)
TRAPPED (Book 4)
ENDURANCE (Book 5)
HAUNTED HOUSE (Book 6)
WEBCAM (Book 7)
DISTURB (Book 8)
WHAT HAPPENED TO LORI (Book 9)
THE NINE (Book 10)
SECOND COMING (Book 11)
CLOSE YOUR EYES (Book 12)
HOLES IN THE GROUND with Iain Rob Wright (Book 4.5)
DRACULAS with Blake Crouch, Jeff Strand, F. Paul Wilson (Book 5.5)
GRANDMA? with Talon Konrath (Book 6.5)

TIMECASTER
TIMECASTER (Book 1)
TIMECASTER SUPERSYMMETRY (Book 2)
TIMECASTER STEAMPUNK (Book 3)

STOP A MURDER PUZZLE BOOKS
HOW: PUZZLES 1-12 (Book 1)
WHERE: PUZZLES 13-24 (Book 2)
WHY: PUZZLES 25-36 (Book 3)
WHO: PUZZLES 37-48 (Book 4)
WHEN: PUZZLES 49-60 (Book 5)
ANSWERS (Book 6)
STOP A MURDER COMPLETE CASES (Books 1-5)

MISCELLANEOUS
65 PROOF – COLLECTED SHORT STORIES
THE GLOBS OF USE-A-LOT 3 with Dan Maderak
A NEWBIES GUIDE TO PUBLISHING

KINKY SECRETS OF MISTER KINK

Carla thought she had it all together.

Then Jake moved in next door.

She never expected to fall for someone half her age. Especially Jake, an escort who specialized in very kinky sex.

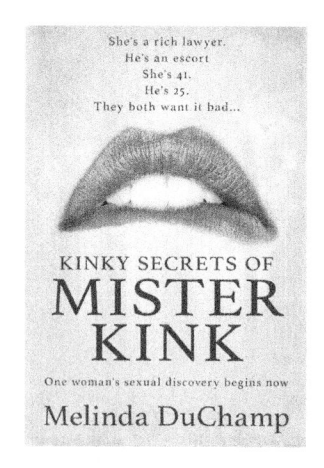

But Carla was curious. And rich. And when Jake accepts her as a client, they each may have gotten more than they'd bargained for…

KINKY SECRETS OF MISTER KINK mixes erotic romance with laugh-out-loud humor. Sexy, funny, and outrageous, this is the book you've always wanted to read. A smart, older woman goes on a journey of sexual discovery, and somewhere along the way finds love. Or at least something equally as tasty.

KINKY SECRETS OF MISTER KINK
It begins where FIFTY SHADES OF GREY left off…

KINKY SECRETS OF MISTER KINK is a 64,000 word contemporary romance by bestselling author Melinda DuChamp. It's hot. It's playful. It's more fun than the last ten books you've read.

Try KINKY SECRETS OF MISTER KINK. You won't be disappointed.

THE COMPLETE KINKY SECRETS OF JEZEBEL

Jezebel is searching for sexual fulfillment, and a soulmate so she can live happily ever after. Her quest leads her up a beanstalk to a fairy tale land where her wildest, kinkiest fantasies come true.

From the debauchery and danger of the Ghastlibad Forest, to finding the perfect partner for her billionaire ex-boyfriend, to indulging in her darkest desires the night before her wedding, Jezebel embarks on a journey of discovery that's nothing like the Mother Goose you grew up with. This adults-only story is for those with sinful desires, who wish to explore erotic excess beyond the plain vanilla of everyday life.

The bestselling erotica trilogy is now compiled into a single, full-length novel, for only the most adventurous readers.

THE COMPLETE KINKY SECRETS OF JEZEBEL

It's erotica for smart people who like to laugh, just like you.

Follow Jezebel up the beanstalk, if you dare...

THE SEXPERTS – THE KINKY GRADES OF SHAY

In the future, some people are still prudes…

But Fanny Leuber and Peter Bonebury, instructors at the Siemann Sex Institute, are doing all they can to make sure everyone can enjoy a healthy, prosperous sex life. Even if that means kidnapping clueless men to teach them how to please a woman, giving BDSM lessons, and creating group sex instructional videos.

But when a gorgeous, naive blond with sexual super powers arrives at the institute, everything Fanny and Peter know will be exposed and turned upside down … including their secret feelings for each other.

Written by bestselling erotica author Melinda DuChamp, THE SEXPERTS – THE KINKY GRADES OF SHAY is another hilarious, romantic, and downright naughty adventure for readers who are daring enough.

It's erotica for smart people who like to laugh, just like you.

KINKY SECRETS OF WITCHES

Here It Is, Nice And Rough…

This is the story of a witch in New York.

Actually, it is two stories.

The first story is an adult paranormal romance. Sweet. Sexy. Funny. It has some steamy parts, a heroine you can root for, and a Happily Ever After.

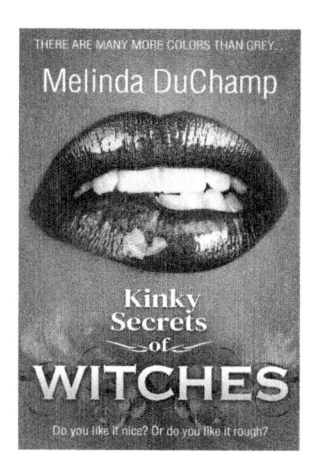

The second story is erotica. Rude. Hilarious. Filthy. It has a lot of kinky parts, and the heroine goes through quite the edging ordeal.

Whether you want a spicy, romantic adventure, or a wicked trip down a very naughty road, KINKY SECRETS OF WITCHES has got it covered…

Printed in Great Britain
by Amazon